The Book
of the
Ring

A novelistic rendition of
Wagner's Music-Drama:

Der Ring des Nibelungen

DAVID PRASHKER

THE ARGAMAN PRESS

AUTHOR'S PREFACE

My goal in this book is not to make an accurate and scholarly translation of the original Nibelungenlied - there are plenty of these about already, by hands more capable than mine - but simply to create a companion narrative to Wagner's highly personal interpretation of that legend. Like Dante, Wagner is believed to be inaccessible to the ordinary mortal, who quite likes the idea of spending a few days in picturesque Bayreuth, and even "taking in the show", because it's one of those cultural great walls that one feels one ought to have climbed; on the other hand, sixteen hours of caterwauling in a foreign language, spread over four days, and not even permitted to take in a picnic hamper, is probably too much. All those diaphragm-heavy women and men in uncomfortable clothing. All those Nazi overtones. No, Wagner may be a cultural icon for the bourgeois aficionado, but I'm going to stick to Stephen Sondheim and Andrew Lloyd Webber, or maybe risk a throw at Verdi or some gentle Mozart. Not Wagner. Not for me.

But the truth is, Wagner is perfectly accessible. For anyone who has read "The Lord of the Rings", or even just seen the movie version, the story of "The Ring" is already totally familiar, though both Wagner and Tolkien have adopted and adapted the source myths to suit their own purposes. It's the music that's difficult, for its inner complexities as well as its length. How much easier, it has always seemed to me, how much easier to approach the music, if one is already completely familiar with the story. Then you can listen, knowing what's happening on the stage in front of you, able to focus where you need to focus, undistracted by trying to make sense of the narrative and following the electronic sub-titles on the screen above the stage.

Here, then, is the narrative, retold in the vernacular, accessible to anyone above the age of basic literacy. I have used Wagner's libretto as my starting-point, keeping his stage directions religiously, telling the tale in precisely the order that he tells it, using his dialogue wherever it's prosaically feasible to do so, paraphrasing libretto into common speech or into narrative wherever his lyrics soar into the ethereal heights of the pre-Raphaelite Romanticism which was his hyperbolous addiction.

This, of course, isn't "The Ring of the Nibelungen", which is a monstrously brilliant piece of Festspiel. This is only a prose account of the plot and action of "The Ring". Once you've read this, you mustn't stop there, thinking you're done. The words are nothing, without the music.

David Prashker

PRELUDE

At its source, the Rhine belongs to Switzerland. It rises in many places in the high mountains, across the canton of Graubünden: most notably at Lake Tuma by the Oberalpe Pass from where it flows down through the Ruinaulta, the Swiss Grand Canyon; and at the Paradiese glacier near the Rheinquellhorn. These tributaries conjoin near Reichenau, and then the Rhine flows north to make a frontier with both Liechtenstein and Austria, before it empties into Lake Constance, re-emerges flowing west through the Rhine Falls, is doubled by the Aare river, turns north at Basel where it becomes the Franco-German border, and at last is Germany's alone just south of Karlsruhe, at Rheinstetten.

Germany is unimaginable without the Rhine. It's the central artery that nourishes its body, from which every minor vein draws blood. When towns were built upon the waterways, the Rhine gave birth to Germany.

And so many towns. Germersheim, whose coat-of-arms is the crowned eagle, because once the Holy Roman Emperor ruled from here directly. Hockenheim, where today the gods drive racing cars. Speyer, where Bernard of Clairvaux preached the Second Crusade. Rheinau. Mannheim. Ludwigshafen. Friesenheim. Heidelberg, at whose university Hegel taught. Würms, where William Tyndale's New Testament was printed, and Martin Luther was brought to trial, and where in the original Nibelungenlied King Gunther had his palace and his bride Brünhild, the Queen of Iceland. Gernsheim. Nierstein. Nackenheim. Ginsheim-Gustavburg. Guntersblum, where not the Burgundian king, but Hagen's brother, saw his tears of guilt transformed into a yellow flower. Mainz, which with Speyer and Würms provided mediaeval Jewry with its diasporal equivalent of the Sanhedrin. Biebrich. Eltville. Ingelheim. Geisenheim. Bingen, where the first opera was written, "*Ordo Virtutum*", by that most unlikely of composers, an Abbess who received visions, the Blessed Saint Hildegard. Boppard. Braubach. Lahnstein. Koblenz. Neuwied. Andernach. Bad Honnef on the slopes of the Drachensfeld - the Dragon's Rock mountains, where you can still visit the cave where Siegfried killed the dragon Fafner. And on, round ox-bows and through gorges and past vast industrial estates: Königswinter which houses the Drachensberg castle; Bonn which for decades after Hitler housed the German parliament; Niederkassel; Wesseling; Cologne; Buchheim; Leverkusen; Dormagen; Neuss; Zons; Düsseldorf; Meerbusch; Krefeld; Duisburg; Moers-Vinn; Rheinberg; Dinslaken; Wesel; Xanten – Siegfried's home town; Rees; and finally Emmerich, before the Rhine is lost to Germany after all, resumed in Holland, searching for the sea, and finding it at last, among the fjordic deltas south of Rotterdam.

"The air grows cool and darkles," wrote Heinrich Heine, one of Wagner's favourite poets, in 'The Lorelei'. "The Rhine flows calmly on; The mountain summit sparkles, In the light of the setting sun."

The story of the "Ring of the Nibelungen" is the story of the Rhine.

PART ONE

DAS RHEINGOLD

SCENE ONE

Deep in the waters of the Rhine, at the foot of the Drachensberg mountains, where the river flows underground through stony caverns and ice-cold waterfalls, a perpetual twilight that is almost green in colour fills the gorges with candescent light. It is much lighter above, much darker below, for the colour changes as the growing darkness mingles with the water that streams restlessly from rock to rock. Where it becomes trapped among the upper slopes and cannot break free, it resolves itself at last into a fine mist, so that the cavern where our story will begin, a cavern of immense height and depth, seems free of any water, for the mist floats like a train of clouds above the gloomy depths, almost to the height of a man.

Though men have never visited this place, nor ever will, except in story.

This underground cavern is enclosed entirely by steep points of rock that jut up out of the chasm. The ground is splintered into a wild confusion of jagged stones, so that there is no level place. On all sides the intensity of the darkness indicates other, deeper fissures in the rock. And on one of these rocks, gleaming brightly in the darkness, sits the Rhinegold, a lump of gold more pure than any other ever mined out of the earth. The Rhinegold is Nature's malign gift to an innocent world, for the beauty of the Rhinegold is irresistible to any creature, human, dwarf, or even god. But the power of the Rhinegold lies in its curse, which will bring down murder, treachery, greed and lust for power upon any who come in contact with it. And on the day our story opens, the fulfilment of that curse is nigh.

In the absence of Father Rhine, his three daughters, the Rhine Maidens, were swimming playfully among the rocks. The first was Woglinde, whose name described the gentle evenness, the balance and the harmony of Nature. The second was Wellgunde, whose body like her name reflected the heavy lime trees that grew along the banks. The third was Flosshilde, the meaning of whose name has not come down to us[1]. By day and by night these three sisters had nothing else to do but serve as guardians of the Rhinegold, swimming among the currents that ebbed and flowed around the precious object, singing lullabies and love songs for their own

---

[1] In Norse, 'hild' is the personification of war and in German flossen means 'to flow'.

4

amusement.

Or for the pleasure of a peeping dwarf, who had crept up on them unnoticed from the dark chasm at the bottom of the river and was watching through a crevice in the rocks.

Alberich, the Nibelung.

It was indeed a most enchanting sight.

There was Woglinde, circling with graceful swimming motions round the central rock. There was Wellgunde, swimming over to join her and then teasing her, the two girls chasing each other back and forth between the rocks. Their very voices were like sirens, luring him towards the rocks.

"Are you watching on your own?" Wellgunde called down from above.

"If you were to join me, that would make two," Woglinde replied.

And hearing this, Wellgunde dived down to the rock to splash her sister playfully.

"How safe is your watch?" Wellgunde asked.

But Woglinde eluded her by swimming further distant.

"It's safe enough from your tricks," she laughed.

And Alberich's eyes could not decide which one to gaze at as they playfully chased each other through the swirling waters.

Until Flosshilde spoiled it, calling down to them, chiding them for not watching properly, for neglecting their charge.

The sisters ignored her though, screaming and playing. Until Flosshilde literally dived between them.

"Is this what you call guarding the gold?" she asked. "You'd better do it properly or you'll both pay."

The girls just laughed, and swam apart again. Flosshilde tried to catch first one and then the other, but they eluded her. Then they turned and together began chasing Flosshilde. O the delight in Alberich's eyes, watching these three gorgeous creatures dart and laugh and play like fish amongst the rocks. Who could possibly stay hidden and unknown for ever?

"Hey," he called, "my beauties."

The maidens at once stopped playing.

"Who are you?" Woglinde asked.

She could hear the voice, but could not see its owner.

"A voice in the dark," Wellgunde gave her own answer, and it was full of fear.

"Look who's below," Flosshilde called, for she had seen and recognized him.

The other two dived deeper down. Now they saw the Nibelung, and shuddered at the sight of him, startled by his intrusion, revolted by his ugliness.

"Look to the gold," Flosshilde instructed, swimming quickly up to her sisters, recalling their father's warning.

The other two Rhine Maidens followed her, gathering quickly around the middle rock, forming a tight circle to protect the gold.

But Alberich was revealed now. The sirens had ensnared him.

"You up there!" he called.

"What do you want?" the three called back.

"Would it spoil your game if I stood here and watched?" he was trying to flirt, but it came across as predatory, not seductive. "Or maybe you'd like to dive deeper, and I can come down and play with you."

Grisly was the word on Woglinde's lips. She wasn't even aware she'd uttered it.

"Did he just say he wants to be our playmate?"

"I think he's mocking us."

But Alberich was entirely serious.

"You shine so brightly in this light," he called. "If one of you were so inclined, I would dearly love to hold you in my arms."

Then it wasn't the gold that he was after. Absurd as it sounded, the ugly dwarf was actually trying to woo them. It was beyond funny.

But funny.

"So much for my fear," Flosshilde sighed deeply, and did indeed now laugh. "The fool's in love," she added.

"The rotten beast!" Wellgunde added.

"Let's go nearer," said Woglinde, thinking how much more fun than chasing Wellgunde it would be to teach this dwarf a lesson.

"Come close to me here," she called, letting herself sink to the top of the very rock whose foot Alberich had just reached.

Now, to get to her, he would have to climb a rocky outcrop full of jagged, scratchy edges. But o the joy if only he could manage it.

And get to her he was determined now to do. He climbed, with imp-like agility but with frequent halts, all the way to the summit of the rock. He slipped repeatedly, slithering on the loathsome, slimy pebbles that made for its surface. It was impossible to stand. His hands and feet simply couldn't fasten or hold on to such treacherous smoothness. Drops of water filled his nostrils. Sneezing could have toppled him altogether.

"Sneezing tells of my love's approach," Woglinde mocked.

"My sweetheart," he was reaching out to try to embrace her. "You lovely child."

Sneezing, slithering, sliding, grasping at jagged rocks to hold his balance.

While Woglinde avoided his outstretched arm, and laughed, and swam up to a higher rock.

"You want to woo me?" she called down to him. "Then woo me up here."

Alberich scratched his head and followed her, but she had already moved on to yet another rock, had escaped him once again. It was too much, and so unfair. She could fly where he could scarcely creep. He pleaded with her to come nearer.

But Woglinde only swam on to another rock, still deeper down.

"Climb to the ground then," she was teasing him. "You never know, I might be yours down there."

So Alberich clambered hastily down. But Woglinde darted quickly to a high rock at the side, and gave him the slip once more.

Wellgunde and Flosshilde were roaring with adolescent laughter as they watched this scene. How stupid the male of the species is before a girl! Just to hear him crying out, wondering out loud how he could possibly catch her in flight, asking her to wait a while, calling her a "timid fish", a "false one". The fool! The stupid fool! Joining in was simply irresistible.

As Alberich clambered hastily down yet another rock in pursuit of Woglinde, stumbling everywhere he went, Wellgunde laughed and called to him enticingly:

"Hey good-looking, can't you hear me calling you?"

Alberich turned around.

"Take my advice," she called to him. "Leave her alone and turn to me."

Alberich stood and looked at her, drinking in her beauty, then clambered hastily along the ground to try to get to her. She was right. This one was far better looking than the shy one he'd been chasing. This one gleamed more brightly. The other looked too thin. If only he could persuade her to come closer.

Wellgunde let herself sink down a little nearer to him, but still not near enough for his appreciation. He wanted to feel her slender arms around him, wanted to caress her body and toy with her hair, to press himself against her ample bosom. He had never spoken to a woman quite so passionately before.

But o the cruelty, the disappointment, of Wellgunde's harsh response.

"Are you bewitched?" she asked. "Is this how you pursue the joys of love?"

She was scrutinizing her would-be lover in a manner that did not bode well for his success. And then, and then.

"Why should I be interested in you? You're a hairy, hunch-backed coxcomb. You're a swarthy and, and a spotted, and, and, and a sulphurous dwarf. Go find a sweetheart who finds that kind of thing attractive."

She'd let him come too close though. Alberich grabbed her arm and tried to take her by force.

"My face may be foul," it was his turn at last to do some taunting, "but my hands hold you fast."

He was wrong though. Wellgunde managed to evade his grasp and quickly swam to the middle rock, which was much higher. The other Rhine Maidens laughed to see how easily she slipped out of his hands. And how distraught he was, crying out angrily that Wellgunde was a deceitful child, calling her a cold and bony fish, shouting after her in his desolation, that if she didn't find him attractive, she could flirt with eels instead.

As if it wasn't like a slippery eel that Wellgunde had slid out of his grasp.

"Why are you grumbling," Flosshilde asked. "Why do you get cast down so quickly? You've tried two, now try the third one. You'll find much sweeter honey from this bee."

Alberich liked this. It took only the simplest calculation to work out that he had a better chance of winning one from three. Especially as alone no girl would choose him.

"Can I trust you?" he'd been bitten twice, and now was shy.

Flosshilde stood, and gleamed. Her answer lay in her eyes.

"Then glide down to me," Alberich beckoned, thinking what luck it was that there were several Rhine Maidens! Surely one of the three must find him attractive? But he was cautious now.

Flosshilde dived down to him, chiding her foolish, senseless sisters for not recognizing his good looks. Alberich quickly approached her. Now that he'd seen the third sister, the fairest of the three, the others appeared to him nothing more than silly, spiteful girls. This was the one he really wanted.

And what was more, she was encouraging him. Allowing him to caress her arms, her hair. Inviting him to whisper sweet nothings in her ear. The Nibelung was almost fainting with excitement. And if she was still gently resisting him, this wasn't really resistance, but coyness, inviting him to make a pass at her, but yet retaining her honour, her integrity. But inviting him. All that flattery. No doubt she was inviting him.

And then, still more, positively drawing him towards her. Tenderly. So tenderly.

"Dearest of men!" she whispered.

"Sweetest of maids."

"If only you were mine."

"If only I could hold you like this for ever."

No one had ever spoken to him like this before. Her words were nuzzling his ear like a tongue. Such ardour in her expression. And in such honeyed tones to be extolling all his virtues: the sting of his glance, the prick of his beard, his flowing mane of shaggy, bristly hair, his toad-like form, his croaking voice.

Flosshilde's sisters had dived down close enough to them to hear each word, and burst out laughing at those final mockeries.

Alberich stared up alarmed.

"You wretches, why are you laughing at me?"

Suddenly Flosshilde darted away from him, swimming quickly to join her sisters.

"Laughter," she said, "is what fits best at the ending of that particular song."

So that he knew she'd been toying with him all along. Just teasing him. Humiliating him. He hardly knew whether to cry or to throw stones in his anger. But what came out was both at once, denouncing all three sisters as despicable, and sly, and lewd, an evil gang. Even the third one had dealt treacherously with him.

Not that this precluded them from further mockery.

"Shame on you, imp," they scoffed together. "We will be faithful to whoever catches us; why did you let us slip through your fingers?"

Then they swam apart, going in different directions, hither and thither, up and down, tempting him to chase them. And in his humiliation, in his desperate longing to possess one of these three women, Alberich was now determined not to leave here thwarted.

Alberich clambered awkwardly, jumping from place to place, falling down and staggering up, his pursuit fuelled by his lust. With what desperate exertions he began the chase. With what terrible agility he climbed the rocks, springing from one to the other, trying to catch first this one, then that one, then the third of the three maidens. But always they eluded him. And always with that mocking laughter that now only incited him to chase them even harder through the pools and rocks, despite the cuts and grazes on his flesh, the wounds their mockery inflicted. Nothing would stop him now. Even when he staggered and fell into the abyss, he simply clambered hastily aloft and renewed the chase again. And sometimes it seemed that he was close to catching them, but it was only that they let themselves sink a little till he almost reached them. And then they sped up to elude him and he fell back again, and it should have been obvious he would never catch them. But he couldn't yield. Again and again he tried to catch them. Until, foaming with rage, he paused breathless and stretched his clenched fist up towards the maidens.

"If I could just catch one of them," he muttered to himself.

But even he could recognize the hopelessness.

So Alberich stood, trapped in speechless rage, desolate and defeated, gazing upward at what would remain forever inaccessible, when suddenly his eye was drawn to an entirely new, a truly extraordinary spectacle.

Through the water from above a continuously brightening glow was breaking. On a high point of the middle rock, that glow kindled to a blinding, radiantly shining gleam. A truly magical light was streaming from this through the water.

The maidens had seen it too, and seen that Alberich had seen it. Morning had dawned in the upper world, and the sun was awakening the Rhinegold, which seemed to smile in the radiance of its own refracted light. Now their previous fear was alerted once again. Together they swam back to the rock, and circled it, continuing to mock him as they did so, increasing their mirth

9

indeed, to distract him from the gold. The water gleamed with golden light. The maidens swimming round the rock merely augmented it.

And Alberich's eyes, powerfully attracted by the gleam, were fixed upon the gold, mesmerized by what he saw.

"What is it?" he demanded.

And had the impudence to call the Maidens "skinny".

The impudence, the arrogance, and still the ignorance.

The sisters ignored the former two, and scorned that ignorance.

"Where have you lived, you ignoramus, that you've never heard of the Rhinegold?"

"Don't you know anything of the golden eyes that wake and sleep in turn?"

"Of the wondrous star in the depths of the water whose glory lightens the waves?"

"Can't you see how blithely we glide in its radiance? And would you, faint-heart, then bathe in brightness too? Come float and frolic with us."

They laughed and sang the ancient poetry, still teasing him, asserting power over him through mockery and incitement of his lust. But Alberich had already transcended lust. Or sexual lust had been transmogrified, into a hunger for a very different possession. Because lust itself is boundless.

"I'm not interested," he scoffed, "in an object whose only purpose is to provide a candle for a childish underwater game."

"You wouldn't be so dismissive," Woglinde chided him, "if you knew its real wonders."

"The world's wealth," Wellgunde added, "can be won by anyone who could fashion a ring out of this gold – for it would be a ring that would grant measureless power."

As if telling a stranger this might ever be the best way to protect the sacred gold.

But the time of the fulfilment of the curse had been decreed, and it was beyond the capacity of the Rhine Maidens to prevent it. They too were the agents of its fate.

"Our father taught us this," Flosshilde spoke, "and made us vow to guard the shining hoard with all our wisdom, so that nobody of false intent should find a crafty way to steal it." Too late she realized how vast a secret she was giving away for free. "Peace, you chatterers," she interrupted herself.

But her sisters still hadn't realised what they were saying. Or perhaps the Norns, who weave the threads of fate, were secretly guiding them.

"Most prudent sister, why do you chide us in this way?" Wellgunde laughed. "You know perfectly well that there's only one soul in all the world who can forge that golden charm."

"He who forswears the sway of love," Woglinde added. "He who forebears the delights of love. He alone can muster the magic that will transform this gold into a ring."

"Then we're secure and free from care," Wellgunde concluded. "For everything that lives loves; there's no one who would wish to be free of love's fetters."

"This lascivious gnome least of all," added Woglinde. "His greed for love is likely to be the death of him!"

Perhaps she was wrong then, Flosshilde thought. Perhaps his lust for women would preclude his gaining of the gold.

"I have no fear of him," she said, and she too went on mocking him.

"Dearest gnome!" they goaded, "won't you laugh with us?"

And so they laughed, and swam, to and fro in the growing light. But Alberich was deaf to their taunts now. His eyes were fixed upon the precious gold, for he had listened very carefully to the sisters' hasty chatter.

"The world's wealth," he was brooding. "By your spell might I win that for my own. If love's denied me, my cunning shall win me all the other delights instead."

"Continue to mock!" he shouted to the Maidens.

It was terribly loud. A new Alberich. And frightening.

"The Nibelung," he warned, "is near your plaything!"

And in a rage, he suddenly sprang towards the middle rock, clambering with terrible haste up to its summit. No slithering and sliding now. No concern for jagged rocks. The three Rhine Maidens in their panic were racing to the rocks from different sides, screaming now, not mocking. But the dwarf was there before them. And the waters churning.

"Save yourselves. The dwarf's distraught. Love's made him lose his wits."

And yet they were still laughing. As though the reality of the impending catastrophe had not sunk in. Or perhaps they still thought they could save the day.

Scrambling upwards, the triumphant Alberich jeered at the sisters, shouting at them to go woo in the dark. With a last spring, he reached the summit. Goading them now, provoking them with taunts, asking mockingly if they were still without fear, he stretched his hand towards the gold. With fearful energy he tore it from the rock, held it aloft, proclaiming that he would be the one to forge the vengeful ring, cursing love to give himself the power. It was impossible, impossible – yet it was true. The Rhinegold had been prized from its rock, by the magic of a dwarf denouncing love. The guardians had failed in their sacred duty. Hastily, Alberich plunged down into the depths, clutching the gold triumphantly - and disappeared. Darkness enveloped the cavern with a suddenness that was terrifying. Mocking laughter echoed from the chasms deep below.

Frantic at their loss, the maidens dived down after the robber, crying "Seize on the spoiler," and "Rescue the gold," and "Help us," and "Woe." But the water only sank down with them, and from the lowest depth nothing could be heard except the shrill, the mocking laughter, of a jubilant, disdainful Alberich.

And high above all this, among the cliffs and precipices of the Drachensberg mountains, the bright sunlight of the dawn of day retreated. All along the Rhine, rocks vanished into thickest darkness. Entire caverns filled from top to bottom with dense, black waves of water, which for some time seemed to go on sinking downward, as though they too were vainly in pursuit of Alberich and the stolen Rhinegold. But the waves gradually evaporated into clouds, which little by little became lighter, and at length dispersed completely, until there was nothing upon the whole surface of the world but mist.

SCENE TWO

The dark waters continued to transform themselves into billowing clouds, and the clouds into fine mist. The theft of the gold had not yet altered the course of the universe, but something else had changed. In the growing light of dawn a fortress had appeared, crowned with glittering pinnacles and with gleaming battlements, where none had ever stood before. Wotan, the father of the gods, slept on, stretched out upon a flowery bank in a clearing in the woods high up in the mountains, dreaming of that very fortress as he'd dreamed of it for years and years. But Fricka, his wife, had woken, and her gaze fell on what was actual brick and stone. What had seemed at first the residue of dream, and then a mirage, now became entirely visible, perched on a cliff that overlooked the valleys where the Rhine flowed, miles and miles of miles and miles, flowing towards eternity.

Fricka rose and gazed hard at the fortress. Nothing so alarming had taken place in generations.

"Wotan!" she shook him. "Wake up!"

But he was dreaming, as he always dreamed, of eternal might and endless fame. How tired she was of these illusions. She shook him again and now he did wake up. He raised himself a little, reassured her that the kingdom of the gods was safe and there was no need for concern. But then he too became conscious of the fortress. Where she was alarmed, Wotan just smiled. For it was done – at last. The completion of his eternal work. At last. There on the mountain top stood the fortress of the gods, just as he'd seen it in his dreams; just as he'd intended it, strong, and beautiful, and majestic.

Fricka was less enthusiastic, however. She feared, she told him, for her sister Freia, the goddess of youth, whom all men craved, and whom Wotan had promised to the builders of Valhalla.

"Now that it's done," she observed anxiously, "payment will be due. Have you forgotten the price? The pledge?"

"No, my dear," Wotan was unperturbed. "I well remember what the insolent builders stipulated."

Fricka scoffed.

"And you intend to pay it?"

"My dear, he's bound us by a contract to build this glorious hall. Thanks to our might, and his skills, there it stands. The cost is immaterial!"

Immaterial? How could he? And how could he ever have signed that contract? Fricka had no time for this display of loveless optimism. Her sister's very life was threatened.

"Had I known of that contract, I, I would have stopped it before it was ever signed," she was so angry it made her voice quiver. "But no, you kept us women at a distance, deliberately, so that you men could bargain with the giants. Rashly, and shamefully, you promised the lovely Freia my sister in exchange. O you men, you were well satisfied with this arrangement. What's a woman, after all, when heartless men go hankering after power?"

Wotan the Storm-God, whose rages were infamous. Yet now he was as calm as a summer's afternoon.

"Was such hankering so far from your mind," he replied quietly, "when you begged me for such a building?"

"It was your infidelity, my husband, that drove me to keep you by my side. I had visions of a splendid home, gorgeously furnished, in which we could relax. But you, you thought only of defences and of ramparts, of dominion and power. Only storm and strife accompanied the building of this fortress."

Amused, Wotan smiled at Fricka.

"That my wife might want to keep me at home," he said, "I would understand, if this were just another normal bourgeois marriage. But as a god, it's my obligation and my duty to conquer the whole world, and for that one needs a fortress. Ranging and changing are life's delights. These are pastimes I simply cannot give up."

"Why, you cold, unloving, disagreeable creature," Fricka retorted. "For the worthless baubles of power and dominion, would you throw away my love and the life of a precious woman?"

"My dear, I forfeited one of my eyes when I wooed you for my wife. I know the sacrifices one must make for love. How stupid of you to scold me now."

Fricka scoffed. The man admired women rather more than she would wish. And as for Freia, surely it had never entered his head actually to give her up?

"Did you?" she asked.

"Did I what?"

"Did you seriously intend to give up Freia when the deal was done?"

But Wotan had no time to answer. For then, precisely then, who should come running towards him but the girl herself. Freia, Fricka's sister, goddess of love and beauty, the most exquisite creature ever born to tempt and tantalise poor frail men. But how curious, to be running wild across the open hills, when what she was seeking was clearly shelter.

Freia rushed in, calling for help, as if in hasty flight. Behind her, coming closer though still scarcely visible, Fasolt the giant was in pursuit of her, ready for the fulfilment of his bargain, desperate to carry her off.

Fasolt the giant. Wotan knew this creature well. Once upon a time he'd been a dwarf and not a giant, the son of King Hreidmar of Norseland, brother of Fafner and…Wotan couldn't remember the third brother's name, and anyway it didn't matter, for he was dead, killed accidentally by Loge, and both remaining dwarves had changed their names when they used their magic powers to transform themselves from dwarves to giants. Good dwarves too, they'd been, Fasolt skilled in teaching men to sow and reap, to work metals and to sail seas; he could tame horses too, and yoke beasts of burden; he could build houses, and he knew how to spin and weave and sew. What better choice to build Valhalla? Why wouldn't he give Freia to such a man?

But now Fasolt had charged in, issuing demands and utterly forgetting how a giant should behave when in the presence of the father of the gods.

"Sit down and calm yourself," Wotan was dismissive of Fasolt's threats. "Have you seen Loge?"

Fricka could scarcely believe what she was hearing.

"Are you still ready to trust that trickster?" she demanded "He's been bad news for the gods ever since the day we first encountered him. But you, you're still captivated."

Wotan was imperturbable. "When simple courage is called for," he said, "I don't need anybody's help. But when jealousy has to be dealt with, only wily subtlety will serve. Loge persuaded me to sign the agreement on the understanding that Freia would be released from it."

"And now you're relying on him and he isn't here. Left us in the lurch just when the giants are approaching. Where's your wily assistant now?"

"And where are my brothers?" Freia called out plaintively.

But neither Donner nor Froh were to be seen.

"Your brothers," Fricka scoffed, "betrayed you when they signed that evil pact, and now where are they? Lying low, I'll bet."

Not far behind Fasolt, Fafner too had come to demand his booty. Both men were of truly gigantic stature, strong, crude and ignorant. Wotan recalled how Fafner, even as a dwarf, had been famous for his powerful arm and respected for his fearless soul. And now he'd added height and muscle to his blacksmith's frame. Now he and his brother went armed with powerful wooden clubs, and a grisly determination to receive what they were owed. Each looked at Freia, and it was obvious from their leering glances that another struggle would be imminent if this one were resolved. For Freia had been promised, but not to two men, that would have been unnatural. Yet two clearly wanted her.

"Strange the things that happen when you're fast asleep," it was Fasolt who spoke first, pointing to the castle, "and others are busy working their balls off. D'you know how many stones we dragged up there? D'you know what it took to make those gates and towers and doors. Ain't no one ever gonna get into that castle who's not an invited guest."

Saying which, he held out his empty hand, and he could have been expecting Wotan to shake it, or he could have been expecting Wotan to fill it. The smile that cut his face was like a scar.

"Take possession, Wotan," he said. "But pay me first."

"Name your fee."

"Name it? It was named long ago, or is your memory that feeble? Freia the fair, Holda the free, to take home with us."

"You must be out of your minds," said Wotan quickly. "I have no authority to give you Freia."

Fasolt stood speechless in angry astonishment.

"Is this betrayal, Wotan? Are the runes on your spear just a joke? Does a sealed contract mean nothing to the father of the gods?"

Fafner had been silent all this while, but now he turned to his brother and, scornfully, asked him: "Do you recognize fraud when you see it?"

Fasolt was wiser than he seemed. They would get nowhere with threats. This needed arguments. He would appeal with Justice, not a sword.

"Wotan," he said, "your authority depends upon observance of the law. Your power may be carefully calculated and you may be clever, but in order to keep the peace you've bound in covenants those who were free. Break those covenants yourself, and you give up your power. I curse your wisdom and I say there'll be no more peace between us, unless you honour this contract. Thus a stupid giant gives advice to a clever god."

"A stupid giant indeed," Wotan replied, "who takes seriously what was contracted as a jest. In any case, what use would a lovely and charming goddess be to such louts?"

Fasolt bristled at this.

"Are you mocking us?" he accused Wotan. "Such injustice! You who attached so much importance to beauty were quite willing to trade a beautiful woman for these turrets of stone. But now it's clear, while the giants, poor creatures, sweated and toiled with callused hands to win a beautiful and gentle woman, neither beauty nor justice meant anything to you."

Fafner had no patience for this idle chatter. Clearly they weren't going to win this argument with words. Nor did they need to. The reality was obvious. Freia was worth little to the giants, but her loss would upset the gods greatly. And right now, betrayed and unpaid, upsetting the gods was precisely what he wanted.

"Golden apples," he enunciated softly, privately, to Fasolt, but wanting to be sure that Fasolt understood his innuendo, "grow in her garden, and she alone knows how to tend them. By eating them, the gods are able to remain perpetually young. But if Freia were taken away, they would become sick and pale, old and weak, and waste away."

And then, aloud, and roughly, for Wotan's benefit, but still to Fasolt.

"Enough of this chatter. Let's just take the girl and leave."

And where, but where, was Loge? Wotan needed to buy time.

"Ask for another form of payment."

"No. You promised us Freia. We want what we're entitled to."

"Come with us. Now!" Fafner instructed her. And saying this he and his brother moved to take her. But just as they did so, Froh and Donner arrived, and Freia called to them to help her. Froh clasped Freia in his arms and Donner planted himself before the two giants, threatening them with his hammer. The giants stood still, mystified. They didn't want a fight, just their fair wages. Yet there was Donner, offering a measured blow with his carefully swung hammer. Until Wotan intervened, stretching out his spear between the disputants.

"Not by force!' he commanded. "This agreement is guaranteed by the shaft of my spear."

"Will you abandon me?" Freia said in shock

"Is that your decision, you cruel man?" Fricka added.

Wotan turned away.

And at that very moment Loge came up from the valley.

At last, Wotan breathed deeply and exhaled an angry sigh that Loge couldn't possibly misinterpret. But just in case, Wotan asked him, measuring his sarcasm exactly as he measured forks of lightning when he targeted the oak trees in the ancient forests, asked him if perhaps he was arriving here in a hurry because he wanted to be sure he kept his promise to sort out the bargain. Loge feigned surprise.

"What bargain," he wondered? "You mean the contract with the giants that the god himself negotiated?"

Wotan hadn't expected this. Such impudence. Such abrogation of responsibility.

"That I negotiated?" he enquired.

But Loge was imperturbable.

"Home and hearth are of no interest to me," he said. "Donner and Froh might worry about board and lodging, especially if they're looking for a marital home. Wotan wanted a stately hall, a mighty castle, and there it stands. Strongly built too. Didn't I check it myself to ensure its quality? I've found Fasolt and Fafner to be entirely trustworthy. Not a stone's out of place. On time and on budget – which is rare enough these days. I've been busy doing the foreman's job these past few hours, not lazing about like others I could name."

"Be careful, Loge," Wotan retorted, not willing to be fobbed off with such pompous talk. "If you betray me." He paused, allowing his eyes to speak what his mouth preferred not to utter formally. But words were necessary too. "Amongst the gods," he resumed, "I am your only friend. I backed you when the others were mistrustful. Now is the time for you to counsel wisely. When the builders asked for Freia as their payment, did I not agree only on the basis of your promise to secure her release?"

Loge looked from face to face, weighing up his answer. But there was nothing on the other scale.

"It's true enough," he admitted finally, "that I did promise to give careful consideration to her release. But how could I promise to find what doesn't exist and can never be found? How could anyone promise such a thing?"

"See what a treacherous rogue he is," Fricka reproached her husband.

"His name should be 'Liar', not 'Loge'," Froh added.

While Donner threatened to put out his flame.

It was plain to Loge that these fools were abusing him only in an attempt to hide their own shame. But what could he do, or say? And while he tried to make his mind up, Donner raised his hammer as though to strike Loge. But Wotan stepped between them, coming to his defence.

"Leave him alone!" he commanded. "He's right to be cautious. His advice is worth even more when it's cautiously given."

"So are contracts, Wotan. So pay up," Fafner demanded.

And Fasolt nodded his agreement.

Wotan turned sharply to Loge, demanding urgently to know what Loge had been doing with his time. Now the two were locked, eye to eye, as if in combat. Had Loge not just told him what he'd been doing? Inspecting the ramparts and the barbicans, checking the reality against the theory of construction drawings, verifying the thickness of the mortar and the quality of frosted glass. The foreman's job, he'd called it. Did Wotan not believe him? No, even in silence, just from his eyes, he could see that Wotan didn't believe him. He'd been elsewhere. The father of the gods had prescience that others didn't have. He saw what others couldn't see. He could recognize the disingenuous.

"Ingratitude has always been my lot," Loge answered at last. "I'm concerned only for your interests, Wotan." But Wotan hadn't let his glance slip so much as a millimetre. "The honest truth?" Loge ventured. "I've been turning the whole world upside down, trying to find a substitute for Freia." Now every eye was fixed on him, not only Wotan's. "But I looked in vain," he added, "and now I realize that there's nothing in the world more precious to a man than female beauty."

Looks of astonishment and perplexity greeted this pronouncement. But none could disagree with him. Nor was Wotan challenging his alibi.

"Wherever life's to be found," Loge continued, "in the water, on the land, and in the air, I've inquired whether anything is deemed more important. But my question only drew derision, for no one seemed prepared to abandon love."

Astonishment and perplexity transformed now into excitement. Loge had never known such an attentive audience.

"However," he went on, "I did encounter one man who'd renounced these favours, who'd sworn to forsake love, in return for gold." Not just an attentive audience. In this moment, perhaps for the first and only time in history, the entire family of the gods was held captive. And not by a blade, but by an impossible idea, an idea so vast and so untenable that, were it true, their own place in the universe might be in jeopardy. "The naïve children of the Rhine," Loge went on, "the Rhine Maidens, told me of their misfortune at the hands of Night-Alberich, the Nibelung. How he wooed them in vain, and then, in revenge, he stole the Rhinegold. And now he values it more highly than a woman's love. Any woman – even Freia."

Wotan hadn't expected this. Now he was irritated. He had his own problems to worry about and was in no position to help others deal with theirs. But on the other hand, if this were true.

"What do they want?" he asked.

"They asked me to bring this appeal to Wotan, that you'll bring the thief to justice and return the gold to the waters, so it can be theirs forever. I promised to inform Wotan of this, and I've kept my word."

Fasolt had been listening attentively to all of this. Leaning close to Fasolt, he whispered in his brother's ear, stating firmly that he begrudged Alberich the gold. Fafner nodded in agreement. The Nibelung had long been a source of trouble to the giants, and yet he'd always managed to avoid capture. Fafner feared even more trouble now he had the gold. This was more serious even than the business of the contract.

"Tell us, Loge, how the Nibelung might benefit from this," he asked.

Loge looked to Wotan for permission to reply. The father of the gods nodded.

"Lying in the water," Loge answered, "the gold's just a plaything. But if someone can forge a ring from it, that ring would give its owner immeasurable power, the utmost power there is. It would win him the world."

Wotan vaguely recalled the legend, forgotten by him for millennia, but now his memory was rediscovering it, and it rendered him deeply thoughtful. The Rhinegold. Yes. And a rumour, or a legend, that immense riches lay hidden within its bright gleam. O yes. He too had heard that a ring such as this could be the source of power and wealth. Loge told lies constantly, for the pleasure, or from laziness, or for self-protection. But this, this was no lie. And if the gold of the Rhine Maidens had really been stolen…

But Fricka had a woman's attitude to gold, and she approached Loge now in confidence, to ask softly whether glittering trinkets made from the gold could be used to adorn women.

"O I assure you," Loge told her, "a wife adorned with such a ring could command her husband's fidelity."

"In which case," Fricka suggested to Wotan, nuzzling against his arm and caressing his chin with her long fingers, "perhaps my husband could win the gold himself."

Wotan didn't answer. He seemed, increasingly, to be under some sort of spell, as though the magic of the ring had already enthralled him. And indeed, he had already recognized the importance of the ring, even though it didn't actually exist as yet, even though it still needed to be forged.

"How can such a ring be forged?" he asked.

"A magic charm turns the gold into a ring," Loge explained. "Nobody knows the charm. But it can easily be mastered by someone who renounces love."

Wotan turned away disconsolately.

"That's not your course in life, Wotan, to renounce love," Loge retorted. "You couldn't do it if you wanted. And anyway, it's too late now. Alberich has the gold and he didn't hesitate. He made the spell, and now he possesses the ring."

"And all of us will become his slaves," Donner remarked, "unless the ring is taken from him."

"Then I must have the ring," said Wotan.

"Can the ring now be obtained without first having to curse love?" Froh enquired. And Loge smiled.

"It would be child's play," he answered.

"Tell us how," Wotan demanded.

"By theft!" came the reply. "What a thief steals, steal back from the thief. Nothing could be easier. But be careful, Wotan. Alberich is wily. It'll be necessary to act with cunning," – this rather more warmly stated – "if the thief is to be brought to justice and the gold returned to the Rhine Maidens."

"The Rhine Maidens?" Wotan replied. "I couldn't care less about the Rhine Maidens."

"Don't even speak their names," Fricka added. "Watery, sluttish creatures. Many a good husband, to my sorrow, lured away by their licentious bathing."

Wotan stood still, and it seemed that he was silently struggling with himself. The other gods fixed their eyes on him in mute suspense.

In the meanwhile, Fafner had been conferring with Fasolt. Obviously, he'd told his brother, the gold would be of greater use to them than Freia could ever be. The gold's magic would confer eternal youth just as effectively, and frankly, if all they wanted was a woman, the power of the ring would bring them all the gorgeous girls their hearts could possibly desire. Fasolt slouched and shambled, and his shoulders drooped. His voice was agreeing with Fafner, but his demeanour suggested he'd been convinced against his will. For Fasolt had his heart set, not on any woman but specifically on Freia. His heart wasn't willing to be convinced.

But Fafner was moving faster than he could move to stop him. Fafner was already giving up the girl.

"Wotan," Fafner approached the father of the gods. "The giants," he said, "are resolved to forego Freia and to settle instead for the Nibelung's gold."

If Fasolt was alarmed by this, Wotan was simply incredulous.

"Are you out of your minds?" he replied. "Your request is shameless. And besides, how could I give you what I don't possess?"

"It was hard to build the fortress," Fafner answered. "But it would be easy by cunning and force to tie the Nibelung down."

"You're shameless. Completely shameless. You greedy fools."

This was too much for Fasolt, who'd been looking for some way to retreat from his brother's offer, and now recognized his opportunity. Taking her by her wrist, he seized Freia and held her tight, pressing his knife against her throat, drawing her with Fafner away from the gods.

"This will be our hostage till the ransom's paid," he called, while Freia screamed, and the gods sat powerless.

Fafner understood what his brother had done, and that he must go along with it. They were committed now. There was no turning back.

"The gold," Fafner pointed with his finger at a spot on the ground, as though this was where he expected to find the gold piled up, "by this evening. Or Freia will be forfeit. Forever."

Freia was distraught. She cried out once more to her sister and her brothers, beseeching them to help her in her plight. But none reacted. Donner and Froh moved not so much as a muscle on their faces, but simply froze, as though ineptitude had turned them into stone. They were waiting for Wotan to make the first move. But Wotan knew that nothing he could do would make the slightest difference. Later, yes, perhaps. It needed thought, and planning. To save Freia, and to win the gold, defeat the giants, keep the castle, stop the Nibelung, keep Fricka happy without yielding everything to her, thank Loge without making his head swell, ensure that everyone respected him and honoured him as father of the gods. All this, by one connected and concerted plan. Too much to resolve at once, even for the father of the gods. And there was Freia, screaming for help again as she was being dragged away, wrestling hopelessly with the hastily retreating giants. The gods looked at Wotan enquiringly, but got no answer. The only sound atop that mountain precipice was Freia's screams as they became more distant.

Loge watched the giants make off with the hapless Freia. Over hill and down dale he saw them go, fording the Rhine, heading for Riesenheim, the home of giants. A pale mist had filled the horizon, gradually growing denser. In it the gods' appearances were becoming wan and aged, as if they too were growing pale, as though the kidnapping of Youth had already left Old Age to rule the universe. Dismayed and expectant they stood now, looking at Wotan, whose eyes were fixed on the ground in unresolved, bewildered thought. Already their cheeks had lost their bloom, their eyes had lost their sparkle. Froh seemed exhausted and Donner could no longer hold his hammer. Fricka certainly wasn't herself either, and Wotan had turned grey, as old age suddenly overtook him. Loge soon realised what had happened. The gods had gone without their daily ration of Freia's apples, necessary to keep them vigorous and young. But the keeper of the garden was now held for ransom. And o, he knew, he knew what this would mean. The fruit would fade and wither on the branches, until it all decayed and fell. Loge himself wasn't affected because Freia was always stingy with her fruit for him and, after all, he was only a demigod. But the giants had understood how dependent the gods had become on the fruit. Without the apples, the race of the gods would become old and grey, hoary and pitiful, withered and the butt of jokes. Without Freia, he knew, the gods would die.

"See what you've done, Wotan," Fricka anxiously castigated her husband. "You take everything so lightly, and now you've brought abuse and shame upon the gods."

For a moment Wotan neither looked at her nor responded. Then, suddenly resolute, he pulled himself together and instructed Loge that the two of them would go down into Nibelheim to win the gold.

"It's good that you're answering the call of the Rhine Maidens," Loge answered.

But Wotan answered violently, "Shut up, you fool. We go to ransom Freia. No other cause."

"This way then," Loge indicated the path down through the mountain to the river.

"No," Wotan replied. He'd already thought this through, and had rejected the idea of approaching Nibelheim through the Rhine. There was another route, a better route, known only to the gods, accessible only to the gods. Dangerous, and difficult, but necessary. Nor did Wotan need to speak it. Loge understood.

"Then come this way," Loge suggested, and at once the two began their descent through a crevice in the rocks from which sulphurous fumes were issuing. Dragon territory. The realm of spiders, goblins, scorpions and trolls. A space of gloom and murkiness, darker even than the minds of men. But what other route was there, if they were to achieve their goal? Both knew, and understood. Loge went first, disappearing into the cleft. Wotan held back a moment, turning to the other gods to say goodbye.

"The rest of you stay here," he gave command. "I will return soon and banish your ageing with redeeming gold."

"Fare well," said Donner.

"Good luck," said Froh.

"Return quickly and safely to an anxious wife," said Fricka.

So Wotan followed Loge into the rock's cleft. The sulphurous vapour that issued from it rendered the whole world invisible, filling it with dense, black clouds. As they descended through the rocks, the vapours darkened into an even more opaque black cloud that extended from the mountaintop right down to the valley floor. Soon they were clambering over the jagged edges of a rocky chasm, moving continually downwards as though their journey wasn't to the Earth but underneath it, to the very bowels of inner Earth. At last a dark red light grew visible, glowing in the distance somewhere, now on this side, now on that. The growing sound of forging became audible, a din of anvils that as quickly died away. They were, they realised, inside some subterranean cavern, open on every side in narrow shafts, but stretching so far out of sight its end was quite invisible. They had come to Nibelheim.

SCENE THREE

Deep in Nibelheim, Alberich was dragging his howling brother Mime from a shaft, tugging him by the hair, threatening to punch him, and to punch him painfully, if the smith didn't finish his work in time.

"But it's done," Mime protested. "Ouch! Hey, stop tugging at my ear. It's done I tell you. Done."

"Where is it then?" Alberich demanded. "Why haven't you produced the work?"

"I, I," Mime stammered, and clenched his fist. "I needed to be sure nothing was missing."

"Missing? What could be missing?"

"You know. Here and there."

"What 'here and there'?" demanded Alberich. "And what's that in your hand. Give it to me!"

Alberich tried to catch his brother's ear again, but Mime dodged and shuffled. Then, in his anxiety, Mime's fist fell open, and out of it fell the metal object he'd been holding in his hand. Alberich picked it up quickly and examined it with care. He seemed well pleased. The object appeared to be perfect in every respect.

"Perfect," he smiled. "Forged exactly as I instructed. Finished and fit. And why was it concealed in your fist? Because, you sly little rogue," he seized Mime by the scruff of the neck and lifted him almost two inches off the ground, "you wanted to trick me, didn't you?" Mime's feet were on the ground again, but now his beard was gripped in Alberich's hand, and he was staring into the blackness of his brother's nostrils. "You wanted to keep this splendid object for yourself. Didn't you?" Alberich spat as he spoke, leaving droplets of saliva on Mime's face. The roots of his beard were aching. "Alberich's cunning taught you how to forge it. Did you really think you had sufficient cunning to steal it from me?"

Saying this, Alberich let his brother go, took the object from his brother's now open palm, and put it on his head. He'd decided he would call it the "Tarnhelm", this magic helmet of the giants which he'd created with the power of the ring. It fitted perfectly. It fitted, surprisingly for an iron helmet, very softly. And now, now was the moment to perform the helmet's real magic, the one thing he'd wisely not told his brother. Now was the moment to pronounce the spell.

"Night and mist," he said, then slowly, magically slowly, "resembling - nothing.'

As the last word was pronounced, so did his form vanish, and in his place there was nothing but a pillar of white mist.

"Can you see me, brother?"

"Where are you, Alberich?" Mime sounded terrified.

"If you can't see me, then you'll just have to feel me instead."

And on that note he began to pound and pummel Mime, until his brother was writhing under the rain of blows, whose sound echoed through the caverns though the scourge could not be seen.

And how the invisible Alberich was laughing, mocking his brother cruelly, thanking his "idiot" brother and commanding the Nibelung to bow to Alberich.

"Now I'm the Lord of Everywhere and Everything," he cried. "Now I shall be the omnipresent and the omni," the word escaped him, but it didn't matter, he was laughing, laughing with the power of the ring he'd forged, and the further power he'd already seized by using it. "I shall be everywhere, watching. I shall never rest again. When you least expect me, I shall be there, watching you." O, this was more fun than he could remember, ever. "All of you will be my subjects. Forever. I am the Lord of the Nibelungen."

Wotan and Loge could hear his voice in the distance as they came down from the cleft in the rock face. Screams and cries answered from the lower caverns, but the voice wasn't Freia's, as they had feared. It was Mime, Loge recognized, and as the cloud of vapour dissipated in the heat and flashing sparks of the glowing anvil, so Loge could now see Mime, cowering in pain as though he were being beaten. But all alone. The sound of Alberich's scolding was already well off in the distance, faint as mist. Yet Mime continued to cower there in pain.

Wotan had come down from the cleft a little behind Loge, and now found him, bent over Mime, cheerfully enquiring why the giant was whining so, what cut him and tormented him?

"Just leave me in peace," Mime moaned back.

"Gladly, my friend," Loge replied. "But I'll help you first."

With difficulty, Loge raised him to his feet, still moaning how nobody could help him now, since he must obey his brother who had put him into chains.

"How so?" Loge enquired.

"Through the golden ring he's forged," Mime explained. "The ring that he made from the Rhinegold. The one he's used to enslave his people. He can cast spells with it that make you tremble. We Nibelungen," Mime was rubbing his eyes and recovering his breath, "we Nibelungen were once a race of carefree blacksmiths, who made ornaments for our women, wonderful jewels and lovely trinkets. We laughed as we worked. Now that villain forces us to labour for him alone. With the help of the ring he can discover what new seams are to be found in the clefts and he forces the Nibelungen to dig them out, to melt and forge and cast and never rest, just to pile up their master's hoard."

"And he beat you for laziness."

"No. It wasn't that. He gave me the hardest task of all, to forge a helmet to his precise instructions. But I understood what I was making. I could see what extraordinary power would fall on him as owned that helmet. I, I, I intended to keep it for myself. I was going to use it to escape from Alberich's tyranny. Perhaps, I thought, perhaps I could outwit my brother and maybe even snatch the ring and become his lord and master! But alas. I completed the work, but I couldn't use the binding spell. And now I've discovered all too well the extent of the helmet's powers. Alberich put it on and simply vanished, vanished out of sight. And invisible he doled out blows upon this blind man. That's the way this foolish Mime has been thanked for all his efforts."

Mime stood there, rubbing his back and arms and legs. But Loge and Wotan couldn't help but laugh.

"This task we've come here for," Loge suggested to Wotan, "it won't be easy."

"I'm relying on your cunning," Wotan answered.

Mime was struck by the gods' laughter, and now, studying them more closely, asked who they were.

"Your friends," Loge replied. "We're here to free the Nibelungen people from their troubles."

As though these words had magically summoned him, Alberich appeared, and Mime, hearing him approach, sank back in terror, began running first this way, then that, as though it were even possible to hide from him who now possessed the Tarnhelm. But Wotan just sat quietly on a stone and waited.

Alberich hadn't in fact appeared, except in the sense of removing the Tarnhelm, for he'd been there all the time. Now the Tarnhelm hung from his belt and he was driving before him, using a brandished whip, a team of Nibelungen laden down with gold and silver that they heaped up in a pile. Abusively, scolding them, he directed his slaves where to pile the treasure, and how much faster he required them to work, then pretended he'd suddenly become aware of Wotan and of Loge – or, at least, of strangers, for he didn't recognize them.

"Have you been prattling to these strangers?" Alberich berated Mime, and drove him with blows of his whip to join the crowd of Nibelungen, sending him off to forge and mould, threatening all of them with further whippings if anyone was idle. Smiling at his own authority, he drew the ring from his finger, kissed it, and stretched it out threateningly as he pronounced a command:

"Tremble and quake, you wretched slaves! Obey, and quickly, the great lord of the ring!"

With howls and screams the Nibelungen, Mime cowering amongst them, went the ways the blows that each received directed them, each into different clefts of the mineshafts, vanishing in all directions. While Alberich gazed mistrustfully at Wotan and at Loge.

"What's your business here?" he demanded.

"We heard of marvels being worked by Alberich in Nibelheim," Wotan replied. "We were anxious to see them for ourselves. Greed has made us your guests."

"Greed?" Alberich mused. "Envy more likely. I can well understand that others might be envious of me. I know well what people are."

"In which case," Loge answered, "you must know who I am. No? Listen to me, Alberich. Without this fire, the caverns of Nibelheim would be cold and dark, and forging would be impossible. I've been a good friend to the Nibelungen, and now I find your manner, shall I say, discourteous?"

"I said I know you, and know you I do, Loge," Alberich replied. "And I see from your companion that the light-elves now consort with gods. If you prove as false a friend to them as you once were to Alberich, then I have nothing to fear from you."

"Do you not trust me?"

"I trust your disloyalty, not your loyalty. And as to me, I defy the lot of you."

"And as to me," Loge replied, "I admire your courage and your power."

He may have meant it disingenuously, but Alberich was too enraptured by that power to notice.

"Do you see the wealth I've gathered?" his arm was pointing from one hoard to another.

"I see it," Loge answered.

"This is nothing," Alberich went on, "compared to what remains to be accrued."

"Yes," Wotan responded, "but what use such treasure when there's nothing you can buy in Nibelheim?"

"Nibelheim exists now to create treasures and to hide them. But with this hoard I shall perform wonders, and then I shall win the whole world."

"I see," said Wotan, most politely. "And how do you intend to achieve that?"

"Up there, amongst the gentle breezes," Alberich replied, "you gods laugh and make love. But with these golden hands I shall make the gods my prisoners. As I've forsworn love, so all living creatures will forswear it. Dazzled by this gold, they'll hanker for nothing but to own it. Others lull themselves complacently on wondrous heights, feasting eternally and despising the dark spirit. They should beware! When their men are subjugated I shall force myself on their women, who shun my attentions now, and foolishly reject my love."

Such laughter, such demoniacal, mocking laughter.

"Did you hear?" Alberich continued. "Beware the nocturnal hoard when the Nibelungen army rises from silent depths to daylight!"

At this Wotan burst out with violent invective but Loge stepped between them and urged Wotan to keep his head. Better to flatter the Nibelung. Better to acclaim him as the mightiest man on Earth. Better anything, than risk his wrath while he still held the Tarnhelm and the Ring.

"We're all seized with wonder," Loge rhapsodised, "seeing this work you've done. Why, if you can achieve everything you hope for from this treasure, why even the moon and stars, the shining sun itself, will serve you! And most of all the race of Nibelungen will obey you. With this ring, you've made your people cower. But what if, in sleep, a thief should creep up on you and snatch the ring, how would you defend yourself? What would you be then?"

"What would I be then? Ah Loge, you think yourself so clever and others stupid. Haven't I also made a helmet to conceal myself?" He pointed to the Tarnhelm hanging on his belt. "With this," he said, "I can assume whatever shape I please. No one will see me and I'll be safe no matter where. Even," he added, "from such a kind, considerate friend as Loge!"

"I've seen much," Loge replied, "but I've never witnessed such a miracle as this. If it's really true, and I must say that I find it hard to credit. But if it's true, then by this means, the Nibelungen really could hold power - forever."

"D'you think I'm lying? D'you think I'm making all this up?"

"I only believe," Loge responded, "what I see with my own eyes."

"Then you're a fool, a puffed up, prudent fool." Alberich was excited at the prospect of demonstrating his superiority. "Tell me what shape you'd like to see, and let me give you proof for your disbelieving eyes."

"In whatever shape you like. I wait to be amazed."

At this, Alberich put on the Tarnhelm and recited the spell: "Giant dragon, wind and curl." And at once he disappeared and, in his place, a giant serpent writhed along the ground. It lifted its head and stretched its open jaws toward Wotan and Loge. Loge pretended to be seized with terror. Wotan simply laughed and offered Alberich congratulations on his transformation. So, just as quickly as he'd appeared, the dragon vanished, and in his place stood Alberich once more, delighted with his demonstration.

Loge continued to feign tremor, and added his congratulations.

"You became so much bigger," he exclaimed with trembling voice, "but could you also become smaller. Which might," he added, "be the best way to escape danger? Perhaps that's too difficult?"

"Too difficult for you perhaps," Alberich rose to the bait. "How small would you like me?"

"Well, I don't know," Loge pondered the question for a moment. "Small enough that you could hide even in the smallest crevice. A toad, say. Yes, why not, a toad."

The challenge for Alberich was irresistible. Once again he put the Tarnhelm on. Once again a spell: "Crooked and grey, crawl toad!"

And the Nibelung disappeared.

The gods saw nothing but a slimy, poisonous toad, perched now on the rocks, crawling now towards them. And then Loge made his move. So quickly, so suddenly, too fast for Alberich to register and respond.

"Quick!" he called to Wotan. "Grab him! Catch the toad!"

Just as quickly, Wotan placed his foot right on the toad, pinning him to the rock. At once Loge reached for the toad's head and seized the Tarnhelm in his hand. Together he and Wotan grabbed the creature and soon enough wrenched off the Tarnhelm. Alberich became visible once more in his own form, but wriggling and cursing under Wotan's foot, moaning that he'd been captured. Then Loge bound his hands and legs with rope and he and Wotan seized the prisoner. Alberich struggled violently, but they managed nonetheless to drag him, writhing desperately to free himself, to the shaft by which they'd come down, and thence into a crevice where they too disappeared, mounting upward through the darkness and the vapours once again, until they'd brought Alberich, bound and now submissive, out of the chasm to the mountaintop.

SCENE FOUR

"Sit there" Loge commanded.

They'd come out in an open space just below the summit of the mountain. The panorama right up to the horizon was shrouded in pale mist.

"There's the world you've taken power over," Loge was minded not just to insult but to torment the prisoner. As he spoke he snapped his fingers, dancing around Alberich, calling him "cousin" as though to mock him. "Look around you," he pulled his beard this way and that, exactly as Alberich had pulled Mime's not an hour before. "The world you intended to rule. Vast emptiness and mist, that's all. Which little corner would you have given me for a stable?"

"You effing thief!" Alberich gave back as good as he was receiving. "You piece of…" but the last word was interrupted by a sharp pull of the beard. Alberich tried again. "You effing…" But another tug prevented that as well. "Loosen these ropes and let me go," Alberich howled. "You'll pay for this, you will. And dearly."

Alberich spat out his abuse, but Wotan merely savoured the moment.

"You're a prisoner," he said. "What you would have done to the world has now been done to you. You want to be set free? That will require a ransom."

And now it was Wotan who snapped his fingers, meaning it to show the scale of the ransom he expected.

Aloud, Alberich berated himself for his foolishness, for trusting that treacherous thief Loge. Now he swore the most terrible revenge. But Loge only laughed.

"If you're seriously considering revenge," he said, "you'd better think first about a ransom. It takes freedom to obtain revenge."

"Demand what you require," came the reply.

"The treasure, and all your gold," Wotan replied.

Alberich was shocked by this, appalled. But then it struck him, that the ring hadn't been named, and if he still possessed the ring, why he could replace the treasure and the gold as quickly next time as he had the last. It would be a salutary lesson to him, and not too high a price to pay. Why not? Why not?

"Have you decided yet?" Wotan demanded.

"Untie one of my hands. I can do nothing bound like this."

Loge untied the rope from Alberich's right hand. No sooner was the hand free than he touched the ring with his lips, and whispered a secret order:

"I summon the Nibelungen here. Their Lord commands them. From the dark to the daylight bring up your hoard." He turned back to Wotan. "Now loosen these bonds that torture me."

No sooner had he spoken his magic spell than the Nibelungen emerged out of the depths of the chasm, dragging the treasure with them, piling it higher and ever higher in a circle round their Lord. Alberich pleaded again for both his hands to be untied, appalled that his minions should see him reduced to captivity like this. But Wotan refused.

"Not until the ransom's paid in full," he insisted.

"They're paying it. They're paying it," Alberich retorted, and shouted at this one to hurry up, at that one where to place it, shouting abuse at all of them, commanding them not to look at him, threatening them with punishment if they were idle, ordering them to get straight back to their smithing once the job was done.

And soon enough it was done, vast piles of gold assembled on the mountain-top, sufficient to rebuild Valhalla if Wotan were so minded. Then, once again, Alberich kissed the ring and stretched it out commandingly. As if struck by a blow, the Nibelungen rushed cowering and terrified towards the cleft and quickly disappeared from sight.

"You have your ransom, so now let me go," Alberich demanded. "But first, give me back one piece, just one piece. That finely wrought helmet, the Tarnhelm, that Loge's holding, give me that."

But Loge threw it on the heap, declaring it to be part of the ransom too. Alberich cursed under his breath, but consoled himself with the thought that he who made the old Tarnhelm could always make another. And again he demanded that they set him free.

"Are you content, Wotan?" Loge asked his master. "Shall he go free?"

But Wotan wasn't content. He pointed to the golden ring on Alberich's finger and claimed that too as part of the treasure.

"The ring?" Alberich replied, horrified.

"To win your freedom, yes, even this ring."

"No," Alberich retorted. "My life, but not the ring."

Wotan smiled. "It's particularly your ring that I require," he said. "What you do with your life doesn't concern me."

Alberich was beside himself, trembling, desperately seeking some way to keep the ring, to convince Wotan and Loge. But what, what could he say?

"If I lose my life," he ventured, "then I must lose the ring. But, but, but my heart, my head, my eyes and ears are truly not as essential to me as is that ring. My ring. I cannot give it up."

"Your ring?" Wotan asked. "Why, you shameless scoundrel! You impudent fool! Tell us first how you got the gold from which the ring was made? Was it your own then, honestly acquired, dug out of the earth with your own bare hands? I fancy the Rhine Maidens would be able to confirm whether or not they gave the gold to Alberich for his own use. I fancy they may suggest you stole it."

"This is a shameful deceit and a monstrous piece of trickery," Alberich retorted. And then, because attack is the best form of defence, he turned on Wotan angrily. "You'd happily have stolen the gold from the Rhine yourself if you'd only known how to harness its power. How convenient for you that I, Alberich, in distress and anger, won this magical thing. Would a royal plaything be so attractive to you if the price of winning it was the renunciation of love? You should take care, Wotan. If this Nibelung sinned, it was only against himself. But you're one of the immortal ones, and you'll be sinning against everything that was, and is, and shall be, if you seize this ring."

Something in this affected Wotan deeply. Perhaps it was true, and he'd now be cursed as owner of the ring. Perhaps it was true, and he too would have to renounce love, even love of Fricka, which she would never tolerate. Perhaps. But yet the ring. The ring. He must possess the ring.

"Give me the ring and stop your prattling," Wotan cried, and seizing Alberich he violently tore the ring from off his finger. Alberich uttered a terrible cry, that he was ruined, crushed – wretched even among the wretched. But Wotan wasn't even listening. His eyes were fixed upon the ring, enthralled by it. It would render him, not just the father of the gods, but more even than that, the mightiest of all the lords. Supreme, in all the universe. Wotan put on the ring.

"Shall he go free?" Loge asked.

"Yes, set him free."

Not looking at Loge or at Alberich. Only, unceasingly, his eyes fixed on the ring.

"Get on home now," Loge commanded Alberich.

But Alberich wasn't minded to leave yet.

Raising himself he asked, and his voice was hysterical with enraged laughter: "Am I? Am I really free? In that case, I'll give you the first greeting of my freedom. As I acquired this ring by means of a curse, so let the ring itself be cursed. As its gold gave me power without limit, now let its magic bring death to him who wears it. No happy man shall ever want to own it. No fortunate man will ever benefit from it. Whoever possesses it will be afflicted with strife, and whoever lacks it will be consumed by envy. All will hanker for its possession, but none will enjoy it to advantage. Its owner will never benefit from it, for it draws him to his assassin. Assured of death, the coward will be in the grip of fear. As long as he lives, he'll thirst for death. The master of the ring will also be the ring's slave, until such time as Alberich wins back what's been stolen from him. This is the blessing with which the Nibelung, in dire distress, invests his ring."

And saying this, he broke out in bitter laughter.

"Guard the ring well, Wotan," he added as he turned towards the cleft in the rock that would lead him back down through the chasm to the underworld of the Nibelungen. But at the entrance he turned back one last time, and angrily spoke one final word.

"Wotan, understand this. You will not and you cannot escape this curse."

So he disappeared quickly into the crevice, slipping away, so Loge thought, as easily as a slimy toad. And even as he vanished, so the thick mist that had shut out the horizon gradually cleared away.

"Did you listen to love's farewell?" Loge asked, sarcastically.

Wotan was sunk in contemplation of the ring on his left hand.

"Let him say whatever his anger needs to say. It's of no consequence."

Moment by moment the sky was growing lighter. Now that he could see beyond his own feet, Loge looked around and realised that Donner, Froh and Fricka were hastening towards them.

"They're here," Froh was the first to speak.

"Welcome, brother," Donner embraced Wotan.

"What news, Wotan?" Fricka asked. "Do you bring joyful tidings?"

Loge, with deep self-satisfaction, pointed to the piled treasure.

"By cunning and by force," he said. "But there's plenty there to ransom Freia."

"Freia's nearby," Donner observed.

"Yes," Froh agreed. "From the sweetness of the air you can tell it's her. The giants must be coming for their gold."

The day grew brighter and still brighter, and with it the faces of the gods too regained their former freshness, as though the very approach of Freia were sufficient to restore their youth. But still a misty veil covered the mountaintop above them. The fortress of Valhalla was invisible.

"Freia!" Fricka called, seeing her sister led between the giants. She would have embraced the girl, indeed hurried to do so, but Fasolt restrained her, refused to let Freia go.

"Hold back woman," Fasolt cried. "She's still ours till the ransom's been paid. And you should know, we only brought her back reluctantly."

"The ransom's ready," Wotan indicated the hoard of gold.

But Fasolt wasn't listening. His eyes were fixed on Freia in just the same way Wotan's were upon the ring. Giving her up would be as hard for him as giving up the ring for Alberich. But there was, he recognised, one way of consoling him.

"Losing her will make me sad," he said. "So, if she's to vanish from my mind, the treasure will have to be heaped up so high, that it hides her completely from my sight."

Fafner smiled at this. And stood. He was waiting for the gods to do what was required.

"By Freia's form, then," Wotan instructed, "measure out the gold."

The two giants placed Freia in the middle of the pile, then planted their staves into the ground in front of her, so they could take the measure of her height and breadth. Loge and Froh hastily heaped up the treasure between the poles, though not quickly enough for Wotan, who couldn't bring himself to watch. Fafner was concerned that the gold be stacked as tightly as was possible. If there were gaps, he said, he would regard himself as cheated. So he stooped, and poked, roughly pressed the pieces of treasure together, looking for fissures, cracks and crevices, arguing with Loge all the while. Wotan turned away moodily, conscious of his own disgrace. But Fricka wasn't minded to let this occasion go by unremarked.

"Look at her," she said, drawing his eyes back to her frail form, walled in almost with gold. "This is your doing, Wotan. You've brought shame on her. You heartless…"

"Put more on the pile," Fafner demanded.

Donner could hardly contain his rage. "Come here, you dog," he shouted, and might even have come to blows with Fafner, but Wotan restrained him, saying calmly that Freia was now completely hidden by the gold.

"And anyway," Loge added, "the treasure's all used up."

Fafner measured the hoard closely with his eye, looking carefully for gaps. "I can see her hair through here. Put that piece on the pile."

"What?" Loge looked to Wotan for an answer. "Even the Tarnhelm?"

"Put it on, quickly," Fafner ordered.

"Put it on, Loge. Let it go."

Loge was astonished. But threw the Tarnhelm on the pile.

So Fasolt took one last look, going up close and peering through the hoard, lamenting the loss of his beautiful Freia. Until he caught sight of an eye. As long as he could still see those lovely eyes, he could not give up the woman.

But Fafner was only interested in filling up the fissures in the pile.

"There's nothing left," Loge protested.

"Not so," Fafner replied.

And pointed to the gleaming, golden ring on Wotan's finger.

"Give me that to fill this hole."

"What? This? My ring?" Wotan was taken aback at the suggestion.

"It isn't his to give," Loge intervened. "This gold belongs to the Rhine Maidens. Only to them may Wotan give it."

But Wotan wasn't prepared for that solution either.

"This is mine," he said. "Mine. My precious. I won it. It's my prize and I intend to keep it."

"I made a promise, Wotan. Evil will befall you if I break that promise."

"I'm not bound by your promises. I gave you no authority to make promises on my behalf. This ring is mine, my booty."

"No," Fafner interrupted, "it's part of her ransom."

"I'll part with anything else in all the world," Wotan replied. "But not for all the world will I give up this ring."

34

This was too much for Fasolt. Angrily he pulled Freia out from behind the pile of gold.

"That's it, the deal's off," he shouted. "Freia was our promise, and Freia it will be. Now she remains with us forever."

In alarm Freia cried out for help and in the same instant Fricka called to her husband to give the giants what they wanted. Froh and Donner too, oblivious of the power of the ring, urged Wotan to surrender it. Fasolt was ready to depart with his female prize, but Fafner held him back. And Wotan. Wotan gazed fixedly into everybody's eyes, one by one, clutching in one hand the ring-finger of the other.

"Leave me in peace," he cried. "This ring I will not surrender."

He turned away in anger. Darkness had fallen by this time, but from a rocky cleft not far behind them a dimly bluish light was breaking through, as though some crack had opened in the ceiling of the underworld. And so it was, for out of this narrow cleft not only light but soon enough the form of Erda gradually appeared, goddess of wisdom and the Earth, mother of Fricka, Freia, Donner and Froh, rising from the ground below to half her height, so that the lower part of her body remained rooted in the earth, while her bust and torso towered like a tall ash tree above their heads. With a gesture of warning, she stretched her hand out towards Wotan, and it was as if a tree-branch had slapped him.

"Yield the ring, Wotan," she instructed. "Yield it! Flee the dead curse which lies on the head of he who wears the ring. Escape the hopelessness and darkness that will bring you only your destruction."

"Who are you, woman?" Wotan called back.

"Everything that's ever been is known to me," Erda replied. "How all things were, and are, and will be. I am the primeval woman of the everlasting world. Erda, the all-wise. Even before the world came into being, I gave birth to three daughters, whom men call the Norns – yes, they who tell Wotan each night what Erda has seen. But now the greatest danger calls me here today. I come myself, so you shall know how grave that danger is. Hear me! Hear me, Wotan. Hear me. All that exists is bound to end. A dark day dawns for the gods. Take my advice. Wotan must yield the ring."

Slowly she sank back into the ground, until only her head and breast were visible. The bluish light began to fade.

"Stay, woman, that I may learn more."

"You know enough already. Ponder in fear and trembling what I've told you."

Saying which, she disappeared completely now.

"I must hear more," Wotan called after her. But she was gone. He tried to climb into the chasm to prevent her leaving, but Fricka and Froh both threw themselves across his way to hold him back.

"What are you raging for?" Fricka grasped his shirt.

"Don't try to follow her, Wotan," Donner implored him. "You know you may not touch a prophetess."

Wotan gazed thoughtfully in front of him, not moving, not speaking, scarcely even breathing. So Donner turned back to the giants to assure them they'd receive their gold, and Freia, hearing this, relaxed at last, truly believing that Donner at least would keep his word. But Wotan wasn't listening. He was brooding deeply over what he'd heard, gazing thoughtfully before him. At length he roused himself from deepest thought, grasped his spear and brandished it as if in token of a bold decision.

"Come to me, Freia," he held out his right hand. Then, when she'd seen his gesture, he brought the right hand over to the left, and slowly, as though it caused him anguish deeper than any he had ever known, he slid the ring from off his finger. "Bought with the gold," he mused. "Bring us your youth again, my Freia. Here, giants, take your ring."

He threw it on the pile.

At once the giants allowed Freia to go free, and joyfully she hastened to the gods, who took her in their arms one by one, kissed her and caressed her, each in turn, savouring her redemption with delight.

Fafner had spread out a huge sack and gone towards the hoard, preparing to pack it all up. No sooner had he begun to stow the treasure, than Fasolt stopped him, demanding his fair share.

"From your lovesick look," said Fafner, "I thought the girl meant more to you than all this gold. But for me, we'd have lost out on this bargain. And if we'd taken the girl, would you have talked to me then of fair shares? I doubt it, lovesick ass. Trust me, I intend to take the greater share of this."

"Shame on you, you thief!" Fasolt replied. And to the gods he said, "I call on you as judges in this matter. How should the gold be shared?"

Wotan turned away contemptuously.

"Let him take the greater part," Loge offered his advice to Fasolt. "Just make sure you get the ring."

Hearing this, Fasolt hurled himself upon his brother, who was busily loading up his sack. Fafner and Fasolt struggled. Hastily, Fasolt snatched the ring, and held it up.

"This," he cried out, "is mine. If I hadn't seen her eyes between the cracks, we never would have had it."

But Fafner wasn't giving up the struggle.

"Don't touch it!" he commanded. "That ring is mine."

Fafner snatched back the ring. But as they continued struggling, Fasolt wrested the ring from Fafner once again. Then Fafner struck out with his staff. With one blow he left Fasolt prostrate on the ground and quickly seized the ring from the clutches of the dying man.

"Now feast on Freia's eyes, you fool. This ring you'll never see again."

He put the ring into the sack, and calmly, as though nothing untoward had taken place, he went on gathering up his hoard.

Appalled, the gods stood by and witnessed, holding themselves with dignity in a long and solemn silence. To Wotan, the truth of the curse had already been made manifest. Loge knew it too.

"Your luck has held, Wotan," he said. "Congratulations. You gained much when you acquired that ring, but you've benefited even more from having it taken from you. Now your enemies are killing each other for the gold you gave away."

Wotan was trembling, gripped by fear of what he'd let loose into the world, but also resolved to learn from Erda how this fear might be mediated. There was, he knew, no other choice for him, but to descend into the underworld once more, and learn from her how care and fear might yet be overcome. Fricka caressed his arm, his hand, cajoling him to go into Valhalla.

"Why do you hesitate? The fortress you dreamed of is yours. The gates await you. You are its Lord. Come, let us take possession."

"It was an evil wage that paid for the building of that fortress," Wotan replied gloomily.

"A sultry veil of mist hangs in the air," said Donner. "It is time for me, too, to use my power."

Saying which the god of thunder summoned up the storm clouds and called forth a thunderstorm to sweep the skies clean. Climbing onto a high rock by the precipice, he swung his hammer. Even as he invoked them, the mists collected around him. Very slowly, he disappeared behind dark clouds. Nothing could be heard except the sound of his hammer as it struck the rock. Until he disappeared completely in an ever-darker, ever-thicker thundercloud. The stroke of his hammer fell heavily upon the rock. A vivid flash of lightning came from the cloud; a violent clap of thunder followed. Froh too had disappeared into the clouds. But just as suddenly the clouds dispersed, Froh and Donner became visible again, and at their feet a rainbow bridge stretched out with blinding radiance across the valley of the Rhine gorge to the fortress of Valhalla, bathed now in the half-light of the setting sun. As Froh pointed out the bridge with outstretched hand, Fafner finished collecting the hoard around his brother's body, hoisted the enormous sack onto his back, and, frightened of the clashing thunder, rushed into the chasm and was gone.

But the gods did not yet move. They stood, overwhelmed by this extraordinary sight, for a long while speechless. It was Wotan who broke the solemn silence.

"The sunlight gleams at eventide," he said, "like gold."

The image wasn't lost on the other gods. Nor was the irony of what he said next.

"In the morning too it glistered, proudly at my feet, Wotan the sun-god. From morning till night I worked, unthanked, in care and fear, to bring forth light. Light! Now night is falling. Now it's night that offers us a shelter from the day's ills."

He paused and, when he resumed, it was as though he'd been struck by a grand idea.

"So do I greet our home, safe from dismay and dread."

And turning solemnly to Fricka, "Come, my wife. Follow me. From now on, we dwell in Valhalla."

He picked up a sword that Fafner had left on the ground when he gathered up the treasure, and took Fricka by the hand.

"Tell me the meaning of Valhalla," she said. "It's a most uncommon name."

"When everything I've dreamed about has come to pass," Wotan replied. "When victory is mine, then the meaning of Valhalla will be clear to us."

Fricka smiled, accepting this temporary answer. Hand in hand, the father and mother of the gods walked slowly towards the bridge, Froh and Freia and Donner following a step or two behind them.

Only Loge remained, standing on the cliff-top staring after the gods. He had listened to their exchanges, but he took no share in Wotan's optimism. Loge knew. He could see the gods hurrying to their doom even though they imagined it was quite the opposite. For collaborating with them he felt nothing but embarrassment. Perhaps he should transform himself into a flickering flame and burn them up, rather than accompany them into oblivion. Perhaps. It was a thought worth dwelling on. Who knew what he should do?

But at last Loge made his mind up and, assuming a carefree manner, sauntered nonchalantly towards the bridge to join the gods. As he did so, the plaintive voices of the Rhine Maidens floated upwards from the valley deep below, unseen.

"Rhinegold, Rhinegold, pure gold, guileless gold! How bright and pure you shone upon us once."

Wotan heard them, even as he was preparing to set his foot upon the bridge. He stopped and turned around.

"What's that mournful sound?" he asked.

"For you and for your brightness we are now lamenting," the distant voices came to him again, doleful but poetic.

"It's the children of the Rhine lamenting the theft of their gold," Loge explained.

"Give us the gold!" the voices called again. "O, give us back the gold!"

"Cursed elves!" Wotan exclaimed.

"O, give us its glory once again."

"Silence them!" Wotan instructed Loge.

"You down there in the water," Loge called. "What are you wailing for? Wotan has a gift for you. The gold may no longer shine on you, but you can bask in the gods' new radiance instead. Look – Valhalla!"

Laughing at this, the gods began to cross the bridge.

But once again the voices of the Rhine Maidens floated upwards, crying plaintively.

"Rhinegold, Rhinegold, pure gold, guileless gold! If only your brightness could shine here in the depths. Goodness and truth dwell but in the deep; false and base are those who dwell above!"

But the gods were already on the far side of the bridge, and the gateway of the fortress stood open for their welcome.

PART TWO

DIE VALKURE

Act One

Scene One

The house was built of wood. Not only its walls, which were made of roughly chopped logs, hewn from some ash tree long before; but the inside of the house too, whose floors were covered here and there with rugs. The house had been formed around the trunk of a gigantic ash, and this vast tree still occupied the centre of the main room, its roots stretching far along the ground. The tree was separated from its upper branches by the hut's roof. In the summer those branches protected the hut from too much heat and light. But on wintry nights, when the gales howled through the forest, the branches of the tree would slap against the roof like fingers, scratching with their nails.

Tonight was such a stormy night, a night that didn't welcome strangers. A stranger there was, however, roaming through the woods, exhausted by the time he came upon Hunding and Sieglinde's house. The storm was abating, but he was desperate for a place to shelter and to rest. He tried the door and found it open, entered, stood a while holding the latch and listening to hear if anyone was home. The fireplace glowed red with several logs that must have been placed there very recently. But he could hear no one. He listened, intently, his eyes circuiting the room as though looking with intensity could enhance hearing. A room behind the fireplace was probably a storeroom. The door beyond must lead into the main part of the house, for it was fitted with a latch; a simple, wooden latch, because this was not a great man's mansion but a simple woodman's hut. Those steps, he guessed, led up to a third door which must be the bedroom.

It would be good to sleep, he thought, in such a bed as he imagined in that room. But no doubt there was a woodman and his wife already sleeping there. Where then? Where could a man find rest whose very dress, whose very appearance declared to all the world that he was in flight, a fugitive? Who would ever dare to give him shelter, fearing for their lives and property? But still exhausted. Hungry, too. On the far side of the room

40

there was a table with a broad bench placed against it, fixed to the wall, and wooden stools the other side. But no food. The man was starving hungry, but there was no food.

The room was empty though. If anybody was at home they must be sleeping in the room upstairs. The man made up his mind. Regardless of who owned the hut, he had to rest somewhere. Seeing and hearing no one, he closed the door behind him, walked, as though with the last effort of an exhausted man, toward the hearth, and threw himself down beside the fire on a bearskin rug. Almost immediately sleep came over him.

Sounds in her sleep had woken Sieglinde. Joyfully, because it meant her husband had come home, and a night alone in that cold bed was suddenly a night wrapped up in his warm embrace instead. Quickly she got up, put on her slippers and a gown, and went downstairs to greet him. But it wasn't her husband. To her surprise, what should be stretched out motionless beside the hearth, but a stranger. Who could he be, she wondered? Had he fainted? Nervously, she approached closer. Was he ill? The stranger stirred slightly in his sleep. Sieglinde leaned over him, close enough that she could almost touch his arm, his shoulder, so that she could see his face. She listened to his steady breathing and knew that he was still alive, had only closed his eyes to sleep. A young man, too, and she a young woman newly married; she couldn't help but note how strong he seemed, even though he'd fallen asleep exhausted.

The presence of the woman had somehow disturbed the sleeper. Suddenly he raised his head and looked at her, asking for a drink. Sieglinde fetched a drinking horn and left the room to fill it. Returning, she handed it to the man. He drank, nodded his thanks, gave back the horn. His eyes were fixed on her with growing interest.

"There's nothing quite like cold water to revive a tired man and to refresh his spirits," he said. "Unless, perhaps, the sight of a beautiful woman. Who are you?"

"Like this house," she replied carefully, "I belong to Hunding." She evaded the naming of her own name; but still polite in answering. The ways of the wood required politeness, even when a strange man came to the home of a young woman, and she was all alone. "You're exhausted," she said. "I can tell. You'll stay here as Hunding's guest until he returns home."

Sensing fear inside the woman's voice, the stranger sought to reassure her.

"I'm unarmed," he said. "When your husband returns, he'll find only a wounded guest."

"Wounds?" Sieglinde replied. "Show them to me."

The stranger shook himself and sprang up quickly to a sitting position.

"My wounds are slight," he said. "Not worth talking about. My body's still intact and my limbs are strong. If my spear and shield had proven half as strong, I wouldn't have had to flee my enemies." Sieglinde was paying close attention, captivated by his tale. So he continued, glad to rid himself of the burden of remembering. "They smashed my spear and shield and then pursued me in a pack. The thunderstorm didn't help. It sapped my strength. But I ran, fast as the wind. Until they gave up chasing me. And now," he smiled, looking deep into her face, "now I seem to have thrown off that tiredness even faster than I fled my foes. Night fell on my eyelids, but now the sun's shining on me once again."

He meant her, of course, for it was still the dead of night. Sieglinde smiled. The man was flirting with her, and she liked it very much.

But she also didn't like it, for she was Hunding's wife, and he had no business flirting with a married woman. And how could she be certain he was unarmed? How could she know he wasn't fleeing from his enemies because he was a thief, or murderer, or worst of all a ravager of women left alone in lonely houses in the middle of the forest? Yet she was not scared. Only – wary.

Sieglinde went out to the storeroom behind the hearth and filled a horn with mead. How exactly she gave it to the man, she knew, would be significant, not only now, but in the way she would tell Hunding. Dismissively, perhaps – here, take it, you're thirsty and I'm duty-bound to hospitality, so drink. Obsequiously – you're the man and I the woman, and so I must stand before you in the manner of a servant. Or ladylike – my dear young sir, since you're in my house, you must sample a glass of mead from my cellar. No, none of these. She couldn't yet figure out the man, but something, something spoke in him, something that she couldn't yet hear. And so she put the mead-horn in his hand with a gesture that conveyed concern for his wound and his tale of flight, but also, in her face especially, a friendly eagerness, to find out more, to know him better.

But the stranger was still flirting with her. He didn't take the horn so much as share the holding of it with her, gently pressing it back towards her.

"You drink first," he said. "Let your lips touch the horn before mine do."

Resist, Sieglinde. You're Hunding's wife.

But she did not resist.

Sieglinde sipped the mead, then gave it to the stranger. Now he took a long draught, all the while looking at her with growing warmth. At last he let the horn fall from his lips and sank slowly down upon the rug. But his eyes did not follow his hand, as eyes normally do, to ensure he set the horn down carefully. His eyes remained fixed on Sieglinde's eyes, and the expression on his face was not exhaustion. But then his mood changed, suddenly. He sighed deeply and gloomily and lets his eyes sink sadly to the ground. His voice was trembling when he spoke again.

"You've taken good care of an ill-fated man," he said. And then, more quickly, getting to his feet even as he said it, "I hope you'll be spared from such misfortune. I'm rested now. I must be on my way."

He started towards the door.

"Who is it," Sieglinde had turned around "that's pursuing you, that you must run away at dead of night?"

The stranger stopped at the door.

"Ill fate and bad luck pursue me wherever I go and catch up with me wherever I stop. Good woman, I pray that it'll stay away from you. And that's why I must go on, elsewhere."

He walked quickly to the door and lifted the latch. Sieglinde knew that she should let him go. But something, something in him spoke to her, though she couldn't yet hear what. Impetuously, as though she'd forgotten who and what she was, she called him back.

"Stay here," she said. "You can't bring bad luck into a house where it already dwells."

This deeply moved the man. Resolved only an instant earlier to leave, now there he was, still standing at the doorway with his hand upon the latch, still looking at Sieglinde, gazing at her face, searching in her features for something that he too seemed to recognise. Sieglinde lowered her eyes, sad and embarrassed. The man turned back towards the room.

"Then let my name be 'Woeful' and let your husband, Hunding, find me here when he comes home."

He came back into the room, leaning against the fireplace, his eyes fixed upon Sieglinde, calm and filled with deep emotion. Slowly she raised her eyes again to him, and now they stood, gazing at one another, silent for a long time, as though each yearned to hold the other in a deep embrace.

Scene Two

Sieglinde started, listening intently. The noise she'd heard outside was Hunding, leading his horse to the stable. Quickly she went to the door and opened it. Hunding came in, armed with a spear and shield, glad to be home at last. But what he saw immediately alarmed him - a stranger, seemingly at ease beside the hearth. He stopped in the doorway and turned to his wife with a look of stern enquiry.

"I found him lying on the hearth," Sieglinde explained. "Distress had driven him to the house. He's wounded."

"Have you tended his wounds?"

"I gave him mead. I treated him as a guest."

The stranger was looking at Hunding, firmly but quietly.

"She gave me mead," he confirmed, "and let me rest. I hope this won't cause trouble for her."

"My house and hearth are sacred," Hunding answered tersely. "I trust you've treated them that way."

Hunding took off his armour and handed it to Sieglinde.

"Prepare some food," he said.

Sieglinde hung the armour on the branches of the ash tree, fetched food and drink from the storeroom, and began to prepare a meal. Involuntarily her gaze alighted on the stranger once again.

But it was Hunding who was staring at the stranger, gazing at his features. He'd witnessed many strange coincidences, but none like this. Every feature - nose, eyes, mouth; the very shape of the man's profile; the way his hair hung on his forehead - every feature reminded him of Sieglinde. The same mark of the serpent glinted in his eye, increasing his mistrust. It was most disconcerting. But he hid his surprise and turned, apparently without disquiet, toward the stranger.

"You must have travelled a long way," he said. "I saw no horse. There are only rough paths into these woods. No wonder you're exhausted."

"The storm drove me," the man replied. "The storm, and desperation. I don't even know what roads I took or how I got here. Through forests and fields, through heaths and thickets. I would be glad to be told where I've arrived."

"Come join me at the table," Hunding had already taken his own seat on the wooden bench. "This roof that covers us, this house that shelters us, belong to Hunding. To the west lie the estates of my wealthy kinsmen, who defend my honour. My guest could honour me in his own way, by telling me his name."

The stranger took a seat at the table, on one of the wooden stools opposite Hunding, and gazed thoughtfully in front of him. Sieglinde had also sat down, next to Hunding, facing the stranger. Her eyes were fixed upon the stranger with a sympathy and intentness that Hunding watched, equally intent, but with far less sympathy.

"Perhaps the stranger's wary of confiding in me," Hunding suggested, watching them both. "If that's the case, maybe you should tell your story to my wife, for I can see she's curious to know you better."

If it was meant to embarrass Sieglinde, it was ineffective. Her smile, her continued gazing at the stranger, confirmed that she was indeed most curious to learn more about their guest.

The stranger looked up, gazed into her eyes and replied gravely.

"I could never call myself 'Peaceful', though I wish I were. 'Cheerful' would be good too. But my name has had to be 'Woeful'. My father was named Wolf. I came into the world with a twin sister. But my mother and sister were taken from me, long ago, when I was still an infant. I hardly knew either of them. Wolf was warlike and strong and made plenty of enemies. As a boy, he went out hunting with the old men. One day they returned from skirmishing, to find the wolf's lair empty. The fine room was burnt to ashes and the oak tree was reduced to a stump. My mother lay slaughtered and my sister was nowhere to be found. This harsh fate was inflicted on us by a cruel band who called themselves the Neidings. My father and I fled into exile. For many years I lived with Wolf in the forest. We were hunted by our enemies but we defended ourselves stoutly. So you see a wolf-cub is telling you his story and it is as 'Wolf-Cub' that I am known to many."

"These are strange and remarkable tales you tell," Hunding remarked. "Woeful the Wolf-Cub! I have, I confess, heard dark rumours of this warlike pair, but I've never come across a Wolf, let alone a Wolf-Cub."

"Where's your father now?" Sieglinde asked.

"The Neidings set upon us. Many of the hunters fell to the wolves, but I got separated from my father and lost all trace of him. I searched everywhere. One day I found an empty wolf's skin in the forest and thought…but there was no sign of my father. Then something made me want to leave the forest. I was drawn to other people, I suppose, but whenever I tried to make a friend, or find a wife, I was outlawed. Ill fortune followed me. Whatever I thought right, others considered wrong. What seemed bad to me, others approved of. I got into disputes wherever I went. I encountered anger, and where I sought joy I seemed only to arouse sorrow. That's why I started calling myself 'Woeful'. Sorrow's the only thing I've ever possessed."

Saying which he turned his eyes to Sieglinde and caught her sympathetic glance.

"Clearly the Norn who allotted you such a wretched a fate doesn't hold out much love for you," said Hunding. "No man would welcome such a stranger seeking hospitality."

"Only cowards would fear an unarmed man travelling alone," Sieglinde responded quickly, almost in rebuke. But more softly she asked him, "Tell us how you came to lose your weapons."

"A young woman in distress called out to me for help. Her family wanted to marry her to a man she didn't love. I went to her defence against her ruthless brothers. And I overcame them. But when the brothers lay dead, the girl embraced their bodies. Grief replaced anger and, in floods of tears, the unhappy bride wept on the battlefield for the death of her brothers. Then her kinsmen attacked me in overwhelming numbers, bent on vengeance. They came from all sides against me, but the girl refused to leave the field. I protected her with my shield and spear until I hewed a number of them to pieces. The others retreated. But I was wounded and my weapons were destroyed. I stood and watched the girl die. Then they attacked me again, furiously, pursued me while she lay dead on her brothers' bodies."

He looked at Sieglinde with sorrowful fervour.

"That," he said, "is why I cannot be called 'Peaceful'."

He stood up and walked to the hearth. Sieglinde looked at the ground, pale and deeply moved. Hunding rose gloomily, deep in thought.

"I too know of a race of savages," he said, "who don't respect the things that others hold sacred. It's hated by others and it's hated by me." His face was harsh and hostile as he gazed at the stranger. "Not long ago," he said, "I was summoned to seek vengeance for a kinsmen's blood. But I arrived too late, and now I've returned home to find the fleeing criminal in my own house."

Hunding stepped forward, close enough to the stranger that a sword could scarce have passed between them.

"Tonight the laws of hospitality require me to harbour you as a guest, to give you shelter for the night, to protect you from your enemies. But tomorrow morning my obligations will be done. Tomorrow, you'll defend yourself with stout weapons, because I still have obligations to my kinsman. It's my right to choose the day of battle and I choose tomorrow. It's your obligation to pay the death-debt for the dead."

Anxiously, Sieglinde stepped between the two men. But Hunding's blood was running hot, and he would not permit her interference.

"Hence from the hall!" he commanded her. "I don't want you here. Go and prepare my night-drink and wait for me in the bedroom."

But Sieglinde did not move. For a long while she stood there, thoughtful and undecided. At last she turned away, but slowly and with hesitation, mincing steps toward the storeroom. There she paused again and stood in thought, her face half-averted, half-watching the two men. Then, with quiet resolution, she opened the cupboard, filled the drinking horn, and sprinkled some carefully chosen spices into it from a box. As she left the room, she looked again towards the stranger, who had never taken his eyes off her. She looked pleadingly, meeting his gaze. Hunding was watching them, conscious of their similarity, conscious they had made some deep connection. Sieglinde turned to the stairs and climbed toward the bedchamber. But on the steps she turned once more, looked yearningly again towards the stranger, and indicated with her eyes, persistently and with eloquent earnestness, a particular spot in the ash tree's trunk. Hunding saw this, started angrily, drove her with a threatening gesture from the room. With a last look at the stranger, she went into the bedroom and closed the door behind her.

"A man should never be without a weapon," Hunding remarked to the stranger, retrieving his own weapons from the branches of the tree. "As to you, wolf-cub, we'll meet tomorrow. Mark my word, and make sure you're ready."

Saying this, Hunding too climbed up the narrow stairs and went into the bedroom, leaving the stranger alone. As he turned back to the dim light of the fire, the sound of the bolt closing on the bedroom door was like that of a sword, clashing with a broken spear.

Scene Three

The stranger was alone. It had become quite dark. The hall was lighted only by the dull fire from the hearth. He sank on the bench by the fire and brooded silently for some time, in great agitation, anxiously recalling that his father had once promised him a sword to serve him in his greatest need. But now he was unarmed, and of all places he had stumbled into his enemy's house. He had seen a woman, lovely and dignified, and strange feelings for her were gnawing at his heart. He felt for her something he had never felt before, had fallen for her sweet enchantment; but she was in the power of a man who treated an unarmed stranger with hostility.

"Wälse!" he cried out in his agitation. "Wälse! My father - where is your sword?"

If only he could draw that strong sword, needed now in his adversity, could draw it from his breast where it lay hidden in his heart. But no fight on the morrow would be won with an if-only.

The logs in the fire were crumbling into one another, flickering and dying. From the flame which sprang up, a bright spark of light struck the spot in the ash tree which Sieglinde had indicated with her look. And there, the stranger saw...a gleam of light, a something silvery, or white. A beam, a flash of light. Perhaps the glance the lovely woman left behind, manifested as light, as though a ghost of love were signalling to him. The stranger stood and stared at it, wondering what it was, this strange magical translucence gleaming in the sinking firelight. Night and darkness, it occurred to him, had closed his eyes. But then her eyes had fallen on him, bringing warmth and daylight. And if now the splendour was already fading, the firelight dying out, still, deep in his breast, a flameless fire was smouldering. For her. The fire in fact was quite extinguished now. The room was completely dark.

"Are you asleep, guest?"

The door to the bedchamber had opened so silently he hadn't even heard it. There she stood now, Sieglinde, in a white nightdress, moving lightly, quickly, down the stairs towards the hearth.

"Who's there?" he replied, taken by surprise, but happily.

Furtively, hastily, Sieglinde answered him: "Hunding's asleep." She smiled, conspiratorially. "Sound asleep. I drugged his drink. Now, under cover of night, fly, save your life."

"I have no other life but in your presence. Here. Now."

"I'll show you where there's a weapon," Sieglinde had no time now for his sentimental flirting. "If you can obtain this weapon, I shall name you the noblest of heroes, for it belongs only to the strongest. It's a weapon of special destiny. Shall I tell you?"

The stranger nodded his assent.

"All of Hunding's kinsmen once sat in this hall. It was Hunding's wedding – yes, to me. To this skin, this bone, at least. Not to this heart. Is a woman truly a wife who marries without a heart? But that's how it was. He was marrying a woman he had never wooed, and who was never asked, but who was forced to be his wife. I sat there miserably while they drank themselves stupid, when suddenly an uninvited guest arrived, an old man in a grey cloak with his hat pulled down to cover one eye. But the glint of his other eye made them all afraid. To me alone his eye revealed a sweet, a longing sadness; tears and consolation combined. He looked at me but glowered at the men, and then a sword flashed in his hand. Suddenly he thrust the sword into the tree trunk, buried it right up to the hilt. The blade, he said, would belong to any man who pulled it from the tree. All the men tried of course, but none of them could win the weapon.

"Guests came and guests went. The strongest all pulled at the blade but it wouldn't budge an inch; it's still there to this day." She glanced over to the tree, indicating where it lay buried. Then, looking closely into his face, she went on, "But I realised who the stranger was who greeted me with so much sorrow. And I knew too for whom the sword was meant. For him who will come from far away to rescue this most wretched woman. Whatever grief she may have suffered, whatever pain she may have felt in her shame and her dishonour, sweetest revenge would make up for all of it. She would regain all she had lost, all she had wept for. She would have won, if only she could find the blessed friend and her arms could embrace the hero."

Even as she spoke these words, the stranger was stepping towards her, and as she finished speaking he took her in his arms, embraced Sieglinde ardently.

"Sieglinde," he said, "even now you're in the arms of that friend for whom both wife and weapon were decreed. I swear that you will be my wife. All I've ever longed for I recognise in you. Everything that's missing in me finds its completion in you. You've suffered disgrace and I've known sorrow. I've been made an outlaw and you dishonoured. But joyful revenge will bring happiness to both of us."

The stranger laughed out loud, holding her against his beating heart.

Suddenly the front door flew open, as though the last gust of the dying storm had spent its dying breath there. Outside a marvellous spring light gleamed. The full moon shone in, throwing its light upon the couple who were able now to see each other clearly. But the sudden opening of the door had startled Sieglinde.

"Who went out?" she cried. "Or did somebody come in?"

"Nobody," the stranger replied, and his eyes and mouth were vivid with a glow of ecstasy. "Nobody went out, but something has come in. Spring,

Sieglinde. Spring."

"Come sit with me," Sieglinde took his hand and led him to the couch, sitting close beside him, snuggled tenderly against his shoulder. The brilliance of the moonlight grew until the light it cast was stronger, warmer even than the fire that had now gone out.

"The winter storms have vanished before the month of May," the stranger whispered, knowing it wasn't the sentimental words he used that mattered, but the gentleness of speaking, and the poetry, the closeness of their bodies. "Springtime," he continued, "shines with gentle light, soft and wonderful. Truly Spring works many wonders. His breath blows over woods and meadows. His eyes are bright with laughter. The lovely songs of birds proclaim him sweetly as he breathes his blissful scents. Gorgeous flowers burst from his warm blood. Buds and shoots grow from his strength. Armed only with the most fragile weapons, nonetheless it's he who conquers the whole world. Winter and storm abandon their defences. To his warm-blooded blows, stout doors yield, for they too would but cannot lock out the Spring. But Spring flies to find his sister, for it's love, true love, that drives him on. Love that was hidden deep inside our hearts but which now smiles blissfully in the light. The sister-bride is freed by her brother. Everything that kept them apart is left in ruins. Joyfully, the young couple greet one another. Love and spring are one."

Sieglinde wasn't sure she understood. And yet, deep down, she did, she understood. She knew. Had known from the first moment she had seen him.

"You," she whispered, "you are the spring I've longed for in the frosty wintertime. When I first saw you, the first time your glance stirred me, my heart was filled with dread. I've only ever known strangers and strangeness in this unfriendly house and wood. But I knew as soon as my eyes beheld you, that you were mine. Everything I've kept hidden in my heart, everything I am, suddenly it became clear to me, as clear as day. It was like the pealing of a distant bell reaching my ear at last, when, in this cold, strange, place, this bleak prison where I live a captive, I first beheld," the last two words resisted her a moment, but only because she so longed to say them, and so feared she might be wrong. But looking in his eyes all fear was banished. And the words came easily at last: "My friend."

She hung in rapture on his neck and gazed deep into his face.

"O sweetest enchantment," the stranger sighed. "Woman most blest."

Their eyes were almost touching.

But for Sieglinde, still not close enough.

"Hold me tighter," she implored him. "Let me look into your eyes and see even more clearly the radiant light that shines from them. You're very handsome, you know."

"This spring moonlight doesn't exactly impair your looks either," he laughed. "Your face, this lovely, waving hair. Now I can see clearly what's enraptured me."

Sieglinde pushed the locks back from his brow and gazed at him in wonder. Caressing his brow, she could see how open it was, and how the veins wound in his temples. It made her tremble with delight, but it also stirred her memory. For it was most strange, and very troubling. She had seen him for the first time this very day, and yet she recognised him. Her eyes had seen this man before.

"I've dreamed of you as well," the stranger said. "A dream of love fashioned in fervent longing. I've seen you before too."

But this was poetry again, and what Sieglinde had recognised was not poetry. She had seen this man before, physically, in the flesh. She recognised him. Not in dream, or poetry, but in reality. Yet how could that be?

"Many times," she said, "I've looked at my image in a stream. I know what I look like, and now I'm seeing me again."

"The same for me," the stranger acknowledged. "Yours is the image that I've long preserved, and sought, within."

But this wasn't it. Not it. This was just love-talk. And there was something more than love-talk here. Sieglinde recognised him, not the soul, the kindred spirit, but the flesh. Quickly she turned her eyes away from him, to hear his voice again, to hear what she was certain she was hearing, a memory from childhood.

"I know that voice," she cried. "I heard it recently when my own voice echoed in the woods. And now I'm hearing it again."

"And I too am hearing it. Your voice, Sieglinde. The sweetest sound I ever knew."

More love-talk. Didn't he understand where she was leading him? Or perhaps he didn't want to understand. Sieglinde gazed rapturously into his eyes.

"That gleam has shone on me before, stranger." She took his face between her hands, holding his jaw fast so he couldn't interrupt her. "The old man at the wedding," she resumed, "the one who looked so kindly at me, consoling me in my grief. By that glance his daughter recognised him and she almost spoke his name."

She paused then, hoping that now, at last, the stranger would understand what she was telling him. But the stranger only stared back, gazing into her eyes adoringly.

"Is your name really 'Woeful'?" she enquired.

"Not any longer," he replied. "Never call me 'Woeful' again, now that I have you. Call me 'Loved' or 'Happy'. Never 'Woeful'."

"Why not 'Peaceful'? You mentioned that name before."

"I will happily be known by any name you choose for me," the stranger answered.

"You said your father's name was 'Wolf'."

"His name, no. But what men called him. For he was truly a wolf to those cowardly foxes. But he whose eyes shone quite as splendidly as yours, my father, his name was 'Wälse'."

Sieglinde was beside herself.

"Wälse!" she exclaimed. "If Wälse was your father, then you are a Wälsung. And it was for you the old man left the sword! Then I shall call you by the name I most love in the world. You shall be 'Siegmund'".

The stranger sprang to his feet and seized the hilt of the sword.

'Siegmund," he repeated. "Victory! A fine name. Siegmund by name and Siegmund by nature. Wälse promised me a sword in my moment of greatest need. And here I stand, grasping it. What higher need than love, yearning love which consuming desire burns brightly in my breast, urging me on to deeds and death. Sword, you too require a name. 'Nothung' I shall call you. 'The Sword of Need', for I found you in my hour of need. Now, my Needful one, show me how sharp your blade is. Slip from your scabbard and reveal your cutting edge."

And with a mighty heave, Siegmund pulled the sword out of the tree and displayed it to an astonished and enraptured Sieglinde.

"Siegmund the Wälsung stands before you," he exclaimed, "and as a wedding gift I bring - this sword. This very sword which won for me the fairest woman in the world. This very sword which will protect us as we fly far from our enemy's house into the laughing, joyous house of spring. Nothung the Sword of Need will protect Sieglinde, even if Siegmund were to die of love."

Love-talk. Poetry and love-talk. He was carried away with his own poetry, already embracing her in order to take her away with him. But did he not understand? Surely. Surely.

Sieglinde tore herself away from his grasp. Intoxicated with love, she stood and faced him. Could this truly be Siegmund who stood before her now? No doubt she was Sieglinde, who yearned for him, to be his wife, his bride, his lover. But if he was truly Siegmund, not just according to the name she gave a stranger, but…her own brother. And yet, what of it? He'd won her and he'd won the sword. The Norns, the Fates, had ordered this.

So she flung herself into his arms, embraced him not with her arms alone, but lips to lips, like lovers.

"Are you really Siegmund?" she asked again.

"Siegmund," he replied. "Your twin brother. And now – your groom."

Then he did know. He did know. And he too understood the Norns, the Fates, had ordered this.

"Siegmund and Sieglinde!" she said.

"Bride and sister, groom and brother, through whom the race of

Wälsungen will flourish for all time."

He drew her to him once again, passionately, fervently.

"For all time," she whispered.

Act Two

Scene One

Wotan's journey in search of his beloved daughter Brünnhilde had brought him, at last, to the summit of a wild, rocky pass. A craggy gorge opened onto a high ridge of rocks, from which the ground sank slowly to a long plateau. Wotan had travelled fully armed, ready for battle, carrying his spear. Brünnhilde too was fully armed, in the regalia of the Valküre.

"Bridle your horse," Wotan commanded her, once the formal greetings befitting a father and his daughter were complete, "a bitter quarrel is about to burst. I'm relying on you to enter the fray and bring victory to the Wälsung. Let Hunding go where he belongs; there's no place for him in Valhalla. Prepare. Ride to the field."

Brünnhilde sprang up at once, shouting her wild battle cry as she flew from rock to rock along the heights and surveyed the scene. Stopping on one of the highest peaks, she looked down into the gorge and called to Wotan.

"Look to yourself, father. You said a bitter quarrel was about to burst, and here it is right now, arriving in a chariot driven by her rams."

Brünnhilde laughed, but only for a moment. The sight of Fricka, of a very angry Fricka, of a Fricka prepared to burst a storm cloud of her own, was not a laughing matter. Beasts grazing on the hill slopes bleated in fear on seeing her. The wheels of her chariot were clattering madly.

"She's coming to pick a quarrel, you mark my words," Brünnhilde warned the father of the gods. "You know I don't like quarrels. A good fight with brave warriors, that's another matter. But if you and she are about to have another fight, I shall leave you to enjoy it."

Brünnhilde howled her battle cry once more and disappeared behind the summit of the mountain, leaving her father to face his consort alone.

No sooner was she gone than Fricka arrived, exactly as Brünnhilde had described her, in a chariot drawn by two rams. She'd come by way of a ravine to the summit of the pass, where she stopped suddenly and alighted. She strode impetuously towards Wotan, who quivered at the sight. The same old storm was brewing, the same old strife. But he was determined on this occasion to take a firm stand.

As she approached her husband, the wise Fricka moderated her pace and placed herself with dignity before Wotan. Anger, she knew well, would achieve nothing. There were better ways of persuading Wotan.

"I've been looking for you everywhere," she sighed. "Did you come to these high mountains just to hide from me?" She smiled, as though this were intended as a jest. "I need your help, Wotan."

"Speak your troubles freely," Wotan replied.

"I've been listening to Hunding's complaints. He called on me as the guardian of wedlock to avenge him. I've made a vow, Wotan, to punish severely the shameless and impious pair who so wronged this husband."

Wotan's throat constricted and his stomach tightened. He breathed deeply, forcing his nerves to calm. He was, after all, the father of the gods. His authority was supreme and unchallengeable. Even his consort, Fricka, had to know her place.

"What wrong can a young couple do," he retorted, "when spring binds them in love? The magic of love enchanted them. I have no authority where love is concerned."

"Don't pretend to be both stupid and deaf," Fricka replied, the conjunctive emphasised rather more strongly even than she had intended. "And don't pretend you didn't already know that his complaint is precisely about the flouting of marriage – a holy vow, Wotan. A holy vow."

She could have been reminding him of his own.

"An unholy vow in this case, my dear," he was determined to maintain his dignity, as well as his authority. "Two people united without love, one of them by force, not by free will. Please don't ask me to intervene in something that's not within my power. And anyway, you know my view on things like this. If tempers are frayed and blood's hot, let them fight it out and may the best man win."

"If," Fricka said, and she was thinking of that remark of Loge's she had overheard, his scathing observation about her own marriage, that 'we all know who wears the horns in that family'. "If, in this tacit manner, you grant respectability to adultery, then you will also have to sanctify the incestuous fruit of this liaison between twins. The very idea stops my heart and causes my brain to reel. Marital intercourse between brother and sister – who's ever heard of such a thing?"

"Clearly you have, my dear. Today. And you should learn from this that things may indeed happen that haven't occurred before. But newness of itself doesn't make it wrong. It's apparent that they're in love, so listen to some sensible advice. True love's so very rare, especially within marriage." That "especially" was his turn to emphasise a word rather more boldly than he'd intended. "You of all people should be smiling on true love and blessing the union of Siegmund and Sieglinde."

Fricka shook her head in disbelief. Her hands were on her hips. The bones of her elbows were protruding.

"Is this the end of the era of the gods?" she spat each word as if it were a stone made out of indignation. "Remember it was you that fathered these riotous Wälsungen. Don't try to silence me. I shall say what must be said. I can read your thoughts, my husband. You no longer care about the sacred kinship of the gods. Everything you once valued you've now cast aside. You break the bonds that you yourself ordained. You laugh, and in doing so you relax your rule in heaven so that whim and pleasure may be gratified by these wanton twins, the licentious fruit of your own unfaithfulness. Why do I even bother to protest about marriage and its vows when my own husband was the first to break them? Don't look away. You've constantly deceived this faithful wife. From the depths of the Earth to the heights of the mountains, you've looked with your lecherous eye for every imaginable opportunity to gratify your fickle fancy and thereby mock and wound me to the quick. Do you think it doesn't grieve me - o but I bear it - when you go into battle with those uncouth girls you fathered, those Valküre. You've just about enough respect for me to make the gang of them, even that Brünnhilde who'd you'd gladly marry if father-daughter marriages weren't equally proscribed, even her you've made respect me as her sovereign and serve me as a handmaiden. But now, now you've gone too far. All this assuming of new names, this roaming the forest like a wolf and calling yourself Wälse. What is this? Demeaning yourself to foster a pair of common mortals born of your own falseness. And now you would debase me too, your own wife, before a she-wolf's litter. Go on, finish your work, fill the cup full and trample on this wife you cheated."

"My dear," Wotan was determined that he at least would not lose his composure, "you simply must learn - and I've tried to teach you because you seem incapable of fathoming it yourself – to recognise events *before* they happen. You only understand the conventional, the what's-been-before, whereas I'm concerned with things that have never yet been known. The father of the gods must be a visionary, a breaker of tradition – else the world will stagnate by tedious repetition. Just for once, listen to me. Mankind requires a hero who's free from divine protection, one who isn't bound by divine law. He alone will be able to perform the deeds that are so vital to the gods but which we, precisely because we are gods, are prohibited from doing."

"Don't try to confuse me with your profundities," Fricka replied. "What lofty deed could heroes possibly perform that couldn't be performed by gods?"

"The freedom of the spirit," Wotan answered. "Does that mean nothing to you? A hero's bravery."

"Freedom of the spirit!" Fricka scoffed. "A hero's bravery! Who breathed life into Mankind? Who inspired them with such heroic thoughts? Who lit up their foolish eyes? Under your protection they appear strong, and spurred on by you they follow their ambitions. That's all. You're responsible for those you now praise to a goddess. This is all just a new trick to try to dupe me, to escape me. But you won't keep this Wälsung for yourself. In him I see only you, because it's only through you that Siegmund can act boldly."

"The boy," Wotan replied, "grew up alone, in bitterness and sorrow. His father's protection never sheltered him."

"Then don't shelter him today," Fricka had caught him out at last. "Take away the sword you gave him."

"The sword?"

"Yes, the sword. The magical, glittering sword you gave your son."

"He won that sword himself," Wotan's composure had finally deserted him. "In the midst of his desperation."

"You fashioned that desperation," Fricka replied, vehemently now, sensing that her husband was on the defensive. Such dejection in his face. This she knew how to manipulate. "You fashioned it, Wotan. You created Siegmund's distress, just as you created the flashing sword. Don't think you can deceive me, who's followed your footsteps at every step of this life's journey. You thrust that sword into the tree trunk so that he would find it. You promised him that splendid weapon. And wasn't it your cunning that contrived to bring him there where he would find it? Don't make angry gestures at me. No one of divine birth," Fricka continued, growing in confidence as she saw the impression she had made on Wotan, "No one of divine birth would battle as an equal with a bondsman. This is simply a case of a free man punishing an outlaw. You have no right to interfere. But if you do, I shall go into battle with you on behalf of Hunding. And Siegmund shall be forfeit as a serf to Fricka."

Again Wotan made an angry gesture, but it was clear to Fricka that he was powerless against her. And he knew it.

"Tell me Wotan," Fricka resumed. "Shall the consort of the most senior of the gods be subject to a bondsman and a slave? Would you scorn me, and shame me, in that manner? An insult to a goddess and an invitation to the base to be more forward still. Surely my husband wouldn't profane his own wife in that way?"

"What do you want me to do?" Wotan enquired, but his voice was heavy with gloom.

"Leave the Wälsung unprotected!"

So heavy that gloom, it was a while before he answered. Wotan looked down into the rocky gorge below, up into the unending skies – but not, for a long while, directly at Fricka. He was ashamed.

But at last, in a voice so subdued it was as if muffled, he gave the answer she was waiting for:

"Let him go his own way," he said.

Another trick? Wotan was so good with words, he could say one thing now, and argue later he had meant something completely different.

"Say that you'll neither shelter nor protect him, when Hunding calls him to the act of vengeance."

"I will not shelter him."

"This is a trick, Wotan. Look into my eyes. Shelter is shelter. Say it clearly. You will remove your protection from Siegmund. That includes the Valküre."

"They're free to act as they see fit."

More tricks. She couldn't exactly say what those tricks were, but tricks they had to be. Fricka was growing animated. But she would have her victory.

"No," she worked it out at last, "they never act as they see fit. Everything they do is in fulfilment of your wishes. Give them an order, Wotan. Tell them, they must forbid Siegmund his victory."

This was too much for Wotan. Torn he was, like a sword from a tree-trunk, leaving behind a gaping wound.

"It's not in my power to overthrow him," he replied at last. "He found the sword."

"But you can destroy its magic. Let it break and leave him defenceless. Let him be left even without a shield."

As she spoke these last words, Brünnhilde's voice reached them from the distance, uttering her jubilant war cry from the mountaintop.

"Here she comes, even now," Fricka observed.

"She comes at my orders. To fetch Siegmund to horse."

Brünnhilde had indeed arrived, leading her horse along the rocky path. But seeing Fricka she halted suddenly, changed direction, slowly and silently led the horse further down the mountain path, and hid it in a cave.

"My honour," Fricka insisted. "My sacred honour, and not Siegmund's bondsman bravery, her shield shall guard today." Her arm was stretched out, her long index finger pointing like a sword blade, as though she were marking the spot where she would cut Brünnhilde down if Wotan didn't yield to her demand "If we are derided by men," she continued, "if we are deprived of our might, then surely the era of the gods will be at an end. And so it will be, if my rights are not protected. My rights, Wotan, the rights of gods, pure and resplendent. Or will you allow that maid to ruin us? For my honour the Wälsung falls today. Now make me that oath."

Wotan had stood up when Brünnhilde first appeared, intending to go out and greet her. But Fricka's words now stopped him in his tracks. He stood, still as a wounded tree, as though he could feel in his own limbs the point where the magic sword had entered. Profound dejection had overtaken him, and now he threw himself down on a rocky seat and looked up into Fricka's face, the way a scolded boy looks at his angry mother. She had defeated him.

"Swear the oath," Fricka demanded.

Brünnhilde's footsteps were approaching. Fricka turned and strode towards her, stood before her, strong and confident. The two women regarded each other for a while in silence.

"The Father of War awaits you," Fricka said at last, choosing that of all his titles, quite deliberately. "He'll inform you which way the dice should land."

Then mounting her chariot, Fricka took up the reins, and with her whip hurried the rams to take her back to Valhalla.

Yet Wotan had not formally pronounced the oath.

Scene Two

Wotan sank back upon the rock, brooding gloomily. Brünnhilde approached him now, wondering and anxious.

"This quarrel seems to have ended badly," she said, "Fricka was laughing as she went, and here are you, downcast. What bad tidings do you have for me?"

Wotan allowed his arms to drop helplessly at his side. His head sunk on his breast.

"I make my own fetters and then she catches me in them," he replied bitterly. "Lord of the world am I, and yet the least free of all its creatures."

"I've never seen you in this state," Brünnhilde answered. "Something's gnawing at your heart."

Wotan gave no answer, just sat there, hopeless and despondent.

"What shame!" Brünnhilde scarcely knew how to express herself. "What shameful distress. For a god to be driven to despair."

Hearing her lament this way, Wotan's expression and gestures grew even more intense. But still he sat quietly, listening.

"For a god to be driven to despair," Brünnhilde repeated. "This is outrageous. This is – reprehensible. I, I, I'm, devastated."

Terrified by what she was witnessing, Brünnhilde threw her shield and spear and helmet down and sank at Wotan's feet in anxious solicitude.

"Father," she cried. "Father, tell me what it is that ails you. Why are you making me, your child, so dismayed? Have trust in me, father. Please, Brünnhilde implores you. Confide in me."

She laid her head and hands with loving concern upon his knees and breast. Wotan looked long into her eyes, then stroked her hair with unconscious tenderness. But slowly, at last, he began to emerge from the depths of his brooding, and gradually, softly, broke his silence.

"If I speak a word of this," he said. "If I even start to tell you what it is that so concerns me, will I be able to keep control of my own will?"

"You're addressing yourself when you address me," Brünnhilde reassured him. "Who am I if not your other self?"

"Then let what I say remain as if unspoken forever. I speak in secret when I speak to you."

Brünnhilde nodded her assent to this. So Wotan resumed, but his voice that was already so soft with sorrow became even more muted as he continued.

"When the pleasures of young love waned in me," he said, "my spirit longed for power. Impetuous desire roused me to madness and I won the whole world for myself. With no thought of integrity I acted as I pleased, unaware that sometimes this meant disloyally, or falsely. I made treaties and alliances that simply concealed evil. Loge's cunning guided me, and Loge - where is Loge when I need him most? But I couldn't let go of love. With all my power, I yearned for love. That child of darkness, that Nibelung Alberich, he managed to liberate himself from the chains of love. He foreswore love and through his curse he won the glittering Rhinegold and, with it, immeasurable power. The ring that he had made I took from him by trickery, but I didn't return it to the Rhine as was my obligation. No, I used it to pay the price for Valhalla, the fortress which the giants built for me, and where I now rule all the world. Erda, who knew everything that ever was, the wisest of women, warned me to give up the ring, warned me of the end of everything."

In speaking, Wotan had managed to give outward form to his inner suffering, and it had begun to purge him. More vehemently now, he continued: "I needed to learn more about that end, but Erda vanished." He was becoming truly animated. "But what she told me, and especially what she didn't tell me but I needed, desperately, to know, it took away all joy from life. As a god I longed for knowledge. I travelled into the depths of the Earth and, with the magic of love, I overpowered that wise woman, overcame her, and she talked to me. I learned her secrets, but she exacted a fee.

"The world's wisest woman," Wotan continued, "bore me a child. You, Brünnhilde, and then your sisters, all nine of you. My Valküre. Through you I sought to avert the dreadful doom that woman told me lay in store – the shameful defeat of the immortals. To protect the gods from their enemies, I sent you out to fetch me heroes, men who were bound to us by law in bondage, mortals whose pride had been curbed and who, through deceitful treaties, were bound to us in obedience."

He was becoming ever more animated, but still this wasn't the powerful Wotan that Brünnhilde knew. His strength was moderated.

"Your task was to spur them into storm and strife," he went on, "to rouse them to want to test their strength in bitter warfare, to inspire armies of bold warriors to gather in defence of Valhalla."

"And this we've done, father. Your halls are filled with heroes. Given that we've never failed you, why are you so worried now?"

"Another ill-tiding," Wotan replied, his voice once more suppressed, "Erda warned me of it. Through Alberich's army the last days of the gods will come to pass. The Nibelung nurses his resentment with a rage born of envy, and yet…" and once again Wotan was becoming enervated, his voice grew strong, his mood defiant. "I have no fear of that force of darkness," he proclaimed. "My heroes will bring me victory." But once again his tone changed, his voice dropped. These changes, it was as though some deep inner struggle were taking place in him, now dragging him down into despair, now allowing him to rise again to self-belief. "But if the ring ever found its way back to Alberich," this was the blackest she had ever seen or heard him, and she waited for what doom-laden phrase would finally emerge. It came at last. "Valhalla would be lost," he said. And it was as if the judge in court had put the black cap on his head and uttered a death sentence. "He alone, he who cursed love, has the power to use the ring's magic," his bones, his flesh, for a moment animated once again, "to break my heroes' faith in me, even to turn them against me, so they would oppose me even in the heat of battle."

He bowed his head again, gazing inwards to his own darkness. It was true what he'd said, that when he spoke to Brünnhilde he spoke in private and in secret. No man nor god had ever spoken so deeply within himself as Wotan now.

"Urged on by fear," he said, "I thought, perhaps, that I could steal the ring myself, to keep it from my enemy. One of the giants, Fafner, to whom I gave the accursed ring as ransom for Freia, he now guards the treasure for which he slew his brother. I'd have to seize the ring from him. But I'm bound to him by sworn agreement. It forbids me to attack him. And if I did, the laws that bind us to these oaths would take away my power. Such," he added bitterly, "are the chains that fetter me. I became a ruler through treaties, and by those treaties I am now enslaved. Only one person can do what I'm unable to do – a hero I've never counselled, a man unknown to me, who acts without my grace, a man oblivious even to my existence, driven by his own need, without command, with the cunning of his own right arm and the guile of his own tongue. Only such a man can do the deed that I must shun, which I'm forbidden even to propose to him, though it be my greatest wish. A man who would fight even in opposition to the gods, though we're his greatest friend become his foe. But where can I find or shape a man like this, a free agent who I've never protected and who, precisely by defying me, will become my dearest friend? How can I make that Other, one who, not through me, but of his own accord, will do what I require? What a predicament for a god to find himself in! What humiliation! With loathing, I see myself in everything I've created. That Other that I long for, that Other I shall never find. A free man must create himself. Wotan can only fashion slaves."

Astonished, Brünnhilde interrupted her father.

"But the Wälsung, father. The Wälsung, Siegmund. Doesn't he act on his own?"

"No," Wotan replied. "I roamed the wild woods with him. Against the counsel of the gods I stirred his spirit, encouraging him to act boldly. Now, against the vengeance of the gods, he has the protection of his sword," Wotan's voice was slow and very bitter, "the very sword which my favour bestowed on him. Why did I trick myself by trying to defraud others? To my deep disgrace, Fricka saw through my deception in a moment. Now I must yield to her will."

"Then withdraw your protection from this Siegmund," Brünnhilde suggested.

"When my hand touched Alberich's ring, I learned what it is to be greedy for gold. I fled the curse, but it runs quicker than I can; there's no escaping it. What I love best, I have no choice but to surrender. And I must kill the one I love, basely betray the one who placed his trust in me."

What was previously only the most desperate pain was now transformed into complete despondency.

"Fade away then, splendour," Wotan continued. "Fade away divine pomp and all the glory of godhood into glittering shame. Let everything I've built fall into ruins. My work is done. But one thing still awaits me. The end. The downfall!" He paused, deep in thought. "And for that end, Alberich is working. Now I understand the hidden meaning in Erda's wild words: 'when love's dark enemy begets a son in anger, the end of the blessed ones will not be long delayed.' I heard a rumour recently, that Alberich had seduced a woman for money, and that woman is now carrying the fruits of the Nibelung's hatred. The child of his spite grows in her womb. What a miracle for a creature who has foresworn love! But I, who ruled by love, I could not beget a free man." Such was his anger that he could no longer sit still. "Take my blessing, son of the Nibelung," he cried out, his voice booming across the gorge for all the world to hear. "What I've most loathed I now bequeath to you. Feed your envious greed upon the empty glory of divinity."

Brünnhilde was shocked, but more than this – alarmed.

"Tell me, father," she implored him, "what task can I perform to thwart this."

"Fight for Fricka," he answered her bitterly. "Guard the sanctity of marriage and its holy vows." Then, dryly, he added: "Whatever Fricka decides is my decision too. What good can my will ever do? I cannot will a free man into life. You must fight now, only for Fricka's subjects."

"No, father," Brünnhilde replied. "Take back those words. You love Siegmund. Knowing how much you love him, I'll fight for him."

"Wrong, daughter. Because you love me you must do what I instruct you. Kill Siegmund and procure victory for Hunding. Be on your guard and summon all your bravery, bring all your skill and boldness to the battle, for Siegmund wields a conquering sword and he won't die a coward."

"No, father," Brünnhilde was as dauntless in this fight as she intended to be in that with Hunding. "Because I love you, because you've always taught me to love Siegmund and he's dear to my heart, I will never be turned against him by my father's self-deceiving words!"

"Dare you defy me?" Wotan's anger had turned now towards Brünnhilde. "Will you flout my orders? Who are you but the fettered, blind slave of my will? When I confided in you, it was because you said that speaking to you was speaking to myself. But now I see that wasn't so. Did I so demean myself that even my own offspring should pour scorn on me? Do you know what it is to feel my rage? Your spirit would be crushed if its withering lash should fall upon you. In my heart lies concealed a fury that could reduce the world that once so pleased me into dust and ashes. Woe to him on whom it strikes. Sad indeed would be his fate, his transformation into misery. I advise you, my daughter, do not provoke my wrath. Pay heed to my command. Siegmund shall die, at your hands. That is the Valküre's task."

Quickly, Wotan stormed away, vanishing among the rocks. Brünnhilde stood for a long time, confused and alarmed.

"I've never seen the Father of War like this," she muttered. "Though I've seen him, many times, provoked to anger by some quarrel."

She stooped down sadly and took up her weapons, arming herself in preparation for the battle. But the weapons that normally weighed nothing on her shoulders now felt heavy. Worry and disconsolation weighed down her spirit more heavily still. Gazing thoughtfully in front of her, she sighed.

"Woe to you, poor Wälsung," she murmured. "In sorest sorrow the one who would remain true to you has now turned false."

She turned slowly, walked even slower, back toward the mountains.

Scene Three

As she reached the rocky pass, Brünnhilde looked down into the valley, where she could see Siegmund and Sieglinde approaching. For a few moments she watched them, then stepped into the cave where her horse was hidden, and disappeared.

Siegmund and Sieglinde had reached the pass by now. Sieglinde was hurrying on ahead, Siegmund trying to restrain her.

"Stay here," he called. "Let's rest a while."

"Not yet. Not yet," Sieglinde replied.

Siegmund took her hand, compelling her to stop running, then turned her toward him and embraced her, gently yet forcefully.

"No farther now," he pleaded, and once more clasped her firmly in his arms.

But even as he kissed her, Sieglinde was struggling to break free, desperate to run further, to run faster. She was terrified.

"Let's stay here, my darling," Siegmund held her tight. "You made us rush away in such haste from our night of love that I can barely keep up with you. Through woods and meadows, over rocks and cliffs, silently rushing on, and my voice calling you in vain."

Trying to soothe her with his voice, to calm her down from her anxiety. But Sieglinde stared wildly before her. The tension in her body was palpable.

"Let's rest here," Siegmund clenched her wrist tighter. But Sieglinde tugged her arm to free herself. Siegmund clenched tighter, now clutching both wrists, so she couldn't get away. "I want to hear your voice," he entreated. Sieglinde pursed her lips. "Just one word." She closed her eyes, as though refusing to look at him might also block his speech. "Your silence frightens me," he said. But did now recognise his tone of voice was wrong, was hindering not helping his attempt to calm her down. Another tack, then. Try another tack.

Siegmund relaxed his grip, allowing his fingers to slip from her wrists into her dangling palms, his fingertips caressing her, softly climbing as they caressed, the whole length of her arms, until he held her shoulders gently, slid his arms around her back, drew her once again into an embrace. His lips pecked kisses on her neck, her ears, her cheeks. His hands were combing knots out of her hair.

"See," he said, "your brother holds his bride. Siegmund's heart is now your home."

Sieglinde gazed into his eyes with growing rapture and delight and threw her arms passionately around his neck. Then, suddenly, she pulled away in terror once again.

"Leave me alone!" she cried. "Leave me alone!" What had previously expressed itself in physical flight, now manifested in a hysteria of words, fleeing from her mouth at once in rage and sorrow, an incoherent passion of confusion and self-contradiction. "Stay clear of me!" she commanded him, "I'm cursed." But held him nonetheless. "This arm that clasps you is unholy. My body's dishonoured, disgraced - dead. Cast it away. Flee from this corpse. Let the wind blow her away who gave herself to you like a, like a whore. When you held me lovingly and I found with you the greatest joy, when you gave me all your love and woke my love as well, when from the holiest heights of sweet bliss you filled my mind and pierced my soul, nothing came forth but loathing and terror, a ghastly shame that gripped me in horror and disgrace, filled with dismay this treacherous woman who once obeyed a man that she belonged to though his bed was loveless. But now I'm dishonoured, cursed. I must abandon you, Siegmund. I'm condemned and worthless. You're the most pure of men. But I must hurry away from him, from you. I can never belong to you, you wonderful man. I bring shame on my brother, disgrace on my friend who's won me."

"Whatever disgrace you may have suffered," Siegmund replied, "will be paid for by that sinner's blood. Run no further, but wait for our enemy here, and let him die at Siegmund's hand. When Nothung strikes his heart, then you'll be avenged."

Sieglinde started in terror and listened. The sound of horns was coming from the distance.

"Can't you hear them? I hear them everywhere. Cries of vengeance. All around us in the woods and vales. Hunding has woken from his sleep. He's assembling his dogs and his kinsmen. Roused to frenzy, the pack's howling. They cry to heaven for the marriage vows that have been broken."

She gazed madly before her like a woman crazed. But it was as if her eyes were closed.

"Where are you, Siegmund? Are you still here, my beloved, my radiant brother? Let the bright lights in your eyes shine on me once again. Do not spurn the kisses of an outcast wife."

Saying this, she threw herself sobbing on his breast. But at that very moment Hunding's horn sounded again. Sieglinde jumped up, terrified. Men were approaching, fully armed.

"No sword will be sufficient when those dogs attack," Sieglinde warned. Her eyes were staring, not into the present but into some imaginary future, bestowed upon her like a vision. Like a woman crazed.

"Let it go, Siegmund! Let the sword go!" she cried, hallucinating. "Siegmund, where are you? There. I see you now."

Siegmund held her in his arms, but she was entirely distracted, her eyes dilated, her face white. He could hardly imagine what terrible sight she was seeing in her mind's eye.

"The dogs are gnashing their teeth for flesh, Siegmund. They're not frightened by the look of a hero. Their teeth have fastened on your feet. You're falling." She screamed. "Impossible! Impossible! The sword has shattered into pieces. The ash tree topples. The trunk breaks. My brother! My brother!"

Sieglinde's strength yielded at last to the power of the vision. Fainting, she sank into her brother's arms, sighing his name as deep sleep took her. Siegmund gave back her name, sighing "Sister! Beloved!", and listened closely to her breathing. She was still alive. He let her slip downwards so that, as he himself sank into a sitting posture, her head was resting on his lap. So he sat now, tending and caressing her in anxious silence, pressing long kisses on her forehead.

Scene Four

All this while Brünnhilde had been resting in the cave. Now she came out, leading her horse by its bridle, advancing slowly and solemnly along the pass. She paused and observed Siegmund from a distance, then, slowly, advanced again, and stopped again, but somewhat nearer now. In one hand she carried her shield and spear, the other rested on her horse's neck. And thus, in grave silence, she watched Siegmund for some time.

"Siegmund," she called out at last. "Look at me! I am she who you must soon follow."

Siegmund looked up at her.

"Who are you?" he asked, "standing there so beautiful and yet so stern."

"Only those doomed to die can meet my gaze," Brünnhilde retorted. "Whoever looks at me must leave the light of life. Only on the battlefield do I appear to heroes. Those whom I greet must follow me into battle."

Siegmund looked long, firmly and searchingly into her eyes, then bowed his head in thought and at length turned resolutely back to her.

"If this is a hero's time to die," he asked, "where will you lead him?"

"To Wotan," Brünnhilde replied. "To the Lord of Battles, who casts the lots and decides men's fates. Follow me to Valhalla."

"And if I do follow you," Siegmund asked, "will I find only the Lord of Battles on the peaks of Valhalla?"

"The hallowed band of dead heroes will greet you there, and make you a warm welcome."

"Does Wälse, my own father, reside in Valhalla?"

"You will indeed find your father there," Brünnhilde replied. And it wasn't the whole truth, but it wasn't a lie either. More than this she couldn't answer him.

"And will I," Siegmund's voice was full of tenderness, stroking the face of his beloved sister even as he looked into Brünnhilde's eyes, "will a woman greet me there affectionately?"

"Wish maidens abound there," Brünnhilde answered. And smiled, because this wasn't what he'd asked; but it was what so many others asked the answer was already waiting on her lips. If I go into battle, and I die a hero, is the legend true that that seventy wish maidens will greet me on the other side, and prove to me that Paradise is Paradise? The naïve fools, ready to give up life for a mere fantasy. No, it wasn't true. And dying in battle for this fantasy didn't constitute true heroism. There was no guarantee of Valhalla anyway for such a warrior. But this wasn't what Siegmund had asked. 'Will a woman greet me there affectionately?' Only Sieglinde. That was all. So Brünnhilde smiled again, and nodded her head. "Yes," she said. "Wotan's daughter will gladly fill your cup."

"You're noble," Siegmund observed. "I recognise who stands before me, the holy child of Wotan. Tell me one thing, immortal. Do brother and sister enter Valhalla hand in hand? Will Siegmund find his Sieglinde when he arrives?"

"Sieglinde's time on Earth is not yet done," Brünnhilde replied. "Siegmund won't find Sieglinde there. Not yet."

Siegmund leaned tenderly over Sieglinde and gently kissed her on the brow. Quietly now, composed, he turned back to Brünnhilde.

"Greet Valhalla for me," he exclaimed. "Greet Wotan and Wälse too, and all the heroes. Greet as well the lovely wish maidens. But I," his voice was resolute, "I will not follow you there."

"You've seen the Valküre's glance," Brünnhilde retorted. "You have no choice but to accompany me."

"Where Sieglinde lives, whether in happiness or sorrow, that is where Siegmund will also stay. The Valküre's glance may wither others, but not me. I'm not frightened. You will never force me to go with you."

"As long as you're alive," Brünnhilde answered him, "you are correct, nothing can compel you. But death will make a fool of you, and vanquish you. It's to warn you of impending death that I've come."

"Whose hand is it will strike me down?" Siegmund enquired.

"Hunding will kill you, fighting hand-to-hand."

Siegmund laughed.

"Bring threats more dire than that," he chortled, "if you would truly frighten me. You stand there hankering for a battle, and you choose Hunding for your hero! Choose him for your victim, Valküre, for it's my belief that he's doomed to lose this fight."

Brünnhilde shook her head.

"Believe me, Wälsung, it's you who has been chosen by the fates to die."

Sieglinde lay resting on his lap. Careful not to disturb her, Siegmund withdrew Nothung, the Sword of Need, out of its scabbard on his hip, and held it out before Brünnhilde.

"Do you recognize this sword?" he asked. "It came from he who is my protector, who promised it would bring me victory? With this I defy your threats."

"He who bestowed it," Brünnhilde spoke each word individually, emphatically, as though spelling it out for him letter by letter, so he couldn't possibly misunderstand, "he who bestowed it has decreed your death, and he has removed the magic power from the sword."

"Silence!" Siegmund berated her. "You'll terrify this sleeping woman."

Though it was more likely that he would wake her with the vehemence of calling Brünnhilde to be silent. He seemed to realise this too. And knew, at once, that his reaction was nothing but the shock of understanding. It must be true what she had told him, this Valküre. Why would she lie? Steeped in sadness, overcome by grief, Siegmund leaned tenderly over Sieglinde, and wept.

"My darling wife, saddest of all faithful women. The whole world is now at war, bent on destroying your tranquillity. In me alone you placed your trust, for me you have defied the world. Am I not to be permitted to shield you and protect you? Must I betray a heroine in battle?" He turned back to Brünnhilde, defiant and indignant. "Shame on him who promised me this sword if he decreed shame and not victory for Siegmund." Emboldened by his own boldness, Siegmund stood up, stepped so close to Brünnhilde he could have done the unimaginable, and seized an immortal in his mortal hands. But his intention wasn't blasphemy, only defiance.

"If I must die," he spoke the words as though they were a solemn oath, "I will not go to Valhalla. Let me remain in Hell forever."

He let the sword drop at his feet and bent low over Sieglinde.

Brünnhilde was shocked, but also moved by this response.

"Do you value everlasting bliss so little?" she enquired of him, and added, her voice slow and hesitant, "Is she everything to you, this hapless, sorrowful woman lying helpless in your arms, careworn and destitute? Is nothing else good or important?"

Siegmund looked up at the Valküre bitterly.

"Strange that you appear so young and fair and dazzling," he said, "and yet your heart is very cold and hard. Death the Deceiver!" he mocked her, then fell silent for a moment, gazing at Sieglinde.

But the presence of Brünnhilde was inexorable, waiting for him, the spirit of eternal patience. Whatever empathy, whatever compassion, may have been visible in her face, she remained the agent of Death, whose task was to bring heroes to Valhalla. Dead heroes. With or without their sister-spouses.

"If all you can do is mock and scoff at me," Siegmund berated her again, "then leave me now, you cruel, you mercilessly cruel woman. Or maybe you're just hungry to gloat over my misery. Go ahead then, feast on my woe and glut your envious heart. But of Valhalla's frigid delights, do not speak a word to me."

Brünnhilde was deeply, genuinely moved.

"I see the distress that gnaws at your heart," she answered him, "and I am sorry for the depths of your sorrow. Siegmund, give me your wife now. I promise to protect her."

"As long as she lives," Siegmund replied, "No one but I will touch her or protect her. If I am doomed to die, then I shall kill her here first in her sleep."

"Wälsung!" Brünnhilde cried, scarcely able to control her own emotions, "This is insane! Listen to me! For the sake of the pledge you gave to her, and for the child your love has conceived, put your wife in my care."

Siegmund drew his sword and pointed it at her.

"This sword," he cried, "this trusted weapon given to me so treacherously, this sword destined to betray me to my enemy, if it cannot prevail against my foe, then let it succeed against my friend."

He pressed the sword's tip against Sieglinde's throat, then thought a moment, and pressed it instead against her heart.

"Two lives are laughing at you here, Valküre. Take them, Nothung, Sword of Need. Take them with one fell thrust."

"Not yet, Wälsung!" Brünnhilde burst out in violent pity. And then she said, not thinking of its implications, not thinking if she had the power, or the authority, but moved by pity: "Listen to me. Sieglinde will live and Siegmund will live with her. That is my decree. The naming of the hour of your death is here postponed. To you, Siegmund, I will grant victory in the coming battle. To you I will grant the bliss your heart deserves. Listen – a trumpet-call. Make ready. Trust your sword and strike without fear. Nothung will be true to you just as the Valküre will surely guard you. Farewell, Siegmund, most blessed. You will see me again, I promise you, on the battlefield."

She rushed away then, mounting her horse and galloping off apace down into the ravine. Joyful and exultant, Siegmund's eyes stared after her.

And in the gathering darkness, where warlike horn-calls echoed through the cliffs and gorges, heavy storm clouds now sank down upon the mountaintop, veiling the cliffs, covering the ravine and rocky pass, until there was only darkness upon all the Earth.

Scene Five

Siegmund bent over Sieglinde, to listen to her breathing. Sleep was good. Like a soothing potion it purged the pain and soothed the grief that previously had so torn her features. Was it the Valküre who had brought this healing balm of sleep? He had no idea. No idea, either, if the furious battle about to be unleashed would wake her, or simply wake again the terror in her heart. She seemed quite lifeless, though her breathing told him she was still alive. And smiling now, in sleep, as though her lips were responding to some pleasant dream.

"Sleep on, my love," his fingers stroked her brow, her lips. "Sleep on until the battle's done, and peace brings joy to both of us."

He laid her gently down upon the rocky seat and kissed her forehead in farewell. Hunding's alarum had started up again, with resolution now, summoning him to fight.

"You call me to prepare for battle," Siegmund thought. "But it's you who needs to make your preparations. For battle and for death." He drew his sword and, looking at it as though he were no longer sure what destiny was planned for him, he braced himself. "Whatever's due, now is the moment," he clenched his teeth. He needed certainty, but there was nothing certain. Wälse had promised him a magic sword, infallible in battle. Brünnhilde had taken away the magic from the sword, then given it back again. But had she? Had she the authority to give it back? Who could he trust, now both his guardians had proven so untrustworthy. Only the sword, and his own courage. These he must trust. Alone, guarded or unguarded. By his own free will. He, Siegmund, alone, must act. There was no alternative.

"Nothung will pay the debt," he pressed his lips against the blade, and swore an oath in his own heart. Siegmund, alone, by the courage of the sword. Let the gods make and alter their decrees. Siegmund, alone, would stand up for his destiny. Even, if necessary, against the gods.

He hurried now towards the cleft in the great rock that would lead him down to the ravine. Down into the dark storm cloud he vanished, the flash of his sword visible for an instant as it refracted a flash of lightning breaking overhead.

And even as he left her, as though she sensed his parting, Sieglinde moved restlessly in her dreams. She was imagining that she was waiting for her father to come home from the woods. The boy was with him. She heard herself calling out, "Mother! Mother!" telling her mother about some strangers, frightening strangers, unfriendly eyes glowering at her. Black smoke and darkness filled the house. Flames flared around her. They were burning down the house. And she was calling out for help. Calling to Siegmund.

"Siegmund!"

A violent clap of thunder and a flash of lightning woke her.

"Siegmund!" she jumped up, calling out his name again, staring about in growing terror. But the world had vanished behind thick, black thunderclouds. Not a sound, save only Hunding's horn-call in the distance, and then his voice, echoing around the mountain passes:

"Wehwalt! Wehwalt!"

For a moment Sieglinde didn't realise who he was calling. Wehwalt – the name Siegmund had given himself when she first asked him. Wehwalt – woeful.

And now Hunding was summoning him to dreadful woe.

"Stand where you are and fight or I shall set my dogs on you!"

"You stand where you are," Siegmund's voice rejoined from the far side of the ravine. "Where are you hiding that I can't find you. Come out, that I may face you man to man."

Hunding, Sieglinde had recognised. And Siegmund. Her heart was pounding as the voices raged and went to war. If only she could see them.

"Run all you can, treacherous cuckolder," Hunding called out. "You can't escape. Fricka will smite you down."

Siegmund had reached the pass by now. He couldn't see Hunding in the darkness of the storm, but from his voice he could place precisely where he stood.

"Are you pursuing me weaponless?" he scoffed. "You spineless creature that has to hide behind a woman's skirts. Do battle in your own name, lest Fricka prove untrustworthy and fail you at the last." No answer. He held up the sword, certain that it would flicker in the darkness when the next lightning flash lit up the sky. So Hunding would see the sword, and quiver.

And then the lightning flashed.

"See, Hunding. From amongst the blossom on the ash-tree in your house, I plucked this sword. Undaunted. Soon you'll taste its blade."

Another flash of lightning illuminated the rock for just an instant, enough for Sieglinde to see the two men locked in mortal combat. With all her strength she called to them:

"Stop, you madmen. Murder me first."

She rushed toward the pass, intending to go down and place herself between them. But suddenly, above their heads, a flash of lightning broke so vividly she staggered as if blinded.

"Strike him, Siegmund. Trust the sword."

It was Brünnhilde, appearing in that flash of light. Closer and closer to Siegmund she flew down, hovering over him, protecting him with her shield.

"Strike him, Siegmund," she urged again. "Trust the sword."

Then Siegmund struck, aiming a fatal blow at Hunding. But the sword hadn't yet reached its mark when a glowing red light broke out of the clouds, and there stood Wotan, close at Hunding's side, his spear held out to thwart the thrust of Siegmund's sword.

"Get back from my spear!" the Father of War called out. "In pieces let the sword be shattered!"

In terror, Brünnhilde recoiled before Wotan, then sank back with her shield. Siegmund's plunging sword could not be stopped however. It searched for Hunding's heart, but found, and snapped, on Wotan's spear. Hunding reacted quickly. He plunged his own spear into the disarmed breast of the defenceless man, and Siegmund fell, dead on the ground. Sieglinde too, hearing his death sigh, fell with a cry on the damp earth, falling as if lifeless, though she had only fainted.

Brünnhilde vanished even as Siegmund fell. Wotan too, disappearing even as Hunding's blade struck home. Once more, only darkness upon the face of the deep. Black clouds. Thunder over the mountain. But in that darkness, Brünnhilde turned in haste towards Sieglinde.

"Flee, woman," she urged. "Take my horse. As fast as you can. Flee!"

Quickly she lifted Sieglinde onto the horse, climbed on behind her, dug in her spurs, and loosed the reins.

Just in time. At that very moment the clouds at last divided, allowing light to seep through. Hunding had fought in that darkness against an unseen enemy, but now his victory was clearly visible. Nodding his head with the satisfaction of revenge, he pulled his spear from Siegmund's chest. And standing on a rock behind him, leaning on his spear and gazing sadly upon Siegmund's corpse, Wotan the War-Father, framed by clouds.

"Go, you wretch," he sneered. "Go kneel before Fricka and tell her that Wotan's spear has avenged her shame. Go. Go!"

But Hunding hadn't even turned around when Wotan waved his hand contemptuously in front of him, and the husband of Sieglinde fell down dead.

And then what dreadful rage overcame the War-Father, seeking the Valküre, his daughter, hearing the sound of her horse's hoofsteps as they galloped away at speed.

"Brünnhilde," Wotan could scarcely contain his fury. "Woe upon you and your crime. This you'll regret, I vow. Your rashness will be punished, if my steed should overtake yours in flight."

And holding out his spear once more, pointing it at the heavens, the Father of War brought forth one final peal of thunder, one final flash of lightning.

Act Three

Scene One

On the summit of that rocky mountain, close by Valhalla, the forests were all of pine. Ancient clefts in the rocks opened on deep caves, where the Valküre stabled their horses and to which they brought the fallen dead of battle, in preparation for their journey to the life beyond. The mountain rose to its highest peak immediately above these caves, opening on a panorama that was unobstructed for as far as the eye could see – even the eye of a Valküre, which could see much farther and much clearer than a human eye. Rocks of various heights and shapes formed a parapet to the precipice, where occasional clouds flew past, as if driven by a storm.

It was on that rocky parapet that four of Brünnhilde's eight sisters – Gerhilde, Ortlinde, Waltraute and Schwertleite – were now ensconcing themselves, returned from their journeys to the distant fields of battle. They wore, as they always did, full armour. En route to Valhalla, each had plucked the body of a hero from the battlefield, and now, as they arrived, they hailed each other.

Gerhilde had climbed up to the very highest point, to look out for her four remaining sisters. Thick clouds passed close by her head. A flash of lightning broke through a passing cloud, and in that light a Valküre on horseback became visible, a slain warrior hanging on her saddle.

"Helmwige! Bring your horse this way."

"Whoa there! Easy."

Helmwige approached the rocky cliff, passing over her sisters' heads, reining in her winged steed as she prepared to land. Gerhilde, Waltraute and Schwertleite called to her as she approached. What seemed like a cloud bearing an apparition disappeared for a moment in the wood behind them.

"Put your stallion next to my mare," Ortlinde called towards the wood. "Your bay will enjoy grazing with my grey."

"Who's that hanging from your saddle?" Waltraute called in the same direction.

"Sintolt the Hegeling," Helmwige's voice came from the wood.

"Then take your bay away from the grey," Schwertleite laughed. "That mare carried Wittig the Irming."

"They were always fighting, Sintolt and Wittig," Gerhilde added, stepping down towards the summit's edge and looking along the horizon for her other sisters who hadn't yet returned.

Suddenly Ortlinde started up and ran towards the wood.

"My mare's being kicked by the stallion," she cried.

Helmwige, Gerhilde and Schwertleite laughed.

"It seems the quarrel between the warriors has now affected the horses," Gerhilde joked.

"Be still Bruno! Hey! Quiet!" Helmwige's voice came back to them from the wood.

But still no sign of the other sisters. They sat, and laughed, and waited a long while. Waltraute took over from Gerhilde as watcher on the summit's edge, and at last she thought she saw something, still off in the distance. It was Siegrune, and two other sisters not far behind. Seven now. But still two missing.

"Here, Siegrune," Waltraute called. "What kept you so long?"

"There was work to do," Siegrune called back, flying down over the wood where her sisters were gesturing to her to land. "Have the others arrived?"

Schwertleite called to her sister, voice being more effective than arm-waving to help Siegrune find the perfect place to land. Waltraute called too, and Gerhilde, adding confusion now, because Waltraute was calling to Grimgerde and Rossweisse, who were just arriving, but Schwertleite was calling to Siegrune, who couldn't decide which voice to follow, and so followed the arm-waving after all. Soon enough Waltraute and Schwertleite were gesturing towards Waltraute, to let her know Siegrune was safe and well and stabling her horse. A flash of lightning sent up by Siegrune added confirmation. But meanwhile Waltraute was still waving her arms and calling out:

"Grimgerde! Rossweisse!"

"They're riding together," Gerhilde said, as though this were something surprising and important.

Rossweisse and Grimgerde came fully into sight, emerging from a bank of clouds, sending out lightning flashes as they passed through it, as though lightning were an amusing game to play, after a battle. Their horses galloped towards the mountain-top, anxious to get home and rest. A slain warrior lay draped across each saddle.

"We greet you travellers!" Helmwige, Ortlinde and Siegrune called together to their sisters. "Rossweisse! Grimgerde!"

They had come out of the wood and stood at the edge of the precipice, waving and calling and gesturing.

Rossweisse and Grimgerde responded with a loud "halloo", an almost yodelling sound, calling from the throat but making the sound vibrate by pressing the fingers back and forth against the mouth, the way a man might use his hand in yawning. The Valküre loved that noise, that game of sounds they'd played since they were babies and War-Father taught them how to do it.

To the halloos of Rossweisse and Grimgerde, then, the responses of

Gerhilde and Waltraute, Schwertleite, Siegrune and Ortlinde. Ortlinde was holding her left arm above the elbow, where the grey mare had kicked her when she tried to separate her from the stallion.

"Leave your horses in the woods to graze and rest," Gerhilde called into the wood.

"Keep the mares far apart," Ortlinde added, "until our heroes' hatred has subsided."

Waltraute and Schwertleite laughed at this, so uproariously that it set Gerhilde and Siegrune laughing too.

"That grey has certainly paid for his hero's anger," Helmwige jested.

And soon enough, as laughter does, it became unstoppably contagious. Now everyone was laughing.

"Were you girls riding together?" Schwertleite asked, once all eight had made their formal welcomes, kissing and embracing.

"We rode separately," Grimgerde replied. "We met up just now."

"If we're all here," Rossweisse started, "then let's not wait any longer. We'll make our way to Valhalla, to bring Wotan his warriors."

"There are only eight of us," Helmwige counted. "One's missing."

"Brünnhilde will still be with that brown-eyed Wälsung," Gerhilde's voice was scathing.

"We must wait for her," Waltraute insisted. "Father would be furious if we arrived without her."

Siegrune was on lookout now. From the edge of the precipice she called out:

"Quick! Sisters! Brünnhilde's arriving even now. She's riding furiously. Something's not right."

All eight sisters rushed up to the lookout, calling and waving and gesturing. Watching too, with growing astonishment.

"She's riding towards the fir trees."

"Grane looks exhausted. I'm not surprised, after galloping that quickly."

"I've never seen such furious galloping by any Valküre."

"What's that on her saddle?"

"That's no hero!"

"She's carrying a woman."

"Where did she find a woman?"

"She isn't even greeting us."

"Heh! Brünnhilde!" Waltraute called to her, as loudly as she could. "Brünnhilde, can't you hear us?"

"Let's help our sister dismount," Ortlinde urged, and immediately Helmwige and Gerhilde rushed toward the wood, with Siegrune and Rossweisse not a pace behind. The other sisters watched, and called.

"Grane has collapsed!" Waltraute exclaimed in horror, staring into the wood. "And such a strong horse."

As though his strength only emphasised how hard Brünnhilde had been driving him.

"She's lifting the woman from the saddle. In a hurry."

Now the remaining sisters also ran towards the wood.

"Sister, sister," they called. "What's happened?"

Breathless, Brünnhilde came out of the wood now, into the clearing beside the precipice. She was leading Sieglinde, supporting her with one arm around her waist and the other around her shoulder.

"Protect me, sisters!" Brünnhilde pleaded. "I'm in the direst need."

All together her sisters questioned her, anxious to know why she was so troubled.

"Why were you riding at such speed?" asked one.

"Where are you coming from?" asked another.

"Only fugitives flee like that," a third observed.

"Is somebody pursuing you?" a fourth enquired.

"I'm running away," Brünnhilde answered. "For the first time in my life I'm running away. The Father of War is hunting for me."

The others were astonished, and again, in their amazement, all spoke at once.

"Have you lost your senses?" said one.

"Tell us everything," said another.

"Hunting for you?" repeated a third.

"Is it from him you're fleeing?" asked a fourth.

"Tell us everything," a fifth didn't even realise she was echoing what had already been said.

Brünnhilde turned anxiously, and went up onto the look-out to scan the long horizon.

"One of you, please, stay on the look out and tell me if he's on his way. War Father. Look to the north. That's the way he's coming."

At once Ortlinde and Waltraute sprang up to the edge of the rocky peak.

"What can you see?" Brünnhilde asked.

"A thunderstorm approaching from the north," Ortlinde answered.

"Gathering clouds," Waltraute added.

But it didn't need look-outs. All the Valküre could see the Father of War, coming ever closer on his sacred steed.

"He's hunting for me," Brünnhilde said. "He's very angry. Protect me, sisters. And save this woman if you can."

Apprehension gripped the sisters, asking all at once that Brünnhilde tell them what had happened.

"Quickly then," Brünnhilde replied. "There's not much time. This is Sieglinde, Siegmund's sister and his wife. Wotan is fuming with rage against the Wälsung. My task in the battle was to prevent her brother from achieving victory. But I protected him with my shield. Wotan's furious. He killed Siegmund himself with his own spear. Siegmund fell, but I fled with his wife. I thought," her voice was trembling with fear, "I thought that if I came to you, you'd hide me, you'd protect me from his vengeance."

Now the other eight Valküre were truly locked in consternation.

"What madness persuaded you to do this?" one exclaimed.

"You're lost," another said.

"You're lost," a third repeated.

"Oh, Brünnhilde!"

But it was Helmwige, Siegrune and Grimgerde who expressed together the deepest shock which all the Valküre were feeling. The word "rebellion" was on all their lips.

"Did you truly disobey the Father of War's commands?"

Gerhilde, Rossweisse and Schwertleite echoed their sisters' words precisely.

Rebellion. Against Wotan. It was beyond their capacity to believe.

"A darkness like the night is coming from the north," Waltraute called down from the look-out.

"It brings a storm," Ortlinde added. "A raging storm."

"I can hear the panting of his horse," one of her sisters responded.

"Me too," another said. "He's coming here. He knows where you are, Brünnhilde."

"It isn't me he's after," Brünnhilde retorted, to her sisters' still deeper astonishment. "It's her." She indicated Sieglinde. "He's decreed the end of the whole line of the Wälsungen. Which of you has the trustiest horse? Will you lend it to her, to save her from his wrath?"

Torn between loyalties, the Valküre didn't know what to say. But time was short, and someone had to say something. It was Siegrune who spoke first.

"Brünnhilde," she said, "you're asking us to defy his rage."

"Rossweisse," Brünnhilde pleaded. "Your horse is fast. Lend him to me."

Rossweisse shook her head.

"He flies fast," she said. "But he's never yet flown from the wrath of Wotan."

Brünnhilde turned to Helmwige, her eyes, her voice, beseeching.

"I don't have the courage to defy our father," Helmwige too denied her.

Now Brünnhilde was growing desperate. She turned to Grimgerde, to Gerhilde, begging them to lend her a horse. To Schwertleite, to Siegrune. Couldn't they see the state that she was in?

"Hold faith with me," she implored each one of them in turn. "As I've always held faith with you. Save this woman. Her grief."

Emotion had rendered her inarticulate.

Then Brünnhilde turned back to Sieglinde, who all this while had been standing, staring gloomily and coldly out in front of her, locked in her grief and lost to the world. Brünnhilde put her arms around the grieving woman, meaning only to protect her. But Sieglinde bristled, shook off Brünnhilde as though a repellent snake had wrapped itself around her.

"Don't waste your tears on me," Sieglinde spoke for the first time since her brother's death. "Death seeks me, and he'll find me waiting, gladly." She looked into Brünnhilde's face, harsh and unsympathetic. "Who invited you to rescue me?" she asked. "If you'd left me there, perhaps I'd have been struck down by the same weapon that killed Siegmund. In the last moment of my life, to be in that way united with him. But you stole that from me. How far away is he from me, and I from him? Shelter me, death, from memory. You want to help me, woman? You want my thanks instead of my curse, added to your father's curse? Then do this for me. Plunge your own sword into my heart. Right here. Right now."

Brünnhilde shook her head. She had seen grief so many times she understood it perfectly. But for Sieglinde, grief at the loss of Siegmund could not be everything.

"You have a duty to life," she replied. "Though Siegmund is dead, his love still calls you. You won a pledge from him," she pressed her palm against Sieglinde's belly, and forcibly, urgently, "you're carrying a Wälsung child. You have to live."

Sieglinde started violently. Brünnhilde had told her this before, but in her anguish she simply hadn't heard it. Now she did, and the whole world was changed. In that one phrase, in that one instant, everything was transformed. Her face lit up with a sublime happiness. But how did the Valküre know? She stared at Brünnhilde deeply, questioning her in silence. And knew the answer without needing words. For the Valküre knew. They were the daughters of Wotan, empowered to know these things. From Brünnhilde's eyes Sieglinde understood. It wasn't simply that Brünnhilde knew now. She had already known, when she made the decision to defy Wotan. She had rescued Sieglinde uninvited, precisely because she knew there was a child. Transformed. It transformed everything.

Now she took Brünnhilde's hands in hers, turned to her, implored her:

"Please, Brünnhilde, brave one. Rescue me. Rescue my child."

Then turning to the other Valküre, she begged them too:

"Guard me, sisters. I need a mighty shield."

But the thunderstorm approaching from the north was growing ever darker.

Waltraute called from the look-out to warn them of its approach. Ortlinde beside her gave counsel for urgent flight. And the other six Valküre, convinced now to assist Sieglinde, but still unwilling to offer any protection that might arouse the anger of Wotan against them, urged her to depart at once.

Sieglinde fell to her knees before Brünnhilde.

"Rescue me, woman," she begged. "Rescue a woman who's with child."

Brünnhilde pulled Sieglinde to her feet. Once more, the Valküre was filled with grim determination.

"Fly now," she said. "Take any horse, but fly. You must go alone. I'll stay here, to face the wrath of Wotan, to draw it away from you. The longer I can hold him here, the better chance you have of fleeing from his fury."

"Which way should I go?" Sieglinde asked

"Which of you came from the east?" Brünnhilde asked her sisters.

It was Siegrune who replied.

"There's a wild forest that way," she informed. "Fafner took the Nibelung treasure there."

"And turned himself into a dragon," Schwertleite added, "with the power of Alberich's ring. He lives in a cave there, keeping watch from dawn till dusk lest somebody should try to steal the ring."

"It's not a fit place for a helpless woman," Grimgerde observed.

"But from Wotan's anger," Brünnhilde replied, "there's no safer shelter than that wood. Our father fears that wood, and keeps away from it."

They were wasting time with these words. From the look-out Waltraute was calling, in a voice latent with panic, that Wotan was getting ever nearer. The Valküre pricked up their ears to listen.

"Brünnhilde," the sisters said together, "it's as though a hurricane were blowing in our direction."

"Fly swiftly," Brünnhilde urged Sieglinde. "Fly to the east. Be brave, and defiant, and be prepared to face great dangers. Hunger and thirst, thorns and rocks. Be sure to laugh, whatever your distress and suffering. Keep just one thing in mind, let it sustain you. In your womb, Sieglinde, you are carrying the noblest hero in the world. Here, take this."

From under her breastplate she drew the shattered fragments of Siegmund's sword and gave them to Sieglinde.

"Keep these safe for the child," she counselled. "I gathered them from where his father fell. All the pieces are here, I'm sure of it. Each broken fragment. One day it will be his destiny to forge this sword anew. One day he'll have cause to wield it."

She took Sieglinde's hands once more, and kissed her on each cheek.

"One last gift I have for you," Brünnhilde smiled. "His name. Let him be called 'Siegfried' – 'Peace through Victory'. Let him fulfil the meaning of his name and live in triumph."

Deeply moved, Sieglinde hailed this sublime miracle and gave back to Brünnhilde kisses equal to those she had received.

"You are," she said, "the most extraordinary woman. You've brought me healing such as no medicine could bring. Thank you. I promise I will save this child, for the sake of him we loved. May my gratitude bring you too the reward of laughter. Farewell. Be blest in Sieglinde's woe."

Sieglinde hastened away towards the cave where the horses were stabled. Even as she ran, black thunderclouds were surrounding the mountain top, a fearful storm approaching from the north. A fiery light lit up the precipice. And Wotan's voice, as loud as thunder.

"Brünnhilde! Stay where you are!"

Ortlinde and Waltraute came running from the lookout, crying "He's here." Brünnhilde didn't move. Simply, she watched Sieglinde as the woman ran towards the cave, then saw her emerge again, leading one of her sister's horses who seemed eager to take the woman on his back. Then Sieglinde mounted the horse, who didn't need to feel the digging of her heels before he bounded forward. Brünnhilde watched, but there was nothing now to see save only wood, and rock. Or not in that direction anyway. Behind her, closer to the precipice, the Father of War was starting to dismount.

"Brünnhilde!" all of her sisters spoke her name at once. But heavily. "He's coming."

As if she couldn't see that for herself.

In fear Brünnhilde looked from one sister to the next.

"Help me!" she implored.

She could have been about to faint.

"He'll kill me," she spoke again. "He's so angry he'll kill me."

Brünnhilde's fear had infected her sisters too. Huddling together, all eight retreated up the rocky point in fear. Brünnhilde let herself be drawn with them.

"Hide among us," they urged, and drew her into the circle they had formed. "Don't let him see you, and whatever he says, don't let it frighten you. We'll hide you."

But a circle of eight women wasn't a forest guarded by a dragon with a ring. Sieglinde might perhaps be safe, but Wotan even now was striding towards the summit of the mountain. Brilliant firelight, against a background of near total darkness, lit his way. Though the women stared in their anxiety towards the wood, it was from the rocks that he was coming.

His arrival, his vengeance, were now imminent.

82

Scene Two

Wotan strode across the plateau from the wood in visible excitement and towering rage, his face, his eyes especially, livid with terrible, wrathful anger.

"Where is Brünnhilde?" he cried out, one word at a time, each one fired like a bolt of lightning as he approached his Valküre daughters on the mountain summit, searching for Brünnhilde. "The rebel – where is she? Would you dare to shield her from my vengeance?"

The Valküre quaked with terror, yet they were determined to do precisely that – to shield her.

"Father," they replied together, "you're frightening us with your fury. What have your children done to waken so much wrath?"

"Don't mock me," Wotan answered. "Take care for yourselves, my daughters, before you speak rashly. I know perfectly well that you're concealing Brünnhilde from me. Hand her over! She's disowned and disinherited from this time forth. By her own doing. She's received what she deserves."

"She fled to us," Rossweisse admitted, breaking the resolve to remain silent and united in their silence. Now all the Valküre felt free to say their piece, and all did speak, but no one waited for the other.

"She begged us for our help," said some of them.

"Your rage dismayed and terrified her," said another.

"The poor dear was seized with fear and trembling," said a sixth.

"Your rage made her shake and tremble," said a seventh. "We beg you, on our sister's part…"

The last of her words were drowned out by the noises of the others.

"Father, we beseech you," one was crying.

"For our trembling sister," another moaned, "we pray to you, father, that the passion of your rage be calmed."

"Soften your anger, father," three of them spoke together.

"Calm now your passion's rage," a fourth.

"For her," a fifth, unaware these very words had just been spoken, "calm now your passion."

It was all too much for Wotan, this cackling of women, shouting and screaming all at the same time, all saying the same thing, and none of it coherent.

"Weak-hearted brood of women!" he let fly at them the rage he'd meant to save for… for the other one, the one whose name he couldn't even bring himself to utter. "I trust you didn't learn this sort of feeble courage at my knee. I nurtured you for battle, shaped your hearts to be keen and ruthless. And now what do I hear, my wild daughters whimpering and whining like ladies of the salon, the moment when my wrath has fallen on a traitor. Yes, traitor. Shall I tell you what her crime was, you lily-livered weaklings? What she did, this creature on whom you're wasting tears of pity. No one but she knew the secrets of my heart. No one but she saw into the springtime of my soul. In her deeds, my innermost desires came to fruition. And now," his anger was subsiding as his spleen was vented; even Brünnhilde, hidden and trembling inside the circle of her sisters, could recognise self-pity when she heard it, the sentimentality of an old man who'd lost through his own foolishness the creature he loved best in all the world.

"And now," Wotan resumed, "she's broken our sacred alliance, disdained it faithlessly, disloyally defied my will. She, took up, arms, against, me."

Such was his continuing disbelief at this eventuality, each word came out with difficulty, alone, as though he had to test it first before he could be certain it was what he meant. But it was. It was precisely what he meant.

"With my own spear that I gave her," he went on, but his rage was lessening. "Do you hear me, Brünnhilde? My water-nymph. Yes, I gave you your name, as well as your helmet and your spear, your fame, your life, your very joys. I, gave, you, these. Can you hear my voice raised now against you? Did I make you the sort of creature who shrinks and hides from her own destiny?"

At this, Brünnhilde stepped forward, out of the band of Valküre, and moved with firm but humble steps down from the rock, until she stood within a short distance of her father.

"Here I am, father," she bowed her head. "Pronounce my sentence."

"I don't pass sentence on you," Wotan replied. "You've pronounced your own sentence. You exist only through my will, and yet most wilfully have you opposed me. You had but one duty – to follow my orders. But you took orders from yourself and disobeyed me. You were my wish-maiden, but you turned my wishes against me. You were the bearer of my shield, but you raised that shield against me. I gave you the power to decide destinies, and you chose to set the fates against me. I made you the inspiration of heroes, and you inspired heroes to rise against me. What you once were, I have now spoken. What you are now, that's for you to say. But you are no longer my wish-maiden, the agent of my will. You were once a Valküre, but from now on, you will have to name yourself what you will be."

Brünnhilde quivered, hearing this litany of complaint and disinheritance. Her body was shaking violently and her lips trembled.

"You've disowned me?" she enquired. "Have I understood you rightly?"

"Never again will I send you on a mission from Valhalla, neither to defend and inspire my heroes in their battles, nor to fetch their bodies from the battlefield to the grave, nor to drink with me in my halls. Never again will you be asked to fill the mead-horn at the festal banquets of the gods. Never again will I kiss you as my child. You are exiled from the heavenly host, and banished from the company of the gods. Our bond is broken. Never again come into my sight."

Shocked, the other Valküre stepped towards the pair. But none spoke. Only they could listen, and not know how to react.

"Will you take from me everything you ever gave me?" Brünnhilde seemed to them calm beyond belief.

"He who overpowers you will be the one to do that," Wotan replied, cryptically. Here, on this mountaintop, you will be confined, defenceless and asleep. Any man who finds you and can wake you – you are his."

Now the Valküre did react, and it was with horror at this sentence. To think their sister should become the victim of any passing man. They came down completely from the rock in anxious groups, surrounded Brünnhilde, who lay half kneeling before Wotan. Each one raised her protest. One by one they called on Wotan not to shame their sister in this way, to shame them through their sister. One by one they pleaded with Wotan to repent and change his judgment, to rescind his curse. Siegrune even dared to call him dreadful; Rossweisse found the courage to say he was hard-hearted. But Wotan was unmovable.

"Haven't you heard Wotan's decree?" he answered them. "Your traitorous sister is banished from your company. Once she rode through the clouds with you – but never again. The flower of her youth will wither away. A husband will win her, and from that day forth she'll belong to him, and obey his will. She'll sit by the fire and spin and be the butt of vulgar jokes."

With a cry, Brünnhilde sank to the ground. Horror-struck, the Valküre retreated from her side.

"Does her fate frighten you?" Wotan asked. "Then fly away from her. She's lost. Keep your distance from her as you would a leper. If any of you dares to disobey me, if any of you befriends her in her misery, that foolish one will share her fate. Hear me clearly and take good notice. And now disperse. Do not return here – ever. Ride from this mountain top as fast as you are able, lest ill-fate should catch you here and punish you."

With wild cries of anguish, the Valküre rushed into the woods, lamenting their own fates as much as Brünnhilde's. Black clouds settled thickly on the cliffs. A rushing sound came out of the wood. Vivid lightning flashes broke from the clouds, and in their midst the eight Valküre flew in a close-packed group, their bridles loose, riding wildly away.

But no sooner had they gone than the wild storm subsided. Gradually the thunderclouds disappeared and the weather became calm again. Gradually a gentle twilight fell upon the mountaintop, and fine weather returned. At last the night came on.

Scene Three

Wotan and Brünnhilde were alone now. Brünnhilde lay motionless at her father's feet, the two of them for a long time unable, unwilling to speak another word. Slowly, Brünnhilde raised her head a little.

"Was my offence," she began, timidly, "so shameful that the offender requires a punishment to match?" Each word seemed to encourage her, to render her voice more firm. "Did I do something so completely base that my father needs to humiliate me this thoroughly? Was my action so dishonourable that it should now rob me of my honour for all time?" Gradually she raised herself to a kneeling position. "Father, look into my eyes, control your rage and explain the hidden guilt which has forced you to exile your favourite child?"

Nothing she could say, however firm, however logical, seemed capable of changing Wotan's attitude, let alone his mind.

"Ask yourself what you've done," he said, his voice grave and gloomy, "and you'll see your own guilt."

"I fought at your command," Brünnhilde responded.

"Did I command you to fight for the Wälsung?"

"You did indeed," Brünnhilde replied. "As Lord of Destiny."

"But you knew I'd withdrawn that edict."

"I knew that Fricka had trapped you into changing your mind, and that you were therefore obliged to adopt her point of view in order to remain friends with her. But in doing so you became your own enemy."

This Wotan could not truly deny. She'd touched the tenderest of all his bruises, and at last it moved him.

"I always knew you understood me better than anyone, and so I put up with your insolence when you defied me. But now I see you thought me cowardly and foolish. Wasn't I obliged to react to your disloyalty? Did you think you meant nothing to me?"

"I may not be clever," Brünnhilde replied, "but this one thing I knew – that you loved the Wälsung. I understood the dilemma, the clash of wills that forced you to drive away your love of him. You could only think of the other one, and sad to say this preyed on your heart so much that Siegmund lost your protection."

"Are you telling me you knew that?" Wotan answered, "and still you dared to offer him your shield?"

"I am your daughter," Brünnhilde answered softly. "My eyes are my father's eyes. I saw what you saw, even when you forced yourself to stop seeing it. Your painful dilemma forced you to deny him, but I held on faithfully nonetheless. As ever, when you went to war, I guarded your back from your enemy, and I saw what you were not allowed to see. I saw

86

Siegmund. I went to him to warn him of the omens of his death. I saw his eyes, heard his words, and realised the depths of his distress. I listened to his loud, courageous lament, so full of boundless love, heartfelt sorrow and terrible defiance. My ears heard, and my eyes saw, what my heart already sensed with awe and trembling. Astonished and ashamed I stood before him," Brünnhilde was growing more animated as her own words spurred her on, "wondering how I might best serve him. Victory or death. These were the options I could share with Siegmund, and I knew that victory was the one I had to choose. One man, father, breathed love into my heart. One will made me the ally of this Wälsung. Faithful to the innermost wishes of that one man, of that one will, I chose to disobey your involuntary command."

"And so you did," Wotan acknowledged, "what I wanted to do, even though necessity compelled me to do otherwise, to act," he hesitated on the word, but got it out at last, "hypocritically. But did you think so lightly, that you believed love's happiness could be attained by causing a burning pain to stab my heart, by rousing my anger out of my desperation, by imprisoning the world of love and my love of the world inside this tortured heart? In my torment, I turned myself against myself. I rose in rage above my agonizing sorrows. Angry longing fuelled by burning desire brought me to a dreadful decision, that in the ruins of my own world I would end my eternal sadness. But you, you drank your draught of love, and laughed, and savoured your fulfilment, smiling while my divine distress was mingling with uncontrollable bitterness? And now," Wotan continued, dry and terse, "you have your carefree heart to guide you. But you've renounced your father. I'm obliged to shun you. Never again will we take counsel together. From this time forth our paths are separate. As long as life and breath remain, this god may never give you so much as a greeting."

"You didn't deserve this foolish girl," Brünnhilde replied. "I was stunned by your commands, and didn't understand them. My own intelligence told me one thing – to love what you loved. Must I then leave you now and, frightened of you, shun you? Must you tear apart everything that once bound us, and banish half of yourself from your other half; a half that was once completely yours? Never forget that, divine lord. You refuse to dishonour the one half; surely you cannot wish to disgrace the other? You would demean yourself by seeing people mock and laugh at me."

"You were happy to follow the power of love," Wotan answered her. "Now follow the one who you're obliged to love."

"At least," Brünnhilde remained unvanquished by his words, "if I am banished from Valhalla, if I may no longer work and govern with my father, if some overbearing man must henceforth be my master, at least don't give me as a prize to some boastful, craven man, some worthless creature."

"You renounced the Father of War," Wotan retorted. "I no longer hold authority over your fate."

A new strategy. Brünnhilde needed a new strategy if she was to change his mind and heart. Like the child she had once been in her father's arms, she leaned towards him now, spoke to him softly, confidentially, as though she were telling him some private secret.

"You gave birth to a noble family," she whispered, "from which no faint-hearted soul can ever spring. The greatest hero, I know, will be born to the Wälsung race."

A new strategy. But not a good strategy. Saying this only made Wotan angry with her once again.

"Hold your tongue about the Wälsungen," he snapped back. "When I cast you off, I cast them off as well. Envy ruined that proud race."

"And I saved them," Brünnhilde countered. "By disobeying you, I saved them."

Confidentiality hadn't worked the first time, but this was the only way that she could say what now had to be said.

"Father," she whispered, "Sieglinde's carrying the holiest child. The look on his face brought a renewed animation to her own. "In sorrow, and in pain such as no woman has ever suffered, she will give birth to he whom fear makes her now conceal."

"Never ask me to protect that woman," Wotan snapped back. "And still less the fruit of her loins."

The strategy would work. It had to. Brünnhilde would not abandon it.

"She also has the sword you made for Siegmund."

"And which I broke in pieces," the god responded angrily. Didn't she know how much it pained him to have to do this to her? Why couldn't she accept her fate, her punishment, and cease this constant making of appeals to him. It hurt him, hurt him deeply, to cast off his child. But what choice had he?

"Don't try to alter my decision by vanquishing my spirit," Wotan's anger had subsided. "You must await your destiny, whatever it will be. I can't change it for you. And now I must leave you, put distance between us. I've stayed with you too long already. As you turned away from me, so must I now turn away from you. I'm not even permitted to know your wishes for yourself. My duty is to see that you are punished."

But calm now. Sad and solemn, even close to tears. Another moment and he would take her hands in his, and change his mind.

"What have you decreed for me to suffer?" she enquired.

"You'll be my sleeping beauty," he replied. "I shall enclose you in a deep sleep, helpless on this mountaintop. He who finds you, he who wakes you, he shall have you for his wife."

Brünnhilde fell on her knees in front of him. If only he would take her hands. Or let her take his hands. But at least there was this softening of his voice.

"If chains of sleep must bind me fast," she said, "leaving me prey even to the most base of men, this one thing you must grant me. I beg you, father, from my deepest anguish. Let my sleep be protected by fearful terrors." And now she did take his hands in hers, and he allowed it. "So that only a truly free and fearless hero will climb this rock and dare to find me here."

"You ask too much," Wotan replied, "too great a favour."

Hugging his knees, Brünnhilde implored him.

"This one thing, father. You must grant me it. Destroy your child who clasps your knees, trample your favourite, crush this girl, let your spear extinguish my very life, but don't be so cruel as to condemn me to this vile disgrace."

Suddenly Brünnhilde leaped up. A wild ecstasy seemed to have come over her. She jumped onto a rock and held her arms out wide, as though invoking the entire landscape as her witness. Her eyes were drawing his to look at every scree and path through which some unexpecting man might climb to find the rock and come upon her sleeping body. This way, through the caves. That way, climbing the steep precipice. Or over there, through the very forest that had carried Sieglinde away. Then she leaped down, behind the rock, and stretched her arms across it towards Wotan.

"Father," she said, "you could command a fire to blaze around the rock, you could surround the entire summit with burning flames whose fiery tongues would lick, whose teeth would bite any unworthy man who dared to approach me sleeping on the rock."

Finished now, she knelt again before him, clutched his knees, as a daughter hugging her aged father, as a supplicant begging at her master's feet.

Wotan could scarcely move or speak. Bending his weary body, reaching his long arms down, he found at last her fingers, hanging loosely on the ground. His fingers clasped those fingers, climbed up them until his palms had found her palms, and slowly raised her to her feet. His heart had swollen; words were beyond difficult. But he found it in him to speak one final word to her.

"Farewell," he said, "you bold, you wonderful child! Once you were the holiest pride of my heart. Farewell."

But he couldn't bring himself to leave.

"Farewell," he said again.

But his fingers were locked between her fingers, and he didn't have the means of separating them.

"Farewell!" he said, a third time.

But it was only words. The stasis of his legs belied him.

And yet, not only words. For now a deeper vocabulary rose to his lips, and with them came a final pouring out of so much, so many years of love for her.

"This I decree, my child," he stuttered. "If I'm obligated to reject you, if I may never greet you again with love, if you may no longer ride beside me as my companion or bring mead to my table, if I must abandon you whom I so loved, the apple of my eye, then such a bridal fire will burn for you as never yet blazed for any bride. A fire shall burn around this mountaintop; devouring terrors shall daunt the fainthearted. Let cowards fly from Brünnhilde's rock, for only one man shall ever win this bride – one who is freer than I, Wotan, the god."

All she could possibly have hoped for, won from her father! Brünnhilde sank forward on her father's breast and now he held her in a long embrace. Or she held him. At last she threw her head back and, still embracing Wotan, gazed with deep emotion into his eyes. Wotan gazed back.

"I love your eyes," he said. "Such brightly glittering eyes that I've caressed so often, and smiled because you let me. Whenever the excitement of battle won me a kiss from you, it was as though I'd won a prize. Whenever I heard the heroes praise you, even in their child-like manner, it seemed to me that poetry was flowing from a laureate's lips. Those gleaming eyes so often flashed at me in storms, as though it was you not me who made the lightning. And whenever my heart was sad with hopeless yearning, whenever I wished for worldly joy to overcome the fears and desperations of the daily world..." Wotan paused, his sentence left unfinished. Nor could it be finished, for departure was required of him, and finishing required staying. "This day," he resumed, "for the last time, lured by their light, my lips shall give your eyes a last farewell. May their star shine for a happier man. But for me, this hapless immortal who must leave you, let them close now in departure."

Because he couldn't bear to have her watch him turn away.

Brünnhilde understood. She closed her eyes as he requested, knowing she would never look on him again. With his divine lips and summoning his godly powers, Wotan pressed a kiss on each of her eyes, a kiss that drew the godhead from her, a kiss so powerful in magic that she fell at once into a deep sleep, cradled on his chest. As she tumbled forward, he gathered her gently in his arms and looked around fastidiously, seeking the best place on which to lay her down. Beside the great rock was a mound, low to the ground and soft with moss, and this he chose. Over it a wide-spreading fir tree cast its shadow southwards, but few branches blocked its northern side. This was the place. Sun would not harm her in the summer, and cold would not bruise her in the winter.

Wotan gazed one last time at his daughter, then leaning forward closed the visor on her helmet. His eyes scanned the whole form of the sleeper, and as he did so a gust of cold wind blew across the mountaintop. He hadn't protected her sufficiently, he realised. So he searched around the fell until he found the great steel shield of the Valküre, discarded by her when she hid among her sisters. This would protect her – nothing could ever do so more perfectly. Laid over her like a blanket, this would protect her.

So it was done, and Wotan turned slowly away.

But no, it wasn't yet done, didn't have to be done already. Wotan turned back, and with a most sorrowful look cast his eyes for one last time upon his daughter. Then, with solemn decision, he strode to the edge of the precipice and pointed his spear toward a large, black rock.

"Loge!" he called, and his voice echoed through the mountains like a thunderclap. "Loge! Can you hear me? Listen to me. I found you when you were nothing but a glimmering flame who blazed and vanished, unpredictable as fire. Once we were allies, now we must work as comrades once again. Loge, I summon you. Appear! Come, waving fire, come wind yourself around this rock and set this mountaintop alight with flames."

"Loge!" he called again, and struck the rock.

"Loge!" a third time, his spear again upon the rock.

And then a fourth time, "Loge!", and as his spear made contact with the rock a flash of flames immediately issued, swelling to an ever-brightening, fiery glow. Flickering flames broke forth, lighting up the world for miles around. Bright shooting flames surrounded Wotan, but the god was mightier than fire, and it simply warmed him. With his spear he described the circumference of the rock, directing the sea of fire to encircle it, building the wall of flames he'd promised to Brünnhilde. Slowly the fire spread, catching dry grass and gorse and thistles, burning them to ashes. But the fire didn't burn out, not even when its fuel was all consumed. Loge had lit it, and Wotan had commanded it. This fire would burn forever, or until its purpose was fulfilled. So on it blazed, until the whole summit of the mountain was enclosed in flames.

"He who fears the sharp point of my spear," Wotan called out, "shall never pass through this fire."

Saying this, he stretched the spear outwards as though it were a wand and he the caster of magic spells, and gazed back sorrowfully at Brünnhilde. This spear had shattered Nothung, the Sword of Need he had created for his perfect hero, his beloved Siegmund. This spear had pointed at Brünnhilde's breast, to name her punishment. And now this spear had set the fire on the mountaintop that would protect Brünnhilde until another perfect hero came and woke her. And where, he wondered, was Sieglinde now, carrying Siegmund's child and the fragments of the Sword of Need? Slowly he turned to leave. Yet one last time he turned his head to look at his beloved, his Brünnhilde. One final time, then vanished through the fire.

PART THREE

SIEGFRIED

Act One

Scene One

The cavern lay concealed deep in the forest. Naturally formed out of the rocks, it contained a smith's forge with a giant bellows. Coal stored beneath the forge burned constantly, keeping the temperature hot enough that metals never hardened until they needed to be hardened, after the smith had worked them into the shapes he wanted. Beside the forge, warmed by it but not so hot a dwarf would burn his fingers unless he was careless, an old and much used blackened anvil echoed to the rhythmic beating of a hammer, as Mime sat and worked his sword blade to a perfect tip. But the work only depressed him. It was heart-breaking bondage, to be fettered like this day after day to a task that never ended, for a spoiled, insolent boy who would never thank him for his work, but who would take the sword as soon as it was crafted, and strike it on the rocks to test its mettle, and break it if he could. Strong enough for giants, these swords he forged. The best swords in the world. But not sufficient for this tyrant.

Mime grew so despondent with his own bleak thoughts that finally he stopped working altogether, threw the sword down on the anvil in a temper, folded his arms across his chest, and sulked. Gazed meditatively upon the ground, he would have said. But he was clearly sulking.

"There's one sword though," the dwarf tended to the nostalgic at his worst moments of gloom, "that even he would never smash. Because he couldn't."

He was thinking of the remnants of Nothung, the Sword of Need. If only he could weld those pieces back together, forge it for the boy, then he would receive due compensation instead of this perpetual shame. But he lacked the skills, however good a smith he was. He sank further back and bent his head in thought. Fafner the savage dragon was lurking somewhere in those woods, guarding the Nibelung treasure with his mighty, monstrous bulk. Siegfried's boyish strength, Mime considered, might well be sufficient to slay Fafner, and then he'd get the Nibelung's ring for himself. Only one sword was strong enough for this. Only Nothung could serve Mime's ambition, placed in Siegfried's all-powerful hands. But Mime could neither weld nor wield it.

He took up the sword once more and went on hammering in deep dejection. "Heart-breaking bondage", he mouthed the words again that echoed constantly upon his lips. "Toil without end." The effort was pointless. The toughest sword he'd ever welded was still useless for the one deed for which it was required. Tinkering and hammering was all Mime could do, and only because the boy made him. And then what did he do? He took the sword straight from the anvil, tested it, broke it, threw it away. And then the tyrant had the gall to berate Mime, as though he wasn't working like a slave.

Boisterous as ever, Siegfried came in from his wanderings about the wood. He wore rough forester's dress, and a silver horn hung down from his neck by a long chain. Behind him, on a rope of bast, he was leading a large, brown bear, who he drove in wanton merriment toward Mime. Mime was expecting this – another of the tyrant's cruel games. Even before he came into the cave, Mime had heard him, coaxing the creature to "get that tinkersmith."

"Tear him! Tear him apart!" the boy had shouted at the bear, and roared with laughter as he watched Mime in his terror drop the sword and flee behind the forge. Siegfried made the bear chase him, round the anvil, behind the coal-store, driving him here, then there, and laughing, uproariously laughing, as though this was the funniest sight that ever took place in the long history of the world.

"Take him away!" Mime screamed. "I don't like this bear!"

Which only made Siegfried laugh still more, and louder.

"I brought him with me," Siegfried chortled, "because two cheerleaders are better than one."

This was an even better joke. Cheerleaders, indeed. Come to shout at him, and beat him, much more likely. Come to pinch him, and to punish him.

"Bruin," Siegfried called to the bear. "Ask for the sword."

"Leave me alone!" Mime implored him as the beast came closer. "Here," he held out the sword he'd just finished forging.

"When?"

"Just now. Today."

"Then today you have your freedom," Siegfried gave the bear a stroke across the back with his rope, and set him loose.

"Away with you, stupid bear," he mocked the uncomprehending creature. "I've got no further use for you. Today's consecrated to – freedom."

O, he was in a wonderful mood. Not that like sourpuss Mime.

The bear ran off into the wood. Mime came trembling from behind the forge.

"I don't mind you slaughtering bears for food," he was still shaking and his voice quivered. "But why do you need to bring them home alive?"

Siegfried sat down to recover from his laughter.

"I was looking for a better companion than the one I've got at home," he said. "D'you want to know what I did? I went into the deepest part of the forest, and blew my horn to see if I could find some cheerful, friendly company. That bear came out of the bushes and stood there growling at me as he listened to my music. A proper critic he was, growl, growl, growl. But I still preferred him to you – at least he listened to my music, instead of talking while I played and looking at the water-clock the whole time in hope that I'll be finished soon and you can get back to your drinking. Maybe I'll find someone even better next time. D'you want to know how I got him here? I simply tied the rope around his neck - and brought him to find out where's my sword."

With that sudden change of tone, Siegfried sprang up and went toward the anvil. Mime anticipated him, took up the sword and gave it to Siegfried.

"I made it very sharp," he said. "You'll like that edge it's got."

He held the sword timidly in his hand. Violently, Siegfried snatched it from him.

"It makes no odds to me," he said, "how sharp it is, unless the steel's hard and true."

He tested the sword, cutting swathes out of the air to feel its weight, its balance.

"What d'you call this?" he cried. "A sword? This is a flimsy toy."

He smashed it on the anvil so its pieces flew about the cave, shards threatening to strike Mime. Mime shrank in terror. One of these days those shards would blind him, and then what would the boy do for a steelsmith?

"There," Siegfried spluttered in his fury, "pick up the pieces. I should have smashed this on your head and spared the anvil. You boast your skills at me, you prattle on about giants and bold deeds and valiant weapons and unvanquishable shields, you tell me you want to forge armour for me and make me swords to win me praise, lauding your skills as though you actually had any. And what do I get? As soon as I lay my hands on what you've made, my hand-grip alone's enough to crush this junk. If you weren't so damned scrawny, I'd throw you on the fire with the sword. You doting, half-witted rogue. I would too, and then my aggravation would be over."

In a rage, Siegfried threw himself down on one of the stone seats in the cave. Mime was cautious now, and kept out of his way. But not so cautious that he didn't dare to speak his mind back at the boy.

"There you go again," he said, "raving like a madman. I never heard of such ingratitude. As soon as you're unhappy about one thing, you forget all the good things what I've done for you." Grammar was not one of Mime's strengths. "You don't remember, do you, not a word of what I taught you about gratitude? You should be obeying me, and gladly, this man as did so much for you."

Siegfried turned his back ill-humouredly on Mime, standing with his face turned to the wall.

"There you go again, see. Don't want to listen, eh. Can't see, can't hear?"

Mime stood perplexed, watching Siegfried from behind. Then he turned to the hearth.

"But I'll bet you'd like something to eat," he said. "Here, come try this meat I've roasted. Or maybe you'd prefer a spot of broth? I cooked it all for you."

He brought a bowl over to Siegfried. But, without even turning round, Siegfried knocked the pot out of Mime's hand and the meat went flying on the ground.

"If I want meat," Siegfried huffed, "I can perfectly well roast my own. You want these slops, go drink them."

This time Mime had had enough. Teenage sulks were one thing, but teenage tantrums he just would not abide.

"So this is the reward I get for so much love!" there was a certain element of whining in his own voice too, he knew. But these things needed to be said. "This is the disgraceful way my effort's repaid. What were you when I found you but a suckling child, a whimpering babe in arms? I brought you up. I made you clothes to keep you warm. Where do you think the food and drink come from? The fairies? I gave you shelter, cared for you as if you were my own." As he remembered, nostalgia tempered Mime's fury, and now he was no longer shouting, but going on a sentimental journey, telling his little boy a bedtime tale. "As you grew," he remembered, "I waited on you, made you a nice soft bed so you could sleep comfortably, made toys for you – d'you remember that first horn? Wonderful ringing sound it made. I was happy to work to make you happy. I helped you with good advice, and learning. Well, maybe not learning, but I sharpened your wits."

Sentimentality had got to Mime's eyes. If Siegfried had bothered to turn around, he would have seen the dwarf was close to tears.

But Mime was still prattling on and on, remorselessly.

"I sit at home, toiling and sweating for you, and where are you, gadding about the world, sowing your wild oats. I worry about you, Siegfried. I'm wasting away for anxiety about your future, poor old dwarf that I am."

Mime was sobbing.

"And for all my worry, and for all my troubles, how do you reward me? Bad-tempered boy that you are, you just scold me. I know you hate me."

Siegfried had watched the show so many times, he knew exactly when the performance would reach its final act, and right on cue he turned around, steadily watching Mime's face and mouthing his last words in harmony with him, as though he were the prompt. Mime didn't even notice. Or not until he finished speaking, dried his eyes, looked up and caught at last the mockery in Siegfried's face. That mockery invariably presaged an outburst. Mime tried to hide the fear in his own eyes, but it was useless. Siegfried simply stared back, until he'd outstared him. Slyly, Mime looked away.

"You've taught me much, it's true," Siegfried replied. "I've learned a lot from you. But what you most wanted to teach me is the one thing I've somehow never managed to learn. How to put up with you! You bring me food and drink, but what nourishes me is my loathing for you. You make me a soft bed, but that doesn't mean that I can get to sleep in it. If your teaching's the source of wisdom, frankly I might as well be deaf and dumb. I look into your eyes, and d'you know what I see? Pure evil in everything you do. I see you standing, shambling about like some sort of cripple, shuffling and nodding and blinking your eyes. All I want is to take you by the scruff of your puppet's neck and put an end to all that nodding. That's how I've learned to love you, Mime! D'you actually have any wisdom? If you do, then help me understand something that I've pondered in vain for years. I run into the forest to get away from you, roam about for hours; why do I come back? The animals mean more to me than you could ever do. Trees and birds, even the fishes in the stream — truly I love them far more than I love you. So why do I come back? If you're so damned clever, tell me that."

Mime attempted to insinuate himself into Siegfried's gentler side.

"That, my child," he said, "just goes to show how dear to you I really am."

Siegfried laughed.

"No," he answered, and his voice was clear and certain. "The fact is, I can't stand you."

Mime went back to his seat beside the anvil, sitting well apart from Siegfried. Clearly he needed a different approach.

"That kind of thinking's because you're a bad boy," he said. "You're wild still, and you have to learn how to control that. Young creatures pine for the nests of the older ones. That's how it is. Love causes it. So you come back to me, because you love me. You yearn for home and hearth with Mime, and so you should. Just as a mother-bird feeds her baby in the nest before the fledgling learns to fly, so you too, you silly child. And so too does clever Mime teach and tend his Siegfried. That's how it is. It has to be."

"Alright, then, clever-clogs," Siegfried replied. "Then explain this to me." His voice had become once more that of the young boy as he continued: "When the birds were singing to each other sweetly in the springtime, courting one another," there was even a hint of tenderness, "you told me, 'cause I asked you, you said that they were wives and husbands. They snuggled lovingly together and never left each other's side. They built a nest, and hatched their eggs in it. Out fluttered young birds, fragile and vulnerable, and the two of them tended their brood together. I saw other things too. Roe-deer mating in the bushes. Even savage wolves and wild foxes. The husband brought food to the lair and the wife suckled the young ones. That's where I learned what love must be. I never took any of the young ones away from their mothers. So where, tell me, is your wife, your loving wife, that I may call her 'mother'?"

"What kind of a question is that, you fool?" Mime replied angrily. "Are you a bird or a fox?"

"No," the boy replied. "You brought me up as a whimpering child and made clothes to keep the little blighter warm. Where did your child come from? Did you make me without a mother?"

Mime was embarrassed.

"You have to trust what I'm going to tell you," he said. "I am both your father and your mother."

"Don't lie to me, you odious wretch," Siegfried's bitterness resumed. But only for a moment. Again it was the little boy whose voice emerged. "I've seen with my own eyes," he said, "how the young always look just like their elders. When I was down by the river, I looked in the water and saw the trees and animals reflected in it. The sun and clouds too, reflected exactly as they really are, right there in the glittering waters. And I looked at my own shape, and I knew it was truly my own shape just the same. But not a bit like yours. I no more resemble you than does a glistening fish a toad, and no fish was ever born to a slimy toad."

"You talk an awful lot of nonsense," Mime was angry with the boy.

"No, listen, I've worked it out myself," Siegfried was growing animated. "It took me ages but I've worked it out. When I ran into the woods to get away from you, I still came back." He sprang up. "It was because I need to learn who my real father and mother were. And only you can tell me."

"What father? What mother? Foolish question!"

Siegfried leaped at Mime, seized him by the scruff of the neck.

"If I have to beat you up to get the answer," he threatened, tugging at Mime's collar, lifting him right off the ground. "I've never learned a thing from you by being gentle. Rely on your goodwill! No chance. I've had to force everything out of you. I'd never even have learned to speak if I hadn't wrung the knowledge from you with my fists. Now tell me, you wretch, tell me who my father and my mother were."

"Let go! You're almost killing me!" Mime gestured surrender with his head and hands. Siegfried released him.

"You could have killed me," Mime sighed, spluttering and struggling to catch his breath. His legs were trembling. "I'll tell you what you want to know," he said, "but first let me sit down and, o you cruel, you thankless child, I'll tell you everything I said, or what I know of it at least. Now sit down and listen, and I'll explain why you detest me. You see," he said, "I'm not your father. I'm not even a relative. And yet you owe me your life. I'm actually a total stranger, though I'm also your only friend. I sheltered you here out of pity, and this is how you pay me my reward? No, I was a fool to hope for thanks. But listen. Here's what came to pass. One day, long years ago, I heard a woman, whimpering out there in the wild forest. I found her, lying on the ground, helped her into the cave and tended her by the warm fireside. She was carrying a child in her womb. Grieving too. In grief she gave birth to the child here. She writhed and writhed, in terrible agony. I helped her best I could. But she was in the most terrible distress. She died, but Siegfried lived."

"Did she die because of me?"

"She gave the child to me, asked me to protect it." Siegfried was listening intently, deep in thought. "Which I did, gladly," Mime continued. "O, I went to no end of trouble out of kindness to relieve that poor girl's suffering." Mime grinned, and started singing, a rich tenor, if slightly out-of-tune: "I brought you up," he sang, "like any whimpering child."

Siegfried interrupted him.

"You've sung that song a hundred times."

Mime smiled, and nodded. The boy seemed to understand.

"Tell me, then, why am I called Siegfried?"

"Because your mother told me to. She said if you had that name you'd grow up strong and handsome." And again he sang: "I made warm clothes for the little child."

But again Siegfried interrupted

"What was my mother's name?"

"Her name? I never knew." He was determined to sing out his song. "Food too and drink I brought for you."

But Siegfried didn't want to hear lullabies.

"I said, tell me her name!" he screeched.

"It's gone from my memory," he said. "No, wait! I remember now. It was Sieglinde," and again he sang, "'the girl who gave you to me in her grief. I sheltered you, as my own flesh and blood.'"

Siegfried had never seemed so excited as he did just now. Not even letting Mime get out a half-line of his dreadful song before he interrupted.

"Now tell me, what was my father called?"

"His face I never saw," Mime answered impatiently.

"But my mother must have told you his name."

"He was killed in battle. That's all she ever said. As the child was fatherless, she left you here with me. As you grew up I waited on you; I made you a bed for comfortable sleep."

"For pity's sake cut out that starling song," Siegfried finally lost patience altogether with the infuriating dwarf. "If I'm going to believe a single word of your story, if any of it's anything but a pack of lies, then show me proof."

"What proof can I show you?" Mime asked.

"I don't believe what my ears hear," Siegfried replied, "only what my eyes see. There must be some piece of evidence."

Mime thought for a long moment, then fetched the two pieces of a broken sword.

"Your mother gave these to me," he said. "She said it was all she had to pay me for the trouble that I'd gone to, feeding her and caring for her and the child. It's a broken sword. She told me it was your father's, that this was the sword he carried when he perished in the fight."

Siegfried looked, and instantly he knew what must be done.

"Forge it for me," he said. "Forge these fragments back together, so that I can wield a real sword. My rightful sword! Come on, get up," he pressed the smith when Mime neither stirred nor answered. "Quickly, Mime! Quickly! I thought you were a master craftsman. Then demonstrate your skill. And no more cheating me with shoddy trash. I'll put my trust only in these fragments. But if I find so much as a flaw, if you play any tricks on me – I know your tricks, Mime, every last one of them, from laziness to deliberate, badly made rivets and steel not hammered accurately. And if you do, believe me, I'll bruise you blacker than you ever saw a bruise before. I'll have your scalp. D'you hear me? I want that sword, today. It's mine. I want my sword today."

"Today? Mime was alarmed. "What do you need a sword today for?

"I shall run away out of this forest," Siegfried replied, "and I shall never come back. O how happy I'll be to be free. Nothing will ever hold me or compel me again." He looked at Mime. "You're not my father. I shall make my home far, far away from here. Your hearth isn't my home, your rocky cave isn't my roof. As fish swim swiftly in the streams, as the finch flies freely in the sky, so shall I swiftly and freely leave this place, waft away like the wind over the forest. I'll blow away and never have to look at you again!"

Saying which, Siegfried rushed out of the cave and vanished deep into the forest.

"Where are you going?" Mime called after him, in great alarm, and with the utmost effort tried to stop him, to call him back. But the boy was gone. Mime stood in the entrance to the cave, gazing in astonishment in the direction Siegfried had gone. But gone without that sword he so desired, so he was bound to come back soon enough. Realising that reassured Mime, who turned now back into the cave, looked at the parts of his smithy as though wondering whether he should start this impossible task that Siegfried had commanded him, and at once sat down in desperation by his anvil. He shook his head. There goes the boy again, he thought, storming about. And me, I just sit here, lamenting the old troubles, burdened now with new ones. He was trapped, and knew it. How was he supposed to help himself now? He had no idea. How was he supposed to keep the boy? That was even more confounding. How was he supposed to lead this hoodlum into Fafner's lair? And hardest of all: how was he supposed to repair the fragments of that unworkable steel? For it truly was unworkable. He'd tried, secretly, many times. Some magic power must have made it, for no furnace fire could forge such an object, no dwarf hammer could shape such solid pieces. Mime put his head into his hands and sobbed. Then, looking up towards the cave-roof and the skies imaginable beyond, he wailed his fate into the emptiness of the world, a shrill cry meant for everyone and no one, meant just to soothe him by expressing volubly his inner pain.

"Not the hatred of the Nibelung," he cried, "nor need, nor sweat, can ever make this Nothung whole again."

But really it was Siegfried he was addressing. Siegfried who was out there somewhere, checking his pride to work out how long he'd need to wait before returning.

"Nothing," the dwarf shouted at the top of his voice. "Nothing can weld that sword together." The tears were pouring from his eyes. "Nothing is not renewable," he sobbed. He'd got Nothung and Nothing confused, which only made his desperation worse. It was all too much for him, too much, and after all he'd done for that poor girl, and for her new-born child. Too much. Unfair. Mime slumped down in despair onto a stool behind the anvil.

Scene Two

The creature had been wandering the forests for so many years, his fellows had taken to referring to him simply as 'The Wanderer'. No one knew who he really was, or where he came from. Round and round the forests he would roam, year after year, searching for something that he clearly wasn't capable of finding. He wore a long, dark-blue cloak and carried a spear which he used as a staff. On his head was a hat with a broad, round brim that hung down so low it hid his eyes.

The Wanderer had not been in this particular corner of the wood for a very long time, and it was a place he generally avoided. But he needed shelter for the night, and there, seemingly inhabited, was a cave that was perfect for his needs. He reconnoitred for a while, until he found an entrance at the rear end of the cave. Better to go in this way, better to surprise its occupant from the inside, where it's so much harder to deny a stranger hospitality.

"Greetings, worthy smith," he saw it was an old and ugly dwarf who lived inside this cave. But even old and ugly dwarves merit courtesy when you hope to share their fire. "I'm a visitor," he went on, "weary from travelling, who requests the favour of your house and hearth."

Mime jumped up. If there wasn't one thing causing him alarm, there was suddenly another.

"Who are you?" he blurted out the question rudely. "What you doing seeking me out like this in the dark forest? Why you pursuing me in these woods?"

The stranger came closer, step by step. Mime braced himself, stooping like a boxer, casting his eyes about for sword or spear. If the man intended mischief, he would need the means to defend himself. But the man wasn't actually threatening him. In fact, the man looked harmless. And he was holding out his hand.

"Men call me 'Wanderer'," he introduced himself. "I've travelled a long way over the face of the Earth and I'm always on the move."

"Then if that's what the world calls you," Mime replied, "my advice is to keep on wandering. And if you're always on the move, then off with you now and don't stop here!"

"Good men have always made me welcome, given me good hospitality," the Wanderer replied. "Even gifts when I departed. Only the wicked fear ill fortune."

"Ill fortune," Mime answered, "already shares this cave with me, and pays no rent. Will you bring still more ill fortune on this poor Nibelung?"

"I've explored this world all my long life," the Wanderer approached closer to Mime, step by step, "and I've learned much. Many times I've been able to teach men wisdom, many times my words have lightened the worries and the sorrows gnawing at their hearts."

Mime understood that he was meant to be impressed. And because impressed respectful. And because respectful generous with his hospitality. But Mime wanted to be left alone. He didn't like guests.

"How very nice for you," he said, "to have travelled so much and thought so much and spied so much. But I don't need travellers here, and I certainly don't need thinkers or spies. I want solitude and my own company. There's no guest rooms at this tavern."

The Wanderer was used to this, and knew how to respond. Step by step he came still closer, never enough to threaten, always enough to make it much more likely his unwilling host would finally relent.

"Many think they're wise," he said, "because they know what's happening in the world. But they have no clue what's going on inside themselves, and so they don't know why they're unhappy. Many times I've been able to assist them. I invite their questionings, and help with answers. Many have benefited from my words."

Too close however. Not so much his steps as this intrusion upon Mime's inner self. The dwarf's face reflected an anxiety so deep, even the Wanderer was cautioned to hold back.

"Many people seek useless knowledge," Mime answered. "I know enough for my needs." The Wanderer had reached the forge now and Mime was biting his lip, breathing heavily. But kept his self-control. "My wits are adequate," he said. "I don't need more. So unless your wisdom needs directions, it's getting late."

The Wanderer sat down beside the fire.

"I would be willing," he ventured, "to stake my life in a contest of knowledge against you. My head's yours, won fairly by you, if I can't teach you something useful. Ask anything you like."

Mime was staring at the stranger open-mouthed. At this suggestion he shrank back, apprehensive. How was he going to get rid of this nuisance who'd already outstayed his welcome? And if he let him stay, if he consented to his game, he'd have to question the stranger very cleverly.

Mime gathered in his courage, for in the end the contest was irresistible.

"I accept," he said. "Your life for my hospitality. But be sure you use that head of yours cagily," he added, thinking that he would have to be just as crafty in the framing of his own questions. "I shall ask three questions," he declared.

"And I shall give three answers," the Wanderer agreed.

Mime set himself to thinking. Three questions that the stranger couldn't answer, so he would be rid of him. The first came easily.

"If you've really wandered so long and far across the world, then you should know what race it is that dwells in the caverns at the deepest depths of all the Earth?"

Too easy. The Wanderer's lips were already opening before he'd got the question out.

"In the caverns at the deepest depths of all the Earth," he answered, "dwell the Nibelungen. Their land's called Nibelheim. They're black elves, spirits of darkness. Black-Alberich was once their lord. He owned a magic ring that had the power to compel his hard-working people into slavery. They heaped rich treasures up for him, shimmering gold in gleaming piles, so that he could win the whole world for his kingdom? What's your second question, dwarf?"

Mime sank into deeper meditation. That answer came to him so easily, no wonder it was so simple for the Wanderer. He must think deeper, more darkly, more obscurely, to find a question that the stranger couldn't answer.

"Clearly, Wanderer, your travels have taken you deep into the bowels of the Earth. So now tell me, what race is it that dwells on the Earth's face?"

Again the Wanderer's lips were ready with an answer as soon as Mime put his question.

"Giants," he said, "live on the Earth's face. Their land's called Riesenheim. Fasolt and Fafner, who were their rulers, envied the power of the Nibelung. They heard about his treasure, and won it for themselves. So they acquired the ring as well. But the brothers quarrelled over the ring. Fasolt was killed and now Fafner guards the golden treasure, disguised as a savage dragon. I believe my life now hangs upon one more question."

Mime was so absorbed in thought, for a moment the Wanderer wondered if his last remark had gone over the dwarf's head. He was about to press him for a third question when Mime looked up, and grinned.

"You know a great deal about the surface of the Earth," he said, "and who lives there. But now be ready to accept forfeit when you lose your bet, for here's my third question. Tell me what race it is that lives among the heights beyond the clouds?"

He had him, surely, with that one. But once again the stranger's lips were moving with an answer even before Mime's lips had closed upon the question.

"Among the heights beyond the clouds," the Wanderer replied, "the gods live in a hall they call Valhalla. They are the spirits of the light, and their lord, Wotan, Light-Alberich if I may call him that, rules over them. Once upon a time, long, long ago, he cut himself a spear-shaft from the primal tree, the sacred ash tree whose trunk may whither but whose limbs, once crafted by a god, can never rot away. With the point of that spear, Wotan rules the world. And on its shaft, carved with binding runes, are sacred treaties, signed with all the races in the universe, acknowledging the authority of he whose hand controls that spear. Wotan it is who clasps it. Before him the Nibelungen army bows. The race of giants has been tamed by his almighty power. All, all must obey him, and forever, for he's the spear's all-potent Lord."

It could have been by accident, or it could have been to make his point, but suddenly the Wanderer struck the ground with the tip of his staff. Mime shrank in terror as a low and distant sound of thunder caused the cave to echo. The Wanderer sat quietly now, and smiled.

"Tell me, crafty dwarf," he said at last, "are my answers entirely satisfactory? May I keep my head?"

Mime stared at him, looking at his shaft especially. There was something, he couldn't find the words for it, but something about this stranger, something not just terrifying, something – Mime got up and busied himself about the cave, seeking in confusion for his tools that seemed not to be where he'd left them, looking about for this or that, turning back shiftily from time to time to catch the Wanderer's calm glance, and turn away again. Something unnameable. He wished the Wanderer would go away.

"Your wager, and your head, you've won," Mime conceded. "Now be off with you."

But the Wanderer sat calmly on his stool.

"Your error, dwarf," he said, "was not asking what you really want to know. I staked my head on telling you. But you don't know what it is you really want to know. So now it's your turn. Return the wager, put up your head as security against my questions. You greeted me without the good grace of good hospitality, and I risked my head in hope of gaining some. By the rules of the wager, your head is mine if you can't answer my three questions. Agreed?"

Mime didn't respond, but nodded, almost imperceptibly.

"Marshal your wits, dwarf," the Wanderer stood up to stretch his back and legs, and walked a circle here and there, deep in meditation, thinking up his questions.

Mime wasn't ready yet, however. Timidity and hesitation struggled with desire to rid himself of this decrepit nuisance. Why not just throw the man out, physically? No, that was a question even the most stupid soul could answer – because he was a frail, old dwarf, and the stranger was tall, and strong, and carried a heavy staff. Only by wit and wile could he prevent the man from trespassing any further in his cave. So he composed himself at last, and nervously, submissively, he gave up pretending to look for tools, and sat down by the anvil.

"I left my native land long years ago," he said. "And I was born long years before that. I knew this Wotan that you spoke about just now. He looked into this cave once. He looked at me. Never did any creature so bewilder me as he did when he set his wits against mine. And now here's you, making the same challenge. Very well. Ask away. Ask anything you want. If I'm lucky, perhaps you'll let me keep my head."

The Wanderer sat down again, relaxing as comfortably as a man at his own hearth.

"Now, honest dwarf," he began. "Give me your best answer. What's the name of the race that Wotan has treated the most harshly, even though," he said this very softly, almost inaudibly – "it's the dearest to him of all the races in the world?"

Mime relaxed too, hearing this question. His face looked almost cheerful.

"As it happens," he replied, "I've done a certain amount of private study on the subject of heroic genealogy. This is a riddle I can readily resolve. You should be thinking of the Wälsungs, the children that Wotan fathered and who he dearly loved, though it's true he didn't always demonstrate that love. Now Siegmund and Sieglinde were fathered by Wälse. They were a wild and desperate pair of twins. And they produced Siegfried, the mightiest of all the Wälsung children. So," Mime asked, "do I get to keep my head this time?"

"Your knowledge," the Wanderer replied in a most friendly fashion, "is impeccable. You've named the family accurately. I see it'll be difficult to catch out such an obviously cunning fellow. But that was only the first question. Now for the second. There was a wise and wily Nibelung into whose care Siegfried was given, to protect him until he was old enough to kill Fafner, and win back the ring, and be the new lord of the golden treasure. Tell me, for my second question, what sword must Siegfried wield if he's to bring about Fafner's death successfully?"

"I know that. I know that," Mime was jumping up and down in his seat, his lips hardly able to contain themselves for wanting to answer the stranger's question before he'd even finished formulating it.

"Nothung," he said, and rubbed his hands with glee. "Nothung's the name of the glorious sword! Wotan thrust it into the trunk of an ash tree, so that it would belong to whoever pulled it out. Not even the strongest heroes could manage it though. Siegmund alone was able to. Bravely he carried it into battle, until it snapped on Wotan's spear. The pieces are now guarded by an extremely wise and honest and charitable and actually a very hospitable blacksmith though sometimes people intrude upon his hospitality and, but anyway this blacksmith knows that only with Wotan's sword will the child – a brave but very stupid child as I happen to know – this Siegfried will be able to slaughter the dragon." He paused, grinning from ear to ear. "So," he asked, "do I get to keep my head a second time?"

The Wanderer laughed and laughed.

"I am completely charmed and enchanted by your wit," he said, recognising the extent to which Mime was malleable with flattery. "I've met many witty creatures, many clever souls – but few to match your talents. But now, if you're so clever, and if with your skills you'd have the young hero do your bidding, there's a third question you must answer. Tell me, wily armourer, whose hand is it that destiny has chosen, to take the fractured pieces of the Sword of Need, and weld them into one anew?"

This seemed to trigger something deep inside Mime, a panic, almost a hysteria, for he jumped up in terror, crying out and nearly fainting.

"What shall I do?" he shouted. "What can I say?" As before, he went hunting in his tool-kit, throwing implements here and bits of broken metal there; but now he was genuinely looking for something particular. "That wretched weapon – I wish I'd never seen it?" he cried as he went on hunting. "I wish I'd never stolen it, it's brought me naught but pain and distress. It's too hard, I can't hammer it. I've tried to solder it, but the rivets are too tough. The finest smiths in all the world couldn't forge that sword again. Who could weld it if I can't? No one can fathom this mystery?"

The Wanderer calmly rose from the hearth and stood in front of Mime.

"You had three opportunities to ask me any question that you pleased. But you chose pointless, empty topics. It didn't occur to you to ask about this matter that lies so close to your heart, something you actually need to know. Now when I tell you, you'll lose your wits and I will have your crafty head. Who'll be Fafner's bold destroyer? You wretched dwarf – you should take heed of this: only one who has never felt fear, only he may forge Nothung anew."

Mime stared wide-eyed at the Wanderer as he turned to go. From the mouth of the cave, the Wanderer turned back a moment.

"Guard that clever head of yours more closely from now on," he called. "You've forfeited it, losing our wager. But I've no use for it, and leave it for him, the one who has never felt fear."

The Wanderer smiled and turned away again, disappearing quickly into the forest.

Mime was oblivious. He had sunk, overwhelmed, onto the seat behind his anvil.

Scene Three

Mime stared out into the sunlit forest. Events of the past hour had shaken him to the very depths, and now the more he thought about them the more his limbs gave way to violent trembling. He cursed the light, which seemed to burn his eyes. The air was on fire, filaments of dust and ashes flickering and flashing, glimmering and buzzing, with minuscule objects floating and spinning and quivering. Something was gleaming and glistening in the sunshine. There was a rustling sound outside somewhere, a hissing and a humming and a roaring. And inside, whether the cave or his head, a rumbling, and a howling, and a crackling, coming nearer. It burst through the forest, heading towards him, so that he jumped up in terror and ran cowering to a corner of the cave. A dreadful mouth gaped at him, all jaw and teeth. The dragon, it was the dragon Fafner! Come for his head.

"Fafner!" Mime managed to get the one coherent sound out of his mouth, before sinking down behind the anvil. The only other sounds that issued from his mouth were screams.

But there was no Fafner. Only in his imagination, in the terror induced by that malicious stranger with his cunning questions and his empty threats to take his head. Mime's screams died down at last. But the trembling of his limbs continued. Nor was he willing to come out from underneath the seat beside the anvil. Not till he was sure that it was safe.

When there came a noise from outside in the forest. Mime listened carefully, and recognised familiar sounds. Siegfried, crashing through the bushes rather than taking the longer way round through the clearing. He would emerge from the forest thicket at any moment.

"Hey there, idle dwarf!" the beloved, hated voice reached him at last. "Have you finished yet?" Siegfried came inside the cave. "What's with my sword? he asked, and paused in surprise, for there was no sign at all of Mime anywhere, no sound, not even his usual whimpering and muttering to himself out loud all day his long litany of moans. Where was he hiding? Had he perhaps sneaked away, frightened of what he knew would happen to him if he failed to forge the sword? The little coward!

"Where are you, Mime? Where are you hiding?"

"Is that you, Siegfried?" a frightened voice hissed from behind the anvil. "Are you alone?"

This was the funniest thing Siegfried had seen or heard in ages.

"Where are you, Mime – under the anvil? What you doing down there - sharpening the sword?"

Mime crawled out, dirty and dusty and utterly befuddled.

"The sword?" he asked, and then, a second time, "the sword? How can I forge it?"

Siegfried was bemused. The old dwarf seemed to have lost his wits completely.

"Only one who's never felt fear, only he may forge Nothung anew," Mime muttered, but it wasn't a line from his regular song, the lullaby he always sang. "This dwarf is much too wise to undertake this work."

"Will you speak sense," Siegfried was getting irritated by this silly nonsense. "Speak sense, or must I help you?"

He raised his hand, as though to strike Mime.

But Mime was oblivious to him. It was as though he couldn't even see Siegfried, was unconcerned about being struck. He'd gone crazy

"Where can I find help when I need it?" Mime asked, whether Siegfried or himself. "I've gambled away this clever head of mine," he went on, staring straight ahead, but seeing nothing. "Forfeited it to one who's never felt fear."

"Is this nonsense for my benefit?" Siegfried asked, impetuously. "Is this your clever ruse to get out of forging my sword? Are you planning to run away from me?"

"I'd gladly run away from someone who knows fear," Mime was slowly recovering his self-command. "But I made a terrible mistake. I quite forgot to teach that to the boy. Stupidly, the one important thing. I wanted you to love me, but even that went wrong. Now, how can I instil fear in you?"

Siegfried had no idea what he was going on about. Pretexts and excuses, that was all it was. Alibis for not doing what he'd been ordered.

"Hey!" he cried, grabbing hold of Mime by the coat-lapels and brandishing his fist in the dwarf's face. "Will this help you?" He shook it and waved it, longed to use it to smash that ugly, stupid face. But something held him back. "What have you been doing all day long?" he asked, and walked away to examine the contents of the anvil.

"I've been worrying about you," Mime replied. "That's what I've been doing. Sunk in my chair distracted, that's what I've been, thinking how I could show you something of importance."

Siegfried laughed. "Sunk in your chair!" he scoffed. "Sunk underneath it from what I saw. What terribly important things did you brush up down there?"

By now, Mime had almost completely regained his composure.

"What I learned," he said, "was fear. And why did I learn it? So I can teach it to you, you stupid boy."

"Fear?" Siegfried wondered. "What's that?"

"Something you've never known," Mime replied. "But something you're certainly going to need if you really plan to go off into the world. Even the strongest sword will be no use to you, if you're not carrying a scabbard full of fear as well."

"It sounds to me like all you brushed up from the floor was scraps of rubbish," Siegfried replied. He had no patience for the dwarf when he was in this mood.

Mime came over to Siegfried. The trembling was passed now. For the first time since Siegfried was a boy, he felt he could address him – yes, like a man who had no fear.

"Scraps was all your mother left me. A little scrap of a child that I brought up as best I could. Scraps of sound advice that I've been repeating to you ever since. And one scrap of a promise, that I made to her, that I wouldn't let her Siegfried go out into the dangerous world until he'd learnt fear."

"If this is a skill I need to know," Siegfried answered vehemently, "why haven't you taught me it already? What is this fear?"

"Have you never," Mime was hamming it up, "been out in the dark forest at twilight, standing in some dark place, and felt a rustling not far off, and then a whistling here, a whispering there, and suddenly a wild roaring booms right next to you, flares flicker all around you, a swirling whirls and flies towards you." Mime was acting out each sound and movement with his body, trying to capture the mood of trepidation; but Siegfried just watched, amused. "Haven't you felt a furious shudder seize your limbs?" he quaked. "Didn't burning fear make you shake, till you thought your heart would burst with pounding?" Mime had terrified himself so deeply that his voice was genuinely quivering now; but Siegfried remained entirely unmoved." If you've truly never felt like that," he said, "then you don't know fear."

Siegfried thought long and hard, but he truly couldn't recall any experience remotely close to that which Mime had described.

"It must be a wonderful sensation," he mused. "But my heart's always strong and firm. This fury and shuddering, this burning and quaking, this fever and dizziness, this pounding and trembling – I'd love to feel such things. Truly, I long to sample the pleasure of each of these. You'll have to teach me, Mime – can you do that? How could a coward like you ever teach me such a thing?"

"Just follow me," Mime replied. "I'll be your guide. I happen to know an evil dragon who slays and feeds on men. This Fafner, he can teach Siegfried fear. All you need to do is follow me to his lair."

"Where is this lair?" Siegfried enquired.

"Niedhöhle, it's called," Mime replied. "The Cave of Envy. It lies east of here, at the edge of the forest."

"Not far then from the human world?" Siegfried considered.

"The human world," Mime replied, "is indeed so close it practically lives inside the Cave of Envy."

"Take me there," Siegfried commanded. "Guide me to this Fafner. I'll have him teach me fear, then head off into the world. Now quick! Forge me my sword. I can't go out into the human world without it."

"The sword!" Mime repeated in desperation. He'd hoped in this way to distract the boy from thinking of the sword. But now – what a disaster!

"Quickly, Mime!" Siegfried urged. "Take me to the smithy and show me what you've done."

Mime cursed the weapon.

"I haven't done it, Siegfried. I can't do it. I don't have the skills. There's magic in the pieces of that sword. Dwarves have no power over that sort of magic. Someone who doesn't know fear might more easily discover the technique."

"Don't try to trick me with your riddles," Siegfried complained. "Admit you're a bungler and I'll forgive you. But trying to lie and cheat your way out of doing things I'll never forgive. Go on, get away from here. Bring me the pieces."

Siegfried strode over to the anvil.

"My father's blade it is, bequeathed to me. So it must yield to me. If you can't do it, I'll just have to forge the sword myself."

Flinging Mime's tools about, Siegfried set himself impetuously to work.

"If you'd paid proper attention when I tried to teach you this," Mime grunted, "you might even be able to do it now. But no, not you. Lazy you were, and flippant, during lessons – now what chance have you got of doing the job?"

"Given that the teacher didn't know how to do it," Siegfried replied. "It wouldn't have been much help for the student even if he were paying attention?" He made a long nose at Mime. "Now go away and stop interfering or I can't guarantee I won't weld various bits of you while I'm at it."

Siegfried heaped up a large pile of charcoal on the hearth and used the bellows to increase the fire. Then he fitted the pieces of the sword into the vise and filed the jagged edges to a smoothness. Mime had sat down at a distance to watch Siegfried at his work.

"What you doing that for?" he simply couldn't help but interfere. "Just use the solder. It's warm and ready for you."

"Take that stuff away. I don't need it," Siegfried replied. "You don't put two halves of a sword together using glue!"

"Siegfried, you've worn the file away to nothing! You've rubbed the rasp to pieces! How are you possibly going to work the steel when it's ground down to splinters?"

"Splinters is precisely what I need," Siegfried replied. "That's how it's broken, that's how I'll fix it."

He went on filing vigorously, while Mime sat there grumbling to himself. An expert was no help here, he could see that. The only help for such a fool would come out of his own folly. Or more likely nowhere. He'd ruin the sword completely. But the boy was certainly putting his back into the task. He'd filed the steel to nothing and he wasn't sweating at all.

Siegfried had gone on fanning the fire until the temperature of the anvil was hot enough to melt the minerals in the cave walls. Mime was as old as the caves and the woods, but he'd never in his life seen anything like this. The heat was melting him as well. While Siegfried continued filing the sword with boisterous energy, Mime decided to move a little farther off. But still close enough to watch. The boy was going to succeed. He just knew it. The boy was fearless. More than that - the boy believed completely in his own abilities, even how to do the things he'd never learned. He was going to restore the sword, Mime could see it. What the Wanderer had said would come to pass. And then what? Where should he hide his foolish head? The boy would surely take that sword and hack it off, unless somehow he could teach him fear. He sprang up, watching some particular hammering technique the boy was using on the sword; he had to bend low to see it properly. As the end of the process was approaching, Mime was growing restless. He needed an answer to his own question: what would happen to his own head if he couldn't teach the boy fear? He'd told the boy Fafner would teach him, and it was certainly a possibility. But Siegfried was destined to kill Fafner and claim the treasure. And how could Siegfried slay the dragon if the dragon taught him to be scared? And how then could he get the ring? This was the terrible dilemma facing Mime: how to get Fafner and Siegfried in a battle to the death of both of them, so he could save his head and steal the ring? Mime cursed fate that had trapped him so inextricably. Advice, that was what he needed. Some sound advice to find some cunning way to get the fearless boy under his thumb.

Siegfried had filed all the pieces of the sword down into powder, and caught them in a crucible which he now set on the fire.

"Hey, Mime!" he called.

Mime was startled from his meditations and turned back towards Siegfried.

"What did you say its name was?" Siegfried asked. "This sword I've just ground down to filaments."

"Nothung," Mime told him. "That's its name. At least, that's what your mother told me."

Siegfried seemed to like that name, or perhaps the fact that Mime learned it from his mother. He sat beside the fire, working the bellows, making up a song as he worked:

"Nothung, Nothung, conquering sword, why did you have to shatter? But your sharp edge and your shining blade are both reducible, to matter, and even now you're nothing more than filings, that are, melting in the crucible." He laughed, at the terribly clever rhymes he'd invented; then laughed some more, until it seemed he'd never be able to stop laughing.

"Blow bellows blow, brighten the dull glow!" That was too easy a rhyme. "Matter" and "that are" was much cleverer, not to mention "reducible" and "crucible". That stupid dwarf Mime could never have thought of rhymes like that. So he laughed still more. He was feeling distinctly pleased with himself. It encouraged him to expand his creative horizon, to think of other things he could make up a song about. So he remembered a tree that had been growing wild in the forest and which he'd felled. "The brown ash burned to charcoal," the line occurred to him, and he looked at Mime, wanting to say something, or to hear Mime say something, about the cleverness of that play on words. But the old dwarf was too stupid to have spotted it, even if he was listening, which he clearly wasn't. "The brown ash burned to charcoal, and now it's lying here, under my control, Siegfried, engineer. Heaped upon the fire, showers of sparks are flaring, on a dragon's bier, flames he'll soon be sharing. O meld and weld the smithied steel, until the sword is held for real. Blow bellows blow, brighten the dull glow!"

Mime was still keeping his distance, sitting well away from the ever-growing heat, nervous of the sparks that could easily singe his hair if one of them flew off any further from the forge. The forge had never been heated quite this hot before, and he wasn't sure the flints would take it, let alone the iron. No point saying anything though, not to Siegfried in this humour. What was certain was the boy was going to forge the sword, and as soon as he'd done so he was going to use it to kill Fafner. Mime could see that, plain as the grin in the Wanderer's eyes when he predicted it. The boy would win the treasure and the ring. But how was Mime then to be victorious? He'd need all of his cleverness and subtlety to get it for himself, and thereby keep his head.

While Siegfried went on singing, uproariously laughing, working the bellows to make the fire hotter still.

And Mime plotted. Siegfried would be exhausted after fighting the dragon. Thirsty too. That would be the opportunity.

"I'll prepare a potion to refresh him," Mime planned, "from a recipe of herbs and flowers I just happen to know. Just a few drops and he'll be fast asleep. Then, with the very sword the boy's just won for himself, I'll dispatch him, and acquire the ring and treasure." He rubbed his hands with delight at his own deviousness. The Wanderer might have considered him foolish but he'd have to admire Mime now. A path to peace, that's what he'd just designed. It only needed now to lay it.

While Siegfried sang on, stoking the fire and laughing as he worked.

"Nothung, Nothung, conquering sword!" he sang again. "Your splintered steel is melting. Swim in your own sweat..." Nothing rhymed with "melting". Except "smelting", but he couldn't find a line that worked with "smelting". He poured the glowing contents of the crucible into a mould and held it aloft. "Soon I shall wield you as my sword," he told it, then plunged the mould into the water trough. Steam billowed out. As the hot steel was instantly cooled it emitted a loud hissing that caused Siegfried to laugh still louder. "In the water flows a fiery flood," he sang. "It hisses burning hate in fiery rage. Once it ran as molten steel like blood, but water's frozen it and now its flow is caged. Stiff as a corpse it lies, stubborn in its hardness like a…" - why the next phrase occurred to him he had no idea, and it was wrong too, but he sang it anyway - "stubborn in its hardness like a dragon who won't just lie down and surrender. But hot blood will soon render…" He couldn't find anything at all to end that line.

He plunged the steel into the forge fire and pulled violently at the bellows once again. At the same moment, Mime jumped up with glee, fetched various jars, shook herbs and spices from them into the cooking pot and attempted to put it on the fire.

"Now sweat once more so I can forge you," Siegfried spoke into the forge. "Nothung, conquering sword," he sang once more, and watched the crazy dwarf, who'd placed his cooking pot among the embers at the far end of the hearth. What in the name of the gods was that idiot doing with his pot? While Siegfried melted steel, Mime was cooking slops!

"When an artist is outmastered by his pupil," Mime read the question in Siegfried's mocking eyes, and answered before it could be phrased, "he knows it's time to take his pension and retire. This old man's been put to shame. So if I'm finished as a smith, I'd best start to earn my keep by cooking for the boy. You make broth of steel, I'll boil eggs."

Siegfried laughed, but this was mockery, not the joyful laughter at his forging of the steel. So the old dwarf had faced up to reality at last, given up the forge for the cooking stove; mind you, if the number of third-rate swords Siegfried had smashed gave any indication of his smelting skills, and cooking was his second trade, then Siegfried wasn't going to let a morsel of that cooking past his lips.

So Siegfried thought, and a great deal more besides. He'd understood more in these last few hours than in all the years gone by before, and he wasn't going to squander that knowledge the way Mime had squandered everything he'd ever had or done. So he drew the mould from the fire, broke it, and laid the glowing steel upon the anvil. Mime wanted to teach him about fear, Siegfried thought. But Mime was a bungler of everything he did. He couldn't even teach bungling without making a hash of it! Someone else, in some far off place, someone else would need to be conscripted to do that.

Siegfried took up his song again, hammering and singing, making up the words to fit the actions to the tune. Rhyme, he'd decided, was plain silly. Grown-ups didn't require rhymes, just meanings, and true feelings. So "Forge me, hammer, a trusty sword," he sang. "Blood once stained the blueness of your surface red. Your laughter was cold but you licked the warm blood cool." No, he was wrong. Even grown-ups did need rhymes. Blank verse led to blank meanings and blank feelings. So he tried again. "Now the fire makes you blush, bright red, soft in your heart however hard outside. But hardness surrenders to the hammer's dread. You shower angry sparks on me who tamed your pride."

Mime listened and observed. The boy was making a sharp sword to slay Fafner, the dwarf's enemy, he thought. But he'd brewed a drink, and drugged it, and he'd kill Siegfried as soon as the boy had finished Fafner. Mime grinned. His cunning would win him the prize. His reward was even now in the forging.

Mime busied himself pouring the contents of the pot into a flask, while Siegfried went on hammering the sword, and singing while he worked. The bright sparks cheered his heart. The sword's valour seemed to increase his own, and still more so as it was strengthened by his burning rage. The blade seemed to laugh back at him, cheerfully, though it appeared to be fierce and angry. The fire and the hammer were forging his good fortune. He'd straightened the sword with hard blows and now its shameful blushes would be swept away like ash. "Be as cold and hard as you can be," Siegfried admonished the sword. He brandished the blade, plunged it into the water trough and laughed loudly as it hissed.

And all the while that Siegfried was fixing the sword in its hilt, Mime trotted here and there, delight at his own guile broadening his smile, the bottle ready in his hand, his plot unfolding. "The gleaming ring my brother made," he mused, "the ring he cast his spell upon to bestow upon himself illimitable power, it will be mine. Mime has won it. Mime possesses it!"

Even Alberich, who'd once enslaved him, even he was now doomed to serve the mighty Mime. He would go back there, Lord of the Nibelungen, and command obedience from all of them. The very hammering could have been the sound of orders being obeyed, or the disobedient being punished. And how Mime grinned! "This dwarf they so despise – how respected I shall be! They'll kneel before me. I'll never have to work again, and others will make me endless treasures. Then gods and heroes will flock to see the treasure I've acquired. The world will cower at my command and all will tremble at my wrath. Mime the brave, Mime the king, lord of the Nibelungen, ruler of the universe! Hey, Mime, you're the world's most happy creature! Who'd have thought it?"

It was almost time. With just a few last blows, Siegfried flattened the rivets on the hilt. And then it was done. He looked at his handiwork, then seized it in his grip and held it up. He had remade the sword.

"Nothung," he cried, "Nothung, coveted sword, now re-set in your hilt."

Mime was too rapt in his own thoughts to pay any attention.

"Never again will I have to work," he shouted loud, though only in his head.

"Once you were broken," Siegfried was exultant. "But now restored. No blow shall ever shatter you again."

"Others will make me endless treasures," Mime thought.

"When my father died," Siegfried cried, "the blade snapped. But his son lived on, to forge a new one. Now its brightness gleams, its sharpness will cut keenly."

"Mime the brave!" the dwarf sang to himself. "Mime the king, lord of the Nibelungen, ruler of the universe!"

Siegfried swung the sword before him.

"Nothung, Nothung, conquering sword!" he cried. "Back to life you are restored." Childish doggerel, but cute! Like a magic spell. So most appropriate. But the next part needed something more mature. "You lay destroyed, ruined, in shards." What in the world rhymed with "shards"? – this poetry was much harder than forging swords. "You lay destroyed, ruined, in pieces. Now you shine defiantly and gloriously."

"Hey, Mime, you're the world's most happy creature!"

"Villains shall see your brightness," Siegfried cried.

"Who'd have thought it?" Mime wondered.

"Strike down the traitor, cut down the knave!" Siegfried exulted. "Look, Mime! You call yourself a smith."

And Mime stopped suddenly, all thought vanished from his head. Fear. Fear was teaching him a new lesson. For there stood Siegfried, brandishing the sword.

"Look what it can do!" Siegfried shouted.

And brought the sword down on the anvil, splitting the iron forge in two from head to base. It fell apart with a tremendous crash. Mime in his state of ecstasy first jumped on to a stool, but now apprehension gripped him, and he fell in terror on the ground. Jubilantly, like a crusader knight who had killed his dragon, Siegfried held the sword aloft, and beamed. The sword was all the poetry he needed.

Act Two

Scene One

In the deepest depths of the forest, close by the entrance to the cave where Fafner dwelled, Alberich lay against a rocky cliff, brooding gloomily. The ground before him rose towards a small, flat knoll, then sank again, so that, lying horizontally as he was, the Earth gave the impression that its end was close, its vanishing point adjacent. Alberich's eyes confirmed this strange impression, gazing through the fissure in the cliff upon what was clearly nothing. He listened hard and watched fastidiously, as though he were the appointed guardian of the Cave of Envy. But something, something was amiss. Intuition, perhaps. A hunch, maybe. Something told him that today was the one he'd sat here for an eternity awaiting. That this was the dreadful dawn, this one emerging from the gloom. Something was amiss. Even the storm, rising through the trees, gave off a bluish light more like the shining of steel than of lightning. What was it? And it was coming closer, flying towards him like a fiery steed, cutting great swathes through the forest. Was this the dragon's killer, come at last? Was this the one who would destroy Fafner? Suddenly the wind subsided and the blue light vanished. No, it wasn't that. The brightness simply concealed itself, under a shelter of returning night. Alberich was most alarmed.

"Who's there?" he called out.

Gradually a figure emerged out of the wood and stopped before Alberich.

"I see a light shining. I know you're there. Say who you are."

"I come to Niedhöhle in the dead of night," a voice came back to him out of the shadows. "To the Cave of Envy. Who sits there in the darkness?"

As though it were a lantern he had tilted towards Alberich, moonlight now broke through. Probably, Alberich told himself, it was just the coincidence of a suddenly dissolving cloud. But he knew it wasn't. Moonlight illuminated the stranger's face, and Alberich recognized him instantly. And just as instantly shrank back in fear.

"You!" he called, exploding in a violent rage. "Why are you here? What d'you want of me?"

Alberich jumped up and dashed towards the stranger, as though he were intending to attack him. But he only pushed him, uselessly, frail hands and fragile arms flailing at the man's unmoving body.

"Get out of my way!" he screamed. "Get out of here, you shameless thief."

The stranger hadn't immediately recognized his assailant. But now he knew him. And he laughed.

"Black-Alberich, is it?" he chortled. "What are you doing here? Did somebody appoint you guardian of Fafner's cave?"

"If you're here to goad your greed to perpetrating still more crimes," Alberich replied, but left the sentence unfinished. Again his feeble hands and arms thrashed at the stranger's body, but it could have been the flailing of a drowning man. "You don't belong here," he cried. "Go on! Get out of here! You've caused enough trouble in the world with all your villainy. Leave us alone now. Traitor!"

"I came here only to observe, not to participate," the stranger answered. "Who would dare to bar the way of The Wanderer?"

"You're a lying, deceitful trickster!" Alberich screamed at Wotan. "If I were still as foolish as I was when you captured me so easily, when you blinded me with your clever tricks, how simple it would be to take the ring from me again. But I'm not, see. I know your tricks now. And I know," there was an edge of mockery now in Alberich's voice, "I know your weaknesses as well. You paid your debts with my treasure, didn't you? You rewarded the giants with my ring for building your fortress for you, your Valhalla." He pointed at Wotan's spear. "Even now, the treaty you agreed with that pair is still inscribed right there, on the shaft of your spear. I know. I know. You paid them my gold as wages, but you dare not snatch it back from them. If you did, that spear would splinter, right down the shaft. In your own hand, by your own hand, that's how these instruments of power are wielded, and disintegrate."

"Whatever may be written on my spear-shaft," the Wanderer replied, "has nothing to do with you, you cretin. No treaty binds us. This spear subdued you to my power, and I'll use it again if you give me cause."

"You're a big talker," Alberich was growing in confidence with every word he spluttered. "You boast and you threaten, but deep down you're the one who's scared. Whoever kills the guardian of the treasure," he exclaimed, "is doomed by Alberich's curse. Remember that, Wotan? Remember, or do I need to remind you? 'As I acquired this ring by means of a curse, so let the ring itself be cursed. As its gold gave me power without limit, now let its magic bring death to him who wears it.' Remember, Wotan? No happy man shall ever want to own it. No fortunate man will ever benefit from it. Whoever possesses it will be afflicted with strife, and whoever lacks it will be consumed by envy. All will hanker for its possession, but none will enjoy it to advantage. Its owner will never benefit from it, for it draws him to his assassin. Assured of death, the coward will be in the grip of fear. As long as he lives, he'll thirst for death. The master of the ring will also be the ring's slave, until such time as Alberich wins back what has been stolen from him. This is the blessing with which the Nibelung, in dire distress, invests his ring.' Until such time as Alberich wins back what has been stolen from him," the dwarf repeated. "Boast on, Wotan. But who's going to win my ring when Fafner falls? Will the precious treasure belong to the Nibelung again? That's what gnaws at you, isn't it? That's what torments you. If Alberich grasps it again, just once in his fist, surely he'll use the power of the ring. But not like those idiot giants, who wasted it, and lost it. Oh no. Let the protector of the heroes tremble. I'll storm Valhalla's heights, guided by the hosts of Hell. Then Alberich shall rule the world!"

Wotan remained unmoved through all this long tirade.

"I'm well aware of your intention," he replied calmly, "but it doesn't worry me. Whoever wins the ring wins the power that comes with it."

"You speak as though this were a mystery," Alberich retorted. "But it's not a mystery to me. I understand the matter perfectly well." His voice was full of mockery as he went on: "Your boldness depends on a hero son sired by your amorous blood. Rumour has it that you've sired a boy who'll pluck a fruit," he paused, and glared, and then, his voice still mocking but risen now to furious anger, "that you yourself don't even dare to touch."

"Don't pick a quarrel with me," the Wanderer remained unflappable. "Quarrel with Mime if you must. It's your brother who's bringing danger to this place, leading a boy here who'll kill Fafner for him. The boy knows nothing of me. The Nibelung's using him entirely for himself. So, I say to you in all sincerity, Alberich should do what's in his own best interest."

Alberich's curiosity was roused by this. A twitch. A movement towards Wotan that threatened violence. But nothing came of it.

"Take careful note, Alberich," the Wanderer continued. "Be on your guard. The boy knows nothing of the ring, and won't know anything, unless Mime tells him."

Another twitch. Another movement towards Wotan.

"Will you keep your hands off the treasure?" he enquired. But it was meant only to threaten.

"I never interfere," the Wanderer replied, "even with those I love. He'll have to look after himself. He'll stand or fall as his own master. Only heroes are useful to the chief of the gods."

"Will no one else fight with me for the ring?" Alberich asked.

"No one but he lusts after the gold," the Wanderer replied.

"But will I win it? Tell me that."

Calmly, the Wanderer moved closer to Alberich.

"A hero is approaching," he said, and his voice was prophetic, "who will set free the treasure. Two Nibelungen covet the gold. Fafner will die and the one who snatches the ring will win it. Would you have me tell you more than this?" He turned to the cave. "The dragon lies sleeping right there. If you warn him that his death is near, perhaps he'll give you his trinkets as a thank you. Let me wake him for you."

Before Alberich could answer or dissuade him, Wotan ascended the rising ground in front of the cave.

"Fafner!" he called, and again, "Fafner! Wake up you lazy dragon!"

Alberich had no idea how to react. Was Wotan mad, or mocking him? Was he waking the dragon in order to set him loose on Alberich so Mime could win the ring? Or was he prophesying honestly? And if so, was it really possible, that Fafner would simply let him have the ring?

"Who's that disturbing my sleep?" Fafner's voice emerged darkly from the gloomy depths of the cave.

"One who has come to warn you of great danger," the Wanderer called back. "Your life will be your reward, but you must recompense him first. He requires the treasure that you're guarding."

He bent his head towards the cave, listening.

"What does he want?" Fafner asked.

Alberich stepped to the Wanderer's side and called into the cave.

"Wake, Fafner! Wake, dragon! A mighty hero is approaching. He wants to test his strength against a dragon."

"Good," Fafner laughed. "I'm getting hungry."

"The boy's bold and strong," the Wanderer said, "and his sword cuts keenly."

"All he wants is the golden ring you're guarding," Alberich added. "Give me the ring and I'll ensure that there's no battle. Then you can keep the rest of the treasure and live long in peace."

But Fafner only yawned and rolled over on his side.

"What I have, I have," he replied. "Now let me sleep."

The Wanderer laughed loudly and turned again to Alberich.

"Now, Alberich," he asked, "what shall we do, since that trick failed?"

Alberich grimaced, looking at Wotan now with a growing understanding that he'd just been mocked.

The Wanderer laughed again. There were so many forms in which a god could take revenge.

"Now stop accusing me of being the villain," he admonished the Nibelung, and approaching him confidentially gave him a reed. "Take care of it," he said. "Everything happens as it's meant to happen. You can alter nothing. I'll leave you now, here, alone. Be on your guard. Fight your brother. Fight Mime. Who knows, perhaps you'll come off better with him than you did with me – or that." He pointed over his shoulder to the cave, and laughed again. Then, as he turned to leave, he added, "As for what's to come, that too you'll learn in due course."

Rapidly, the Wanderer disappeared into the forest. In his wake a dark storm rose out of the still night, a bright glow as of lightning flashed across the sky. And as quickly both vanished. Alberich stared after the Wanderer as he rode swiftly away. He'd achieved nothing. The Wanderer had left him nothing. Or only anxiety and humiliation, which was less than nothing. And anger. Burning, seething anger.

"Go on laughing!" he shouted into the empty distance. "Go on mocking, you pleasure-seeking, self-serving gang of useless gods. Immortal, are you? One day I'll see the lot of you in Hell." An idea amused him, growing from the words he'd uttered. "One day eternity will end," he shouted, "and then where will you be?" And quietly, to himself, "As long as the gold goes on gleaming, I who know about it will keep guard, and my tenacity will get the better of the gods."

He slipped into a cleft in the rock face and sat down there as the day began to dawn.

Scene Two

Mime and Siegfried reached the same place in the forest just as day was breaking. Siegfried was carrying the newly reforged sword, hung in a girdle made of rope around his waist. Carefully, Mime looked around. The clearing they had entered lay deep in shadow, but where the ground rose towards the cave an early light was visible, a hint of dawn at the end of the long night.

"This is the place," Mime decided. "You stay here."

Siegfried sat down under a large linden tree and looked around him.

"Is this the place where I'm going to learn fear?" he asked. "You've led me a long way. All night long walking through the forest, all alone, or just the two of us. Now I want you to leave me, Mime. But if I don't learn what I need to know here, believe me, you'll be walking all alone forever, just the one of you." He smiled. "Mind you, that way I'd be shot of you."

"Believe me, my little darling," Mime used the affectionate term he'd used when Siegfried was a child; but it was empty now; all affection had expired, "if you don't learn fear, in this place, at this time, there's no other place and no other time where you'll ever learn it. D'you see the dark opening of that cavern? A dragon lives behind those rocks, a fierce and savage dragon, huge he is, and grisly like a bear." That was a good word to add, Mime smiled at his own cleverness, remembering how Siegfried had brought that bear to taunt him. "Huge," he repeated, "and with a horrible set of jaws, wide enough to gobble a creature up with just one gulp. Hair and skin, all in one swallow."

Siegfried remained unmoved, sitting calmly under the linden tree, nodding his head in thought.

"Best bet then's to close his jaws," he said. "But maybe I'll just stay clear of them."

"The beast drips poisonous venom," Mime continued. "One drop of that saliva touches you, you're gone, eaten away, skin and bone."

Siegfried was still thinking deeply, planning his approach.

"I'm not worried about any poisonous venom," he said. "It won't hurt me, 'cause I'm going to attack him from the side where he can't drip on me."

"Yes," Mime replied, "but he has a sneaky, snaky tail which he can thrash about until he catches you. If he coils it around you and gets a proper grip on you, your limbs will break like glass."

"Then I'll just have to keep my eyes wide open," Siegfried answered, "and not let him use his tail. But tell me this, Mime. Does this monster have a heart?"

"A cruel, hard heart," Mime responded. "He's merciless."

121

"But does it beat in the usual place? Like any man's or beast's?"

"Be sure it does," Mime replied. "Right there like yours and mine. Are you beginning to feel something there? Is it beating harder, faster? Are you beginning to feel fear?"

Siegfried had been lying indolently beneath the linden tree. Now, suddenly, he sat up.

"What I'll do," he grinned, and his heart was as tranquil as his voice. "I'll thrust Nothung right into his heart – is that what fear is? Hey, old man? Is that it? All of it?"

Mime gave no answer, only saw the look of contempt on Siegfried's face, and turned away.

"No, that's not that's what fear is," he said, "but it's all you have to teach me, isn't it? Be on your way, old man. No one's going to learn fear here."

"Wait a while," Mime counselled him. "What I'm saying may sound to you like empty babbling, but wait till you see and hear the beast yourself, and then I promise you, you'll lose your senses. When your eyes start to dim, and the ground sinks under your feet, and your heart starts beating in your chest so hard you'll think an earthquake must be shaking you," Mime had never sounded quite this friendly before, "then you'll thank me for bringing you here. And then you'll know how much Mime loves you."

"I don't want you to love me," Siegfried shouted back angrily. "How many times do I have to tell you? I want you to get out of my sight and leave me alone. If I hear one more word from you about, about love, I won't have it, d'you hear? All that nodding and bowing, all that twitching of your eyes – I don't ever want to see it again. D'you hear me?"

Mime smiled inwardly. The boy hadn't yet learned fear, but he had certainly learned impatience. How that would serve him when he fought the dragon!

"Are you still here?" Siegfried screamed. "I don't want to see you any more."

"I'll leave you now," Mime acquiesced. "If you need me, I'll just be down there, waiting by the stream. You stay here. Soon, when the sun is high, watch out for the dragon. He'll have to pass this way when he comes out of his cave to get a drink of water from the stream."

Siegfried laughed.

"That's right, Mime," he said, animated. "You go wait by the stream. And for sure he'll pass that way to get his breakfast. And when he does I'll plunge Nothung into his heart, but only after," Siegfried's staring into Mime's eyes rendered his meaning obvious, "he's had something more solid to eat and needs to wash it down. If I were you, I mean, if you really want a rest, I'd stay well clear of the stream. Go further away. As far as you can get. And don't come back."

"Wouldn't you like me to bring you some refreshment after the fight,"

Mime responded.

Siegfried turned away, clenching his fist and snarling at Mime.

"Call out for me," Mime tried a different tack, "if you need counsel."

Siegfried repeated the same gesture, but even more violently this time. But Mime was not done.

"Or if fear should overtake you…"

This was too much for Siegfried, who jumped to his feet and began to drive Mime away, pushing him with his fists and making angry faces.

Mime was delighted. He'd pushed Siegfried to the very edge of danger, and now it only needed to await the outcome.

"Fafner and Siegfried," he thought, as he disappeared into the safety of the forest. "Siegfried and Fafner." If only they would kill each other!

Siegfried sat down again beneath the linden tree, watching Mime as he departed, stretching out on the ground until he'd made himself comfortable. The knowledge he'd now acquired, the knowledge that Mime wasn't his father, had filled his heart with joy. He was liberated. At last he could enjoy the forest's coolness and feel the smile of daylight on him, knowing that the ugly dwarf was gone, that he'd never have to see that wretch again. This new knowledge changed everything, gave him so much to think about. He wondered how his real father had looked, concluded that it must have been like him. "If Mime had had a son," he reflected, "wouldn't he be the perfect likeness of Mime? Just as grizzly and gruesome and grey, small and crooked, hunch-backed and hobbling, with droopy ears and bleary eyes?" Away with the goblin! He never wanted to see him again.

Siegfried leaned farther back against the linden tree and looked up through its branches. The world lay in deep silence. He could hear the forest murmur.

As he sat there, waiting for the moment when fear would come and introduce itself to him, Siegfried wondered what his mother had looked like. He couldn't imagine her at all, but he was sure, and it induced a deep tenderness in him just to think of it, that her eyes would have gleamed brightly, shining like a doe's eyes. Only - even more beautifully. The boy was close to tears for thinking how she must have borne him in such sorrow, for wondering why she had to die. "Do all mothers die giving birth to their sons?" he wondered. What a sad world that would be, if it were so. "If only I'd seen you, mother!" It was hard to equate the word "mother" with a living creature.

The boy sighed softly and leaned still further back, slouching now against the linden tree's trunk and its obtruding roots. Deep silence occupied the world. Above him the murmurs of the forest were increasing. In the branches overhead a woodbird sang a happy song, so much sweeter than Siegfried's thoughts, that Siegfried sat up and listened, as though he were trying to understand the meaning of the bird's song. Strange though, he thought he knew all the birds that inhabited these forests, yet here was one he'd never seen before. Perhaps it didn't live in this forest, but somewhere farther away. And then, if he could only understand its language, perhaps it could tell him something – about his mother. Had the dwarf not told him once that birdsong was their way of talking and could be understood – that one could learn it. Yet how would this be possible? He thought as hard as he was capable of thinking, squeezing his brain muscles tight, squeezing his eyes tight, clenching his fists tight, shuddering with the intensity of thought. And then, when he opened his eyes again, he saw a clump of reeds growing not far from the linden tree, and it was obvious. He would simply recreate the bird's song, and talk to it in its own language. He would copy its notes on a reed pipe. If he got the words wrong but copied the tune, he would still be singing its language and, perhaps, perhaps he could learn what the bird was saying.

He ran to the nearby spring, cut off a reed with his sword and quickly whittled it into a pipe. Again he stood, listening intently. The bird stopped and listened too, as though it were waiting for Siegfried to say something. Siegfried blew into the pipe, but the sound he made was harsh and dissonant. He cut the pipe again, shaping it more carefully this time, to procure a purer sound, then blew again. But again the sound was rough and unharmonious, a mere noise. He shook his head and once again he cut the pipe. And once again he tried it. But now he was getting angry. He pressed the reed with his hands, moulding it and shaping it, and tried again. But stopped. It didn't sound right. He simply couldn't get the lovely tune to work on the pipe. His own stupidity had let him down. Learning from this creature was beyond him.

The bird was singing once again. Siegfried watched it, ashamed that the rascal had been listening to him in vain, had heard him play so badly. Or not playing at all, in truth. "Then let him listen to my horn," Siegfried flung the silly reed away. He had no skills with that, but on the horn he was a master. Now the bird would hear a real forest tune, one that he could really play – a cheerful one. He'd used it to try to attract a female companion, but nothing better than wolves and bears had ever answered him. Now he'd see what it would bring him. Perhaps a friend whom he could love.

Siegfried took the silver hunting horn from his hip and blew on it. With each of the long-sustained notes, he looked expectantly at the bird.

But it wasn't the bird that was aroused by his playing. Almost at the first note, loud and penetrating through the woods and rocks, there came a sound of movement in the woods beyond. Instead of the bird, he'd disturbed a very different creature, for it was Fafner who emerged now from his lair deep in the cave, Fafner in the shape of a monstrous, serpentine dragon. He lurched from his cave and broke through the underwood bushes, dragged himself up to the higher ground until the front part of his body rested upon it, then uttered a loud sound that may well have been no more than yawning. But it caused his jowls to open wide, the entirety of his sharp teeth and his cavernous throat to become visible. Siegfried looked around at just that moment, and fixed his eyes on Fafner in astonishment. The great creature was standing on the knoll, staring at the one who'd dared to break his sleep with so much trumpeting. But the trumpeter just smiled. His call had worked. His tune had brought him something lovely! He'd summoned up a playmate!

"What's going on here?" Fafner called.

"Are you an animal?" Siegfried retorted. "And yet you can speak to me. Perhaps then you could teach me something. There stands before you," it was hard to know exactly how to say this, "one who does not know what fear is. Can you enlighten me?"

"Are you being impudent?" Fafner asked

"Impudent?" Siegfried retorted. He didn't know the word, but playing games was so much fun. "No," he said, "just plain and ordinary pudent. But I want to know what fear is. Teach me, or I'll make mincemeat of you with this."

He put his hand on the hilt of his sword. But Fafner simply snorted, emitting a sound like laughter.

"I came out for a drink," he said, "but now it looks like lunch is served."

Once again he opened his jaws and showed his teeth.

Siegfried was impressed.

"That's a fine mouth," he commented. "Excellent teeth, dainty palate. A little bit too much gap in the throat. Why don't you let me close it up for you – with this?"

"My mouth's good for many things," Fafner replied. "But empty chatter isn't one of them. Gobbling impudent strangers is however."

And he threatened Siegfried with his tail.

But Siegfried was expecting this. Mime had warned him about the tail.

"You're a cruel and merciless brute!" Siegfried shouted. "And I have no intention of providing you with lunch. Rather, I shall use my sword to carve you up for sandwiches."

"Oh you splendid little braggart," Fafner roared with laughter and put out his arm. "Come, let me embrace you."

Siegfried drew his sword and leaped towards Fafner.

"Beware, you bag of noise!" Siegfried cried. "The braggart's coming!"

Heroically, Siegfried stood defiant on the high knoll in front of Fafner, legs wide, left arm at his side, right arm holding out the reforged Sword of Need. The lizard dragged himself farther up the knoll and spat at Siegfried from his nostrils. But Siegfried ducked to avoid the stream of fiery mucus, sprang closer, took his stand again on one side. Fafner tried to reach him with his tail, but the distance was too great. Siegfried thrust with his sword at the same moment, taking advantage of the dragon's distraction, and nearly struck. The dragon tried to turn, but Siegfried sprang over him at a single bound and struck him in the tail. Fafner roared and pulled his tail away, raised the front part of his body in order to throw its full weight upon Siegfried. But doing so, he offered his breast up to the sword. Quickly, Siegfried sought the precise place of the dragon's heart, and thrust his sword in, right up to the hilt. Fafner reared up in agony, then sank back down upon the wound as Siegfried let go of his sword and sprang aside.

"Lie there, you merciless brute!" he shouted. "Lie there now with Nothung in your heart."

"Who are you?" Fafner asked, his voice weak, his body already failing. "Brave boy," he muttered. "My heart is pierced. Who incited your childish courage to commit this murder? It can't have been your brain that planned this act."

"There is still much that I don't know," Siegfried admitted. "Not even who I am. But as to who incited me to murder you – why, you yourself, dragon. You incited me to fight you to the death."

Fafner shook his dying head. "Then let me tell this bright-eyed boy, who knows so little about himself, who it is he's murdered. There were once two giants, two brothers, Fasolt and Fafner, who ruled the world, and both are now dead because of the accursed gold that they acquired from the gods. Fafner am I, who killed Fasolt to obtain the gold, and now as a dragon I guard the treasure. But I, I've fallen to a pink-cheeked boy. Watch your step, my little hero. Whoever prompted you to do this deed is plotting your death even now. It's the destiny of the treasure to kill whoever lusts to own it."

Fafner rolled on his side, his legs too weak to stand, the muscles in his neck no longer able to support his head. Blood poured from the wound in his chest. Now, with his last gasp, he issued his final warning.

"Mark how it will end," he prophesied. And with his last breath, Fafner looked up at the boy: "Think of me," he said.

But Siegfried wasn't ready for the beast to die. There were still things that he yearned to learn from the dragon, his own origins, his father's name. The beast in his death throes seemed to be the possessor of much wisdom. The dragon had asked his name. Then perhaps he would recognise it, and be able to enlighten him.

"I'm still nobody," he said. "But I'm called Siegfried."

Fafner raised himself slightly, trying to speak. But all he could manage was the repetition of the name, "Siegfried."

Then his head fell back on the ground and the beast expired.

"The dead have nothing to tell us," Siegfried mused out loud, gazing contemptuously at the creature. "But my sword lives on. Now it must lead me."

Fafner had rolled completely on his side in dying, leaving the sword accessible, and whole. Siegfried drew it out of Fafner's breast. Blood sprinkled his hand. He drew it quickly back, for the blood burned like fire. Involuntarily, he put his finger to his mouth to suck away the blood. As he gazed thoughtfully in front of him, the song of the forest birds came once more to his ears, and it seemed as if the birds were talking to him, as though his tasting the blood had cast some kind of spell on him that gave him the power to understand their language, as he had so longed to do before. Now his eyes scanned the branches, seeking actual birds. A thrush, a finch, an owl lurking in the shadows. None spoke to him. A woodbird, crouching on the branches of the linden tree, high above his head. Siegfried looked up, and the woodbird caught his gaze and called to him.

"Hey, Siegfried!"

Siegfried stared back, astounded.

"So it's you who owns the Nibelungen treasure now," the woodbird proclaimed. "Go into the cave, the whole hoard's there. If you can find the Tarnhelm, it'll help you to perform great deeds. If you can find the ring, it'll make you master of the world."

Siegfried listened, holding his breath, amazed.

"Thank you," he muttered, softly and with great emotion. "Thank you, dearest bird, for this advice. I take it gladly."

He turned toward the rock, climbed down inside the cave, and disappeared into its darkness. Dark too the destiny of the Nibelungen treasure that now awaited him.

Scene Three

Mime had watched every moment of this encounter from his hiding-place among the trees. Now he crept forward to the knoll, peering timidly about to assure himself that Fafner really was dead. Alberich too had been watching the encounter, from a cleft in the rock on the opposite side. The Wanderer had warned him, and he'd warned Fafner – but in truth he hadn't expected it all to come to pass. Yet there the dragon lay, blood coagulating on his scaly torso. And there was Mime, himself looking around in search of Siegfried, moving towards the cave. Alberich rushed over to him, blocked his path.

"Where are you slinking off to so quickly, you sly villain?" Alberich called as he seized his brother by the arm.

"To hell with you!" came back Mime's equally vituperative answer. "I don't want you. You're not needed here."

"Tell me, you rogue," Alberich squeezed his brother's arm so hard his fingers left indentations in the flesh, "are you trying to steal my gold? Have you acquired a fancy for my property?

"Leave me alone," Mime tried to free his arm. "This place belongs to me. What you doing here anyway?"

"Catching you in the middle of a dubious little enterprise, that's what I'm doing here."

"What I've obtained by hard work, you're not going to steal from me," Mime replied.

"Oh," mocked Alberich, "so it was you was it, who went down into the Rhine and stole the gold from the Rhine-Maidens? It was you who worked the gold into a magic ring?"

"And I suppose it was you," Mime responded, "who fashioned the Tarnhelm that changes people's shapes? You may have wanted it, but you didn't make it. I did."

"Made it!" Alberich mocked. "You couldn't make a fart in your own trousers if someone didn't show you how. The skill to make the Tarnhelm came from the magic ring. My ring."

"And where's that ring now?" Mime taunted back. "The giants took it from you, you cretin. What you lost, my cunning will recover."

"So your plan, you pathetic creature, is to profit from what the boy's done. By stealing it. That brave boy's now the master of the ring, not you."

"I raised that boy," Mime replied. "He owes me. All my sweat and suffering on his behalf. He owes me. It's been a long time coming, but this is my reward."

Alberich shook his head. "Let me get this clear," he said. "For rearing the lad, you now have the nerve to make yourself a great man? A king? You scrubby, sleazy, scurvy, pathetic serf. The most miserable dog has more right to the ring than you. Trust me, you'll never get your hands on the ring of power."

Mime scratched his head.

"Then you have it," he said. "You keep the ring. But look after it well. You be the master, but make sure you treat me as your brother. You have the ring, and I'll take the Tarnhelm that I made with my own hands. That way, we share the booty. We both get our reward."

He rubbed his hands confidently, pleased with the compromise he'd negotiated. But Alberich only laughed, that mocking laughter Mime had heard so many times before.

"Share it with you," he laughed. "What, and the Tarnhelm too? You devious little toad. Give you all that, and I'd never sleep soundly again."

Mime was beside himself with rage at this.

"Not even an exchange?" he asked. "Not even a share? Must I go empty-handed, with no reward?" He was whining now. "Can't I have anything?"

"Nothing," Alberich replied. "Not a trinket. Not even a nail to hang your hat on!"

This was too much for Mime. All his life his older brother had bullied him, and had his way. But this was too much. Too much. Passionate now, he turned on his brother with a fury Alberich had never seen before.

"If I get nothing," Mime hollered, "then you get nothing either. Not the ring and not the Tarnhelm. Now it's me who says no to sharing. You just wait while I call Siegfried and his valiant sword to come to my aid. This treasure's his. He won it when he killed the dragon. He won't allow you to steal his prize. He'll give you your reward."

"Turn around then," Alberich responded, seeing Siegfried emerge from the cave as though summoned by the shouting of his name.

"He'll have chosen the most childish playthings, you mark my words," Mime seemed to have forgotten his quarrel for a moment.

"He's got the Tarnhelm," Alberich noted.

"Yes. And the ring," Mime saw.

"The ring!" Alberich cursed under his breath.

Mime laughed maliciously. This was a much better bargaining position.

"If you're very nice to him," he mocked, "maybe he'll give you the ring. If I haven't already obtained it for myself."

Even as he said this, Mime slipped back into the forest, and Alberich, remembering what the Wanderer had told him, acknowledged, to himself at least, that the ring would have eventually to be surrendered to its master. Then it was beyond his power to obtain it, even now. Or was it? Was it? If he was clever, cunning, perhaps. Alberich followed the wise counsel of his stupid brother, and slipped back into his hiding-place inside the rocks.

*

Siegfried came out of the cave, carrying both the Tarnhelm and the ring, deep in thought as he regarded his booty. What was he to make of them? He'd taken them from the pile of golden treasure because this was the advice the woodbird gave him, and he felt that he could trust the woodbird. Either way, their beauty would serve as a souvenir of his exploits – every hero won trophies, even if they were only pretty trinkets, and these were proof that he'd fought and killed Fafner, though he still hadn't learned fear. He hung the Tarnhelm on his belt and slipped the ring onto his finger. The silence in the woods was palpable. Once more, Siegfried's attention was drawn to the voice of the woodbird as it broke the silence, and he listened to the bird with bated breath.

"So Siegfried now has the helm and the ring," the woodbird chirruped. "Let him not trust Mime, who's the falsest and most perfidious of friends. Let Siegfried listen carefully to Mime's treacherous words. He'll be able to hear what Mime really means in his heart. Tasting the dragon's blood has given him that power."

Siegfried's mien and gestures told the woodbird that his words were heard and understood. Siegfried stood quite still, beneath the trees, upon the knoll outside the dragon's cave. There was Mime, approaching through the forest. Siegfried leaned on his sword, observing and self-contained. Let the auguries of the woodbird prove their worthiness.

The dwarf crept forward and watched Siegfried closely, wondering if he was weighing up the value of his spoils. Perhaps the Wanderer had hung about and chatted to the boy, counselling him with crafty runes and magical prophesies? He would have to be doubly clever now. He would have to set his cleverest trap and fool the insolent child with friendly and deceptive speeches. This wasn't going to be as easy as he'd imagined.

But feint heart never won a magic treasure!

"Siegfried, welcome!" Mime called out to his protégé. "Tell me, my hero, have you learned fear?"

"I haven't even found a teacher yet," Siegfried replied.

"But the grim dragon – have you slain him? That must have been a battle worth the watching."

"He was fierce," the boy replied. "Fierce and very spiteful. But his death saddens me, to tell the truth, when there are scoundrels far wickeder than him still living. He who brought me here to kill Fafner, I hate him more than I could ever hate the dragon."

Gently, Mime. Friendly, and gently. It's the only way.

"Calm down," he said, "You won't be seeing me for much longer. Very soon my eyes will close in everlasting sleep. You've done well. What I wanted from you has been accomplished. Nothing else is left for me," he continued, unaware of what he was actually saying, unaware that Siegfried's new-found power let him hear the thoughts behind his words, and not just the words themselves. "Nothing's left for me but to claim my share of the spoils, which shouldn't be hard since you were always such a booby."

"Then you are planning to harm me?" Siegfried asked.

"What? Did I say that?" Mime replied, astonished. "Siegfried, my dear friend. Listen to me." But the words he wished to say, the tenderness with which he wished to say them, were not the words or tone that issued from his mouth. "I've always hated you and all your kind," was what came out. "Loathed you. D'you think it was from feelings of love that I raised such a pest. The treasure in Fafner's care, the gold, that's what I've been working for." Mime held out his arms, as though to embrace Siegfried, paternal arms cuddling his beloved son. But his mouth wasn't in his control. "If you won't give me the treasure," he said, and lightness, jocularity, belied his speech, "Siegfried, my son, I'll have no choice but to kill you."

"I'm pleased to hear you hate me," Siegfried answered. "But do I really have to give you my life as well as the treasure?"

"Did I say that?" Mime replied crossly. "You haven't heard me properly." He took out the flask and, struggling to conceal his true feelings, offered it to the boy. "Look, you're tired after such strenuous efforts. There's a fever burning in your blood. I knew it'd be that way, after such a fight with such a dragon, so while you were smelting the sword, I made you this. Now drink it," Mime didn't mean to, but he was tittering, "and then I'll win the sword, and with the sword I'll have the Tarnhelm and the treasure too."

Siegfried nodded his head, understanding everything.

"So you'd steal the sword and the ring and all the loot as well?" he said.

Mime was bewildered. He knew exactly what he'd said, and it was none of this. He'd wooed the boy, and courted him, offered him loving words and affectionate gestures. Why was the boy choosing to mishear him, deliberately misinterpreting everything? He didn't understand.

"You mistake me, Siegfried," he tried to say the words as tenderly as possible, but they came out in a rage. "Tell me, am I not speaking clearly? Am I stammering or slobbering at the mouth? I've gone to the greatest imaginable trouble to hide my true intentions by flattery, and you, silly boy, you've got it all wrong. Open your ears and listen carefully, then you'll hear exactly what your Mime means."

Siegfried smiled. His ears were open, he was listening carefully. Hearing Mime's secret thoughts like this, he did indeed know exactly what his Mime meant.

"Here," Mime offered the flask again. "Here, take this, and drink the cordial. You've always liked my cordials in the past, even when you acted in a surly way and pretended to be cross. Even when you were in a bad temper, you always drank them."

"You're right," Siegfried replied. "I'm always glad of a nice drink." And then it struck him that the power the dragon's blood had given him could be used to his advantage. All he had to do was ask. "How did you make this one?" he enquired.

How amusing to see Mime's reaction, the gaiety of his explanation, his merry jesting, as though he were describing a state of pleasant intoxication which the potion was to bring about, when what he was actually describing was his effort to poison his adopted son. But Siegfried's face remained unmoved. Simply, he listened.

"Just drink it," Mime said, "and trust my skill." But thought was thought, and it couldn't be silenced. "Your senses will soon fail. Your mind will vanish into night and mist and you'll fall down on the ground, unwaking and unconscious, your limbs prostrate as if the muscles have collapsed entirely. While you're lying there, I could easily take the spoils and hide them. But if ever you woke up, o then I'd never be safe, even if I had the ring. So, with the sword that you've made so strong and fine and sharp," the exuberance of his joy was staggering, "I will hack off your head, my little child. Then I shall have peace *and* the ring."

Mime went on tittering to himself, thinking how sly and clever he was being with all the words of flattery and insincere affection he was speaking. But Siegfried seemed not to hear these.

"So you'll kill me when I'm asleep, is that correct?" he asked.

"I'll do what?" Mime was furious. "When did I say anything like that?" The boy was mad. But Mime was cleverer than the boy. All he needed now was to take still more pains to make his voice and manner tender. His most charming voice would win the silly child over.

"Let me be absolutely clear," his thoughts came through his lips. "One word at a time, so there's no misunderstanding. I, shall, chop, off, your, silly, childish, head! There, is that meticulously clear enough?" And demonstrating heart-felt solicitude for Siegfried's health, he went on, "even if I hated you a little less, even if your insults and my shame and trouble didn't give me so much to avenge," the voice so gentle saying it, "still I wouldn't hesitate to get you out of my way. Otherwise," and he was laughing now, "how would I get the loot, since Alberich has his eye on it too?"

Mime poured the draught into the drinking-horn and offered it to Siegfried urgently.

"Now, Wälsung – you are a Wälsung, aren't you? Now drink and choke yourself to death! And after this last drop, you shall never need another."

How Mime laughed then, knowing he'd done the deed, killing an imitation dragon with tricks that Siegfried might have used against the real dragon, and spared himself the need to fight.

But Siegfried didn't take the drinking-horn. He reached for his sword, and held it threateningly in Mime's face.

"Taste this instead," he cried. "You loathsome babbler."

Seized by violent loathing, he struck Mime a sharp blow with the sword. A single blow, but quite sufficient. Mime fell down at once, dead on the ground. And from a deep cleft in the rocks, the echoing sound of Alberich's mocking laughter.

But Siegfried didn't hear the laughter. As he stared at the corpse on the ground, he put his sword back in its belt. This was how it had to be. Mime the loathsome babbler had tasted the sword. Nothung had paid the wages of hatred, for which purpose it was forged. He picked Mime's body up and carried it to the knoll in front of the mouth of the cave. Here he threw it down and here, now, it would lie, guarding the treasure it had so deviously sought. Siegfried smiled at his own thoughts, and spoke in his heart to Mime. "Now you're the lord of all this splendour," he exclaimed. "And you'll have a watchdog too, to protect you from robbers." He laughed. With great exertion he rolled the dragon's body in front of the entrance to the cave so as to stop it up completely. "Lie there, grim beast," he spoke in his mind to the dragon. "Guard the glittering treasure, together with your greedy enemy. So you shall both find rest."

He looked thoughtfully down into the cave for a time, then turned slowly away, as though all this effort had exhausted him. He looked up into the sky. It was noon, the sun was high, shining straight down on his temples from the blue above. All that hard work had made him hot. He wiped his hand across his forehead. A storm was racing through his fiery blood and his head was even making his hand feel hot. He needed rest, and shelter.

Siegfried stretched himself on the ground under the cool shade of the linden tree, and once again gazed up through the branches. He longed to hear the sound of the woodbird once again, but worried that, perhaps, all the disturbance that had taken place here might have driven the bird away. But no, there it was, happily perched on a branch above him, twittering and fluttering, with its brothers and sisters flying lovingly around it. The sight of that little family induced a moment of nostalgia in him, of regret for the family he'd never had, the loneliness he felt, deprived of siblings, his mother dead, his father fallen in battle – and suddenly, as though for the first time, it registered deep within him that his parents had never seen their son. Only one companion had he ever had, a horrible dwarf – and yet the thought of him kindled something warm in Siegfried, a surprising warmth, but a recognising warmth, that there'd been some goodness there, some kindness there, even if it had never blossomed into love. But the coldness in his heart quickly overcame the momentary warmth in his nostalgia. The evil dwarf had set cunning traps for him, and so Siegfried had had to kill him. That was how it was.

With painful emotion, Siegfried looked up into the branches, and spoke to the friendly woodbird.

"I come to you now," he said, "in the hope that you can help me find a good companion. I need your wise counsel to guide me in the right direction. I've so often sought a companion but I've never yet found one. Perhaps you can do better for me. Your advice has served me in good stead thus far. Now sing again, and I'll hearken to your counsel."

And at once the voice of the woodbird came back to him across the forest, chirruping in a language that Siegfried was magically capable of understanding.

"Siegfried has struck down the evil dwarf," the woodbird sang, "and now he may be told about the most marvellous woman. She lies asleep, high on a rocky precipice, and a fire burns around her home. He who can walk through the fire and wake the maid, this maid, Brünnhilde, will be his."

Siegfried jumped up impetuously from his seat, overcome by excitement.

"O song of joy!" he exclaimed exultantly. "O splendid melody! O breath of sweetness!"

The meaning of the words the bird had sung burned into his longing breast, tugged violently at him and inflamed his heart. Something new was being born in him. But what? But what? He begged the woodbird for an explanation.

"Cheerful in grief," the bird replied, "I sing of love. I weave in woe to create bliss. Only those who understand longing can understand my meaning."

Siegfried didn't yet understand, but something new was being born in him, and already it was driving him onwards, making him want to shout for joy, to rush out of the forest and up towards those rocks. But what was it? What was it?

"Sing to me some more, sweet bird. Tell me, am I the one who'll break through the fire? Can I awake the bride?"

He listened again and again the bird sang to him.

"No coward can ever win this bride," it chirruped. "Brünnhilde is meant only for one who knows no fear."

Now Siegfried was jubilant. He danced. He sang. If only in his heart.

"That stupid boy," he called back to the woodbird, "the one who knows no fear. Why, that's me! Only today I tried with all my might, but still in vain, to study fear at the school of Fafner. Now I burn with desire to learn it from Brünnhilde. How do I find the way to the mountain?"

The bird fluttered up, circled around Siegfried, and flew about him hesitantly. Siegfried understood. The bird would show him the way.

"Wherever you fly," he called, "I follow."

He ran after the bird, which teased him a while, leading him hither and thither as though it too wasn't quite certain of the way. But at last it set a course, flying off towards the mountains, an exuberant Siegfried in pursuit.

Act Three

Scene One

A wild landscape rose steeply upwards from the foot of a rocky mountain. The night was stormy, full of rain with lightning flashing and violent thunderclaps that gradually abated. Not the lightning though, which flashed and flashed among the clouds, so those who understood would know The Wanderer was journeying among them.

He had, in fact, come to the mouth of a deep cave that opened in the rocks. Now he stood there, leaning on his sword, and called toward the entrance.

"Wake up, Wala!" he summoned her. "Wala! Erda, goddess of the earth. Wake from your long sleep. I command you. Rise now. Rise from the deep chasm where sleep holds you prisoner. Erda! Erda! Goddess of wisdom. Rise from the depths of night and silence where you sleep. Let my song rouse you – waken and answer me. I need your sleeping wisdom. All-knowing one. Guardian of wisdom. Erda! Erda! Omniscient goddess! Wake now, Wala. Wake!"

At last the mouth of the cave began to grow brighter with a bluish light.

"You call so loud!" her voice was dimly audible, deep down inside the cave. "Mighty spells arouse me. From the dreams that bestow wisdom I have been woken. Who summons me? Who is foolish enough to scare sleep away from me?"

Her voice, and she herself, became clearer as she climbed slowly towards the entrance to the cave, climbing from the very bowels of the earth which she inhabited. Her face and body appeared to be covered with hoar frost; her hair and garments glittered and shimmered like frost or snow-flakes against moonlight.

"It's I who broke your sleep," the Wanderer replied. "With spells that could rouse you from however far away, and break whatever chains sleep used to hold you in its grip. I wander the earth in search of knowledge. Not information, Erda - primaeval wisdom. So I've come to you, the fount of knowledge. No creature alive surpasses you for wisdom. You know what's hidden in the depths, what's contained within the mountains and the valleys, the air and the water. Wherever there's life, there will your spirit also be encountered. Wherever minds are active, your mind directs them, nurtures them, makes them fruitful. All things, men say, are known to you. So, to seek the wisdom of your counsel, I've woken you from your sleep."

"My sleep," Erda replied, "is dreaming. My dreams are thoughts, and in thought is wisdom found. But while I sleep, the Norns are awake. Piously they weave the ropes and spin the webs of knowledge from my deepest thought. Why do you not ask the Norns?"

"The incidents of the world," the Wanderer retorted, "impinge upon the spinning of the Norns, determining their patterns. They cannot alter or reverse events. I come to you to learn how I may stop a revolving wheel."

"Human actions cloud my mind," Erda answered, "and sink me into darkness. With all my knowledge, I too was once mastered by a despot. I bore a wish-maiden to Wotan. At his behest she chose heroes to wage war for him. She too is brave and clever. Why do you wake me when you could seek knowledge from the child of Erda and Wotan?"

"Do you mean the Valküre maid Brünnhilde?" Wotan asked. "She defied the Master of Tempests at the very moment when he had assumed complete mastery of the universe. What the Lord of Battles most yearned to do, but refrained from doing, forbade himself from doing, the stubborn girl Brünnhilde dared to accomplish in the heat of battle, even against his will. The War Father punished the girl. He pressed sleep on her eyes. Now she lies asleep upon a rock, and will only waken when a man woos her for his wife. What value would there be in questioning her?"

For a long while there was silence. Erda brooded in deep thought. "I am dazed with sleep still," she spoke at last. "How wildly off-kilter the world's course is. The Valküre daughter of the Wala sentenced to fetters of sleep while her all-knowing mother slept, and did not know! Does he who preached rebellion now punish rebellion? Does he who conceived the deed become angry when it is done? The defender of justice and the guardian of oaths, does he shun justice now and govern by breaking oaths? Let me go back into my cave. Let sleep seal up my wisdom."

"No, mother earth," the Wanderer retorted. "You shall not go back into your cave. I wield sufficient magic power to prevent you. All-wise one, it was you with your timeless knowledge who plunged the dagger of worry into Wotan's dauntless heart. Your knowledge of the future filled my spirit with fear of shameful, catastrophic downfall. If you are truly the world's wisest woman, then you must tell me how a god can overcome his dread."

"You are not who you say you are," Erda replied. "A god! Dauntless? These are not words I expect to hear from the War Father. A turbulent spirit? Why did you come so wild and storm-like to disturb the Wala's sleep?"

"And you are not who you dream yourself or think yourself in dream to be," Wotan responded. "The primaeval mother's wisdom and all primaeval knowledge will come to an end if it contends my will. Do you know what I intend?"

Once again the Wala brooded long in silence. But when no answer came, the Wanderer berated her once more.

"Because you are less wise than either of us imagined, I shall open your ears and you may sleep carefree forever. I intend the downfall of the gods, and it does not fill me with fear, because this is what I most desire. I resolved to do this when I was mad with sorrow, when my mind was lanced upon the horns of a dilemma, when anguish and despair had overtaken me. But joyfully and freely do I now put my plan into effect. In rage and loathing I gave the mastery of the world into the hands of that greedy Nibelung, but now it's to a glorious Wälsung that I bequeath the inheritance. One who never knew, though I have chosen him. A boy of fearless bravery, untaught by me, unaided by my counsel, such a boy has acquired the Nibelung's ring. Happy in love, innocent of envy, his noble nature is immune to Alberich's curse, for fear is foreign to him. She whom Erda bore, our child, Brünnhilde, she will be awakened by this hero. Then she will do as a child of the mother of all wisdom should – she will redeem the world. So sleep now, Erda. Close your eyes and sleep. And in your dreams you can watch the Wanderer's downfall. Whatever may befall them, whatever may become their destiny, to the ever-young this god is glad to yield. Go down, Erda, go down into your cave. Mother of primaeval fear and source of the world's sorrows, go down now, go down to everlasting sleep!"

Erda's eyes began to close, even as the Wanderer spoke his last words of command. Down into the cave, down into the earth she sank, deeper, ever deeper down, until she had disappeared completely. The entrance to the cave turned dark. The wild landscape, the rocky mountain, all turned dark. But in the distance, high above them, on a rocky precipice close to the mountain-top, dawn with its rosy fingers touched the edges of the canvas of the day, and painted it a fiery orange. The storm had ceased.

Scene Two

For hours Wotan wandered through the forest. At last he came to the cave where Siegfried had slaughtered Fafner and then Mime. The storm had washed away the blood of the two murders, but marks on the ground, damaged reeds, misplaced stones, all continued to bear evidence of what had taken place. Wotan leaned back against the rocks, looking this way and that into the forest. He knew that Siegfried was long gone, following the woodbird to the mountaintop to face his final destiny in fire and in the arms of Brünnhilde. How surprising, then, to see Siegfried approaching. Wotan remained without changing his position at the cave, watching and wondering. Siegfried's woodbird fluttered toward the cave, stopped suddenly, flapped its wings in alarm, then disappeared again, deep into the density of the wood. Soon afterwards, Siegfried himself came into the clearing beside the cave. Out loud, but to himself, he was lamenting that his bird had left him. Happily it had shown him the way at first, but now it had vanished, leaving him right back where he'd started, in a place he no longer wished even to remember, let alone revisit. What choice did he have now, without Mime, without the woodbird, without parents or siblings, but to make his own way in the world? And if he was to find the mountaintop, if he was to walk through fire and claim the maiden of his destiny, well, quite simply, he would have to find the way himself. He would seek again the path his guide had shown him, and then adventure on alone. So he muttered, and so Wotan listened, and approved. But it wouldn't have been Wotan if he didn't also interfere.

"Say, boy, where are you travelling?"

Siegfried stopped and turned around.

"Who's there?" he called, and then, realising that help might be at hand, "Can you show me the way?"

He approached the Wanderer, but didn't recognise him.

"I'm heading into the mountains," he explained. "I'm looking for a rock that's surrounded by fire. There's a woman there, asleep on the rock. I'm going to wake her."

"Who told you to seek this rock?" the Wanderer enquired. "Who spoke of a woman and made you desire her?"

"A singing woodbird," Siegfried replied, "gave me good advice."

"A singing woodbird?" the Wanderer mused. "Woodbirds chatter about all sorts of things, but no human can understand it. How is it you could make sense of what it sang?"

"Through the blood of a savage dragon," Siegfried answered, "which I killed here, at the Cave of Envy. His fiery blood had scarcely touched my tongue than I understood the language of the birds."

"And who suggested you should challenge such a mighty foe and fell this dragon?"

"That came from Mime," Siegfried answered, "a deceitful dwarf, who wanted me to learn what fear is. But it was the beast himself who prompted me to plunge my sword into his heart. He snapped his jaws at me. He provoked me."

"And who," the Wanderer persisted with his questions, "who made the sword so sharp and hard that it could fell so fierce a foe?"

"I forged it myself," Siegfried answered. "The blacksmith couldn't do it, so I had no choice. I would have been swordless without it."

"But who made those powerful splinters that you used to forge the sword?" the Wanderer questioned.

"What do I know of that?" Siegfried replied. "I only know the splinters would have been no use to me if I hadn't forged the sword anew."

The Wanderer burst out in joyful, playful laughter.

"That's my opinion too," he laughed, looking at Siegfried with deep pleasure.

"Why are you laughing at me, old man, and asking all these questions?" Siegfried gave voice at last to the surprise he'd been feeling all along. "Stop mocking me, and stop delaying me with all your chatter. If you can point out the way for me, then kindly do so. If you can't, then hold your tongue."

"Good youth, be patient," the Wanderer laughed on. "If I look like an old man to you, then treat me with the respect old men deserve."

"Respect the old – are you serious?" Siegfried replied, an edge of anger in his voice. "All my life, I've had an old man standing in my way. Now I've got rid of him. If you insist on blocking my way, old man, then you'd better watch out," he gestured to the sword hung on his belt, "or you might go the same way as Mime."

He stepped closer to the Wanderer, his manner threatening, fearless.

"Show me what you look like then," he said, and reached towards the string that held the cowl around the Wanderer's head. "Why do you wear such an enormous hat? Why does it droop over your face like that?"

Equally undaunted, the Wanderer held his ground.

"This is the Wanderer's habit, when he goes abroad in windy weather."

Siegfried examined him still more closely, poking his face right into the Wanderer's face, seeking inside the cowl, below the hat.

"You're missing an eye," he declared at last. "What happened? Did someone knock it out when you insisted on blocking his way? Take yourself off now, or you risk losing the other one as well."

"I see, my son," the Wanderer rejoined, "that although you're extremely ignorant, you do at least know how to look after yourself." He smiled. A riddle perhaps would be the best way to placate this foolish boy. "With the one eye that I'm missing," he said, "you yourself are looking at the eye that still remains for me to see through."

Siegfried listened to this slow and thoughtfully. He liked riddles. This one was just stupid though. How could he be looking through the old man's missing eye? He burst out laughing.

"You're good for a joke you are," he scoffed. "But I don't have time for jokes and riddles. So, enough, either show me the path, and then be off on it yourself, or else. I've no other use for you, so speak, or trust me I'll send you packing."

A fearless boy, so Erda had spoken. A fearless god too, who continued to stand his ground against this – bully.

"My child," he chose the term deliberately, determined to arrest such impudence, "if you'd recognised me, if you knew who I am, you'd spare me such insults. Being so fond of you, your threats make me sad and even disappointed. I've always loved the human race. You're such eternal optimists, despite the evidence. You keep your sunny disposition, even when you're shrinking from me in my rage. But you, my boy, you are especially dear to me, my paragon of heroism. Do not arouse my wrath today. It could destroy the both of us."

But Siegfried wasn't listening. Or if listening, not understanding. Or if understanding, then not prepared to hear.

"I thought I told you to hold your tongue, you unmannered creature?" he said. "Move out of my way now!" He held the Wanderer's cowl in one hand, and with the index finger of his other pointed over the Wanderer's shoulder. "That's the way that leads to the sleeping woman. That much I already know, from the woodbird who abandoned me here."

But even as he spoke, even as his threat became latent, suddenly the skies grew dark.

"That woodbird left you," the Wanderer burst out angrily, "for the sake of its own salvation. It recognized the Lord of the Ravens and knew how it would suffer if I caught it. The path that it showed you – you may not take it!"

Siegfried stepped back, astounded but defiant.

"May not!" he repeated. "Ha! May not! And who are you to try to stop me?"

"I am the guardian of the rock," the Wanderer replied, "whom you should fear. The sleeping girl lies imprisoned by my power. He who wakes her, he who wins her, will render me powerless forever. A sea of fire flows around the woman. Bright flames lick the rock. He who craves her for his bride must climb that blazing rock, and pass unblemished through the fire." He pointed with his spear towards the summit. "Look up there. D'you see that light?" As he spoke, a flickering glow appeared, high up on the rocks, and gradually increased in brightness. "Its glare increases, see. Its lustre spreads. Clouds of smoke and flaring flames roll and scorch and crackle down the mountain, coming towards us. Look, a sea of light surrounds your head like an aureole. You'll be devoured by ravenous flames if once they seize you. Go back, you reckless boy. Go back."

"Go back yourself, you stupid babbler!" Siegfried replied. "I said show me the way, and now you have. Right there, where the blaze is burning, that's where the maiden sleeps. That's where I'm going."

He attempted to set off, but the Wanderer barred his way.

"Have you no fear of the fire? Then my spear must block your path. My hand still holds this holy sceptre. Know that the sword you're brandishing was once shattered on this shaft. For a second time then, let it now break on the eternal spear."

He stretched out the spear and Siegfried drew his sword.

"So it was you," he said. "You were my father's enemy. You killed him. How glorious is the vengeance that I'm granted now. Brandish your spear and I'll break it with my sword."

With a single blow, Siegfried severed the Wanderer's spear in two. A flash of lightning sprang out of the shattered haft and darted up towards the rocky summit where the glow of ever-brightening flames blazed now with increasing brightness. A clap of thunder echoed in the tail of the lightning flash, then quickly died away. The fragments of the spear fell at Wotan's feet. Quietly, sadly, he stooped to pick them up. The boy was still standing there, waiting for the old man to yield his ground. He could have walked around of course, but he wanted the surrender, the act of yielding. Wotan understood this, and with his head downcast, gazing at the shattered fragments of his erstwhile authority, he stepped aside.

"Travel on," he said. "I have no power to stop you."

And even as he spoke those words, darkness descended utterly, and the Wanderer quite simply disappeared.

Siegfried was astounded and bemused. Where had he gone? Had the coward just run off, now that his spear was broken? But it didn't matter. He could see the sea of fire growing brighter, blazing down the mountainside. A fire to warm a man's spirit and his heart, regardless of what it might threaten against his body. A marvellous, marvellous fire, shining bright to light his way, radiant and open. A bath of fire, to dip his valour in the way he'd dipped the splinters of the sword into the forge, and made them strong and new again. A fire in which to find a bride. Yes! Yes! Now he could win a true companion. Now he could learn what it really was to love.

Siegfried raised the horn to his lips and plunged into the sea of fire, which now appeared to be climbing up the mountain, not descending from its heights. If the Wanderer were following him with his one eye, he would soon have lost sight of him, ascending intrepidly towards the summit. The firelight too had reached its zenith and had now begun to fade, gradually dissolving into finer and still finer mist, lit up as if by the red light of dawn.

Scene Three

The clouds had dissolved into a fine, rose-coloured veil of mist. Now, as they began to break up altogether, the higher clouds disappeared entirely, dissipating until the whole sky was turned bright blue, and daylight covered it. On the edge of the rocky summit, now becoming visible, a light veil of reddish morning mist hung on, hinting at the magic fire that still glowed just below it. And there, under the wide-spreading fir tree, Brünnhilde lay asleep, still wearing her full armour, her helmet on her head and her long shield serving as a blanket.

Weary from the long, slow climb, Siegfried at last reached the rock which fringed the summit, and lifted the upper part of his body over the topmost rock, so that he could see the plateau of the summit. For a long while he gazed about, astonished. What an extraordinary haven of bliss to have stumbled on, so high in the mountains! He pulled himself over the last jagged rock and stood now on the plateau of the summit, on a rock at the very edge of the precipice, and gazed with surprise at what presented itself to his eyes. He looked into the wood, but there was nothing there but trees. But then he saw something lying in the shadow of the trees. It was a horse, standing fast asleep as horses do. Slowly he walked forward, then stopped in utter amazement, for there, some short way off, there lay the form of Brünnhilde. Or at least, something shining – some piece of gleaming metalwork. For a moment he wondered if perhaps he wasn't simply dazzled by the fire. A coat of shining armour. His, maybe, for the taking.

Carefully he lifted the shield, and there, beneath it, lay Brünnhilde. A man, he guessed, armoured for battle. A splendid creature, made for the nobility of heroism. The face was covered by the helmet though, the noble head confined by it. The sleeper would be more comfortable without such headgear. Again with great care, Siegfried unbuckled the helmet, and removed it from the sleeper's head. Now he was truly amazed. Long, curling tresses of hair tumbled out. Siegfried started back, moved to a tenderness he'd never known before, fascinated by the beauty of this sight, sunk deep in contemplation. It reminded him of shimmering clouds, hovering on the waves of the bright sea of heaven. So beautiful was he, this young warrior, it was as if the gleaming sun were laughing through his features as it flowed in streams of light across the cloudy waves.

He bent lower over the sleeping form, whose breast heaved gently as the warrior breathed. Perhaps he should remove the tight breastplate? Cautiously, lest he startle the man awake, Siegfried tried to loosen the breastplate, but the metal was too hard. He drew his sword, the great Nothung that had slaughtered Fafner and broken the spear of that troublesome Wanderer. A sword more than strong enough to cut the iron rings that held this breastplate shut. First on one side, then the other, Siegfried cut away the chain mail that enclosed the breastplate, and lifted it off. Next the greaves, the iron gauntlets holding the man's arms almost to the elbows. But this was no warrior, no hero armed for battle. What lay revealed before him now, clothed in soft female garments, was…startled and astonished, Siegfried jumped back.

"This isn't a man!" he cried out, and it was as if his voice had escaped from his heart unbidden.

He gazed at the sleeping form with great excitement. A magic fire was burning in his breast. Burning anxiety had blinded him. His heart was feeble, dizzy. He'd been seized with – but he didn't even know what he should call it. Tightness of the stomach. No, deeper than that. Constriction of the very bowel. And yet, deeper even than that. Perhaps, perhaps this was fear.

Twice over, too. The impact of the woman on his very being. The utmost desperation he was feeling, having no idea who he could turn to now for help.

"Mother, mother," he cried, "think of me!"

Almost fainting, Siegfried sank down upon Brünnhilde's body. For a long while he lay there, snuggling in her breast the way a suckling child might. The silence was as slow and rhythmic as her breathing. But at length he raised himself with a sigh, wondering how he should wake the girl, and if he should actually watch her eyes unclosing. Eyes unclosing – the very expression that had occurred to him moved him so much, that he repeated it out loud. And when her eyes did unclose, would he not he be blinded by the sight? Was he rash enough, bold enough, to dare? Could he bear the brightness? He was dizzy and reeling, swaying on his legs. The anguish of longing burned his senses. His hand trembled, pressed against the woman's pounding heart. Yet something was wrong. He'd never felt this urgent pressing in the lining of his stomach. Was this - cowardice? Was this - fear?

"O mother," he cried. "Mother, this is your brave child!"

And as though his mother were with him now, there to heed and listen to him, he spoke with all the gentleness this sleeping woman had engendered in him.

"A sleeping woman, mother, has taught me to be afraid! How do I arrest this fear? How steel my heart?"

But he knew. In those same depths where fear had even now been born in him, he knew. If he himself was to waken, then first he must wake up the girl.

Once again, as he approached her sleeping form, he was overwhelmed by the beauty of her face and features, overcome by emotion more tender than any he had ever felt before. He bent closer. Her flower-shaped mouth was quivering sweetly, their gentle tremors so attractive, even in his new-found fear. Her breath against his cheeks was warm and fragrant. Yet delight also engendered desperation.

"Wake up!" he called, yet only in a whisper. "Wake up, holy maiden!"

He gazed at her, but she couldn't hear him. Slowly, with constrained expression, he recognised that he himself must draw the life from those sweet lips, even if the kiss might kill him – for what if she were sleeping there because of poison? He sank, as if dying, on the sleeping figure and, with his eyes closed, fastened his lips on hers.

Brünnhilde opened her eyes. Siegfried jumped up and stood gazing at her. Brünnhilde raised herself slowly into a sitting position, sat upright, spread her arms with stately gestures as though to greet the sun, and then the light, and then the radiant day. Slowly consciousness returned to her.

"I've been asleep a long time," she spoke softly to the stranger towering over her. "What hero are you who's woken me?"

Siegfried was entranced by her look and her voice. He stood, as if rooted to the spot.

"I struggled through the fire that blazed around the rock," he told her. "I unbuckled your tight helmet. My name is Siegfried. It's I who woke you."

Brünnhilde sat upright. Good child of the gods and goddesses that she was, even waking from a millennial sleep like this, she knew her first responsibility was to say her morning prayers, to offer thanks up to the gods for bringing her to another day. So she pronounced the blessings now, upon the world, upon the shining Earth, and Siegfried understood those stately gestures she had made before. They too were forms of prayer, blessings upon the sun, the light, the day.

But now it was him that she was gazing at. And smiling.

"My sleep is over now," she said and held her hand out to him. "I'm awake and I can see that it's you, Siegfried, who's woken me."

Siegfried was overwhelmed. His heart could have burst, so full was it, so gripped by ecstasy. How to express what he was feeling? It was impossible. Taking his cue from the woman, he made a kind of prayer, blessing his mother who had borne him and the earth that gave him food. But it was insufficient. Words couldn't express what lay beyond words, unfathomable in a distance beyond distance. All he really wanted was to stare into her eyes, and not express, but simply feel the joy their radiance bestowed on him.

Brünnhilde too was stirred by equally deep emotion. Taking her cue from him, she spoke a blessing to her mother who had borne her and the earth that gave her food. But what use blessings when his eyes were fixed on her like that, adoring her, desiring her – awakening her.

For a long while the two remained like that, their eyes and bodies filled with glowing ecstasy, lost in mutual contemplation.

"Siegfried," Brünnhilde pronounced his name again, as though to test it on her tongue, to see how well it fitted with her own name. "Siegfried!" she said again, but this time the name was beyond testing, already approved, assimilated alongside her name, as though they were already one. "My blessed hero!" she added one more phrase of prayer to the liturgy already established. "You've woken me into life with," she smiled, seeking a pun that she could make upon his name. "Siegfried," she mused again, "victory and peace." And then she found the words she needed. "You've brought the victory of wakefulness over sleeping, and the peace that comes when light repulses darkness." She smiled again. Another pair in symbiosis – metaphorical perfection – victory and peace, symbiotic in his own name! "Joy of the world!" she whispered to him. "If only you knew how long I've loved you. You've been in all my thoughts and all my cares. I fed you tenderly before you were conceived. My shield protected you, before you were born. That's how long I've loved you, Siegfried."

Siegfried was bemused, bewildered. Was this? No – it couldn't be? And yet.

Softly and timidly he asked, "Are you my mother? Didn't you die, after all? Have you, simply, been asleep?"

Brünnhilde smiled and once again stretched out her hand to take his in her fingers.

"What a delightful child you are!" she said. "No, I'm not your mother, and your mother won't come back. But you and I are one, or will be, if you'll declare you love me as I know I love you. And whatever you're not, and don't know, you'll find in me, and know from me. Two become one, and in the becoming complete each other. I'm made wise only because I love you. So shall you be in me. O Siegfried, Siegfried! Victory and peace, the conquest of light over darkness. I've always loved you, Siegfried, from the moment when I divined Wotan's great idea, his secret plan, an idea that I could never name, nor even think about, but only felt. But I fought for it, I struggled for it and did battle for it. For the sake of that plan I disobeyed him and was punished, confined by his sentence because I didn't think of it but only felt it. That idea – can Siegfried guess it? – was my love for you!"

Siegfried was barely listening, understanding not a word of what he heard. But words were nothing to him. It was the sound of her voice, the miraculous sound of her glorious voice, that he was focused on. Her voice, and the light glowing in her eyes, and the touch of her warm breath. Her voice was so sweet to hear, then so what if he didn't understand a word she said? His senses were alive to her, his feelings gravitating towards her. This was enough. She could have been telling him tales from ancient times for all he knew – he was transfixed in the present world, of gazing at her beauty. "I'm yours," he yearned to say. "You've bound me in fetters that even Nothung couldn't break. Make me a hero once again, for you. For you."

And only after he'd spoken did he even realise he'd spoken. His courage

145

hadn't failed him. The words he yearned to say, but feared to say – they had been spoken.

Deeply moved, he remained gazing upon her. Brünnhilde gently turned her head aside and stared into the wood. There, among the firs, she recognized her favourite horse, Grane, grazing happily. Siegfried's kiss had woken him too, when it had woken her.

Siegfried didn't move, not even to follow her eyes as she pursued her horse amongst the firs. His own eyes were transfixed upon her exquisite lips. With a passionate thirst, his own lips were burning with desire to kiss her eyes, her lips.

Brünnhilde gestured towards her weapons, the shield that used to shelter heroes, the helmet that once protected her own head. She was defenceless now, and knew it. Her maidenhood defenceless now. No shelter, no protection. And none, her smile indicated, none needed any more.

Siegfried shook his head in wonder. He too was defenceless, stripped of shield and helmet. No shelter against the lances with which this glorious girl had pierced him to the heart. No protection against the wound this woman had inflicted on his mind. No need, either. No need.

"Tell me what happened," Brünnhilde asked. "I can see there the shining steel of my breastplate." Her voice grew sadder as she saw what love had already destroyed, just in the course of being born. "A sharp sword has split it in two," she mused, "and with it has removed the defences of my maiden's body. I have neither sword nor shield with which to guard myself. An unarmed maiden is the world's most miserable creature."

This was almost too much for Siegfried. His passion for this maid was absolute.

"I came to you," he said, "through blazing fire. I wore no breastplate of chain mail to protect my body. And now that fire has planted itself inside my heart. My blood's boiling in a blaze of passion. A scorching fire's been kindled in me. The very fire that encircled Brünnhilde's rock now burns deep in my breast."

Absolute, and absolutely uncontrollable.

He took her in his arms, holding her close and tight.

"Extinguish this fire," he implored her. "Still this passion that's blazing in me."

Passion had overwhelmed him.

But Brünnhilde jumped up in terror. Her arms resisted him. With all the strength she could muster she pushed him away, until she was able to break free of his grip and flee from him.

"No god ever dared to come so close to me!" she cried. "Heroes humbled themselves before my maidenhead. I was chaste," she affirmed, "when I left Valhalla. You've shamed me, disgraced me." But with each exclamation, her tone changed. Anger diffused into quiet desperation, reconciliation. Now, as she spoke, her head was nodding slowly, acceptingly. This too was part of Wotan's plan, which she had divined. This too was fate. "He who wakes me wounds me," she pronounced the gnomic words of recognition. "He who broke my breastplate and my helmet, he will break my – I am Brünnhilde no longer."

"For me," Siegfried replied, "you're still the dreaming girl. Brünnhilde's sleep hasn't ended. But you're right. The girl must sleep in order that the woman may awaken. Awake now, and be my wife."

Brünnhilde was still too shocked, her senses too confused, her knowledge stifled.

"Is this the end of wisdom?" she asked aloud. "Must all my understanding fail?"

"But didn't you say," Siegfried wished he'd listened more closely, "didn't you say that all your wisdom was just the light of the love you have for me?"

Brünnhilde gazed before her. Something was changing in her. As though love had rendered her mortal. Wasn't she herself a limb of the World Tree, the one that Wotan had planted in Hunding and Sieglinde's house – or had love severed her, as woodcutters sever the limbs of trees they need for kindling? She had gone to sleep a maiden, but just as Wotan prophesied a hero had fought his way through the enchanted forest, climbed the insurmountable summit, braved the fire to reach her, woken her with a kiss. This, this was how her life was meant to be. She must accept. She must be reconciled.

But it was hard.

"What is it?" Siegfried asked her, tenderly.

"I don't know. A melancholy darkness clouds my sight. I feel as if my eyes are growing dim, as if their light has been extinguished. As if the night had seized me in its grip. It's a most turbulent mixture of fear and confusion that rises in me, out of mist and misery. I'm frightened, Siegfried. Very frightened. Terror rises, grows, hardens, towers above my head. My maidenhead."

Impetuously, she covered her face with her hands. But Siegfried had begun to understand, and gently he removed her hands, held them in his.

"Night," he said. "It was the night that frightened your enchanted eyes. You've been asleep a long time, fettered in darkness. But when those fetters break, so must your gloomy fear. Drive out the darkness, Brünnhilde, and you'll see, the day is bright with sunshine."

"Bright enough for all the world to see my shame," Brünnhilde replied in great agitation. "Bright as the sun on my disgrace. Siegfried, Siegfried, can you not see how frightened I am?"

But her face belied her words. What he was seeing was a woman in whose mind a pleasing picture had just formed. What could it be? Certainly not the horror she had just described. But now she turned again and looked with tenderness on Siegfried.

"I've always lived," Brünnhilde said, "and I live now, in the bliss of sweetest longing, with only one passion, to make you blessed." Her voice seemed to have taken on the quality of the fire that Siegfried had walked through to get to her; yet there was tenderness as well. "Siegfried," she went on, "Splendid man. Treasure of the world. You make the earth live, you, the laughing hero. But you must go. You must leave me alone. Don't approach me with your overwhelming passion. Don't force yourself upon me just because you have the physical strength to do so – it would destroy our love." She paused, needing a different stratagem. "Did you ever see your reflection in a clear stream?" she asked. Siegfried nodded. "And did it please you?" Again a nod. "But if you'd disturbed the surface, you'd have created ripples in the stream and lost sight of that reflection. Nothing would have remained but the eddying and flowing of the surge. So it is with you and I. Don't try to touch me, you'll create ripples, you'll make us both unhappy. Let us remain like this, and you'll see yourself forever happy in my eyes, because you'll see them smiling happily upon a blessed, happy hero. O Siegfried, you child of delight. Love yourself for who you are, and turn from me. Leave alone what makes me me. Don't destroy what already belongs to you."

All this was too complex for Siegfried.

"I only know that I love you," he replied. "And if only you could love me too! I'm no longer who I was before. If only I had you! White water pours before my eyes. With all my senses I can see and hear and feel and touch nothing, nothing but that extraordinary, devastating flood. If it disturbs my reflection so that I can no longer recognise my own face, so be it; I burn for the fire of my passion to be cooled in those waters. Now, right now, just as I am, let me jump into the stream, let its blissful torrent swallow me, until my longing's been consumed entirely by the tide. Awake, Brünnhilde! Awaken, virgin maid! Laugh and be alive to the sweetest of joys. Be mine! Be mine! Be mine!

"O Siegfried," Brünnhilde replied with passion deep as his, "I'm yours already."

"Already mine, then be mine now," Siegfried took her hands once more in his, his eyes pleading with her, his whole being engaged in the act of seeking to persuade her.

"I'll be yours forever."

"Forever is tomorrow. Be mine now, today, this very instant." He took her in his arms and held her close. "This close we are already, breast to breast, your heart pounding against mine. Our eyes look into each other's, and catch fire. My breath devours yours, and yours mine," he clasped her body tighter still, and kissed her mouth. "Eyes to eyes and lips on lips.

That's how we know what each means to the other, already and forever, yesterday and yes tomorrow. Because now. No more doubts and no more questions then. Be mine, Brünnhilde. Be mine, now. Are you mine?"

"Am I?" Brünnhilde answered. "Am I yours? Divine peace floods in waves inside me. Purest light blazes in the fire of passion. The wisdom of heaven streams away from me, because the cry of rapture at the joy of love has chased it from me. Am I yours? O Siegfried, Siegfried. Can't you see me? When my eyes devour you, how is it that the light is not so strong it makes you blind? When my arms embrace you, how is it that my fire doesn't leave you scalded? When the blood coursing through my veins surges towards you, how is it that you aren't simply overwhelmed by fire? Aren't you afraid, Siegfried? Aren't you afraid of the wildness and passion of this woman?"

And now Brünnhilde loosed the reins with which she'd been trying all this while to bridle her own passion. Her arms around his neck, her mouth pressed against his mouth, her body clutching his body, she embraced him fervently.

And Siegfried, at once delighted and astonished, returned each of her embraces with a passion equally unbridled. His blood was on fire, kindled by hers. His eyes gazed into hers, blazing her and being scorched by her. His arms embraced her body fervently. And in the act of love, so did he regain the boldness of his heart. And as to fear? That fear that he had never learned, that fear that he had witnessed momentarily through her; through her he had transcended it already.

"Fear!" he pronounced the word that Mime had conjured up, like a magic potion to destroy him with. "Fear! I wondered what it was, and longed to have it. Now I fancy I've forgotten what it is."

With these last words, but involuntarily, Siegfried let go of Brünnhilde. But she, she only laughed at him, laughed loud and wild and joyfully, in the utmost joy of love.

"You're such a child!" she said. "Such a delightful child! You're my foolish lord of the most glorious deeds. Don't look at me like that; I'm laughing because I love you. I love you so much, I'd go blind laughing. Let the whole world laugh at us until we die, and laugh still as we're buried."

"I like your laughter," Siegfried said, "because now I know you're ready to awaken to me."

Brünnhilde laughed again, acknowledging his meaning. In love, he would awaken her from immortality. Eternal love, but mortal – that was the price. So in her heart she bade farewell to the glorious light-giving realm of Valhalla. But in their love another kind of mortality would be born, for this was Siegfried the hero, born to be the destroyer of the gods, to plunge Valhalla into twilight. Let it be that way, if it must. Let the proud fortress crumble into dust. Let the grandiloquent pomposity of the gods be over.

End in ecstasy, immortals. Let the Norns break their runic ropes! Let the twilight of the gods – the Götterdämmerung – rise through the dusk. Let the night of their annihilation rise up through the mists. So she thought, and in her heart accepted it. She was bathed in Siegfried's starlight. He was hers eternally, always hers: her inheritance, her own, her one and all, her radiant love and laughing death!

Siegfried held her in his arms and gazed into her eyes. How happy he was to see this glorious woman, simply alive, joyfully laughing. His heart too was singing, greeting the day that shimmered now around them, greeting the sun that lit their way, greeting the light that had arisen from the night, greeting the realm Brünnhilde still inhabited. She was waking now, alive, and smiling on him, laughing with him. Like two great stars in the firmament of the heavens, his starlight fell on her, and hers on him. He was bathed in Brünnhilde's starlight. She was his eternally, always his: his inheritance, his own, his one and all, his radiant love and laughing death!

"Radiant love and laughing death!" she swooned into his arms.

"Radiant love and laughing death!" he held her joyfully.

"Radiant love and laughing death!" their two voices, with their breathing, and their bodies, became one.

PART FOUR

GÖTTERDÄMMERUNG:
THE TWILIGHT OF THE GODS

Prelude

Close by the summit of the mountain, Siegfried and Brünnhilde had found a cave, and here they slept the long night of their marriage, man and demi-goddess locked in each other's arms, mortal flesh, immortal love. While they slept, Erda's daughters, the Three Norns, weavers of the destinies of men and gods, came to inspect the fire at the summit of the mountain, for rumour had reached them that the fire had been breached. They arrived at dead of night, tall women dressed in dark clothing, their heads and faces draped in veils. At first it seemed that rumour must be false, for firelight still glowed where Loge's armies had emblazoned it. But soon enough the truth revealed itself to them. Inside the citadel of fire, no prisoner. She had escaped, or somebody had liberated her. The Three Norns had no need to ask, for all knowledge was in their custody, without requiring rings of fire. They knew. Even without witnessing the events, they knew. What had taken place, and worse, its meaning, its implication for the future of the world. Nothing so significant as this event had taken place since light first broke out of darkness, and chaos was transmuted into order on the face of the deep. Their mood was gloomy. Silence and stillness hung over them. Conscious that destiny had been wrenched from their power, none wished to speak. But silence could not endure for ever.

The First Norn, the eldest of the three, had found a place to lie down on the ground beneath a spreading fir tree.

"What light's that?" she asked.

"Daybreak already?" the Second Norn wondered, stretched out on a rock in front of the cave where Siegfried and Brünnhilde were still sleeping.

The Third Norn, the youngest of the sisters, had found a place to sit upon a rock below the summit.

"Loge's armies," she pointed to what was not yet daybreak, but the same fire spirits who had blazed around the rock since Wotan gave the order to protect Brünnhilde. No longer needed, no one had instructed them to stop blazing. "It's still night," the Third Norn observed. "Why don't we spin and sing?" But her voice conveyed little enthusiasm.

"If we're going to spin and sing," the Second Norn observed, "we'll need somewhere to fix the rope."

The First Norn untied a golden rope that hung like a spider's girdle round her waist, and fastened it at one end to a branch of the fir tree.

"For better or for worse," she said, gloomily, understanding that the duty of song lay first with her. But what, what should she sing, who knew the time of singing was now nearly over? She wound the rope. If this was now the end, what better song than that of the beginning. So her hands wove, and her voice, plangent and melancholy, sang the saga of the beginning of the world. "I used to weave," she told, "at the foot of the world ash tree, when it was large and strong, and its trunk put forth so much vegetation it was as if one tree alone were quite sufficient to adorn a forest with its noble branches. In its cool shade gushed a spring. It whispered wisdom as its waters flowed. My song was sacred then, holy as the holy place it honoured. Then one day a valiant god came to drink at the spring, and forfeited one of his eyes as payment for what else he did there. Yes, Wotan. He broke off a branch from the world tree. Using all his strength, he cut a spear shaft from the trunk. In the course of time, the wound blighted the tree, and because the tree spread its foliage so wide, the blighting of the tree blighted the entire forest. The faded leaves dropped. The tree withered and died. Sad and dry was the fountain. And as to the lady who wove in the shadows of the world tree, sad at heart became her song." She stopped singing and looked across at her sisters, sighed deeply, as though exhaling nostalgia and returning to reality. She took up her rope and wove it busily. And in a voice intended to express reconciliation, "So," she added, "if today I no longer weave beside the world ash, a fir tree will have to suffice to tether the rope. Your turn now, sister. What happened next?"

She threw the rope to her sister. The Second Norn passed the rope around a rock that projected at the mouth of the cave, and she began to sing. "The terms of binding treaties," she recounted, "were recorded by Wotan in runes on the shaft of the spear, which he wielded as the guardian of the world. But a bold hero broke the spear in battle. The sacred testament of treaties fell in pieces. Then Wotan sent the heroes of Valhalla to the world ash. They chopped its withered trunk and branches into pieces. The ash tree fell and the holy spring dried up forever. Today I anchor the rope to this jagged rock, for I have no other place to anchor it." She stopped. "Here, sister," she threw an end of rope towards the cave. "Your turn now. Tell us what happened next."

The Third Norn caught the rope and threw its loose end out behind her. "The fortress built by the giants still stands," she sang. "Wotan sits there in the hall with the gods and heroes as his sacred companions. Chopped logs that were once the world ash stand heaped around the walls in a huge pile. When that wood catches fire there will be a conflagration such as men and gods have never seen before. It will burn brightly and terribly, the flames will utterly consume that splendid hall. Then the eternal gods will fade into the twilight, and be lost forever. Do you want to know more? Then pass the rope again. Here, from the north," but the attempt to lift their mood with a jest was unsuccessful. The Norns were locked in gloom that much resembled desolation. Still, she threw the rope to the Second Norn who passed it to the First, and she in turn untied the rope from the branch and fastened it to another one.

"Sing, sister. Spin and sing," the Third Norn urged her eldest sibling.

But the First Norn had never in her life been more reluctant.

"Is that the dawn breaking?" she asked, "Or is it just the firelight?" and it was as if she'd quite forgotten that she'd asked this question once already. "My eyes are growing dim," she rubbed them with the back of one hand while her fingers held and wove the flecks of rope. "I think it's sorrow," she too tried to make a jest of it. "Tears obscure vision. Old age too. You know, I can no longer remember clearly the sacred days of old, when Loge sprang up in bright flames and set the universe on fire. Do either of you know what happened to him?"

The Second Norn held out her hand to take the rope, and wound it once again around the rock. "Wotan tamed him with his magic spear," she told. "He served the god as counsellor; but he also gnawed and nibbled at the runes carved on the spear to try to gain his freedom. Wotan never forgave that treachery. But Wotan also needed Loge, and when it came time to protect Brünnhilde, no one but Loge had the magic power. Pointing the spear at him so he couldn't resist, Wotan commanded him to set his fires around Brünnhilde's rock. Does my sister know what will happen to him?"

The Third Norn caught the rope and threw it behind her again. "One day" she sang, "Wotan will thrust the splinters of the broken spear sharp into Loge's breast. An all-consuming flame will flare up from them. The god will hurl it at the remnants of the world ash, piled together. If you want to know what happens after that, wind up the rope."

She threw the rope back to the Second Norn, who wound it as her sister had suggested, then threw it to the eldest Norn, who once more fastened the rope around a branch of the fir tree.

"The night is fading," she observed lugubriously. "My eyes are growing dimmer. I can scarcely feel the strands of the rope any longer. The twine has all come loose and now it's tangled. I keep seeing things, blurred but horrible, visions that trouble and confuse my mind. What happened to Alberich, after he stole the Rhinegold?"

The Second Norn caught the rope from her elder sister and tried to tie it round the rock. Aware that time was slipping from their grasp she moved quickly, busily, but still in vain. The sharp edge of the rock cut into the rope, pulling its threads apart. There was no more tension in its fraying strands and the twine was tangled. But like her elder sister, appalling visions were appearing, darkening her mind. The Nibelung's ring, rising out of hatred and distress, pulling at the rope of destiny, destroying it. An avenging curse was gnawing through its plaited strands. The Second Norn looked anxiously at each of her sisters, trying to describe it. But it was indescribable.

"What will become of this?" she asked in terror.

The Third Norn quickly reached out for the rope her sister threw to her, but it was too slack now, it no longer reached her.

"If I'm to point this to the north," she said, and panic was latent in her voice, "it has to be pulled tighter." She tugged hard at the rope. And the rope broke.

The three Norns were terrified. All at once, as one voice, each spoke the same words, their voices cracked with disbelief:

"It's broken. The rope of destiny. It's broken."

They grasped the pieces of the broken rope and, with them, tied their bodies each one to the other. For the last time they spoke, not words of destiny, not visions of the future, but a terrible lament, for this was the moment of their passing into history, and the world would never be the same again.

"The era of universal knowledge is now gone," they spoke the words as one voice. "Never again will the world benefit from our wisdom."

"Let us go down to our mother," the Third Norn advised.

"Yes," the Second Norn agreed, "to Erda."

The First Norn nodded her assent. "Let's go down," she echoed.

And even as the dawn began to rise on the horizon, the Three Norns, the weavers of destiny, vanished into the underworld beneath the earth.

*

Day had dawned. The morning sky grew pink, then rose, then crimson. The firelight below continued to glow faintly. As the sun finally emerged from under the horizon, so did Siegfried and Brünnhilde emerge from their cave, Siegfried fully armed, Brünnhilde leading her horse on its bridle.

"My beloved hero," Brünnhilde snuggled against Siegfried, "I know you long for new adventures. And my love for you would be poor indeed if I tried to stop you setting out. But one thing makes me hesitate, one worry – that you've been so poorly rewarded for winning me. What I've learned from the gods I've given you – sacred charms in great quantity – but my strength lay in my maidenhood, and everything I inherited from the gods is lost now, yielded to the hero to whom I now submit. I'm drained of knowledge but strong in will, rich in love but destitute of strength. You mustn't despise this poor creature who begrudges you nothing but has nothing more to give."

"You wonderful woman!" Siegfried replied. "You've already given me far more than I know how to keep. Don't scold me if I'm still ignorant despite your lessons. Of one piece of knowledge I'm fully aware," his voice was filled with passion, "that Brünnhilde lives for Siegfried! One lesson I found very easy to learn, never to stop thinking of Brünnhilde."

"If you want your love for me to truly bless me," Brünnhilde replied, "then you should think only of yourself, of your adventures, the ones you had to live through first to win me. Think of the raging fire that you walked through fearlessly, though it burned around the rock…"

"To win Brünnhilde," Siegfried interjected.

"Yes, to win Brünnhilde. And think of the woman underneath the shield, the one you found there fast asleep, whose fastened helmet you broke open…"

"To wake Brünnhilde," Siegfried interjected.

"Yes, to wake Brünnhilde. And think of the vows we've made that make us one, the troth we've plighted, placing each other in the other's holy trust. Think of how we live for love. Think of all that, and then Brünnhilde will burn forever like a sacred fire in your breast."

She put her arms around his neck, reached up on tiptoe to embrace him.

"Now I must leave you," Siegfried broke away. "Leave you," he added, "in the safe protection of this holy fire."

Even as he said these words, he was removing Alberich's ring from his finger. Now he held it at the tip of the fourth finger of her left hand, as though he were the chamberlain appointed to put on the crown. But he didn't put it on. Rather, he pressed it into her palm, and closed her fingers round it.

"In exchange for all your teaching," he spoke the words as if a wedding vow, "I give you this ring. All the virtue of my deeds lies in the power of this ring. I slew a vile dragon that had long and angrily guarded it. Now you must guard it, and its power, as my sacred pledge of trust."

Rapturously, Brünnhilde put on the ring.

"This ring will never be taken from my hand," she swore. "And in exchange, take Grane, my horse. Once he bore me boldly through the skies, but now like me he's lost his magic powers. Never again will he fly among the clouds, in thunder and in lightning. But wherever Siegfried takes him, even through fire, Grane will follow fearlessly. From now on it's you, my hero, that he'll obey. Look after him well, he knows our voice, he'll do what you require of him. Remind him of Brünnhilde often."

"Everything I do now," Siegfried replied, "every deed that I perform, will be inspired entirely by the virtue of Brünnhilde. You'll choose my battles; my victories will all be in your honour. On your horse, protected by your shield, I'm no longer Siegfried, I'm Brünnhilde's arm."

"And I'd be your soul and spirit too, if my deepest wishes could be granted."

"You are, my love," Siegfried replied. "Because my courage is kindled by you."

"Then you are both Siegfried and Brünnhilde."

"Yes," he replied. "For wherever I am, there shall we two be together."

Brünnhilde laughed. "Then my rocky home may not be empty after all."

"Since we are one, it will contain us both."

Brünnhilde had never reached such heights, such steep, unfathomable heights, of inward intensity, of emotion inexpressible except through poetry. This, this was what it meant to abandon immortality and become like mortal men and women, in order to discover immortality again through mutual love. But how, how to express it, how to inform the gods of what a terrible error they had made, when they foolishly chose eternal lovelessness rather than this ephemeral bright flickering of heaven? Out loud she summoned them, addressing them as they expected to be addressed, "the sacred gods, majestic beings, race of eternals" and called on them to feast their eyes upon this blessed pair. "Parted," she challenged them, "who could separate them? Separated," she proclaimed, "they would never be apart."

And for Siegfried too only the poetic words seemed to do justice to his deep emotions, the language of the ancient marriage ceremony, binding them as one.

"I hail you, Brünnhilde," he pronounced the formula, "as my goddess of the morning star."

"I hail you, Siegfried," Brünnhilde responded, "as the conqueror of light and fire."

"Farewell, resplendent love."

"Farewell, resplendent life."

"Farewell, my guiding, shining star."

"Farewell, my conquering light."

How many more times did they bid each other fond farewells, still holding hands, still not departing? At last Siegfried took hold of Grane's bridle, led him quickly to the edge of the ravine. Brünnhilde followed him, alone now on the mountain top, watching as he led the horse down beyond the projecting rock, beginning his descent into the ravine. Soon, from far below, the sound of a horn reached her, Siegfried blowing one more adieu from deep down in the valley. Brünnhilde listened, trying to find his shape among the distant trees. She stepped further out onto the precipice, and suddenly she could see him, waved furiously, waved still more when he returned her greeting, stood for a long while, sad yet joyful, hoping for one last glimpse.

But he was gone.

Act One

Scene One

Our story moves now to the Great Hall of the Gibichungen, on the Rhine, the fortress of King Gibich and Queen Grimhilde, where Gunter ruled, guided by his sister Gutrune and his half-brother Hagen, son of Alberich and Grimhilde. From the windows of the fortress' great hall, the view over the river was quite magnificent. A wide expanse of water on which occasional fishermen could be seen, or farmers bringing their cattle down to drink; and beyond it, looming in the distance, rocky heights enclosed the shore. Gunther and Gutrune were seated on high thrones to one side, a table set with drinking vessels in front of them. Hagen sat on the far side of the table, his usual grim expression on his face.

"Tell me, Hagen," Gunther enquired, "and tell me honestly. Is my name honoured along the Rhine? Am I considered a worthy successor to King Gibich?"

"I confess that I'm envious of your title and your merits," Hagen replied. "But our mother, the Lady Grimhilde, taught me to respect you."

"Strange that you should envy me," Gunther observed, "when I have nothing but envy for you, and you have no cause to be jealous. I may have inherited the throne by right of being the firstborn, but you alone were given wisdom. The rivalry of half-brothers was never better resolved than you and I have found the means of doing. When I enquire about my reputation, I'm really only praising your good judgement."

"Then I must criticise my own judgement," Hagen responded, "because your reputation still leaves something to be desired. I know of some particularly valuable treasures that the Gibichungen haven't yet acquired, but which we ought to have."

"If you've been keeping something secret, Hagen, I shall not be pleased."

"The race of King Gibich has entered its summer," Hagen chose his words carefully. "His children are in their prime and their maturity, and yet Gunther is unmarried and Gutrune too has not yet found a husband."

Gunther and Gutrune sat awhile in silent meditation. Marriage was certainly one of their eventual intentions, but who, that was the question, who was worthy of welcome into the Gibich race?

"Who would you have me marry, that would enhance my reputation? Gunther enquired.

"I know of a woman," Hagen replied, "a truly splendid woman, beautiful and noble. Her home is a high rock in the mountains, and a fire blazes all around her dwelling. Only by passing through the fire could a man be this Brünnhilde's suitor."

"Brünnhilde," Gunther tried the name on his own tongue, and liked the taste. "Perhaps you think I'm not brave enough?"

"Sadly, she's been destined for a man stronger than you."

"And who might that be?"

"Siegfried, the offspring of the Wälsungen. He's already been chosen for the task. It can only be done by the strongest of heroes, and, you see, a pair of twins, Siegmund and Sieglinde by name, driven by love, bore this noble son. He grew up in the forest, and he grew up very strong and very brave. I would venture he would make Gutrune an excellent husband."

"What has this Siegfried done," Gutrune began shyly, "to warrant this description as the most glorious of heroes?"

"There was a dragon, Fafner by name, who guarded the Nibelungen treasure at Niedhöhle, the Cave of Envy. Siegfried closed his fearsome jaws for him. Killed him with his sword. It was this not unexceptional deed that secured his fame as a hero."

"I've heard of this Nibelungen treasure," Gunther replied meditatively. "It's something greatly to be desired."

"The man who knows how to use it would have the whole world in his power," Hagen agreed.

"And Siegfried won it in a fight?" Gunther enquired.

"That's right. And now the Nibelungen are his slaves."

"And only he can win Brünnhilde?"

"Right again. The fire will yield to no one else."

Gunther rose angrily from his seat. "Why do you stir up doubts and quarrels? Why do you raise my hopes for something I can never have?" He walked to and fro in agitation. But Hagen, without so much as leaving his seat, yet with an expression on his face that seemed full of hidden meaning, held Gunther's attention fixed as he approached him.

"What if Siegfried were to obtain the bride, but for Gunther not himself. Wouldn't that give you Brünnhilde?"

Gunther turned away again in doubt and anger. "What could possibly persuade a happy man to win a bride for someone else?"

"Just asking him should be sufficient, if Gutrune were his wife, and he therefore your loyal vassal."

"Why you wicked…are you joking?" Gutrune knew Hagen well enough that very little shocked her. But she was shocked. "How would I be able to charm this Siegfried, let alone seduce him into marriage? If he is, as you say, the most glorious hero in the world, then the loveliest women on Earth would long since have won his love."

Hagen leaned confidentially towards Gutrune. "Remember a certain potion that you have in your secret cabinet. And speaking of secrets," he leaned still closer, whispered in her ear: "Trust me. I'm the one who brought it home, I know what it can do. It'll bind in love whichever hero you desire."

Gunther had come back to the table and, leaning on it now, listened attentively.

"Let Siegfried come to Gibichung," Hagen continued, "and taste that little cocktail. He'll pretty soon forget entirely about any woman he might have seen before Gutrune, even the idea that any woman ever took his fancy. Nice plan, eh?"

Gunther grinned broadly, excited and well pleased.

"The gods be praised for our Lady Grimhilde," Gunther raised his head in mock solemnity towards the heavens, "for giving us Hagen as a brother."

"I should very much like to see this Siegfried," Gutrune observed.

"How might he be found?" Gunther continued her thought.

At that precise moment, the sound of a hunting horn reached them, very loud but distant. Hagen listened, and smiled conspiratorially, as though by some enchanted means he had contrived this answer to his brother's question.

"He's out there looking for adventures," Hagen observed wryly. "He treats the whole world as if it were one vast enchanted forest, and he the restless hunter always seeking dragons to slay and damsels in distress to rescue. He'll come to Gibich-on-the-Rhine soon enough."

"I'll gladly welcome him." Gunther declared.

Again a horn was heard, coming closer but still distant. Gunther and Hagen listened.

"It's coming from the Rhine," Gunther observed.

Hagen gazed along the riverbank, trying to see downstream.

"There's a man and a horse," he said, "approaching in a boat. He blows a pretty horn."

The horn sounded yet again, even nearer now, so that it was clear the man was signalling to them. Gunther had been following Hagen to the window, to try to see; but stopped halfway, and listened. There was no need to see this for himself, for Hagen was taking delight in describing the entire scene.

"He pulls a powerful stroke, whoever he is. Not a small boat either, but for him it's no effort at all. Look how fast he's driving the boat against the current. That sort of massive strength propelling an oar can only belong to one man, and that's the man who slew the dragon Fafner. This has got to be Siegfried himself, and no other."

If Gunther was meant to be impressed, or frightened, it didn't show. If anything, his excitement to meet so awesome a hero outweighed any reservations he may have had about Hagen's hidden motives. He simply worried that the stranger might be rowing by, and not stopping.

"Is he coming to us?" he asked.

"Ahoy there! Hey, you!" Hagen called across the stream through cupped and hollowed hands. "Where are you bound? Who are you seeking?"

"The mighty son of Gibich," the stranger called back from the river.

"Then park your boat, man. Here he is. Waiting to give you a warm welcome. Here, come on shore."

Scene Two

"Welcome," Hagen called down from the jetty as Siegfried brought his boat to shore. He threw a metal chain to Hagen, and the Lord Chamberlain himself made the boat fast. Siegfried sprang on shore, leading Grane behind him.

"Welcome, Siegfried" Hagen shook the stranger's hand.

Gunther too had come down to the riverbank to offer his welcome to the stranger. Gutrune had remained in the high hall, seated on her throne, but with a clear view of the jetty and the hero who was landing there. She gazed at him now in astonishment; as each of them, indeed, was gazing at the other, mute in contemplation, wondering where all of this would lead.

Siegfried hadn't let go his horse; rather he was grooming him with his hand, helping him get back his land-legs after the uncomfortable journey on the river.

"Which one of you is King Gibich's son?" he asked.

Gunther nodded. "I'm the man you're looking for," he said.

"They speak your name and fame the whole length of the Rhine," Siegfried offered what was more than just a diplomatic compliment. "Now fight with me or be my friend," he added, and offered his gauntleted hand.

"Leave the fighting," Gunther replied. "Be welcome."

"Where can I leave my horse?" Siegfried enquired.

"Leave that with me," Hagen replied. "I'll find a stall for it."

"You addressed me as Siegfried," the stranger commented. "Have we met somewhere before?"

"I recognised you simply by your strength," Hagen replied.

"Take good care of Grane," Siegfried said to Hagen as the Chamberlain lead the horse away. "You'll never hold a nobler horse, either by rein or bridle."

Siegfried looked thoughtfully after Hagen, but in truth his mind was on the horse, and not the man. So he didn't see Gutrune in the window of the castle, nor the gesture Hagen made to her, indicating to her to leave the great hall of the throne, to wait in her own room. And besides, Gunther had slapped him on the shoulder, taken his hand in his again to shake it, or perhaps to test its strength against his own. Gunther was pointing at the castle gate, where liveried valets not armoured soldiers waited to welcome a stranger in.

"Wandering hero," Gunther permitted himself the polite formalities of chivalry, "allow me to extend to you the bounty of my father's house. Wherever you walk, whatever you see, treat it as your own. My birthright, my inheritance, land, people, goods are yours. I pledge myself to you, body and soul, in oaths of blood."

Evidently he was ready to cut open a vein and make the words flesh. But Siegfried wasn't in the same state of readiness. For he had nothing in exchange to offer. He had come in search of a master he could serve, not a blood-brother.

"I have," he responded, "neither land nor people, no paternal house, no grounds. My entire birthright is this body, and the more I live, the more it wastes away. All I own is a sword, forged by my own hand. Let my sword stand for my oath. That I'm glad to offer, with myself, for my allegiance."

"I've heard it rumoured," said Hagen, who had now returned from stabling Siegfried's horse and speaking privately to Gutrune, "that you're the new master of the Nibelungen treasure."

"D'you know, I'd completely forgotten about that treasure." He laughed. "That shows you how lightly I treasure it."

Hagen laughed too, then glowered at Gunther until he also joined the raucous laughter at this clever play on words, and slapped Siegfried on the back, and congratulated him on the virtue of indifference.

"I left it lying in the cave," Siegfried explained, "where that dragon used to guard it."

"And you took nothing at all?" Hagen wondered.

Siegfried pointed to the piece of metalwork hanging from his belt.

"Nothing but this," he said. "And I don't even know what it's for."

Hagen nodded his head and smiled in recognition.

"This," he said, "is the Tarnhelm, the most skilful piece of work a Nibelung has ever undertaken."

His fingers were clenched into fists, as though he were having to fight back the desperate desire to touch the helmet, to hold it in his hands, to put it on. But other than his fists, his outward calm was absolute.

"It works," he went on, and if only he could do it by example, if only he could demonstrate, "it works by putting the helmet on your head, and it'll change you into any shape you choose. If you hanker for some distant spot, it'll take you there in a twinkling. Did you really take nothing else from the treasure?"

"Just a ring," Siegfried replied.

"A ring," Hagen was finding it hard to keep his breath under control. "I trust you've put this ring in a safe place."

"Ah yes," Siegfried replied, and the thought of Brünnhilde filled his heart with tenderness, "I gave it to the most wonderful woman in the world."

Brünnhild...the name was on Hagen's tongue, and half-pronounced, until he managed just in time to make a cough of it. Mercifully Gunther realised the near-mistake in time and came to his half-brother's rescue, slapping Siegfried on the back once more and guiding him, in the true comradely manner of chivalric heroes, to the window, to demonstrate the vastness and the grandeur of his estates.

162

"You need not give me anything," he declared, "by way of allegiance. If you were to exchange that helmet for everything I possessed, you'd be receiving dross for gold. Our friendship needs no rewards. We serve each other freely."

While Gunther spoke thus to Siegfried, Hagen had gone to Gutrune's door and opened it. Dressed like a queen, but carrying a drinking horn as though she were a servant, the king's sister made such formal entry that Siegfried could out of politeness only stand and look. To her slight curtsey he made bow. To her radiant smile he gave back his own most handsome face. To her perusal of his muscular form, he thought only and intensely of Brünnhilde.

"Welcome, guest, to the house of King Gibich," Gutrune had been well-trained in the formalities of courtly life. "The king's daughter offers you a drink."

Siegfried bowed once more, in his friendly manner, and took the drinking horn. He held it out meditatively, the way a priest might hold a blessing cup. But the blessing he was minded to recite wasn't for the bountiful gods, but for she who had surrendered her godhead for his sake.

"If I were to forget everything I've been taught," he spoke the words into the air, but his eyes turned first to Gunther, then to Hagen, finally to Gutrune, for he spoke them for their benefit as well, "there is still one lesson I would never, could never forget. This drink, the first I've tasted since we parted, is offered to Brünnhilde, my true love."

He put the drinking-horn to his lips and drank a long draught. Finished, he gave the horn back to Gutrune, who lowered her eyes in what might have been the manner of a serving-girl, or perhaps the embarrassment and confusion of a royal princess.

But Siegfried fixed his gaze upon the woman, and where Brünnhilde had filled his inner sight before, now, suddenly, it was Gutrune who had inflamed his most intense desire.

"Look at me," he said to her. But she kept her head bowed. "My eyes are burning from looking at you, as if I've been struck by lightning. Why do you lower your eyes in front of me?"

Blushing, Gutrune lifted her eyes and met his.

"O but you're beautiful," Siegfried exclaimed with ardour. "You were right to close your eyes. Or veil them, at least. Their beams are burning my heart. I can feel rivers of flame scorching me and kindling my blood."

Certainly something was scorching his heart and kindling his blood. His whole body was trembling.

"Gunther," he enquired, "what's your sister's name?"

"Gutrune," Gunther replied.

"Gutrune," Siegfried repeated softly. "And do I dare to read good runes in your name, as I've read good omens in your eyes?" He took her hands in his and held them ardently. "I offered to serve your brother, but in his pride he's rejected me. Will you deny me too if I offer you my hand in marriage?"

Involuntarily Gutrune caught Hagen's eye. Humbly, modestly, she bowed her head, allowing Siegfried to know how much she felt unworthy of his offer. The empty drinking horn was in her hand, and she, her movements seemed to say, a king's daughter, yes, but also a serving-maid. She couldn't answer such a question now. With faltering steps she left the hall. Siegfried followed her with his eyes as if entranced. Hagen and Gunther watched Siegfried watching.

"What about you, Gunther?" Siegfried enquired. "Do you have a wife?"

"Not yet," Gunther replied. "Nor is there much point trying to find one. You see, I've set my heart on somebody, but winning hers beyond me."

"Beyond you?" Siegfried retorted. "Come now, there's nothing you can't win with me to help you."

"Her home is on a high rock…" Gunther began to tell.

"Her home is on a high rock?" Siegfried repeated, interrupting in astonishment.

"A fire blazes round her dwelling…"

"A fire blazes round her dwelling?" Siegfried echoed the words again.

"Only he who can pass through the fire…"

Siegfried was struggling to remember something that these words evoked. Struggling, with intense effort. But he couldn't find it. "Pass through the fire. Pass through the fire." Whatever it was, it was gone.

"…can be Brünnhilde's suitor."

It was clear from Siegfried's expression that the name Brünnhilde already held no meaning for him.

"I," Gunther said, "can never climb that mountain, for the fire will never let me pass through."

This was the cue that Siegfried had been waiting for. The chance to serve, that was why he'd come to Gibich. To find a master, who would send him out to labour in the world, as King Eurystheus had once sent Hercules. To prove himself a hero against dragons, beasts and monsters, against gods and goblins. Gunther had asked only for friendship, but could Siegfried not serve him just as well and just as valiantly in friendship as in vassalhood? This recognition woke him from his dreamy state, and now he turned to Gunther with almost excessive gaiety.

"I'm not afraid of fire," he said. "Let me win the woman for you. Then I'll be your vassal, and your Hercules, and in exchange, Gutrune for my wife."

"Gutrune I give you, gladly," Gunther answered.

"Then this Brünnhilde shall be yours."

"How will you trick, I mean persuade her?"

"By the magic of the Tarnhelm," Siegfried was so excited he could barely

164

wait to start. "I'll disguise myself as Gunther."

"Let's swear an oath," Gunther ventured.

"Blood-brotherhood," Siegfried concurred.

Hagen filled a fresh drinking horn with wine and offered it to Siegfried, then to Gunther. Now, as convention prescribed, each drew his sword and pricked a small cut on the lower arm, just above the wrist. Where others sealed their bond by pressing blood to blood, wrist to wrist, at Gibich oaths were sworn by holding the open wound above the drinking horn, allowing its mouth to sup. Then each placed two fingers on the horn that Hagen held between them.

"Renewing blood," Siegfried recited the formal liturgy of oaths, "refresh and nourish life through each of these drops I shed."

"Let our blood," Gunther responded, "boldly mixed in brotherly love, flourish in this cup."

And then together, for their oath was oneness in a bond of blood-brotherhood:

"Trust in my friend."

"Trust in my friend."

"Free and carefree let our bond be proclaimed."

"Free and carefree let our bond be proclaimed."

"We are blood-brothers."

"We are blood-brothers."

"But if a brother breaks his oath," Gunther began, but didn't complete the phrase, for Siegfried interrupted him, rendering the last words unnecessary.

"If a friend betrays his trust," he said, and he too left his sentence incomplete.

"The drops of blood that we in true friendship have solemnly drunk today," the two recited the words in harmony, "will flow in streams if either of us should turn traitor."

Gunther took the horn and drank.

"I swear that oath," he proclaimed.

Then he handed the horn to Siegfried.

"I swear that oath," Siegfried drank and gave the empty horn to Hagen, who placed it on the window sill, and severed it in two with his sword. Gunther and Siegfried clasped each other's hands, acknowledging thereby that each accepted the other's oath. So it was done.

Siegfried turned to Hagen, who had stood behind him during the oath ceremony.

"Why did you take no part in the oath?" he enquired.

"My blood would spoil the drink," Hagen responded. "Unlike Siegfried's, mine is neither pure nor noble. Rather it's obstinate and cold, like stagnant water inside me. As you can see, it doesn't even redden my cheeks. That's why I steer clear of hot-blooded promises."

"Leave the poor unhappy fellow to his misery," Gunther laughed, handing to Siegfried the shield he'd laid aside to make his oath.

"Let's make a prompt start," Siegfried ventured, putting on the shield. "My boat's right there. It'll take us at full speed straight to the rock." He stepped closer to Gunther and pointed through the window to the mountains. "We'll have to spend one night by the riverbank, on board. Then you can bring your bride home."

He turned to go, and beckoned Gunther to follow him.

"Don't you want to rest first?" Gunther asked.

"The end of labour is rest," Siegfried replied. "Let's labour first."

And saying this, he set out at once for the shore to cast the boat loose.

"Stay here, Hagen, and guard the hall," Gunther instructed his Chamberlain, and followed Siegfried to the shore. The two blood brothers laid their arms down in the boat, put up the sail and made ready for departure.

Inside the castle, Hagen had taken up his spear and shield when Gutrune appeared at the door of her chamber. Through the high windows she could see Siegfried pushing off the boat, which immediately floated into the middle of the stream.

"Why are they leaving in such a hurry?" she asked.

Hagen took up his sentry post in front of the hall, holding tight his shield and spear.

"They're sailing off to court Brünnhilde" Hagen grinned.

"Siegfried?" Gutrune was astonished.

"It would seem he's in a great hurry to have you for his wife."

"Siegfried mine!" she exclaimed, and in a state of much excitement went back to her room.

Hagen sat motionless outside the great hall of the Gibich fortress, leaning his back against the doorpost, gazing out across the Rhine. What he'd achieved already, what he could see unfolding before him, gave cause to sit contentedly, and wait. There was Siegfried, seizing an oar and pulling it with mighty strokes, driving the boat downstream so fast it was already almost lost to view. And there was he, Hagen son of Alberich and Grimhilde, rightful heir of the Nibelungen treasure that his father had brought up from the waters of the Rhine, rightful inheritor of the ring of power and the magic Tarnhelm, both of them his father's reward for renouncing love. His, not yet, but very soon. So he continued to sit on watch, guarding the house as Gunther had commanded him, defending the hall against its enemies.

"For Gibich's son," he thought out loud, "the wind's blowing and he's gone a-courting." He laughed, like a man counting his blessings, and discovering he has accrued interest. "What better fortune could a man ask for? His tiller's guided by a mighty hero who'll face every danger he

166

encounters for him. He'll bring his bride back down the Rhine, but for Hagen he will also bring the ring. My ring. My precious. Sail on, you sons of freedom; happy companions, sail on. You think me base. But why base? Wherefore bastard? When this is done, all of you will serve this Nibelungen son."

Scene Three

High up in the mountains, on the rocky height where Wotan once built her prison and Loge guarded it with fire, Brünnhilde sat waiting, silently contemplating Siegfried's ring. Each time another happy memory overwhelmed her, she covered the ring with kisses. But then, off in the distance, she heard the sound of thunder. She looked up, listened, then looked down at the ring again. A flash of lightning. Again she listened, peering off into the distance from where a dark thundercloud was rapidly approaching.

Brünnhilde recognized another sound, likewise distant, but very familiar, a sound as if in greeting to her. A winged horse was hurrying towards her, using the storm winds to propel it even faster, flying down now through the clouds towards the rock.

"Who are you?" Brünnhilde called out loudly. Then, in a softer voice, as though speaking to herself, "Who is it wishes to disturb my solitude?"

"Brünnhilde! Sister!" the voice from far away was Waltraute's. "Are you sleeping or awake?"

Brünnhilde jumped up from her seat, recognizing Waltraute's voice, anticipating happy news. "Is that you, sister?" she cried out, waving her arms to help her sister find a place to land. "Why so fast?" But Waltraute gave no answer, just kept on hurrying. Brünnhilde hastened to the edge of the ravine. "There," she pointed, "in the wood. You can dismount there and leave your horse to rest."

She ran into the wood, where a noise louder than a thunderclap greeted her. But also her sister. Brünnhilde was overwrought, leading Waltraute towards the rocky clearing. Such was her excitement, she simply failed to notice that Waltraute was in a state of anxious fear.

"Have you come just to see me?" she asked. "You're terribly brave. I don't just mean the storm. Aren't you scared of repercussions for bringing greetings to Brünnhilde?"

"It's only because of you I've hurried here," Waltraute replied.

"You mean you dared to break War Father's orders, for my sake, for the love of Brünnhilde? Or maybe, is it possible, has Wotan rescinded his edict against me? O Waltraute, when I disobeyed the god and protected – failed to protect - Siegmund, I knew that I was doing what he really wanted. And I know his anger must have abated too, for even though he put me here to sleep, imprisoned on this rock, left for any passing man to find and waken me, yet even so he granted me my pitiable plea. He surrounded the rock with scorching fire that barred the way to cowards and craven men. So my punishment was transformed into happiness when the most marvellous hero won me for his wife. Can't you see how happy I am? I live in light and laughter, blessed by his love."

She put her arms around Waltraute, embraced her joyously. But Waltraute had no patience for this sentiment. She tried, but failed, to break away.

"Was it my happy fate that made you come here, sister?" Brünnhilde enquired. "Did you want to see for yourself the delight that destiny has given me, and share in it yourself? Is that why you came?"

"Why would I want to share the hysteria in your addled brain?" Waltraute expressed herself more vehemently than she'd perhaps intended. "Do you not understand the anguish and the dread I've suffered, even thinking of breaking Wotan's command and coming to you here?"

For the first time Brünnhilde realised, recognised, her sister's desperately agitated state. But why? But why?

"Anguish?" she echoed the word her sister had used. "Anguish? And dread? Are these your fetters? Then Wotan hasn't revoked his sentence. Are you afraid he'll be angry with you too now?"

"If all I feared was his rage," Waltraute replied gloomily, "then that would be the end of dread and anguish."

"I'm, I'm shocked, Waltraute. I don't understand."

"Then calm yourself down and listen to me carefully. My fear drives me back to Valhalla, just as it was my fear that drove me here."

Shocked, frightened, Brünnhilde laid her palm on her sister's wrist. "Has something happened to the immortal gods?" she asked.

"Just listen to me," Waltraute pulled her hand away and clenched her fist, struggling to control her breath. "Listen carefully to what I'm telling you. From the moment that Wotan left you here, he refused to give the Valküre battle orders. We fought, but randomly, chaotically, bewildered. He refuses to meet any of the brave heroes in Valhalla. He rides out on his own, without pause or rest, raging around the world dressed as the Wanderer. Then he came home, holding the fragments of his spear; some hero had shattered it. Without explanation, by some secret sign, he sent the heroes of Valhalla to the forest, to cut down the world ash. The sacred trunk was chopped in pieces, and the logs piled in an enormous heap around the hall of the blessed. Then he called a council of the gods and took his seat on the throne. They came in fear and consternation. He told them to sit beside him. The heroes sat around the hall in a great circle. So he sat on his majestic throne, speaking not a word, silent and grave, with the shattered fragments of his spear grasped in his hand. They're sitting there even now. He won't touch Holda's apples. The gods just sit there, motionless, frightened and astonished, overwhelmed by fear. He's sent off his two ravens. If ever they return with good news, then, for one last time in eternity, perhaps the god will smile. The other Valküre, they don't know what to do, they just sit there, clutching his knees. But he's blind to their weeping glances. We're all of us consumed with fear and unending anxiety.

I put my arms around him once, weeping" – Waltraute hesitated as she told this part – "and then his eyes softened and he spoke of you, Brünnhilde. He sighed deeply, and he closed his eyes and – it was as if he was dreaming - he whispered the words: 'If she would give the ring back to the Rhine Maidens, the gods and the world would be saved from the burden of this curse.' I thought about this for a long time. Then I made my mind up. I stole away. I slipped through the silent ranks of gods and heroes, secretly and hurriedly mounted my horse and rode as fast as I could get here to Brünnhilde. Now, sister, I implore you," she threw herself down before Brünnhilde, "whatever you can do, whatever you dare to do, have courage and do it now, and put an end to this eternal misery."

Brünnhilde lifted her sister's face and looked at her, took her hand in hers and held it gently. Then, quietly, calm now, she replied: "Such dreadful dreams and anxious fancies you've told me. What sadness in your face! But I in my folly have been cast out from the palace of the gods, evicted from the clouds of heaven. I don't understand what you're telling me. Your tale seems dark and confused and almost meaningless to me. I look in your eyes and I see tiredness, the fires that usually glow there barely flickering. Your cheeks are pale. What does my white-faced, wild sister want of me?"

Now it was Waltraute who took Brünnhilde by the hand, held it firmly, pointed at the ring on her fourth finger.

"This is what you can do," she urged her sister vehemently. "Listen to me. For Wotan's sake, throw it away."

Brünnhilde was astonished.

"The ring? Throw it away?" she said.

"Give it back to the Rhine Maidens."

"To the Rhine Maidens? I...the ring...Siegfried's love token. Are you insane?"

"Listen to me. Listen to my fears. The ill fortunes of the world are hanging on this ring. Throw it away. Cast it into the water. You have the power to end Valhalla's misery, by throwing this accursed ring into the river."

Brünnhilde was incredulous. "Do you know," she asked, "what this ring means to me? No, you can't know, because you've never experienced love. This ring means more to me than all the pleasures of Valhalla, more even than the glory of the gods. One glance at its bright gold, one gleam of its majestic brightness, is worth more to me than all the gods and their eternal happiness. For this ring, this holy ring, is Siegfried's love. Do you understand? Siegfried's love. If I could just explain to you the joy it brings me. Just having this ring."

Her fingers were stroking it, caressing it, as though by some magic power she could conjure up the real Siegfried. Waltraute let her sister's hand go free, clenched her own fists again, desultory now that she had failed in her mission. One last time she looked into her sister's face, hoping even now to convince the selfish girl. But Brünnhilde was adamant.

"Go back to the gods," she said. "Go and inform their secret council. Tell them this about my ring. Tell them," she spoke each word slowly, underscoring it so there could be no question Waltraute had understood what she had said, "tell them, Brünnhilde will never give it up, neither the ring, nor love itself. They won't take love from me, not even if the radiant splendour of Valhalla itself should collapse in ruins."

"So much for your loyalty," Waltraute shook her head in sadness. "I never thought you of all people would be the one to abandon her sisters to lovelessness and mourning."

Such bitterness only made Brünnhilde angry now.

"Go fetch your horse," she said. "Go on, it's time to leave."

But Waltraute didn't move. Eyes met eyes, glowers met glowers. As though she could convince her sister by looks, now that words had failed. Her eyes pleaded, implored, beseeched, but all in vain. Brünnhilde merely glowered back, and refused to cower.

"Go," she said again. "You'll not win the ring from me."

Waltraute burst into tears of sorrow, crying woe for herself and her sisters, woe for the gods and for Valhalla. Or was it simply one more stratagem? No, Brünnhilde could see that this was genuine. But there was nothing she could do. She who'd been banished had been saved by love. She would never betray her rescuer. Never.

Waltraute hurried away. Soon a storm cloud rose out of the forest. Brünnhilde watched the brightly flashing cloud as it disappeared into the distance, and prayed out loud that clouds and lightning, carried on the wind, should leave her now forever and not come back again.

Evening had fallen. Brünnhilde looked calmly out over the landscape. Below the cave, where her prison had once been, twilight filled the sky and the firelight seemed to shine more brightly – or was that perhaps just an illusion caused by growing darkness? But no, it was no illusion. The firelight was coming nearer and tongues of flame, growing continually brighter, were darting up over the edge of the rock. Brünnhilde wondered out loud why the defensive wall of flames was flaring up so angrily. A tide of fire was gushing over the summit of the rock. Then she sat up in delight as a horn-call sounded in the distance. Siegfried! She listened ecstatically. Siegfried had returned! It was his call that she was hearing, his arrival that had kindled the guardian flames, as though to welcome home their conqueror. Now she jumped up, straightened her clothes, her hair, readied herself to meet him and to fall into the arms of her god!

Overjoyed, she ran to the cliff-edge. Flames shot about her. And out of them leaped Siegfried, finding a safe landing on a high rock. At once the flames fell back and now they flared only below the cliff edge, at the top of the ravine. Siegfried it was surely, but with the Tarnhelm on his head, so that it hid the upper half of his face, leaving only his eyes free. But the form, the body, was not Siegfried. Brünnhilde shrank back in terror, and ran to the safety of the cave. She fixed her eyes, speechless and astonished, upon Siegfried.

"I'm betrayed!" she cried. "Who are you? How did you get here?"

Siegfried remained where he had jumped, upon a large stone near the guardian rock, leaning on his shield, motionless, watching Brünnhilde.

"Brünnhilde!" he called out, feigning a voice much rougher than his own. "A suitor has come to court you. One who doesn't fear your fire. I come to claim you as my wife. Will you follow me of your own free will."

Brünnhilde trembled violently.

"Who are you?" she called out, "who has dared attempt, undaunted, what only the bravest hero may attempt?"

"I am such a hero," Siegfried replied, in the same gruff, manly voice he'd used before, "and I will take you by force if you resist me."

Now Brünnhilde was truly seized with fear. It seemed to her it was some beast or demon standing on that rock. Or maybe some bird of prey had flown down to devour her.

"Who are you, you monster?" she screamed. "Are you human? Are you one of Hella's night creatures?"

"I am a Gibichung," Siegfried replied, again using that gruff voice, with a slight tremble at first, but then with growing certainty. And Gunther is the name of the hero whom you, woman, must now follow."

Brünnhilde was desperate now. She cried out, but not to the monster who was threatening her. Her cry like her despair went deeper far than that. The monster was just a monster, whereas Wotan.

"Wotan!" she screamed his name so loud it could have reached Waltraute on her way home to Valhalla. "You're a cruel and vengeful god. Now I see the nature of my punishment. You've banished me to mockery and derision."

Siegfried sprang down from the rock and came closer.

"The night is falling," he declared. "In this cave you must be married to me."

Brünnhilde stretched out her finger threateningly, showing him Siegfried's ring.

"Go back!" she commanded him. "Beware this ring has magic powers! You cannot force me into shame while this ring still protects me."

"By conjugal right, that ring must be given to Gunther. With it, let the two of you be married."

"Go back, you robber," Brünnhilde held her ground, "you villainous thief. I dare you to come near me. This ring makes me stronger than steel

172

and you will never steal it from me."

"Perhaps you could teach me how to take it from you," Siegfried mocked her, and at once he moved towards her, attempting to seize her ring hand, taking and then losing hold of arm, thigh, hair. At one point she fell, and they wrestled together on the ground, but Brünnhilde wrenched herself free, then fled, then finding good ground turned round to defend herself. Siegfried seized her again, and again she fled, and again he caught her. Now their wrestling was truly violent, as Brünnhilde gave no quarter. She pulled his hair, scratched him with her fingernails, and when he chased her again he did so limping. But his strength was more than hers, and soon enough Brünnhilde wearied. Her feet no longer found themselves steady on the stones. Her body had great difficulty balancing as she leaped from rock to rock. So Siegfried caught her, gripped her by the hand and pushed her to the ground. As she knelt there, exhausted, her head dropped earthwards but her right arm was still raised high, the wrist bent backwards as he held her in his power. And now Brünnhilde yielded. The pain in her wrist was more than she could bear. So painful was it, she could scarcely feel the drawing of the ring from off her finger. Siegfried knelt down beside her, gloating as he held the ring close to her face, compelling her to acknowledge that he'd taken it. Brünnhilde shrieked violently. As if crushed, she sank down in a feint, and what could have been worse even than the theft of the ring, he caught her as she feinted, and as her eyes half-consciously met his, he let her limp body sink onto the stone bench in the entrance to the cave.

"Now," he announced in triumph, "now you're mine. Now, Brünnhilde, Gunther's bride, show me the way to your chamber."

Half-feint still, Brünnhilde stared in front of her. She was exhausted. How, now, could a miserable, wretched woman defend her honour? Siegfried had made her get up again, was driving her on now with words and gestures of command. Trembling and with wavering steps Brünnhilde went into the cave. Siegfried drew his sword.

"Now, my Sword of Need," he invoked Nothung in his own voice, "bear witness that I wooed honourably. Now preserve my fealty to my brother, let the sword protect the bride."

Holding Nothung before him, he followed Brünnhilde into the cave.

Act Two

Prelude and Scene One

That same night, Hagen sat leaning against one of the wooden pillars of the hall of the Gibichungen, on guard in theory, in fact fast asleep with his arm around his spear and his shield at his side. The Rhine flowed away in front of him, as languid as sleep itself, and on the other side, had his eyes been open to see it, a rocky height cut by several mountain paths. There Fricka's altar stone was visible, higher up a larger one for Wotan, and on the side a third for Donner.

From behind dark clouds, the moon suddenly appeared, throwing a vivid light on Hagen and the objects immediately surrounding him. Amongst these was the figure of his father, Alberich, returning from a visit to the statues of the gods, crouching on the ground in front of him, leaning his arms on Hagen's knees.

"Hagen!" Alberich jostled his son gently, to try to wake him. "Are you asleep, son?" he asked softly. "Are you so fast asleep you can't even hear me, me whom rest and sleep deserted long ago?"

Hagen remained motionless, so that it appeared that he was still asleep. But his eyes were open.

"Yes, I hear you, you sly dwarf," Hagen replied in a whisper. "What do you have to say that's so important it needed to disturb my sleep?"

"Don't forget the majesty that you possess," Alberich replied. "You can have it, if you're as brave as the mother who gave birth to you."

Hagen didn't shift from his sleeping position. Simply, he looked at his father out of half-closed eyes, and yawned. "Just because I inherited half a throne from my mother doesn't mean I have to thank her for giving in to your deceits. Look at me. Old before my time, sallow and pale. I detest happy people. Personally, I've never experienced one moment of happiness."

Alberich beamed, like any proud father. Still crouched at Hagen's knees, he clapped his hand on one of them, and stroked him, so hard the boy almost kicked his father trying to shrug his tenderness away.

"It's good to hate happy people," Alberich found the knee again, and stroked it even harder. "Me," he said, "I'm not just joyless, I'm burdened with sorrow, so you should have plenty of love for me." Not rubbing now, but gripping the knee so tight he could have been trying to hurt him. "Be strong, be bold, and be cunning," his fingers had found the nerves on either side of the knee joints, and were squeezing so tight Hagen's leg was almost numb. "Them as we're engaged in battle with," he said, "we use the weapons of darkness against them. They'll know soon enough what envy is, and what it means to be hated. That treacherous bandit, Wotan, the one who stole my ring, I hear he's been defeated by his own offspring. That's right. Lost all his power and authority to a Wälsung. And now, d'you know what he's doing? Sits around all day, feeling sorry for himself, him and all the other grand company of the gods, nothing else to do all day but sit there fearfully anticipating their own downfall. Well I for one am no longer afraid of 'im. Let 'em all fall together! Are you asleep? Hagen? Wake up, son."

Hagen still didn't move. "And who will inherit the power of the immortals?" he asked.

"Me and you!" his father replied. "Unless I'm very much mistaken about your loyalty, this world belongs to us now – if you share my fury and my desolation. Wotan's spear was shattered by the same Wälsung who killed Fafner the dragon in battle and in all innocence found himself possessor of a ring. A ring of power and authority he doesn't even know he has." Alberich crouched higher, his hand still on Hagen's knee, still clenched, but now his mouth pressed close to Hagen's ear, so the fringes of his beard brushed the boy's face, more irritating even than the hand upon his knee. His father's breath stank.

"Valhalla and Nibelheim bow down before him," he whispered, as though he were trying to excite Hagen with the mystery of power. "I cursed that ring, you know. But him, on him the curse is powerless. Because he has no inkling of the value of the ring. He has all that power, and no idea he has it, and no ambition neither. He's burning away his life, laughing in the fires of love. There's only one solution, and that's to destroy him. Are you asleep? Hagen? Wake up, son."

"He's well on the way to his own destruction," Hagen replied. "I have him working for me towards that end."

Alberich nodded and smiled. "We must get the golden ring. By robbery if necessary. Listen, there's a woman, a very clever woman, who lives for the Wälsung's love. If she ever advised him to go to the Rhine Maidens – and trust me I know those Rhine Maidens, they once beguiled me down in the watery depths – if she persuaded him to give them back the ring, the gold would be lost and nothing we could do, however cunning, would ever get it back. So no delays, boy; you must work to get the ring. I bred you for this purpose, to stand firm fighting heroes. I wasn't strong enough to confront the dragon; he was destined only for the Wälsung – but I raised you to be fierce in hatred, so you'd avenge me, so you'd win the ring for me, and in doing so subject Wotan and the Wälsung to derision. Swear you'll do this, Hagen."

"Don't worry, dad," Hagen replied. "I'll get you the ring."

Though dawn was breaking and an early morning twilight glowing in the distant heavens, the dark clouds that had previously blocked out the moon, rendering Alberich invisible, were also closing up the sky again.

"Swear to me you'll do it."

"I've already sworn it for myself. Stop fretting."

"Loyalty, Hagen. Loyalty." Alberich had already become little more than a shadow. Now, as the clouds thickened, he was gradually disappearing deeper and deeper into the shadows. "Loyalty, my son." His voice was becoming less and less audible. "You're my son and trusty hero. Be true, Hagen. Be true!"

But he'd quite disappeared, lost in the shadows of his own darkness. Hagen still hadn't moved from his position, leaning against one of the wooden pillars of the hall of the Gibichungen, on guard in theory, in fact fast asleep again, with his arm around his spear and his shield at his side. The words "true" and "loyalty" reverberated in his head, causing him to smile. Could untruth serve truth and thereby legitimise the lie? Could loyalty be demonstrated through acts of disloyalty. Why not? If one truth was higher than another, then the higher must subordinate the lesser, and the ends would justify the means. Hagen stared, his eyes fixed and his body still, toward the Rhine, over which the light of dawn was slowly brightening.

Scene Two

Hagen fell asleep, and at least once in his sleep his body twitched in a convulsive spasm, as though some powerful force had passed in front of him. Until there, without warning, was Siegfried, stepping suddenly from behind a bush beside the riverbank, returned to his own form, though the Tarnhelm was still on his head. Now he removed the Tarnhelm and hung it on his girdle as he walked toward the Chamberlain.

"Hagen!" he called. "Wake up, sleepyhead. Did you see me coming?"

Hagen stirred himself slowly, opening first one eye, then the other.

"Greetings, Siegfried," he replied. "You're back this quickly? Where were you..."

"Brünnhilde's rock," Siegfried interrupted. He was looking well pleased with himself. "When you heard me call your name, that's where I still was, and that's how fast I was able to get back here. The other two are following more slowly by boat."

Siegfried roared with laughter. As Hagen looked behind him, seeking a boat along the Rhine somewhere, but failing to see one because they were still many, many miles away, the Rhine itself was becoming more and more deeply coloured by the glowing red of dawn.

"Are you telling me you won Brünnhilde?"

"Are you telling me Gutrune is awake?"

"Gutrune!" Hagen called into the hall. "Wake up and come outside. Siegfried's here. Come on, woman, get a move on."

Siegfried turned toward the hall, anxious for his betrothed's arrival.

"When she gets here," he said, "I'll tell you both how I overpowered Brünnhilde."

And soon enough Gutrune came out from the hall, looking radiant even though she had just woken, dressed hurriedly, had had no time to put on make-up or brush her hair a hundred times as normally she did each morning. But radiant, in Siegfried's eyes, for all that.

"Come and give me a proper welcome," he took her hands and held her close. "I have good news for you."

"I bid you welcome, noble hero, in the name of Freia who gives honour to all women."

Siegfried smiled. "Be generous and kind to him, my Gibich maid. I'm a very happy man. Today I won you for my wife."

Gutrune returned Siegfried's smile, and if it was less ardent than her lover's, perhaps this was because she'd just woken. And besides, Siegfried was here, but not the others.

"Is Brünnhilde following with my brother?" she asked.

Siegfried grinned. "She's his, if that's what you mean. He wooed her, and he won her."

"And the fire didn't scald him?"

"Oh, be sure the fire would have devoured him, had he tried to go through it. But I went through it for him. Because I wanted to win Gutrune."

"And you're unharmed?" Gutrune asked, genuinely concerned.

Siegfried laughed. "To be honest I rather enjoyed it. It was, how shall I say it, a most arousing experience. It led me to you."

"And Brünnhilde thought you were Gunther?"

"I resembled him to the last hair. The Tarnhelm did it, just as Hagen predicted."

"I always give good advice," Hagen interjected.

"And did you take the woman by force?" Gutrune wondered.

"By force, yes. But not mine, Gunther's."

"But she gave herself to you?"

"She spent her wedding night with her rightful husband."

"But rightful properly meant you."

"Siegfried was with Gutrune."

"And yet Brünnhilde was beside you."

"Between east and west," Siegfried demonstrated with his sword, "lies this much north. Brünnhilde was so near and so far."

"Then how did she come from you to Gunther?"

"When dawn came up, she followed me through the dying flames of the fire, down the misty rock to the valley. When we got close to the shore, Gunther swapped places with me. Then, using the Tarnhelm's magic powers, I wished myself here and at once arrived. A strong breeze is blowing the lovers up the Rhine. You should get ready now to receive them."

"Siegfried," Gutrune declared. "You are a man of mighty powers. You frighten me."

While they spoke, Hagen had gone down to the shore, to see if the boat was yet approaching. Now, in the distance, he could see the outline of a sail.

"They're coming," he called.

"Grant the herald thanks," Siegfried replied.

"We must prepare a proper welcome for Brünnhilde," Gutrune proposed, "to make her feel this is a place she wants to live, and where she'll be happy. Hagen, call the men together. Tell them there's to be a wedding today at the court of the Gibichungen. The women will be delighted. I myself will call them to the feast; they'll gladly attend to share our happiness." She started back inside the hall, but at the doorway turned around again. "As to you, my faithless hero, should you not rest?"

"Helping you is all the rest I need," Siegfried responded. And taking her hand in his, he followed her into the hall.

Scene Three

Hagen had climbed onto a rock above the riverbank, to watch the boat come near. As they approached, he put the cow horn to his lips and sounded it, summoning the men of Gibich urgently.

"Every man in Gibich!" he called. "Gather now. Gather quickly. Come armed. Bring weapons. Call your neighbours. Arms. Weapons. The best you have. Spit and polish them. Sharpen them for battle. Urgently. Come armed. Gather now. Gather quickly."

Once again he sounded the cow horn.

From different paths, armed vassals came rushing, at first just one man on his own, followed by another. But as the word got out, they came running in droves, until the whole Gibich race was gathering.

"Why's the alarm being sounded?"

"Who gave the call to arms?"

"We've come armed. With weapons. Hagen - what's the emergency?"

"What enemy's coming, Hagen? Who's attacking us?"

"Is Gunther in danger?"

"What's the crisis?"

Every man had brought his sharpest and most powerful weapons – swords, spears, shields.

"Where's the battle, Hagen? Where's the enemy? What's the emergency?"

Hagen stood on his rock, and struggled to avoid erupting into laughter. Men were so susceptible, so gullible. You could twist them any way you wanted, if only you knew how. First Siegfried, with a potion. Now the vassals, with a ruse.

"Get your weapons ready and don't hang about," he instructed. "I've summoned you here to provide a proper guard of honour to welcome back our hero Gunther. He's taken a wife!"

Stupid as they were, stupid enough to be tricked by such a ruse, they were far too stupid to understand that they'd been tricked.

"Yes," one cried, "but where's the crisis? Who's the enemy?"

"There is no enemy," he replied. And thought, but didn't express the thought out loud, that this may not be correct; Gunther was bringing home a Valküre, a proud and independent woman. But no enemy. "Gunther," he proclaimed, "is bringing home a wife."

But the alarm had been sounded. The men were convinced there was an enemy.

"Is her family in pursuit?" they asked.

"Has he stolen her and they're coming with arms to fetch her back?"

"No one's following Gunther," Hagen explained. "Just Brünnhilde."

"Then has he already overcome the danger? Did he win the battle? Tell us what happened."

Hagen sighed deeply, laughing inside himself at such ignorant, malleable creatures.

"The dragon-killer overcame the danger," he explained. "Siegfried the hero kept Gunther safe and brought him to his bride."

"Why did you summon us with arms then?" one of the vassals had finally twigged.

"Yes," a larger group of men echoed him. "Why did you call out the army?"

"Because we're going to need a lot of sharp swords to slaughter enough sturdy bulls to feed us all. Let's make Wotan's altar run with their blood."

The men at last understood, and raised a cheer, for Hagen, and for Gunther, and for Siegfried.

"What else should we do, Hagen? they clamoured to assist.

"What else, Hagen? What needs to be done?"

"Sacrifice a boar for Froh," Hagen instructed them, "and a prime goat for Donner. And make sure you sacrifice sheep for Fricka too, so she'll bless the marriage."

Now that they'd fully understood, the men were ready to join in the hilarity.

"Then what, Hagen?" they called out. "What else needs doing?"

"Then get your wives to fetch mead and wine and fill the drinking horns."

"Then what, Hagen? What should we do once we've got a drinking horn in hand?"

"Then what?" Hagen laughed. "You need me to tell you? Then get drinking, until you're so drunk there's not a god left in Valhalla who could claim you haven't honoured him. Then you can be sure they'll grant the couple a good marriage."

The vassals burst out in peals of laughter. "If even fierce Hagen is this happy," someone cried out, "then good luck and universal health are about to break out all along the Rhine."

This caused still more cheers to go up.

"Yes," another responded, "and as of today the hawthorn doesn't prick any more. Hagen, you're officially promoted to proclaimer of weddings!"

Hagen had tried to keep a straight face through this excessive hilarity. Now he climbed down from the rock and stood among his vassals.

"Enough laughter," he said. "You're good men, but there's serious business to attend to here. We have to prepare a proper welcome for Gunther and his bride. And here they're coming, even now, Gunther with Brünnhilde."

He pointed along the Rhine to where the boat was visible. Some of the men hastened to the high ground, while others arranged themselves along the shore to witness the arrival. Hagen approached a small group of them, clapped hands on this one's shoulders, then the next.

"Love your new mistress well," he commanded. "And give her your loyalty, your support. If she's wronged, take vengeance quickly."

He turned away, leaving them to reflect upon his words.

Soon enough the boat came fully into sight, and all along the river bank men raised their hats and waved them, cheering Gunther and his bride back into Gibichung. Those who had been looking out from the high ground come down to the shore, adding their waves and welcomes to the general greeting. Some of the men even dived into the water, to help pull the boat to land. The crowd pressed closer to the bank.

Scene Four

Gunther stepped out of the boat, leading Brünnhilde ceremoniously by the hand. Crowds of men and now women too had ranged themselves along the river bank to receive them with the honour and respect worthy of the Gibich king and his new bride.

"Welcome, Gunther," some cried, waving their hats in the air.

"Health to you and to your bride!"

"Welcome, bridegroom! Welcome, bride!"

"Welcome!"

And with the loud cries, a clattering of metal as people clashed their swords together to offer loud applause.

One by one, along the row of his most senior military and civilian officers, Gunther made formal presentation of Brünnhilde. The words he spoke, though formally addressed to her, were meant for them however: the ceremonial of introduction in the language of courtly protocol.

"Brünnhilde, fairest wife, I bring you here to the shores of the Rhine. No man ever won a nobler wife. The good grace of the gods has long shone down upon this Gibich realm, and now they've given us you. Now our race will attain the ultimate height of its fame."

Brünnhilde followed him, with pale face and downcast eyes. But the men and women of Gibichung went on saluting, revelling in their good fortune, creating a cacophony of applause with their weapons.

Gunther led Brünnhilde to the castle gate, and through it, into the hall of the Gibichungen. Not once since she'd alighted from the boat had Brünnhilde raised her eyes. So she didn't immediately see who it was who came out now to greet them: her Siegfried, but not with open arms to welcome her, his lover; rather he stood side by side next to Gutrune, attended by her women, as though this were already his home, and she his bride.

"Greetings, hero!" Gunther took Siegfried's hands in his. "Greetings, my beautiful sister." He took her hands, kissed her on each cheek. And letting one of her hands go, he took one of Siegfried's again, placed it in Gutrune's and wrapped his two hands tight around them. "I'm glad to see this man beside you," Gunther proclaimed, loudly enough that everyone could hear, "for he has won you as his wife. Two happy couples, side by side, each blessed, each radiant." He drew Brünnhilde forward, "Brünnhilde and Gunther, Gutrune and Siegfried."

Only now, hearing that name so sacred to her heart, did Brünnhilde look up, in astonishment, and see Siegfried. Where should she look, if not at him? But not in love, in joy at seeing him again; only in amazement. Gunther felt the trembling of her hand, recognised the pallor in her face, the shock in her expression. He too was amazed. The whole court, bewildered and amazed. Gunther let go her trembling hand - or perhaps it was Brünnhilde, who pulled her hand away - and looked in consternation at his bride's expression. What's wrong, some asked, and others wondered, loud enough their words were audible inside the hall, what sort of behaviour was this? Had she become deranged?

While Brünnhilde went on trembling.

Siegfried calmly took a few steps towards Brünnhilde and asked why she looked upset.

Brünnhilde was scarcely able to command herself.

"Siegfried," she stammered. "Here? Gutrune?"

"She's Gunther's younger sister," Siegfried explained, "betrothed to me, just as you are to Gunther."

"I," Brünnhilde retorted, with fearful vehemence. "To Gunther. You're a liar."

She swayed, almost staggered, looked as though she were about to faint. When she put out her arm, seeking support, Siegfried took her in his arms and held her. She shook her head, as though trying to clear confusion out of it, squeezed her eyes shut in the same manner, opening and closing them as if, somehow, the terrible vision she was seeing might yet disappear. But there was only blackness.

"The light's fading," she muttered.

Held by Siegfried, she looked up at his face, still close to fainting.

"Do you truly not recognise me?" she asked.

"Gunther," Siegfried turned to his friend and lord, "your wife is unwell."

Gunther stepped forward, unsure what exactly he should do. "Pull yourself together, woman," he ventured. "Here stands your bridegroom."

Brünnhilde didn't look at him. What she was seeing was the ring on Siegfried's outstretched finger.

"The ring!" she began, but more than that she couldn't manage. Only: "He? Siegfried?"

All around the hall, and beyond it, where men and women were gathered on the river bank and report of what was taking place inside the hall was being passed in whispers, voices wondered what she meant by this. A woman brought to wed a king, and this behaviour. No one had ever experienced the like of it.

Hagen had been outside among the crowds, and coming back into the hall now realised his help was needed.

"Silence!" he called. "Give ear to the woman. Let's hear what she has to say."

Brünnhilde tried to do as Gunther had advised, but what she'd seen had startled and unsettled her completely. Taking a deep breath, clenching her hands, she tried to restrain what was a most terrible agitation. And it wouldn't pass. For there, right there, on Siegfried's hand...

"I saw a ring on your hand," she spoke to Siegfried. "It doesn't belong to you. It was taken from me, forced from me, by another man." She pointed to Gunther. "This man. How is it possible this ring is on your finger now?"

Siegfried looked carefully at the ring.

"I didn't get this ring from him," he said.

Brünnhilde turned to Gunther. "You took this ring from me, when you forced me into marriage. Demand that he return what's yours, or give me back my pledge."

Gunther was most perplexed. "I never gave Siegfried that ring," he said. "But clearly you recognise it."

"Then where have you hidden the ring that you wrenched from my hand?"

Gunther, embarrassed and bemused, stayed silent.

Brünnhilde pointed at Siegfried. "This is the man who snatched the ring from me," she exclaimed, bursting out in anger. "This man. Siegfried. You're a thief."

Everybody looked at Siegfried, who was lost in his own thoughts as he contemplated the ring.

"No woman gave me this ring," he said, "nor was it from a woman that I acquired it. I know precisely when and where I won it. This was the prize I took at Niedholm, at the Cave of Envy, when I slew the monstrous dragon."

But just then Hagen stepped between them.

"Brünnhilde," he said. "Brave wife. Are you sure you recognise this ring. If it's the one you gave Gunther, then it belongs to him, and Siegfried must have obtained it by a trick." Hagen turned to the crowd of courtiers, gathered in the hall. "Siegfried must pay for such disloyalty," he proclaimed.

Brünnhilde responded with a shriek of the most terrible anguish. "Cheats!" she screamed. "Swindlers. Traitors. Shameful betrayal. How shall I be avenged?"

"Treachery?" asked Gutrune. "To whom?"

All the men and women of the court echoed her question.

But Brünnhilde didn't look at any particular individual. Rather, she turned her head up to the skies, and spoke directly to the immortals in Valhalla.

"You holy gods, rulers of heaven. Was this part of your divine plan? Do you want me to suffer as no one has ever suffered? Do you intend for me a shame such as no one has ever borne? Then bring me also a revenge that has no equal. Ignite in me an anger that will never abate. Let Brünnhilde's heart be broken, if that will also break the man who has betrayed her."

"Brünnhilde," Gunther implored his wife. "What are you saying? Calm down."

"Leave me alone, traitor," she pushed him away. "Self-betrayer," she added. And then, turning to the court, "Let every man and woman present know." She pointed to Siegfried. "I am not married to Gunther, but to him."

Astonishment seized the court again. Whispers of incredulity filled the hall, and rumour quickly reached the crowds outside as well. "To Siegfried?" they muttered. "She's married to Siegfried. Impossible."

But Brünnhilde was adamant. "He," she pointed again. "He forced himself on me. He made me satisfy his lust for love."

"Do you value your own name so lightly?" Siegfried responded. "Do you have so little self-respect? Your tongue utters nothing but tittle-tattle and slander. Must I accuse a woman of lying? Let any man declare that I have broken faith. I swore blood-brotherhood with Gunther, and Nothung, my worthy sword, guarded that oath of loyalty. Its blade kept me apart from this wretched woman."

"You are devious and deceitful," Brünnhilde retorted. "You call your sword to witness, but you are false. I know how sharp it is, and I also know the sheath in which it lay so peacefully against the wall – Nothung, the true friend, when its master was wed to his beloved."

Hearing this, the men and women of the court crowded together in indignation. Had Siegfried broken faith, they asked each other? Had he tainted Gunther's honour? Was he a traitor? But no one was more indignant than Gunther.

"Cast this slander back in her teeth," he commended Siegfried, "or I will be shamed, publicly disgraced."

Gutrune too, aware of the inference for her, equally indignant.

"Have you been faithless, Siegfried, false to your oath? Bear witness now. Prove that this woman accuses you unjustly."

Such was the shock at the accusation made by Brünnhilde, men and women seemed to forget protocol entirely.

"Clear your name," one called out, "if she's wronged you."

"Silence her accusations!" called another.

"He's sworn an oath," other voices called and echoed.

"I will silence her accusations," Siegfried proclaimed. "The oath is sworn already, but I will swear another. Who will give me his spear as ward and witness?"

At once, Hagen raised his spear.

"I will," he said, holding its point towards Siegfried. "Swear on this. My spear will be your witness, and it will defend your oath with honour."

The courtiers formed a circle round Siegfried and Hagen. Hagen held out his spear and Siegfried placed two fingers of his right hand on the point.

"Shining steel, sacred weapon", he uttered once again the formal liturgy. "Preserve in memory for all time this my binding oath. On this sharp spear-point I make my oath. Spear-point, you are my witness. If I am destined to die by the spear, let it be your sharpness that pierces me and ends my life; if I am destined to die now, let it be you that strikes me down, if this woman has accused me justly, if I broke faith with my brother."

This was too much for Brünnhilde. Enraged, she burst into the circle, tore Siegfried's hand away from the spear, and seized the point with her own.

"Shining steel, sacred weapon," she echoed the words Siegfried had used previously. "Preserve in memory for all time this my binding oath. On this sharp spear-point I make my oath. Spear-point, you are my witness. I dedicate your power to striking this man down. I bless the sharpness with which you'll cut him, for this man has broken every vow he ever swore, and this last one was pure perjury."

This was too much for the courtiers. Men and women called on Donner to help them, to pour down his storms and silence this monstrous disgrace. And as to Siegfried.

"Gunther," he called. "Look to your wife, who is shamelessly, scandal-mongeringly lying. She's a wild mountain woman who needs time and rest to calm her rage. Some mischievous plot or wicked demon has focused her rage on all of us." He turned to the crowd. "Go home all of you. Leave all these squabbling women. Better to make a tactical retreat when tongues start waging war." He stepped close to Gunther now, close enough to whisper in his ear. "Believe me, I'm angrier even than you that our little deception on the rock has proven less than perfect. I can only presume the Tarnhelm didn't disguise me properly. But don't worry, angry women soon calm down. Give her a little time, and no one will be more grateful that I won her for you." He turned again to the men of the court. "Go, celebrate," he called. "Cheer up and follow me. It's time to banquet." And to the women, "Come and enjoy the wedding. Lend your hands, there's much to do." One by one he put an arm around a shoulder, took a hand and steered a woman in the direction of the celebrations, charming every one of them. "Come on, ladies, time to laugh and be happy." He was determined to lead them by example. "In the hall and in the fields you'll find me the cheerleader of the cheerful today. If you believe in love, then come and share in mine. Let the happiness in my heart infect yours. Love is contagious, you know."

Exuberantly merry, Siegfried threw his arm around Gutrune and drew her away with him into the hall. The Vassals and their women, carried away by his example, followed him. Only Brünnhilde, Gunther and Hagen stayed behind. Deeply dejected, ashamed and confused, Gunther sat down at one side and hid his face.

Brünnhilde gazed sadly after Siegfried and Gutrune as they left the hall, then let her head fall.

Scene Five

Brünnhilde stood, absorbed in meditation, trying to understand what mischievous cunning was at work here, what sorcerer's magic spell had stirred up this storm. Where would she find the wisdom needed to fathom such a mystery? Where were her magic spells to undo this riddle? From joy, everything had turned to misery and disaster. She has passed all her knowledge to him, and now she had nothing left but self-pity and regret. The more she thought about her predicament, the closer her emotions came to breaking point. Because it wasn't just betrayal of love that they'd foresworn, one to the other. Circumstance had rendered her his prisoner, held in his powerful clutches, fettered in bondage to him like some piece of booty. He was rich now, a man of power and importance in the world; she could lament her disgrace to all and sundry, but he'd given her away with gay abandon, and there was no one now to offer her a sword with which to cut these shackles?

Or perhaps there was such a man. Hagen, Gunther and Gutrune's half-brother, Lord Chamberlain of the Gibichung king. He certainly looked honest, and sincere, coming over to her now and offering her his counsel.

"Trust me," he said, and if not him, who else was there to trust? And if he was whispering, wasn't that wise considering what he had to say? "You've been cheated and mistreated," he pronounced each word with the contempt it rightfully deserved. "I will take vengeance on your betrayer."

"On whom?" Brünnhilde asked, looking around wearily.

"On Siegfried who's betrayed you," Hagen replied.

Brünnhilde smiled bitterly. "On Siegfried? You? One look from his flashing eyes would turn your greatest courage to fear. Even I was fooled by it, when it fell on me, through his deceitful disguise there on the rock."

"But he swore his perjury on my spear," Hagen reminded her.

"Truth and falsehood, faithful oaths and perjuries – they're all just empty words. You'll need something stronger than words to sharpen your spear on if you're going to defeat that champion."

"I know how great a warrior he is," Hagen replied, "and that he'll be hard to kill in battle. So you must advise me. How may I overcome this hero?"

"What a thankless, shameless reward to have received for loving somebody," Brünnhilde lamented. "I have no skill, no magic spell, nothing that hasn't served to protect his life. Without his even knowing it, the magic that brought him to me also protects him against wounds. I can do nothing."

"Is there no weapon that can hurt him?" Hagen asked.

"Not in battle, no" she replied. "But if he were taken from behind...Not that he would ever turn his back upon an enemy, or run away, or even show his back. That's why I withheld my spells there."

"And there," Hagen declared, "my spear will strike." He turned quickly to Gunther. "Stand up, Gunther. Noble Gibichung. Here stands your brave wife – why are you wallowing in misery?"

Gunther started up passionately. "I'm shamed and disgraced," he said. "I'm the most wretched of men."

"Wretched I can't say," Hagen replied. "But shamed. Yes. That's where things lie."

"You're a coward," Brünnhilde reproached him, "and a false friend. You hid behind a hero, so he would win the prize of prizes for you. When a family sires such faint-hearts as you, truly they've sunk to the bottom of the pit."

It hardly needed Brünnhilde to say all this; Gunther was already beside himself with desperation.

"I've cheated and been cheated," he said. "Betrayed and been betrayed. Now let my bones be crushed and my heart broken. Help me, Hagen. Help me for the sake of my honour. Help me for the sake of our mother, for she bore you as well as me."

"No brain can help you here, Gunther, however clever; nor any hand. The only remedy is – Siegfried's death."

"Siegfried's death," Gunther repeated, gripped with fear.

"Nothing else redeems your shame."

Gunther stared in front of him.

"We swore blood-brotherhood together."

"Then the breaking of that oath must be atoned in blood."

"But did he break the oath?" Gunther asked.

"Yes," Hagen replied, "when he betrayed you."

"Did he betray me?" Gunther wondered.

"Yes," Brünnhilde responded. "Siegfried betrayed you, and now you're all betraying me. If life were just, all the blood in the world wouldn't wipe out your collective guilt. But let this one death suffice for everything. Siegfried shall die to expiate the sins of the whole world."

"His death," Hagen whispered privately to Gunther, "will be your salvation. Gunther, you'll have enormous power if you can just obtain that ring, and death alone will enable you to do so."

"Brünnhilde's ring?" Gunther asked, uncomprehendingly.

"It's the Nibelung's ring," Hagen explained.

Gunther sighed deeply, but finally nodded his head. "Let this be the end of Siegfried," he decided.

"We'll all benefit from this death," Hagen reassured him.

"But what of Gutrune?" Gunther asked. "I've just given her Siegfried for a husband. If we punish her husband like this, how will we ever face her?"

Brünnhilde was furious at these words.

188

"What has wisdom taught me?" she wondered. "What have I read in the signs and omens? This. In the helplessness of my misery I now understand," her voice rose to a new height of passion as she said, "Gutrune is the sorceress who enticed my husband away. Let terror strike her!"

"Siegfried's death will leave Brünnhilde distraught," Hagen suggested to Gunther. "So let the deed be done in secret. Tomorrow morning we'll set off with a hunting party. In his enthusiasm our hero will rush on ahead to capture the first boar. Perhaps a wild one'll be the end of him."

"So let it be," Gunther agreed. "Let Siegfried die this way."

They looked to Brünnhilde for confirmation. Brünnhilde nodded her assent.

"So let it be," she echoed Gunther's words. "Let Siegfried die this way."

"So he will pay for the disgrace he's brought on each of us," Gunther concluded.

"And the shame of his crime will be expiated," Brünnhilde added.

So the three stood, agreed and committed to their plan, Brünnhilde in full trust of their support and their complicity. But in his heart Hagen was singing a very different song, a song of triumph and of deep ambition. Now, he knew, the prize was within his grasp. Soon, very soon, he would have it in his hand, to hold for ever. From Siegfried's hand he himself would take the ring. So, in thought, he turned to Alberich his father, the fallen prince, the night-watchman, the lord of the Nibelungen, and spoke as if in prayer: "Look at me, Alberich. The time has come to summon once again the Nibelungen hoards. Call them to obedience, Lord of the Ring!"

His face remained impassive however, or showed only such emotion as was fitting to the words that Gunther and Brünnhilde spoke.

"He has betrayed an oath of loyalty," were Gunther's words.

"He has broken his holy vows," were Brünnhilde's.

"And now," they made an oath together, "let him atone with his own blood. All-seeing god of vengeance, guardian of oaths and lord of vows, Wotan, look down on us. Summon the awe-inspiring hosts of heaven to hear this oath of vengeance."

Gunther turned impetuously towards the hall. Brünnhilde followed him. But even as they went in, they met the bridal procession coming out. Boys and girls, waving branches of flowers, leaped joyously in front. Men carried Siegfried on a shield, and Gutrune beside him on a seat. On the rising ground behind them, serving men and women carried the implements and animals for sacrifice by various mountain paths towards the altars, which others had adorned with flowers. Siegfried and the Vassals sounded the wedding-call upon their horns.

Seeing her, the women invited Brünnhilde to accompany them to Gutrune's side. Brünnhilde stared blankly at Gutrune, who beckoned her with a friendly smile. As Brünnhilde was about to step back impetuously, Hagen stepped in and forced her towards Gunther, who seized her by the hand, and then allowed himself to be raised on a shield by the Vassals. And thus the procession, scarcely interrupted, began its journey towards the high ground.

Act Three

Scene One

The waters of the Rhine flowed between steep cliffs in the shadows of the Drachensberg mountains. At a certain point, a little upstream from what is now the town of Würms, the river opened on a wild and woody, rocky valley, and here the three Rhine Maidens - Woglinde, Wellgunde and Flosshilde - came up to the surface of the flowing water and swam in circles, as if in a dance, and paused, and sang. Their hymn was not of joy but mourning and lugube. They sang in honour of Dame Sun, who had once poured down her beams of light over the created world; but now it was darkness once again that covered the whole face of the deep. They sang of the past and faded glory of the sun's rays, when they were brightened by their father's gold that glistened there, safe and majestic. Ah, the Rhinegold, that shining gold, how brightly it once gleamed, the noble star of the deep. But gone now. Lost.

So they resumed their swimming, dancing as though around the rock that had once enthroned the gold. And as they danced they sang. "Weialala. Weialala" – an echo of the name, 'Woeful', that Siegmund once gave himself. But the woe was theirs, not his.

Suddenly, out of the distance, a horn call made them stop. They listened intently, each acknowledging to the other her recognition of the sound. They had waited for this for almost an eternity. And now, now they were hearing it, at last. Joyously they resumed their splashing about in the water. Joyously they resumed their singing. But it was a different hymn now, a chant of hope, calling on Dame Sun to send them a hero who would give them back their gold. Let it be theirs, they cried, and they would no longer envy the sun's bright eye. Rhinegold, shining gold, how gladly it would gleam then, the free star of the deep.

The horn they'd heard in the heights belonged to Siegfried.

"Can you hear?" Woglinde called.

"He's coming," Wellgunde answered.

"Let's make a plan," Flosshilde advised.

Quickly, the three Rhine Maidens dived down into the rushing water, as Siegfried appeared on the cliff above them, fully armed. He seemed angry, somewhat crazed, shouting out loud as though he were scolding somebody, some servant who was carrying his bags, some dwarf who'd failed to forge a sword correctly. But he was actually alone.

"Some elf has led me astray," he moaned, "and now I've lost the path.

Hey, you," he shouted down to one of the three Rhine Maidens, "you, you little beggar. Tell me in which of these mountains you've hidden my quarry?"

The three Rhine Maidens surfaced again as if in a dance, and called out Siegfried's name.

"What are you grumbling about?" Flosshilde asked.

"Which elf are you so cross with?" Wellgunde teased.

"Or maybe some troll's been teasing you? Woglinde suggested.

"Tell us, Siegfried," they called out as one. "Speak to us."

Siegfried looked at them and smiled.

"Is it you then," he enquired, "who enticed my shaggy companion into getting lost? Is he your sweetheart now? In which case, I leave him to you."

The Rhine Maidens laughed loudly.

"What would you give us," Woglinde asked, "if we were to reveal your quarry?"

"I haven't caught a thing today," Siegfried replied, "so name your price."

"You have a golden ring glinting on your finger," Wellgunde pointed.

"Give us that," all three asked him at once.

"I slew a monstrous dragon to obtain this ring," Siegfried responded. "Must I now exchange it for a wretched bearskin?"

"Are you that stingy?" Woglinde teased.

"Miserly, and mean," Wellgunde taunted.

"When a man's out shopping for women," Flosshilde added, "Generosity's the key."

"If I spend my money on you," Siegfried retorted, "I rather think my wife would not be pleased."

"Is she a shrew?" Flosshilde asked.

"Does she beat you?" Wellgunde wondered.

"Maybe you've already had a touch too many?" Woglinde laughed.

And the others laughed with her, loud guffaws of raucous laughter, as though nothing but joy had ever been their habit, as though nothing quite so funny as this had ever been thought or said.

"Go on," Siegfried pouted, "laugh all you like. But I promise you I'll leave you miserable. Crave this ring all you want, you'll never win it from me with mockery."

Once again the Rhine Maidens joined hands and resumed their dance.

"Isn't he handsome," Flosshilde sang.

"And such muscles," Wellgunde sighed.

"What girl could resist him?" Woglinde teased.

"What a pity he's so stingy!" they all called out together, and laughed, and dived down underneath the foam again.

Siegfried climbed down towards the water's edge, wondering how to respond to their grudging compliments, and why he'd let himself be so insulted? If they came back to the water's edge, he decided, he would let them have the ring.

"Hey! Hey!" he called loudly to them. "Water maidens! Come quickly and I'll give you the ring."

He drew the ring from his finger and held it out towards them. The three Rhine Maidens surfaced again. Their faces were grave and solemn.

"Best keep the ring," Flosshilde told him. "Keep it, and look after it well, until you understand the peril…"

"…of possessing it," Wellgunde and Woglinde finished their sister's sentence for her.

"Then you'll be well pleased to let us free you from its curse."

Siegfried calmly put the ring back on his finger.

"Reveal what you know," he ordered them.

"Siegfried!" each of them called out at the same time, as though each had something of significance to say. "An evil destiny we see." But it was Wellgunde who was granted precedence by her sisters.

"You wear the ring at your peril," she explained.

"It was fashioned…" Woglinde interrupted.

"…from the pure gold of the Rhine," Flosshilde finished the phrase for her.

And now all three were speaking at once, so that Siegfried really couldn't follow anything, let alone understand a word of it. But got the gist.

"The one who cleverly forged it…" Wellgunde said.

"…and shamefully lost it…" Woglinde added.

"…laid a curse on it," Woglinde and Wellgunde spoke together.

"…that forever brings death to he who wears it," the triple chorus sang for once in harmony.

"Just as you slew the dragon," Flosshilde spoke as if delivering an oracle.

"…so will you be killed as well," Wellgunde's voice echoed her sisters.

"This very day," the three saying it together made it appear so much more certain.

"So now we prophesy. If you will not give us the ring…"

"…to sleep forever in the deepest waters of the Rhine…"

They didn't say what, but their voices portended something dark and inconsolable, something too great for one man to allow.

"Only the flowing waters of the Rhine can wash away the curse!"

"Enough!" Siegfried held up his hand as though to hold off their barrage. "You're wily and cunning women, but hold your peace now! I wasn't persuaded by your flattery and your threats impress me even less."

"Siegfried!" Woglinde called, and Wellgunde too, "Siegfried!"

"We speak the truth," Flosshilde insisted.

"Turn, Siegfried!" Woglinde implored him.

"Turn from the curse," Wellgunde beseeched.

"This curse," Flosshilde explained, "was woven in the dead of night, night after night, woven by the Norns whose task it is to weave the rope of elemental law."

Now it was Siegfried's turn to scoff. "My sword," he told them, "once severed a spear. And Nothung will sever your elemental law and its unending rope if those Norns try to weave their curses into it. It's true though, a dragon once warned me that the ring was cursed – a dragon who couldn't even teach me fear." He contemplated the ring. "With this ring I've acquired possession of the world," he proclaimed. "But I'd give it up gladly for the gift of love; I'd give it to you Rhine Maidens in exchange for your gift of love. But when you threaten my limbs and my life – though they're worth less than a finger to me – still you won't get the ring. As for that life and these limbs, see" he picked up a clod of earth from the ground, held it above his head, and tossed it behind him. "See? I would throw them away as easily as that."

"Quick, sisters!" cried Wellgunde. "Get away from this madman."

"He thinks himself wise and strong," Flosshilde whispered to Woglinde, but Woglinde wasn't listening.

"He thinks himself wise and strong," she tried again with Wellgunde, who nodded, took her hand, bad her swim away.

"But he behaves like a captive and a blind man," Flosshilde was still trying to explain this unprecedented phenomenon that was Siegfried. But Wellgunde just wanted to get away. She held her sister's hand even tighter, dragged her away. So they swam, wildly excited, making wide circles until they reached the shore.

"He's sworn oaths," Flosshilde still wasn't done, "but he doesn't keep them."

Wellgunde was pulling her arm so hard it could have come out of its socket.

"He knows mysteries and yet he pays no heed to them." Wellgunde had had enough of this. But Flosshilde wasn't finished.

"A glorious possession was granted to him…" she began again.

"A glorious possession was granted to him…" Wellgunde echoed her sister, hoping in this manner to persuade her to shut up. But Flosshilde looked at her, and suddenly Wellgunde realised that her sister wasn't simply serious, but prophesying. Frivolity had cost them dear with Alberich. Frivolity might cost them dear again with Siegfried. Suddenly her anger and her impiety were gone, and in its place the Rhine Maiden reassumed her dignity.

"A glorious possession was granted to him…" she agreed.

The three sisters looked at each other, then spoke in unison:

"And he doesn't even realise he's lost it".

"Only the ring…" Flosshilde began.

"…which will bring about his death," Wellgunde completed the sentence for her.

"He'll never surrender the ring," the sisters said together.

"Farewell, Siegfried."

"A proud woman will inherit your wealth today. She'll give us a better audience. Let's go to her."

Saying this, they turned back quickly to their dance, swimming leisurely out of Siegfried's sight along the Rhine. Siegfried watched them swim away, and smiled. Then he placed one foot on a piece of rock upon the shore and stood, with his chin resting on his hand. The song of the Rhine Maidens played in the wind and the air. "La weiala, la lei wallala," they ululated, their voices becoming more distant. "Leia la, leia la". Until they were gone.

So on water, as on land, Siegfried told himself, he'd learned the ways of women. He who dares defy their flattery will have to endure their threats. And then if he defies their threats, he gets their scolding tongue instead. And yet – even as they disappeared into the distance and their song became little more than susurration on the wind, still their fragrance lingered, and the aftertaste was on his tongue. If it hadn't been for Gutrune's trust, the troth he'd plighted to her, why he could easily have seduced any one of these gorgeous women.

Siegfried gazed yearningly after them. But they were gone, their voices still audible, but now from far away. Up above, another sound was coming closer, the bellowing of hunting horns. And Hagen's voice, calling for Siegfried. The horns sounded closer and still closer. Siegfried started from a dreamy reverie, and answered the call with his own horn.

Scene Two

The voices of the men of Gibichung reached Siegfried where he stood upon that rock above the Rhine, watching the Rhine Maidens vanish. He called and waited to see who would appear. It was Hagen, above him on the cliff.

"At last we've discovered where you've been hiding," Hagen's voice was duplicitous with friendliness. But Siegfried had come to trust his friend.

"Come down," he called. "It's fresh and cool here by the river."

Large numbers of men had followed Hagen and Gunther to the cliff, so it was a great crowd that now descended to the river.

"This is as good a place as any to rest and cook a meal," Hagen announced. "Put down the game you've caught and bring out the wineskins and the drinking horns."

Such little game as had been caught was set down on the rock. Hagen looked at Siegfried, then at Gunther and the other men, an expression of resigned disappointment on his face.

"I'm afraid Siegfried scared most of the game away," he added, laughing. "So we'll have to make do with his tales of his own success."

Siegfried laughed. "I'm so ill prepared for a meal," he answered, "I shall have to beg some of your food."

"You killed nothing?" Hagen asked.

"I went hunting for forest game," Siegfried recounted, "but the only thing I found was waterfowl. If I'd been properly warned in advance, I'd have had three wild water birds for you in my bag."

Hagen and Gunther were perplexed. What on earth was he hinting at?

"Down there, along the Rhine," Siegfried continued, "they told me I'll be murdered today."

Gunther started and looked darkly at Hagen. Siegfried lay down on the bank, between the half-brothers.

"It would be a poor hunt indeed," said Hagen, "if the lurking beast were to catch the hunter, and not the hunter catch the beast."

"I'm thirsty," Siegfried said, and reached out for the drinking horn that Hagen had filled and was now offering to him.

"I've heard it said," Hagen observed, "that Siegfried understands the language of birdsong. Can that be true?"

"It's been a long time since I paid any attention to their twittering," Siegfried replied, taking the drinking horn and drinking deep. Then he turned and offered it to Gunther.

"Drink, Gunther, drink. Your brother offers you a drink."

Gunther looked into the horn with terror written on his face.

"It's too thin and pale," he said, and then, more gloomily even than his first remark, "the only thing that I can see in it is Siegfried's blood."

Siegfried laughed, thinking this was just, perhaps, a jest. "Then let's mix our drink and blood together," he ventured.

Siegfried poured ale from Gunther's horn into his own until it overflowed. Then he raised his horn to offer up a toast.

"Now that it's mixed, the cup runs over. Let it serve as a libation for good Mother Earth."

"You're much too happy," Gunther sighed deeply.

Siegfried was perplexed. "Is Brünnhilde giving you trouble?" he asked, in a low voice.

"I wish Gunther understood her as well as Siegfried understands birdsong," Hagen replied, his voice equally low.

"Now that I've heard the song of women," Siegfried answered, "I've quite forgotten the song of birds."

"But you did understand them once?" asked Hagen.

Siegfried turned, animated, towards Gunther, aware that his blood-brother was in a most miserable mood.

"Would it cheer you up to hear some stories of my boyhood?" he asked.

"It would," Gunther replied, and Hagen too urged Siegfried to recount. So they, and many of the other men, made beds along the grassy bank, and lay down close to Siegfried, who alone sat upright.

"I was raised," Siegfried began, "By a bad-tempered dwarf, whose name was Mime. Hatred had driven him to make me strong enough to kill a dragon for him, one that lazily guarded a treasure in the forest. He taught me smithing and metal smelting, but the one job the craftsman couldn't do, this bold apprentice had to do himself. The fragments of a broken sword had to be worked anew. It was my father's weapon, and I forged it afresh. I made Nothung as hard as nails. The dwarf judged it fit for battle, and took me into the forest, where I killed Fafner the dragon. Then something strange happened. The dragon's blood burned my fingers and I put them to my mouth to cool them. My tongue had hardly touched them when the birds started to sing and I immediately understood them. One sat on a branch and sang:

"'Hey, Siegfried now owns the Nibelung treasure. He'll find it in the cave. If he wants to take the Tarnhelm it'll help him work wonders. And if he can get the ring, that will make him master of the world.'"

"Did you take away the ring and Tarnhelm?" Hagen interrupted.

"Did you hear the bird again?" one of the men enquired.

"I picked up the ring and Tarnhelm and then listened again to that wonderful warbler. It sat in the trees and sang:

"'Siegfried now has the helm and the ring. He mustn't trust Mime who is treacherous. He only wants to steal the treasure and is slyly lurking, waiting for Siegfried whose life he's after. Oh, Siegfried mustn't trust Mime.'

"Was this good advice?" Hagen interrupted again.

"Did you settle scores with Mime?" another of the men asked.

"Mime came to me with a drink made of poison. But he was full of fear, and stammering, and gave the game away. Nothung dispatched the wretch!"

Hagen chuckled coarsely. "What he couldn't forge, Mime could still taste!" he laughed.

"What did the bird say next?" some of the men asked.

In the meanwhile, Hagen had taken another drinking horn and filled it, squeezing the juices of a herb into it when Siegfried wasn't looking.

"Drink some more, Siegfried," he offered the horn. "Then tell us the rest of your tale. I've mixed it well for you and it'll awaken your memory properly. You won't forget what's past once you've drunk this."

He handed the horn to Siegfried, who looked thoughtfully into it, and drank slowly, gazing at the treetops again in sorrow, and listening.

"There sat the bird," he resumed, "singing that Siegfried had killed the evil dwarf and could now be told of the most marvellous woman. 'She's asleep high on a rock,' the bird sang, 'and a fire burns around her home. If he can walk through the fire and wake the bride, then Brünnhilde will be his.'"

"Did you take the bird's advice?" Hagen wondered.

Gunther had been listening with growing amazement throughout the tale. But now, hearing Siegfried speak about Brünnhilde, something even deeper than amazement caused him to sit up. How would this end, this tale, this blood-brotherhood? And what had Hagen mixed in Siegfried's drink.

"I set off without delay," Siegfried was telling, "until I reached the fiery rock. The flames were nothing. I walked through them and there was my reward. Even as I saw her, I found myself sinking more and more into a state of ecstasy. A marvellous woman, sound asleep, clothed in shining armour. I took the helmet off this glorious maiden and awoke her with a daring kiss. But now true flames engulfed me. I seemed to be burning as I was enfolded in the beautiful Brünnhilde's arms."

This was too much for Gunther. He jumped to his feet, shocked by what he was hearing. But to what end? He had no idea. Simply he stood there, amazed, transfixed. And terrified.

At that precise moment, two ravens flew up from a bush, circled over Siegfried's head, and took wing towards the Rhine.

"Do you understand the cry of the ravens?" Hagen asked.

Siegfried jumped up and looked after the ravens, turning his back towards Hagen.

Then Hagen saw the only opportunity he might ever have. And seized it.

"Vengeance, they cry to me!" he exclaimed, and plunged his spear deep into Siegfried's back.

Gunther and the other men rushed towards Hagen, but it was too late.

The wounded Siegfried swung his shield on high with both his hands, as though to smash it down on Hagen. But his strength failed him. The shield fell backward and, with a crash, he himself fell down on top of it.

Four men, who had tried in vain to restrain Hagen, cried out in desperation at what the Chamberlain had done. Others simply cried out in their consternation, muttering incoherently, unable to raise an accusation to their lips. It was horrifying.

"Speak naught!" Hagen instructed them, and pointed at the body that lay prostrate on the ground. "I have punished falsehood as falsehood merits punishment."

Saying this, he turned calmly aside and walked, alone, out of sight over the cliff. Gunther and the men watched, stupefied. But none dared to pursue him. Slowly he walked away through the twilight that had begun to fall at the moment when the ravens first appeared.

Gunther bent down, stricken with grief, at Siegfried's side. The other men stood sympathetically around the dying man. Then two stooped down to help Siegfried, who was trying to sit up. His eyes were open radiantly.

"Brünnhilde," he spoke the name so gently, looking into the void beyond, that several turned to follow his gaze, convinced that she was actually standing there. "My holy bride, awaken now," he stretched out his hand, as though to touch her. "Who has put you back to sleep? Who has bound you in this fearful slumber? Your awakener came and kissed you awake, and when the bride's bonds were broken, Brünnhilde's joy smiled on him. Ah, those eyes, opened forever! Ah, that wonderful breath!" But his own breath was intermittent now. Each word was an agony. "Leaving is sweet, trembling blissful." His fingers trembled indeed, in one last effort to reach her outstretched hand. And then his arm fell to his side. One more time he tried to raise it, but the effort was too much. Only the corners of his mouth rose up the merest trace, answering her smile. "Brünnhilde offers me her greeting!"

But there was no one there. Only his imagination, hallucinating from the poison Hagen had made him drink, and the anguish of the spear wound in his back.

The pain was too much for him. He fell back on the ground, and Gunther could see his friend was dead. The men stood over him in sorrow. But no one moved.

Scene Three

Night had fallen. At Gunther's mute command, the men raised Siegfried's corpse onto his shield and slowly, in solemn procession, carried it away over the rocky high ground. Gunther followed, a small distance behind the corpse. The moon was breaking through the clouds, illuminating the funeral procession more and more brightly as it approached ever closer to the summit. A mist rose from the Rhine, gradually filling the whole valley, climbing too, as though it too had joined the sad cortège delivering Siegfried's body. Over the steep mountain ridge they walked, the men taking turns to carry Siegfried's shield. Until they reached the other side and, as the mist gradually dispersed, there was the Gibichung palace, nestling peacefully on the banks of the Rhine.

Moonlight reflected on the river. Gutrune had come out of her chamber and into the hall, thinking she'd heard Siegfried's horn sounding in the distance. She listened intensely, but no, he still hadn't come home. Nightmares had disturbed her sleep, or one mare in particular, Siegfried's magnificent horse Grane, which was neighing wildly in her dreams. Then Brünnhilde's laughter had awoken her. Was that Brünnhilde she could see now, walking to the river-bank? She was afraid of Brünnhilde. But perhaps it wasn't her; perhaps she was still inside. Gutrune listened at the door and called out softly:

"Brünnhild! Brünnhild! Are you awake?"

She opened the door timidly and looked into the inner room. It was empty, so it must have been Brünnhilde whom she saw walking by the Rhine. She shuddered, listening again to the sound of a distant horn. Was that his horn? No, someone else's. Or nobody's. Just her imagination, hearing what she longed to hear. The whole world was deserted; she must be imagining it. She looked anxiously out. If only Siegfried would come soon. She started to go back to her chamber, but then she heard the voice of Hagen, coming nearer. So she paused, stood motionless for some time, gripped with fear.

Hagen's voice came nearer.

"Wake up!" he was calling. "Wake up! Wake up! Bring torches, bright torches."

So she'd been correct when she thought she heard a horn. The men were coming back, bringing home the spoils of the hunt. The light from glowing torches showed nothing specific though. Just men, arriving. Carrying whatever it was men carried when they came home from the hunt. Dead meat, borne on the biers of their shields.

"Gutrune!" Hagen called out as he entered the great hall. "Gutrune, rise and welcome Siegfried. The mighty hero is coming home!"

But something in his voice alarmed her.

"What's happened?" she asked, gripped with fear

It wasn't Siegfried's horn she'd heard. It wasn't Siegfried's horn. What could it mean?

Men and women were rushing about in great confusion, with lights and flaming torches, joining the procession that was returning with the spoils of the hunt. Gunther was amongst them. Something in his face alarmed her too.

"I didn't hear Siegfried's horn," she said.

"The hero's pale and can't blow his horn now," Hagen replied. "He can't go off hunting or to battle now. And he can't pay court to lovely women."

Gutrune understood. But wouldn't allow that understanding to rise into her consciousness.

"What is it they're bringing?" she asked, with mounting horror.

The procession halted in the centre of the hall, where the men set down the corpse upon a hastily erected dais.

"They have a wild boar's victim," Hagen's composure only made the horror worse. How could he, how could he be so calm, if what she knew was true was indeed true?

"Is it – Siegfried?"

"Yes, Siegfried, Gutrune's dead husband!"

Gutrune shrieked, and threw herself upon the corpse. All around, the hall was filled with men and women, shocked and grieving. Gunther had arrived now, searching for his sister, determined he would be the one to tell her. But it was too late. There she lay, faint, collapsed rather, stretched out across her husband's body. What could he say or do now? Perhaps implore her to open her eyes and speak to him. But it was no use.

At length Gutrune came to herself again, and looked up, ready now to confront the horror of Siegfried's death. Gunther, her brother who'd brought this destiny upon her, Gunther was leaning over her, trying to console her. But she pushed him away, violently pushed him away from her. She hardly knew what she was doing. Words were coming from her lips unsummoned, calling him faithless brother, accusing him of murdering her husband. Her hands were thrashing at his body.

"They've killed Siegfried," she cried.

"Direct your lament to him," Gunther wasn't looking at her, but at his half-brother, "not to me. He's the cursed boar who gored this noble man!"

But Hagen was impassive.

"Are you angry with me?" he enquired, as though he were being accused of drinking too much mead, or tearing some unimportant fragment of her bridal gown.

"I curse you!" Gutrune exclaimed. "May you know only fear and bad luck forever!"

Then Hagen stepped forward, his face defiant. "Yes, I killed Siegfried," he said, and truthfully he sounded proud of it. "I, Hagen, struck him dead. He was stabbed by the very spear on which he perjured himself. He was my rightful victim and I've now claimed him." He turned to Gunther. "And for this act he now demands the ring!"

"Stand back, Hagen," Gunther ordered. "What has fallen to me, you will never take."

Hagen called on the men to support his action. But no one moved.

"Will this shameless son of an elf touch Gutrune's legacy?" Gunther demanded.

Hagen drew his sword. "It's an elf's legacy, and yes, I will take it."

He rushed forward toward Gunther. But Gunther had anticipated this, and quickly drew his own sword, stood ready to defend himself. And how they fought! Men tried to throw themselves between the brothers, to separate them, but in vain. First one sword-thrust, then another. Gunther advancing upon Hagen, Hagen turning the tide back against Gunther. A cut. A graze. But then a blow. And it was Gunther, Gunther who was lying dead, felled by a stroke of Hagen's sword.

Gutrune shrieked as Gunther fell. Women shrank back in terror. Men stood motionless. But Hagen lunged for the ring and grasped at Siegfried's hand, ready to slice the finger off if necessary. But the finger raised itself menacingly. Terrified, Hagen stepped back.

And then, through the crowd of men and women, Brünnhilde's voice was heard, firm and solemn.

"Cease this wailing!" she called out to them. "Cease this woeful clamour."

Lost still in the crowd, few could see her. But all heard her, even Hagen, who stood silent now, gazing at that finger.

"You've all betrayed this woman who has come here for her vengeance," Brünnhilde spoke with such authority that all were bowed. "His wife," she emerged now from behind the throne, her arm raised towards Gutrune. "I've heard you whining like children for their mothers when milk's been spilled. But not a lament befitting the noblest of heroes."

Gutrune raised herself from the ground and faced her.

"You're soured by jealousy," she cried. "You brought this tragedy on us. You turned the men against him. Woe that you ever came near this house."

"Stay silent, poor wretch!" Brünnhilde replied. "You've never been his true wife – only his whore. I was his lawful wife. Siegfried swore eternal loyalty to me long before he set eyes on you, Gutrune."

It was true too, Gutrune knew it now. But o, what misery. Brünnhilde was the beloved that the drink made him forget. And Hagen. Hagen.

"You!" she thrust her arm toward him like a sword. "You suggested the drug that took away her husband."

She was broken now, reduced utterly to despair. And shamed, shamed for her part in this travesty. Turning timidly away from Siegfried, she bent over Gunther's dying body, motionless now, and as it seemed, for ever. But Hagen stood defiantly, leaning on his spear and shield, sunk in deep thought, on the other side of his half-brother. And Brünnhilde, alone in the centre of the throng, gazing absorbed in contemplation of Siegfried's face, at first profoundly shocked. But soon she too was overwhelmed by desperation. Except. Except that this was Brünnhilde, Wotan's daughter, an immortal by birth, not some cringing, weeping woman. As she had been Brünnhilde when Siegmund faced Hunding, as she had been Brünnhilde when her father came to condemn her, so she was still Brünnhilde now. In solemn exaltation, she turned now to the men and women, took command of herself by taking command of them, gave instruction for the funeral, ordered them to pile up stout logs along the banks of the Rhine.

"The fire on which the noble body of this great hero burns shall blaze high and bright," she declared. "Bring me my horse, which shall follow the warrior with me. The hero's sacred honour is to be shared. My own body craves it."

So the younger men began to erect an enormous pyre in front of the hall beside the Rhine. Women went to their homes, and came back with rugs to adorn it, spices and flowers to scatter on it. Again Brünnhilde stood lost in contemplation of the dead man's face, speaking to any who would listen of this wondrous man whom she had known. Her face gradually became transfigured with tenderness and light as she described how his radiance had shone on her like purest sunlight.

"He was most pure," she told them, "and yet he betrayed me. He cheated his wife, but he was loyal to his friend. And from his own beloved – his only love – he kept apart with his sword. No truer man than he ever swore an oath; no more loyal man than he ever made a bargain. No more honest man ever fell in love. And yet," the conflict of emotions in her ran so deep it was impossible to remain coherent, "and yet, all his oaths, all his bargains, his truest love, he betrayed as no one ever did. Does anybody know why this was so?"

No one could answer. Only they could stare at this remarkable young woman, and empathise with her in her grief and her confusion.

Looking upward, Brünnhilde called on her father, Wotan, Wälse, Wanderer, father of War, the solemn guardian of oaths on high, to turn his glance toward her welling sorrow and recognise his eternal guilt.

"Majestic god," she cried, "you must hear my complaint. By the hero's bravest action, which you, the god, desired, he was caught up in the ruinous curse of the ring. And I, I had to be betrayed by this pure one in order to become wise. Do you think I know now the needs of the god? Everything is known to me, everything has become clear. I can hear the flapping wings of your ravens. I send them home with news, both feared and desired."

Waving her own arms as though to shoo the lazy ravens from the hall, she signalled to the men to lift Siegfried's body onto the pyre. At the same moment she drew the ring from off his finger, and gazed at it. The ring. The cursed ring.

"The god should be at peace now," she resumed her private dialogue with her father. "My legacy I have accepted for myself. But this accursed ring, this terrible ring! I seize its gold and now give it away. Thank you, wise sisters of the depths – the Rhine's swimming daughters – for your sound advice. What you desire I shall give you. Claim it yourselves from my ashes. The fire that burns me will cleanse the curse from the ring. Those in the water will dissolve it and carefully preserve the bright gold that was vilely stolen from them."

Brünnhilde put on the ring, then turned to the pile of logs that formed the pyre on which Siegfried's corpse lay stretched, a pile of logs as large if not as old as those that Wotan had gathered from the sacred ash tree. Then she snatched a torch from one of the men and, waving the firebrand and pointing to the mountains in the background, bad the ravens to fly home.

"Tell your master what you heard by the Rhine," she instructed them. "You'll travel past Brünnhilde's rock, where another fire's still blazing. Send Loge to Valhalla, for the end of the gods is now approaching. Thus do I throw the torch at Valhalla's proud fortress."

She hurled the torch onto the woodpile, which quickly broke out into flames. Two ravens flew up from the rock on the shore and disappeared into the mountains.

Then Brünnhilde saw her horse, Grane, which two young men had just led in. She sprang toward him, seized him, quickly removed his bridle. She bent affectionately toward him and spoke lovingly to him, asking if he knew where she would take him?

"Your master lies there," she stroked his face and neck, "shining in the fire – Siegfried, our glorious hero."

Grane neighed, and threw up his head.

"Are you neighing because you're eager to follow your friend? Are you drawn towards him by the laughing flames? My breast burns too. Bright fire has seized my heart. I'm longing to embrace him, Grane, to be clasped by him, and united in infinite love. Heiajoho! Grane!" Brünnhilde cried out exultantly as she mounted the horse. "Greet your master now. Siegfried! Siegfried! Blissfully, your wife greets you!"

And saying this, she dug her heels into the horse's flanks, and pulled his mane. So Grane leaped, with a single bound, into the burning pyre. Immediately, the flames blazed up so high they filled the whole square before the hall, and it seemed as if they too had been set on fire. Men and women fled away from it in terror.

Scene Four

The whole world appeared to be filled with flames: the logs on Siegfried's pyre and those that Wotan had gathered in the hall of the heroes in Valhalla. Siegfried's pyre wouldn't burn forever though. Soon enough the fire-light died down and only a cloud of smoke was left, drifting towards the river where it lay on the horizon like a dark bank of cloud. But the fire had affected the river too, causing it to flare up in the way that only rivers can, bubbling and flowing like the flaming torrent of a geyser. The Rhine had been transformed into a pyre of water, in which the lovely maidens of the Rhinegold would surely drown, if nothing happened to abate them. Faster and more furiously did the waters surge, until the Rhine had overflowed its banks in an almighty flood which rolled over the fire. On its waves the three Rhine Maidens appeared, swimming to the surface, standing now precisely where the pyre had previously stood.

Hagen had witnessed Brünnhilde's death with ever-growing concern for his own fate. Now he was seized with even greater alarm. The Rhine Maidens. How often had his father, Alberich, told him about the Rhine Maidens. Why were they here now? He knew. He knew. Quickly, he threw aside his spear, his shield, his helmet, and rushed wildly into the water.

"Give back the ring!" he cried. "My precious!"

Woglinde and Wellgunde twined their arms around his neck. Swimming backwards, they drew him down into the depths as they swam away, until he was no more. Flosshilde, swimming in front of the others, had sought among the watery ashes on the pyre, had found Grane's black bones, and then Brünnhilde's, found at last the charred skeleton of a finger upon which a golden ring still shone, untarnished. Jubilantly she held it up. Jubilantly she swam after her sisters.

So the teeming waters of the Rhine fell back.

And now, through the cloudbank on the horizon, a red glow broke out with increasing brightness. Illuminated by this light, the men and women of Gibich, and all the other towns on that stretch of the Rhine, could see the three Rhine Maidens, swimming in circles, merrily playing with the ring on the calm surface of the river, which had returned to its natural bed.

But this was not yet the end. From the ruins of the fallen hall they watched, with great anxiety, the growing firelight in the heavens. The logs of the sacred ash tree were still burning, brighter now, and brighter. So bright, indeed, the inside of the great hall of Valhalla could be seen, with the gods and heroes assembled, seated, the heroes in a great circle around Wotan, the War-Father himself on his majestic throne, speaking not a word, silent and grave, with the shattered fragments of his spear grasped in his hand, and all the other gods beside him, motionless, frightened and astonished, overwhelmed by fear. The age of Man was dawning in the pink and orange light that issued from the heavens in the twilight of the gods. Bright flames set alight the great hall of the gods, until the gods and heroes were completely hidden by the flames. Now it was the end.

ABOUT THE AUTHOR

David Prashker was born in London in 1955 and has lived in France, Israel, Canada and the United States, where he is currently based.

He is the author of thirty books, including contemporary and historical novels, short stories, poetry, songs, plays and scholarly works. You can follow his blog at apps.theargamanpress.com/Blog/ or find him at his website Davidprashker.com.

For more information about his books, go to:

theargamanpress.com.

www.ingramcontent.com/pod-product-compliance
Lightning Source LLC
Chambersburg PA
CBHW070825180626
46818CB00001B/396